D0117499

CARTOON HANGOVER

BRAVEST WARRIORS

™

CREATED by PENDLETON WARD

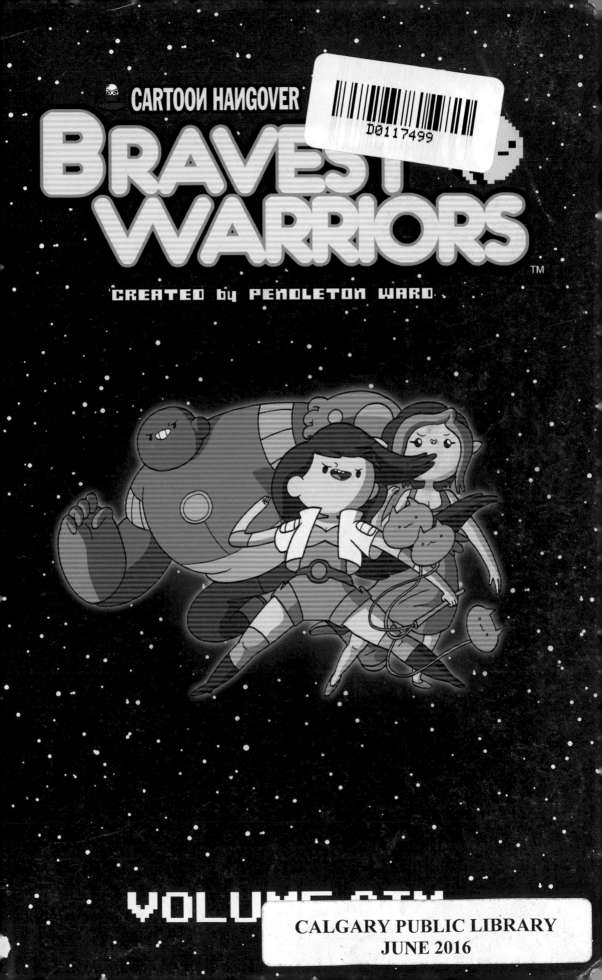

VOLUME SIX

CALGARY PUBLIC LIBRARY
JUNE 2016

www.kaboom-studios.com • www.youtube.com/cartoonhangover

ROSS RICHIE CEO & Founder • **MATT GAGNON** Editor-in-Chief • **FILIP SABLIK** President of Publishing & Marketing • **STEPHEN CHRISTY** President of Development • **LANCE KREITER** VP of Licensing & Merchandising • **PHIL BARBARO** VP of Finance • **BRYCE CARLSON** Managing Editor • **MEL CAYLO** Marketing Manager • **SCOTT NEWMAN** Production Design Manager • **IRENE BRADISH** Operations Manager • **CHRISTINE DINH** Brand Communications Manager • **SIERRA HAHN** Senior Editor • **DAFNA PLEBAN** Editor • **SHANNON WATTERS** Editor • **ERIC HARBURN** Editor • **IAN BRILL** Editor • **WHITNEY LEOPARD** Associate Editor • **JASMINE AMIRI** Associate Editor • **CHRIS ROSA** Associate Editor • **ALEX GALER** Assistant Editor • **CAMERON CHITTOCK** Assistant Editor • **MARY GUMPORT** Assistant Editor • **KELSEY DIETERICH** Production Designer • **JILLIAN CRAB** Production Designer • **KARA LEOPARD** Production Designer • **MICHELLE ANKLEY** Production Design Assistant • **DEVIN FUNCHES** E-Commerce & Inventory Coordinator • **AARON FERRARA** Operations Coordinator • **ELIZABETH LOUGHRIDGE** Accounting Coordinator • **JOSÉ MEZA** Sales Assistant • **JAMES ARRIOLA** Mailroom Assistant • **STEPHANIE HOCUTT** Marketing Assistant • **SAM KUSEK** Direct Market Representative • **HILLARY LEVI** Executive Assistant • **KATE ALBIN** Administrative Assistant

BRAVEST WARRIORS Volume Six, February 2016. Published by KaBOOM!, a division of Boom Entertainment, Inc. Based on "Bravest Warriors" © 2016 Frederator Networks, Inc. Originally published in single magazine form as BRAVEST WARRIORS No. 21-24. ™ & © 2014 Frederator Networks, Inc. All rights reserved. KaBOOM!™ and the KaBOOM! logo are trademarks of Boom Entertainment, Inc., registered in various countries and categories. All characters, events, and institutions depicted herein are fictional. Any similarity between any of the names, characters, persons, events, and/or institutions in this publication to actual names, characters, and persons, whether living or dead, events, and/or institutions is unintended and purely coincidental. KaBOOM! does not read or accept unsolicited submissions of ideas, stories, or artwork.

A catalog record of this book is available from OCLC and from the KaBOOM! website, www.kaboom-studios.com, on the Librarians Page.

BOOM! Studios, 5670 Wilshire Boulevard, Suite 450, Los Angeles, CA 90036-5679. Printed in China. First Printing.
ISBN: 978-1-60886-794-3, eISBN: 978-1-61398-465-9

CREATED BY
PENDLETON WARD

WRITTEN BY
KATE LETH

ILLUSTRATED BY
IAN McGINTY

COLORS BY
LISA MOORE

LETTERS BY
STEVE WANDS

SHORT MISSIONS

"THE LITTLEST LEAGUE"
WRITTEN BY **MAD RUPERT**
ILLUSTRATED BY **TORIL ORLESKY**
COLORS BY **WHITNEY COGAR**
LETTERS BY **KEL McDONALD**

"STINKY SCREAMING MAN"
WRITTEN BY **MAD RUPERT**
ILLUSTRATED BY **KAT LEYH**

"ESCAPE FROM JUNK RAT ISLAND"
WRITTEN BY **MAD RUPERT**
ILLUSTRATED BY **CAREY PIETSCH**

COVER BY
TYSON HESSE

DESIGNER
KELSEY DIETERICH

ASSISTANT EDITORS
**CAMERON CHITTOCK
& WHITNEY LEOPARD**

EDITORS
**REBECCA TAYLOR
& SHANNON WATTERS**

WITH SPECIAL THANKS TO BREEHN BURNS, ERIC HOMAN,
FRED SEIBERT, RUTH MORRISON, NATE OLSON, AND ALL OF
THE CLASSY FOLKS AT FREDERATOR STUDIOS.

CHAPTER 21

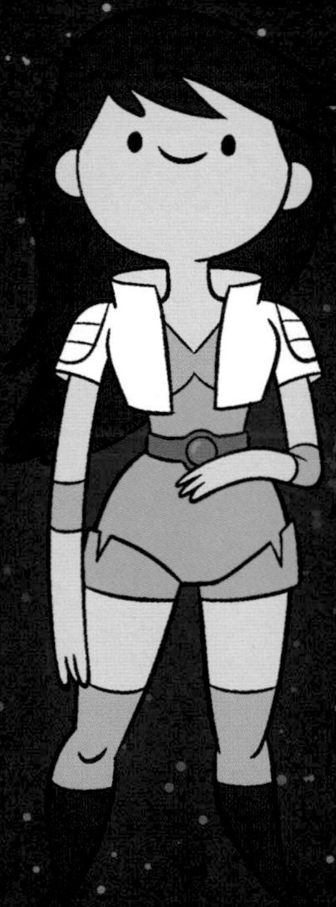

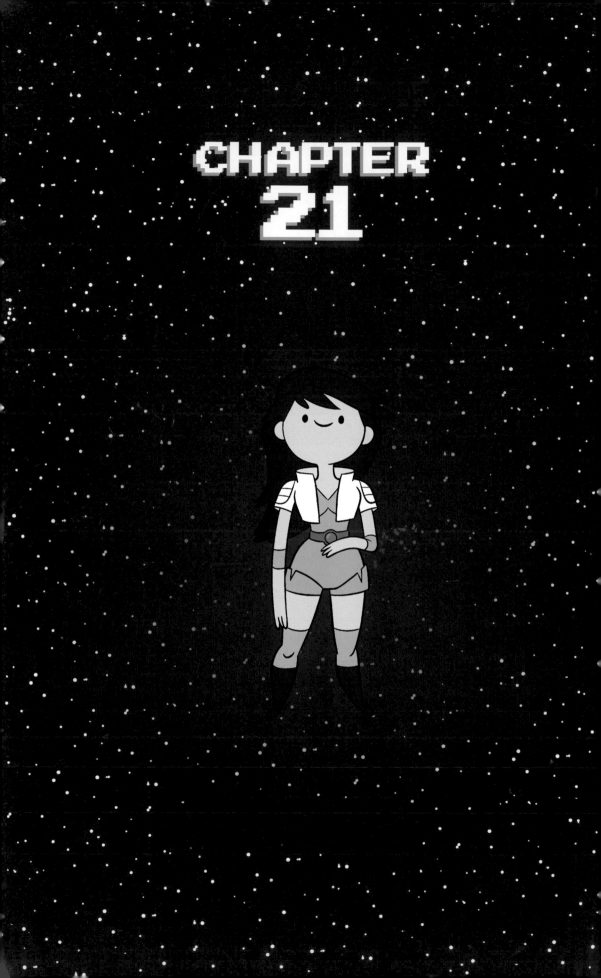

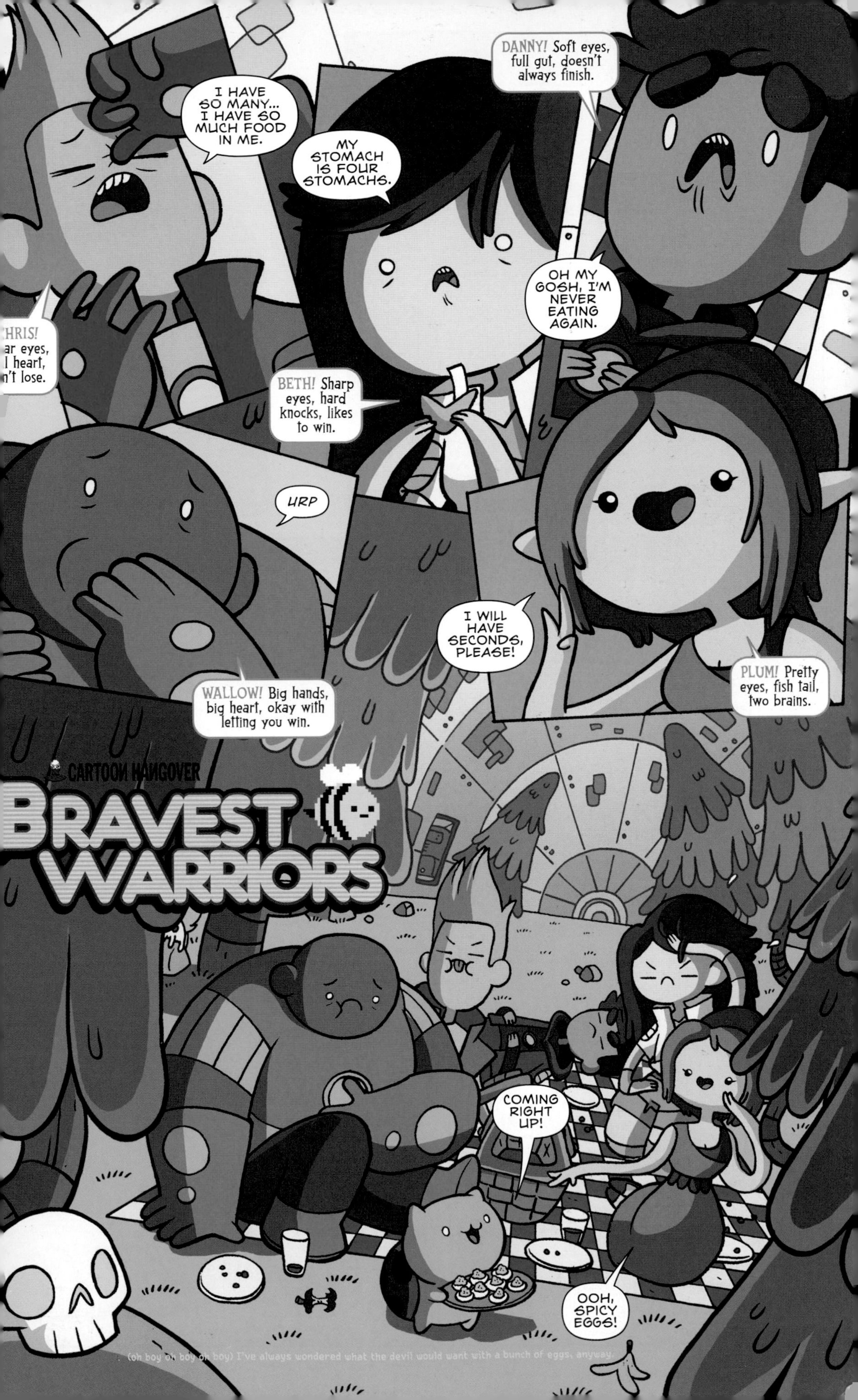
I HAVE SO MANY... I HAVE SO MUCH FOOD IN ME.
MY STOMACH IS FOUR STOMACHS.
DANNY! Soft eyes, full gut, doesn't always finish.
OH MY GOSH, I'M NEVER EATING AGAIN.
BETH! Sharp eyes, hard knocks, likes to win.
URP
I WILL HAVE SECONDS, PLEASE!
PLUM! Pretty eyes, fish tail, two brains.
WALLOW! Big hands, big heart, okay with letting you win.
CARTOON HANGOVER
BRAVEST WARRIORS
COMING RIGHT UP!
OOH, SPICY EGGS!
(oh boy oh boy oh boy) I've always wondered what the devil would want with a bunch of eggs, anyway.

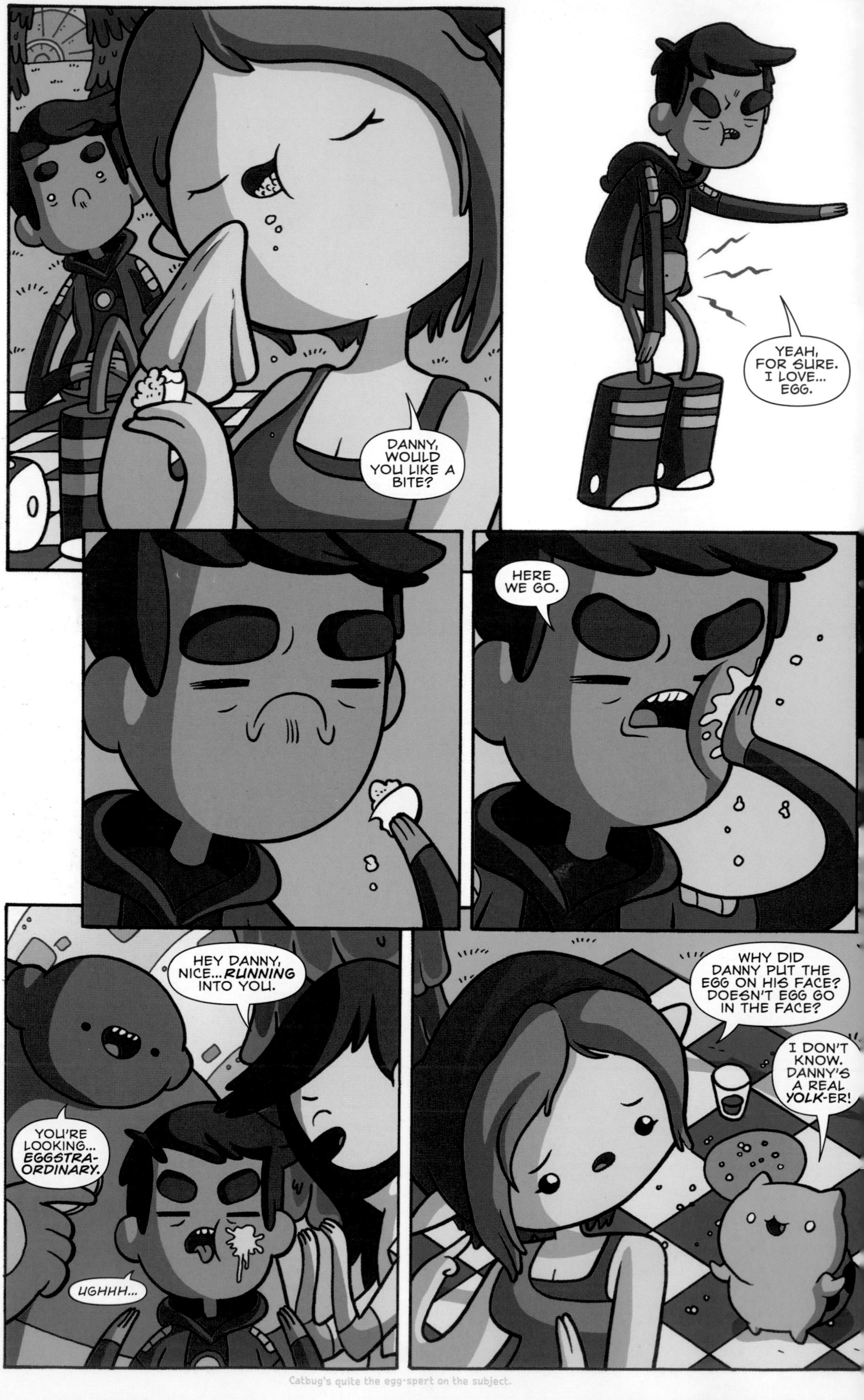
DANNY, WOULD YOU LIKE A BITE?
YEAH, FOR SURE. I LOVE... EGG.
HERE WE GO.
HEY DANNY, NICE...RUNNING INTO YOU.
YOU'RE LOOKING... EGGSTRA-ORDINARY.
UGHHH...
WHY DID DANNY PUT THE EGG ON HIS FACE? DOESN'T EGG GO IN THE FACE?
I DON'T KNOW. DANNY'S A REAL YOLK-ER!

Catbug's quite the egg-spert on the subject.

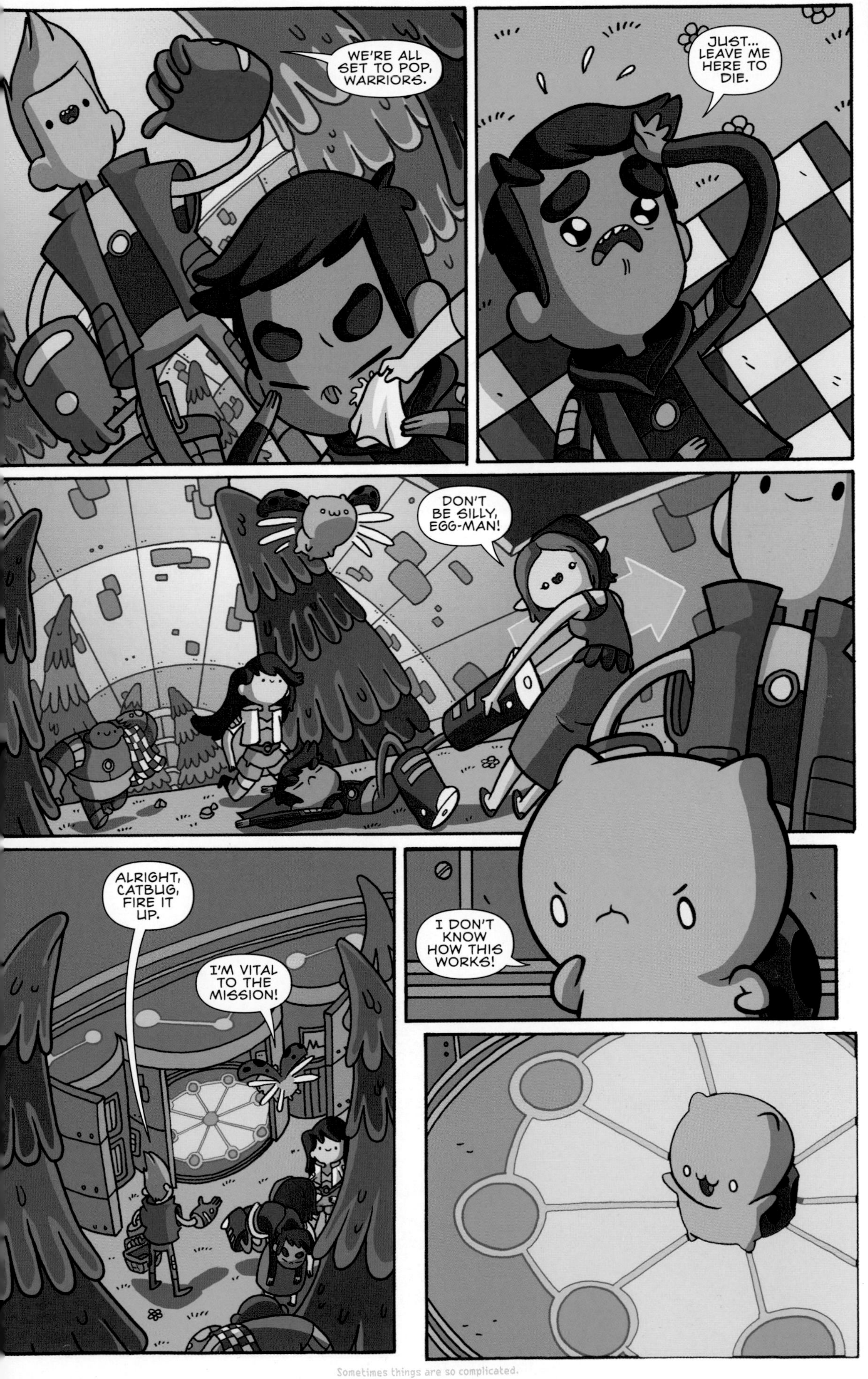
WE'RE ALL SET TO POP, WARRIORS.
JUST... LEAVE ME HERE TO DIE.
DON'T BE SILLY, EGG-MAN!
ALRIGHT, CATBUG, FIRE IT UP.
I'M VITAL TO THE MISSION!
I DON'T KNOW HOW THIS WORKS!

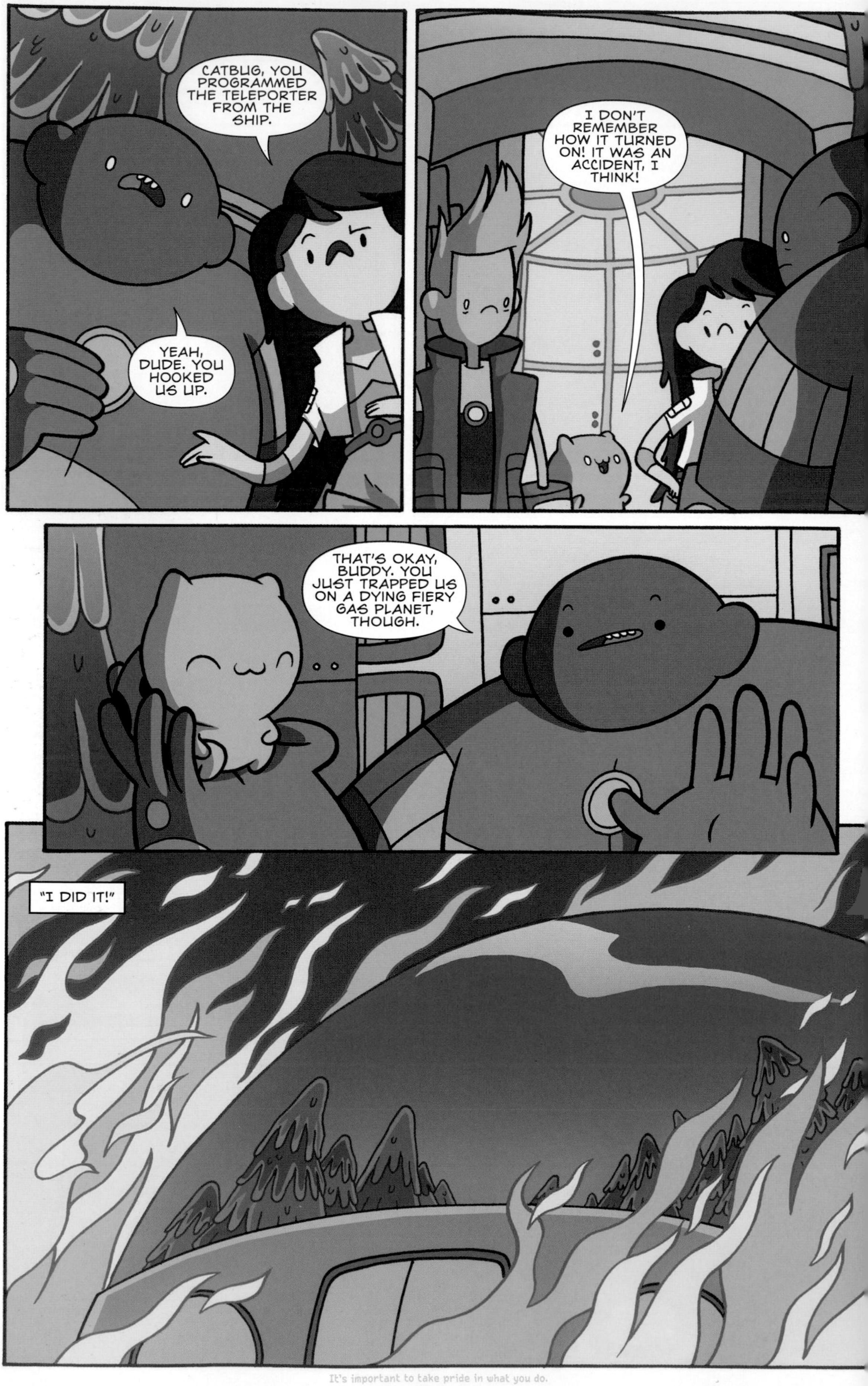
CATBUG, YOU PROGRAMMED THE TELEPORTER FROM THE SHIP.
YEAH, DUDE. YOU HOOKED US UP.
I DON'T REMEMBER HOW IT TURNED ON! IT WAS AN ACCIDENT, I THINK!
THAT'S OKAY, BUDDY. YOU JUST TRAPPED US ON A DYING FIERY GAS PLANET, THOUGH.
"I DID IT!"

It's important to take pride in what you do.

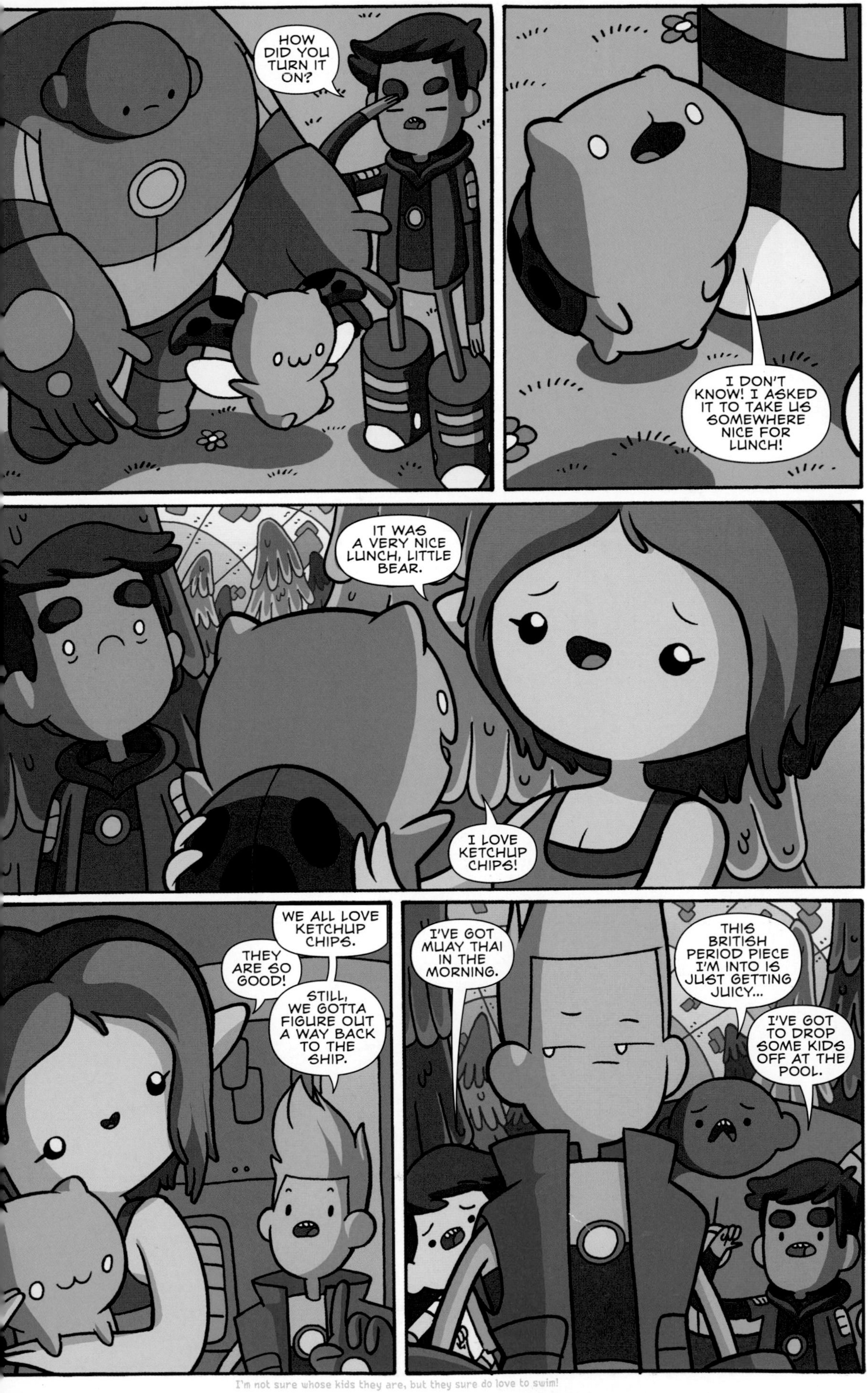
HOW DID YOU TURN IT ON?
I DON'T KNOW! I ASKED IT TO TAKE US SOMEWHERE NICE FOR LUNCH!
IT WAS A VERY NICE LUNCH, LITTLE BEAR.
I LOVE KETCHUP CHIPS!
WE ALL LOVE KETCHUP CHIPS.
THEY ARE SO GOOD!
STILL, WE GOTTA FIGURE OUT A WAY BACK TO THE SHIP.
I'VE GOT MUAY THAI IN THE MORNING.
THIS BRITISH PERIOD PIECE I'M INTO IS JUST GETTING JUICY...
I'VE GOT TO DROP SOME KIDS OFF AT THE POOL.

I'm not sure whose kids they are, but they sure do love to swim!

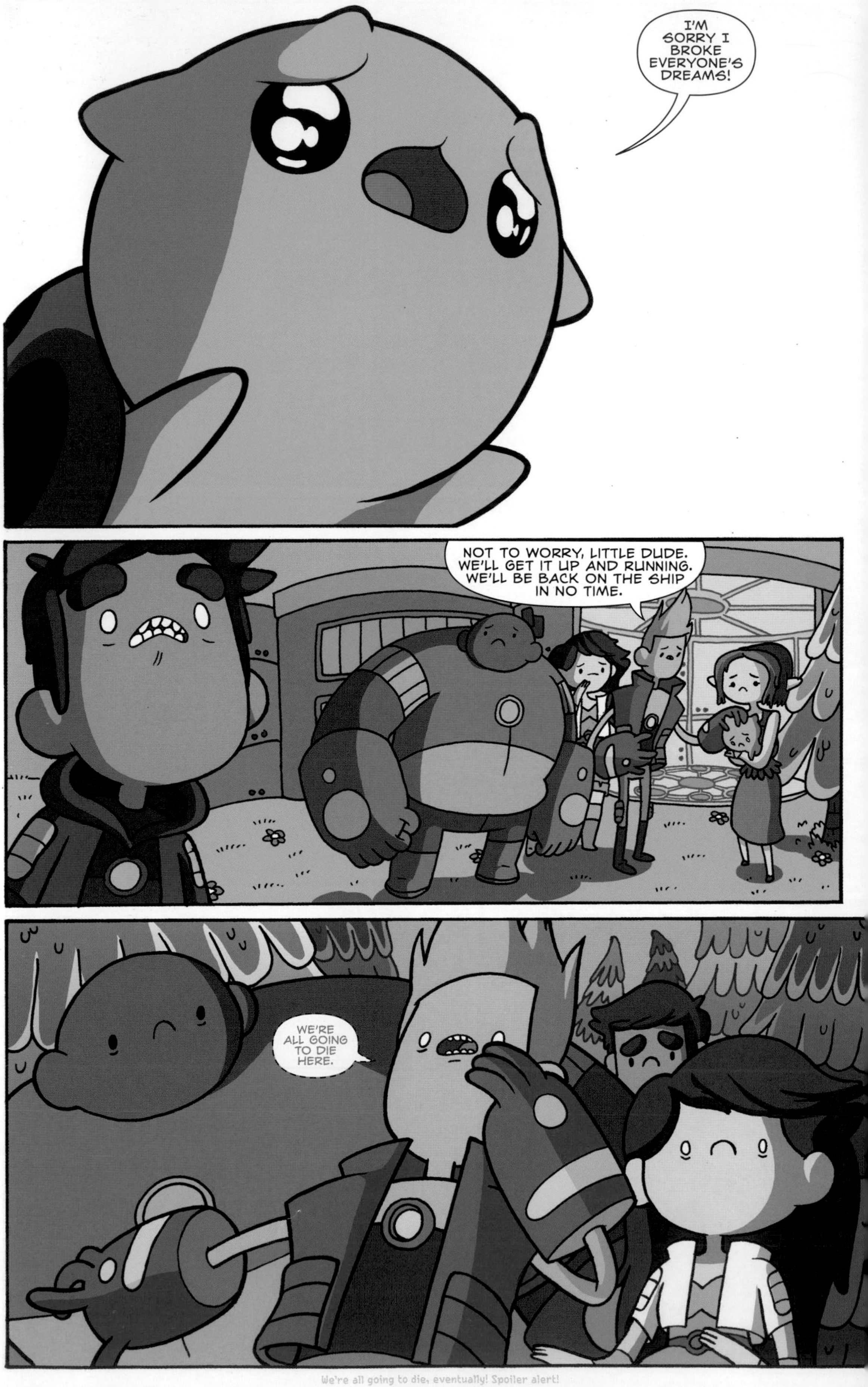
I'M SORRY I BROKE EVERYONE'S DREAMS!
NOT TO WORRY, LITTLE DUDE. WE'LL GET IT UP AND RUNNING. WE'LL BE BACK ON THE SHIP IN NO TIME.
WE'RE ALL GOING TO DIE HERE.

We're all going to die, eventually! Spoiler alert!

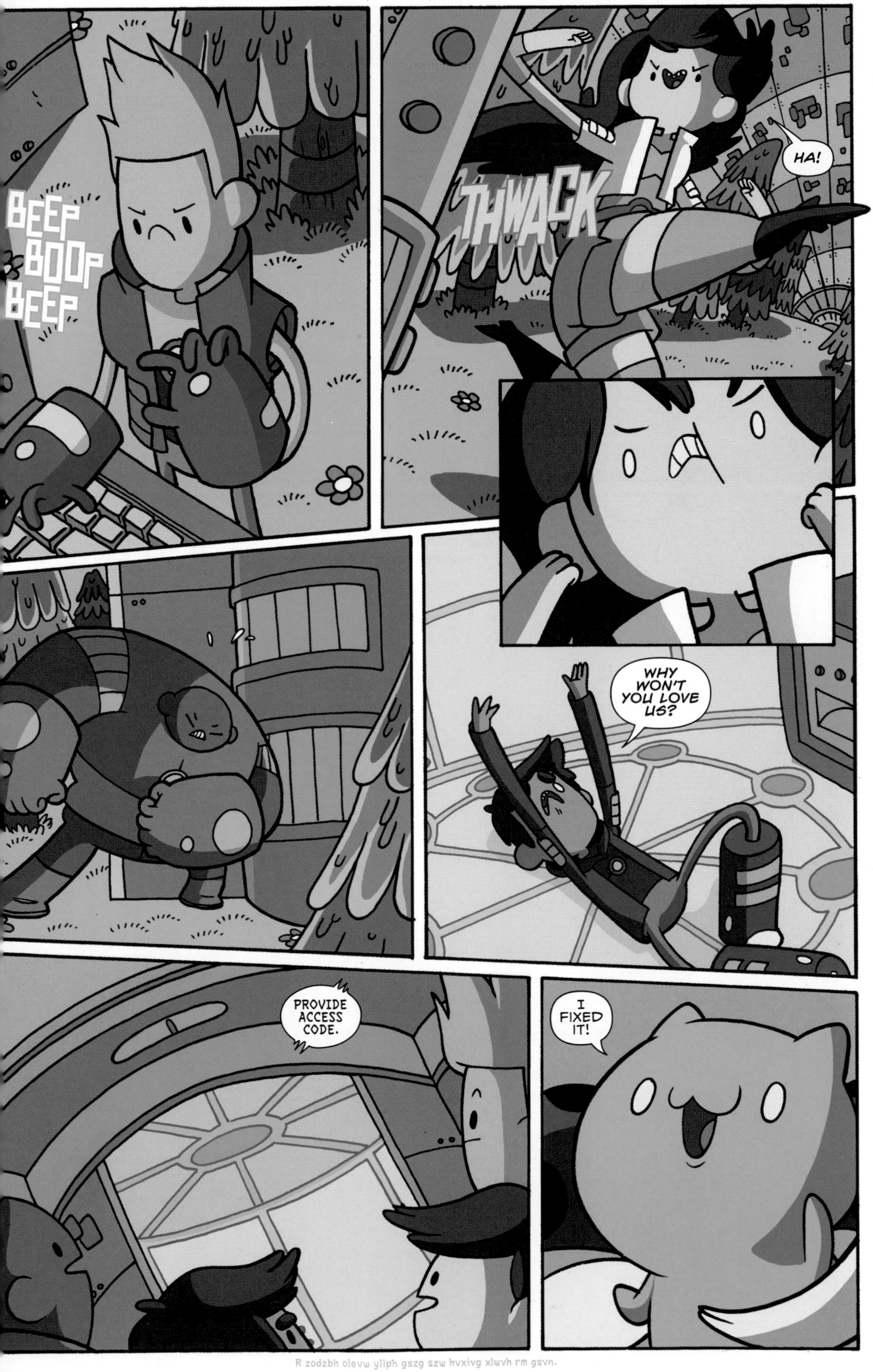

BEEP BOOP BEEP
THWACK
HA!
WHY WON'T YOU LOVE US?
PROVIDE ACCESS CODE.
I FIXED IT!

R zodzbh olevw yllph gszg szw hvxivg xlwvh rm gsvn.

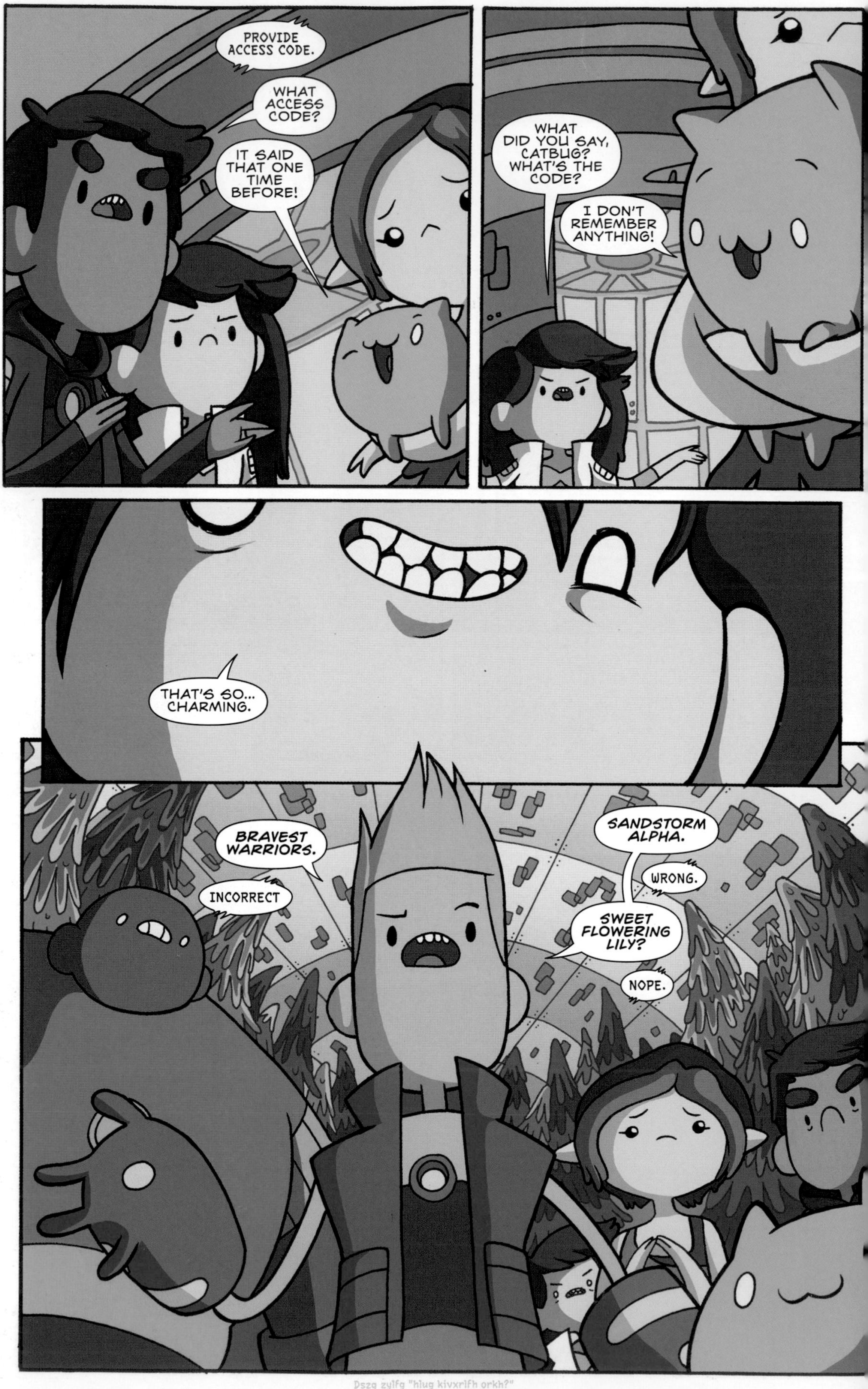
PROVIDE ACCESS CODE.
WHAT ACCESS CODE?
IT SAID THAT ONE TIME BEFORE!
WHAT DID YOU SAY, CATBUG? WHAT'S THE CODE?
I DON'T REMEMBER ANYTHING!
THAT'S SO... CHARMING.
BRAVEST WARRIORS.
INCORRECT
SANDSTORM ALPHA.
WRONG.
SWEET FLOWERING LILY?
NOPE.

Dszg zylfg "hlug kivxrfh orkh?"

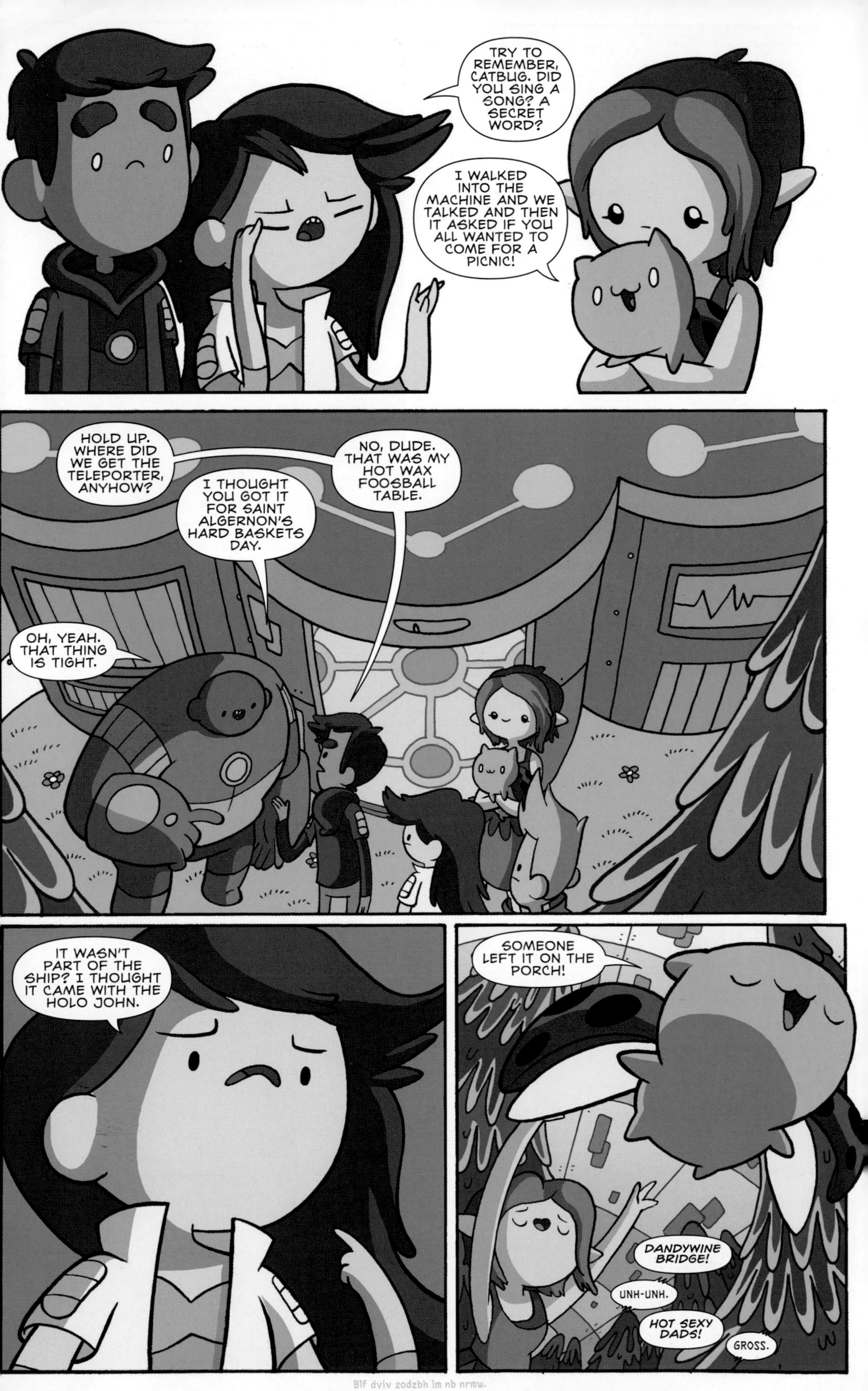
TRY TO REMEMBER, CATBUG. DID YOU SING A SONG? A SECRET WORD?
I WALKED INTO THE MACHINE AND WE TALKED AND THEN IT ASKED IF YOU ALL WANTED TO COME FOR A PICNIC!
HOLD UP. WHERE DID WE GET THE TELEPORTER, ANYHOW?
I THOUGHT YOU GOT IT FOR SAINT ALGERNON'S HARD BASKETS DAY.
NO, DUDE. THAT WAS MY HOT WAX FOOSBALL TABLE.
OH, YEAH. THAT THING IS TIGHT.
IT WASN'T PART OF THE SHIP? I THOUGHT IT CAME WITH THE HOLO JOHN.
SOMEONE LEFT IT ON THE PORCH!
DANDYWINE BRIDGE!
UNH-UNH.
HOT SEXY DADS!
GROSS.

Blf dviv zodzbh lm nb nrmw.

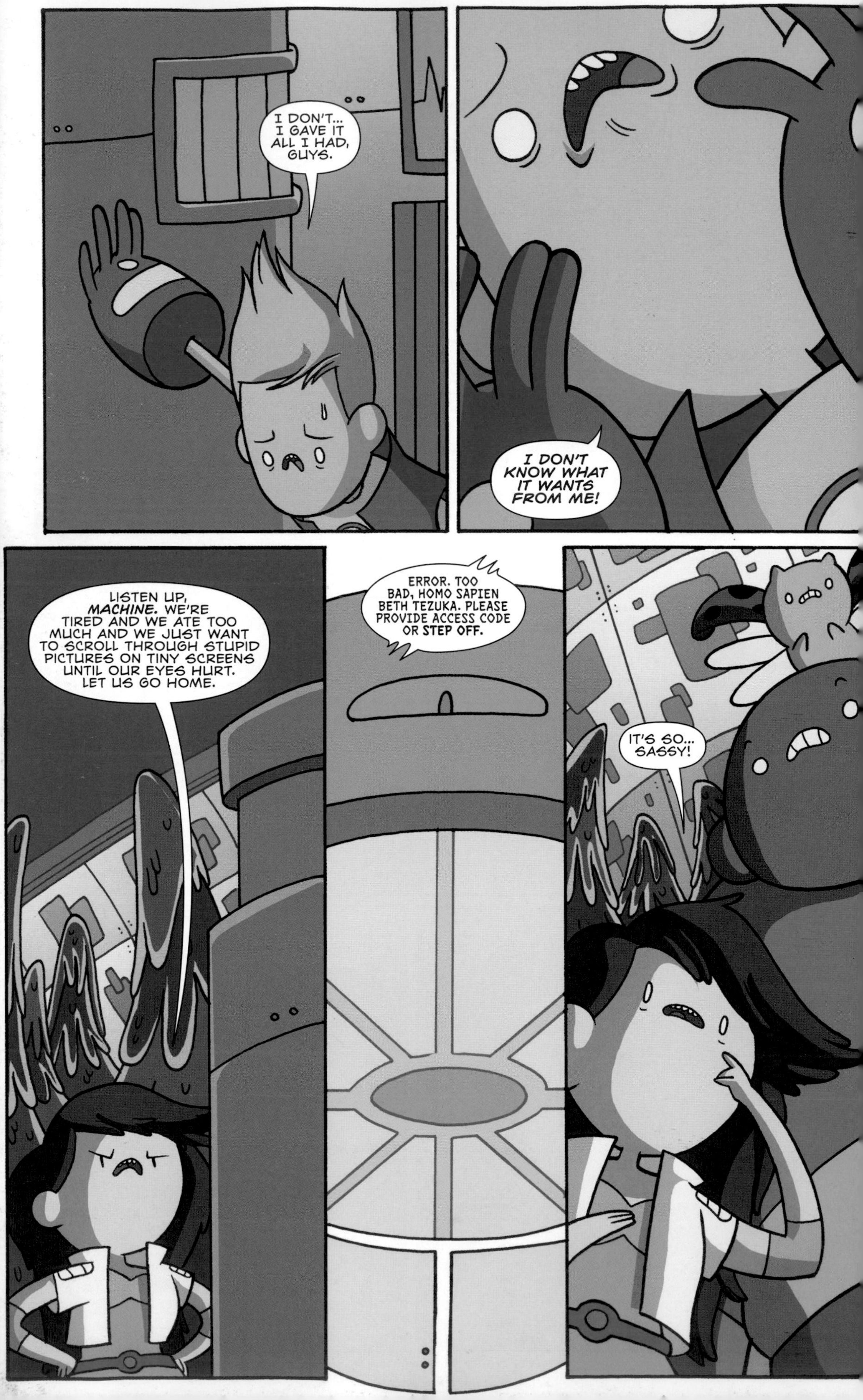
I DON'T... I GAVE IT ALL I HAD, GUYS.
I DON'T KNOW WHAT IT WANTS FROM ME!
LISTEN UP, MACHINE. WE'RE TIRED AND WE ATE TOO MUCH AND WE JUST WANT TO SCROLL THROUGH STUPID PICTURES ON TINY SCREENS UNTIL OUR EYES HURT. LET US GO HOME.
ERROR. TOO BAD, HOMO SAPIEN BETH TEZUKA. PLEASE PROVIDE ACCESS CODE OR STEP OFF.
IT'S SO... SASSY!

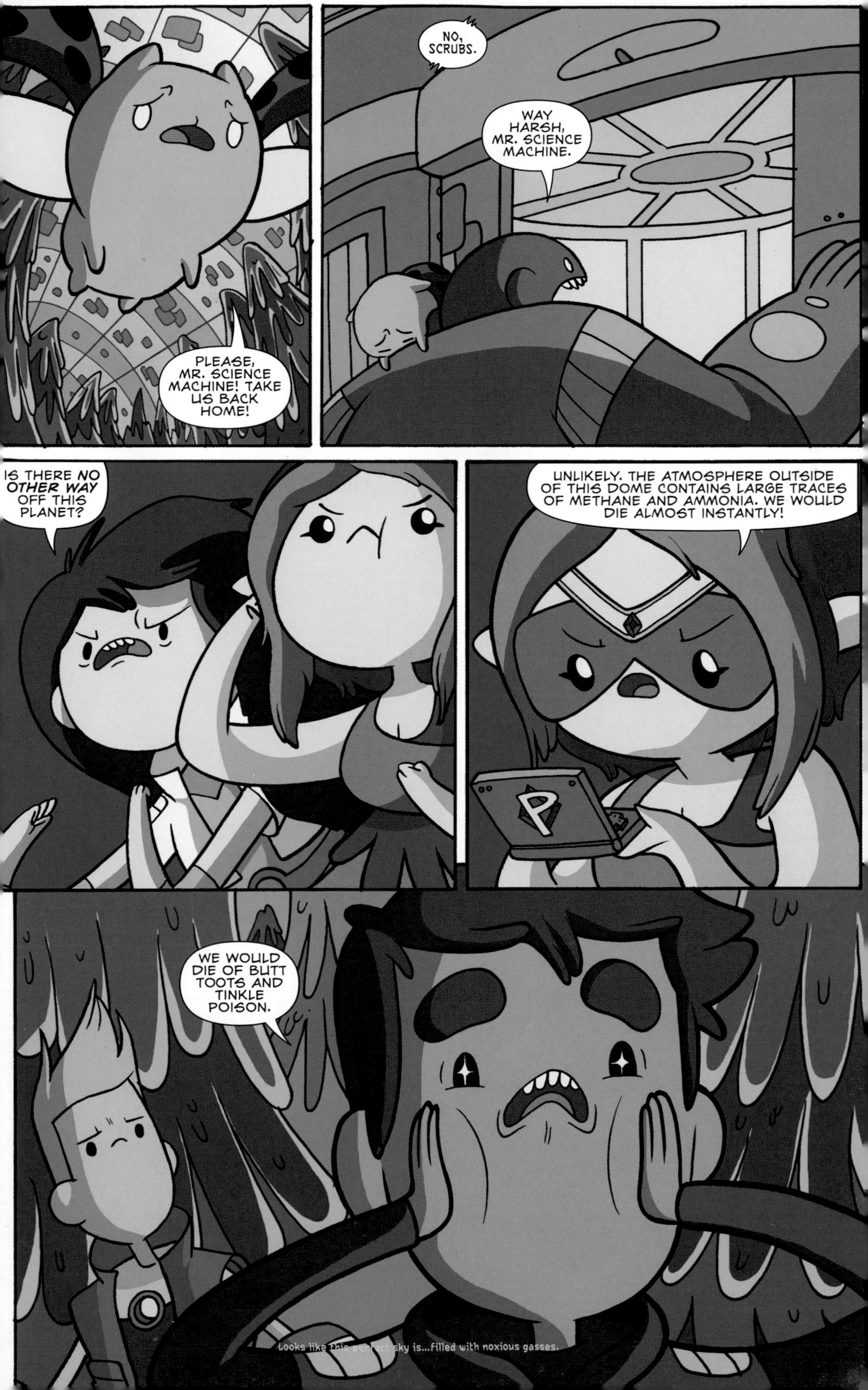
PLEASE, MR. SCIENCE MACHINE! TAKE US BACK HOME!
NO, SCRUBS.
WAY HARSH, MR. SCIENCE MACHINE.
IS THERE NO OTHER WAY OFF THIS PLANET?
UNLIKELY. THE ATMOSPHERE OUTSIDE OF THIS DOME CONTAINS LARGE TRACES OF METHANE AND AMMONIA. WE WOULD DIE ALMOST INSTANTLY!
WE WOULD DIE OF BUTT TOOTS AND TINKLE POISON.
Looks like this perfect sky is...filled with noxious gasses.

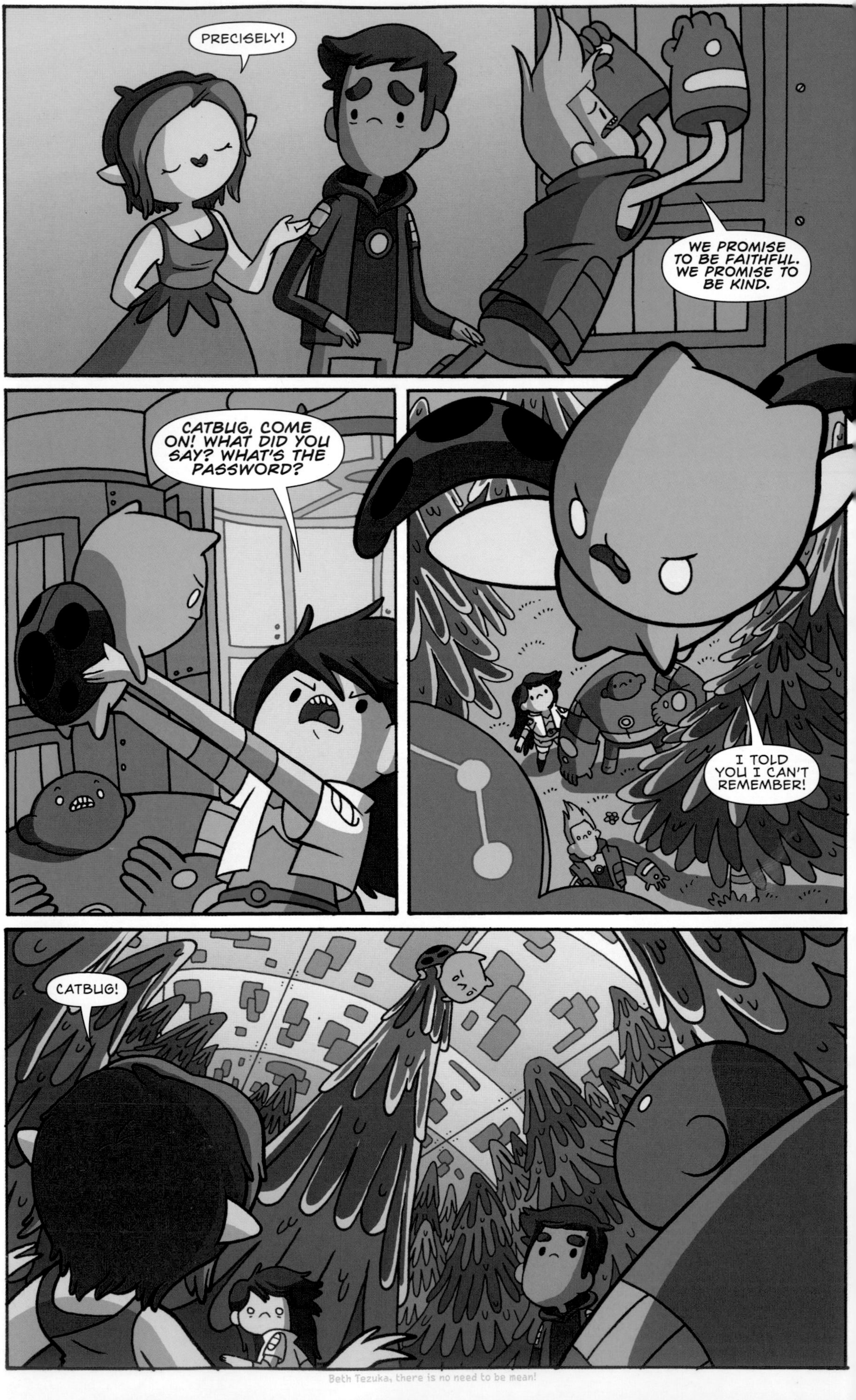
PRECISELY!
WE PROMISE TO BE FAITHFUL. WE PROMISE TO BE KIND.
CATBUG, COME ON! WHAT DID YOU SAY? WHAT'S THE PASSWORD?
I TOLD YOU I CAN'T REMEMBER!
CATBUG!

Beth Tezuka, there is no need to be mean!

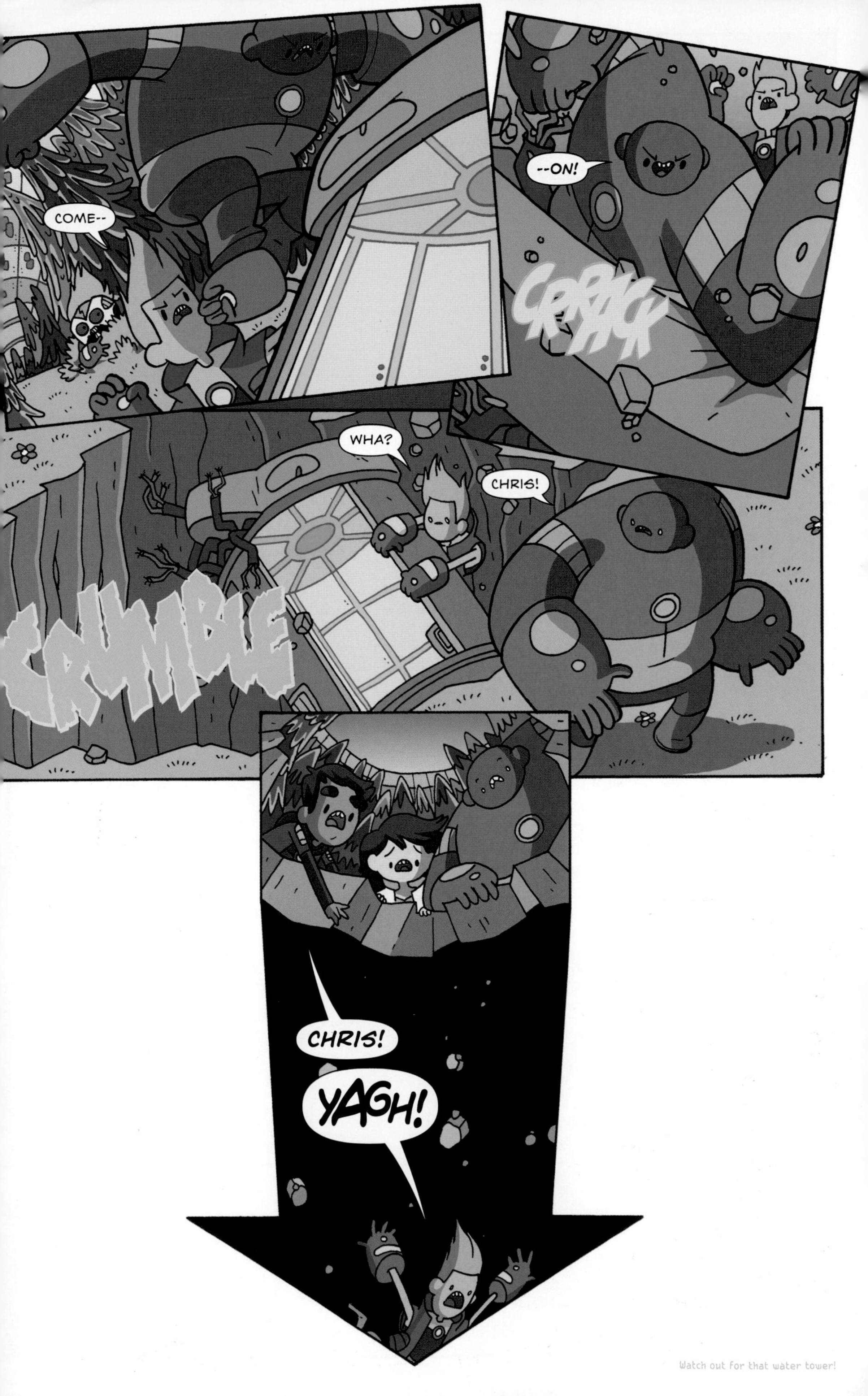
COME--
--ON!
CRRACK
WHA?
CHRIS!
CRUMBLE
CHRIS!
YAGH!

Watch out for that water tower!

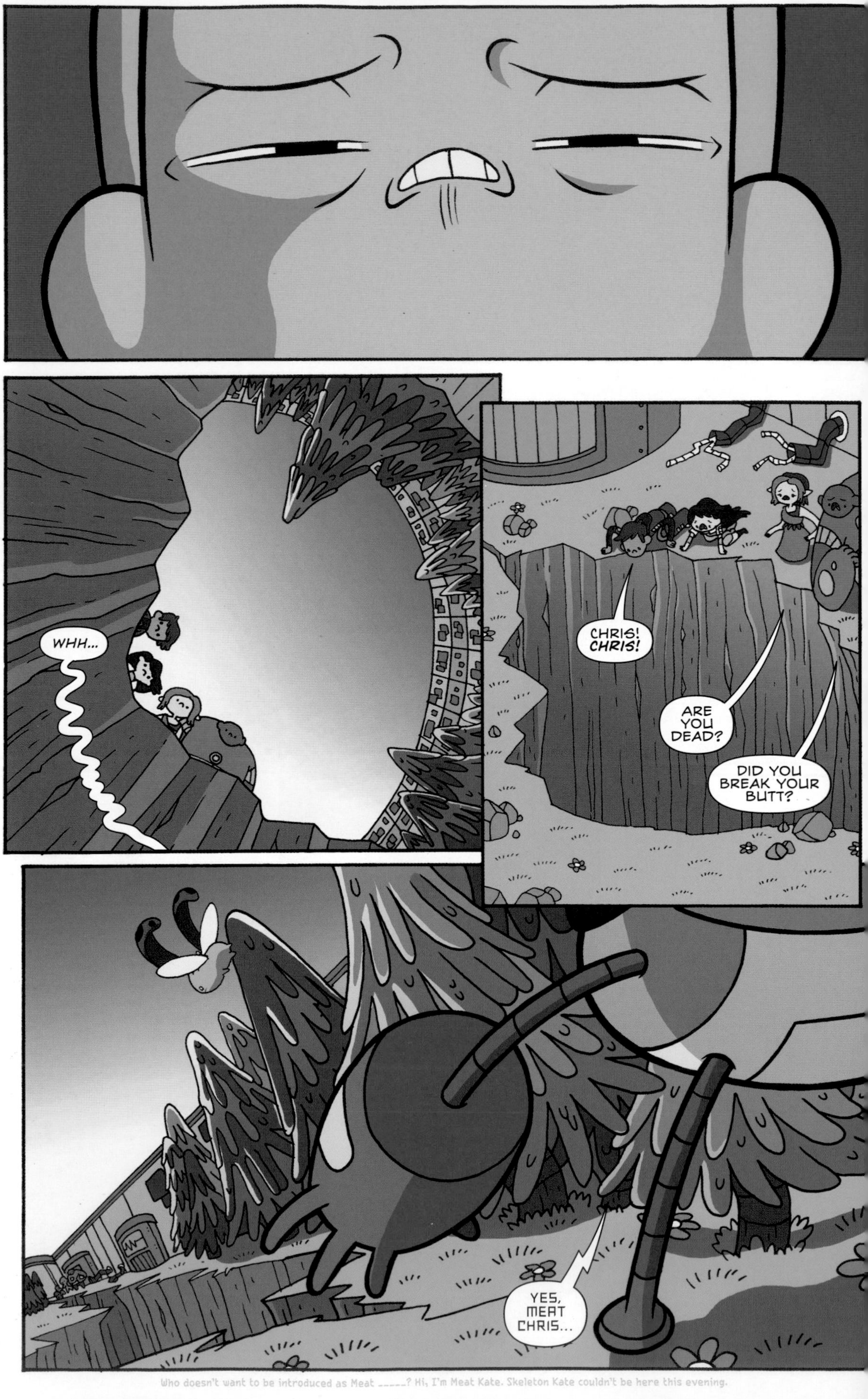
WHH...
CHRIS! ***CHRIS!***
ARE YOU DEAD?
DID YOU BREAK YOUR BUTT?
YES, MEAT CHRIS...

Who doesn't want to be introduced as Meat _____? Hi, I'm Meat Kate. Skeleton Kate couldn't be here this evening.

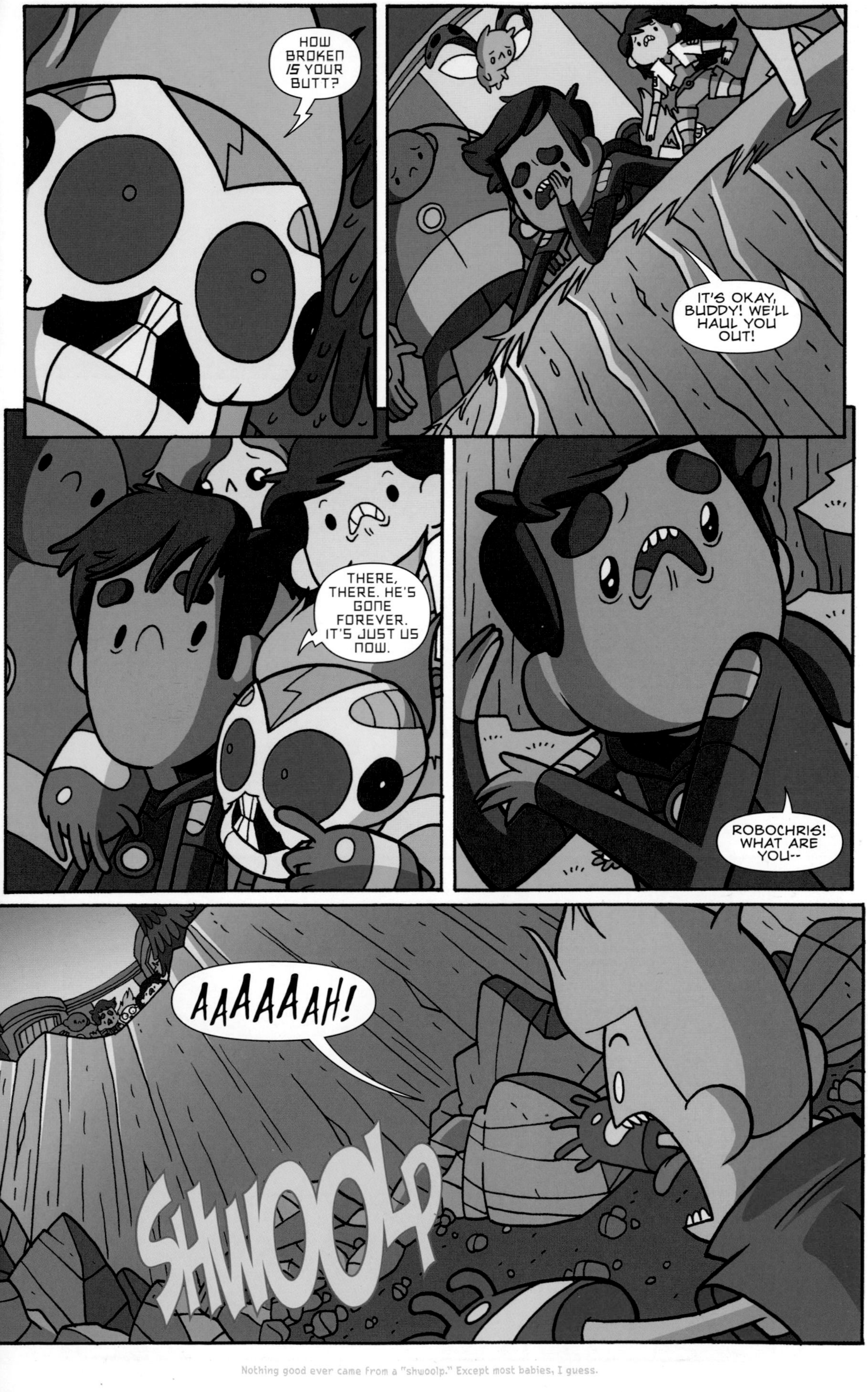
HOW BROKEN IS YOUR BUTT?
IT'S OKAY, BUDDY! WE'LL HAUL YOU OUT!
THERE, THERE. HE'S GONE FOREVER. IT'S JUST US NOW.
ROBOCHRIS! WHAT ARE YOU--
AAAAAAH!
SHWOOLP

Nothing good ever came from a "shwoolp." Except most babies, I guess.

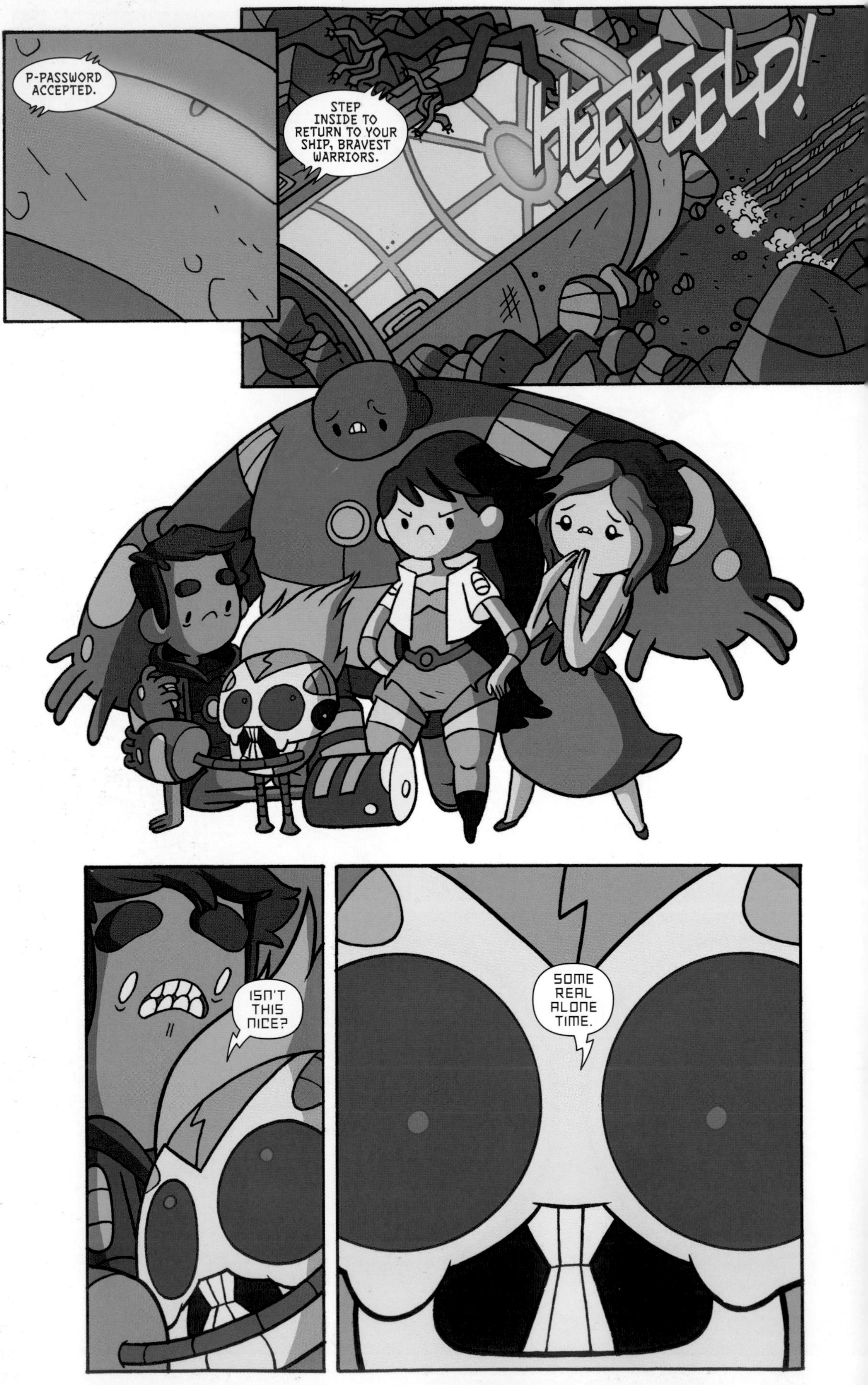
P-PASSWORD ACCEPTED.
STEP INSIDE TO RETURN TO YOUR SHIP, BRAVEST WARRIORS.
HEEEEELP!
ISN'T THIS NICE?
SOME REAL ALONE TIME.

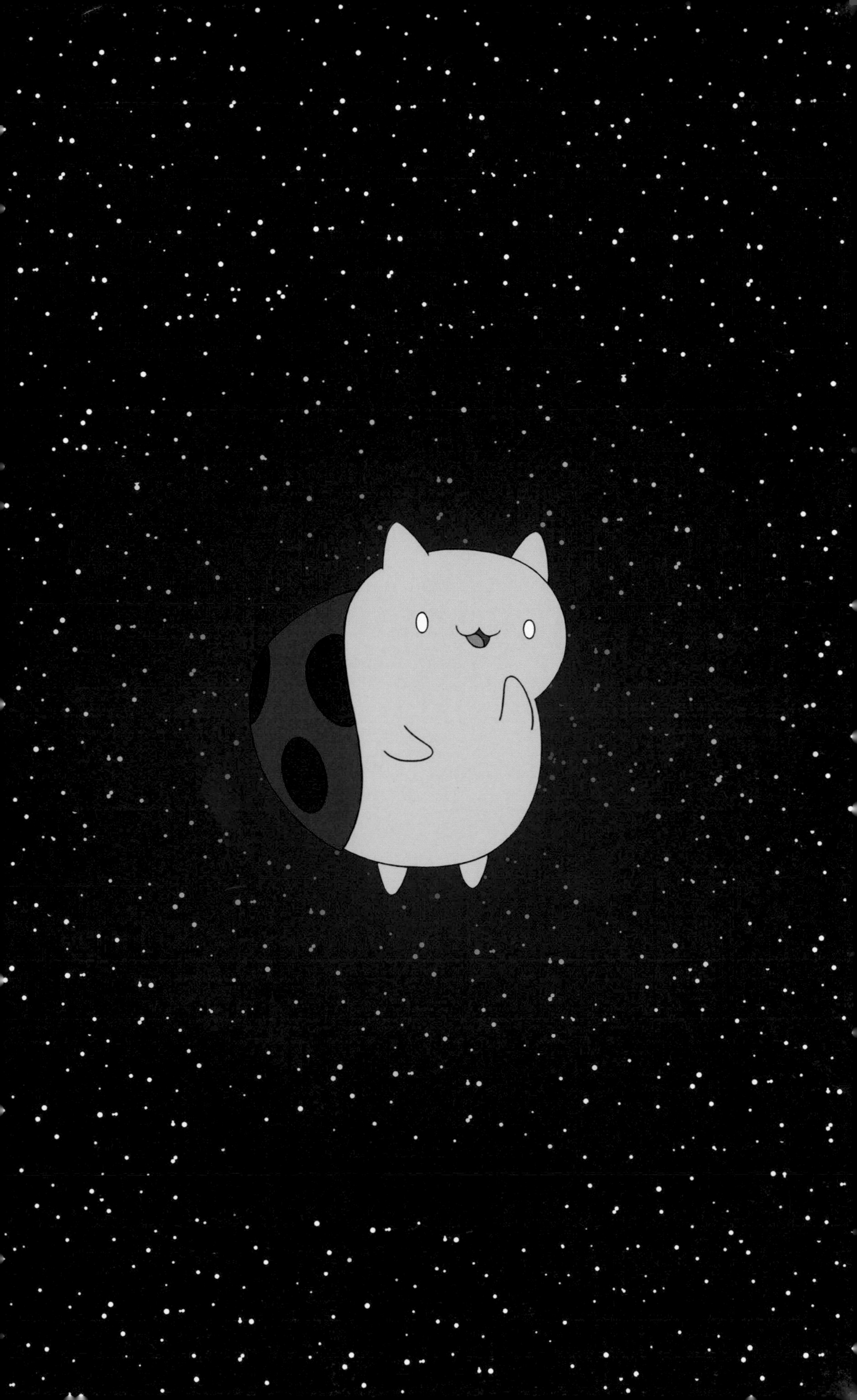

CHAPTER 22

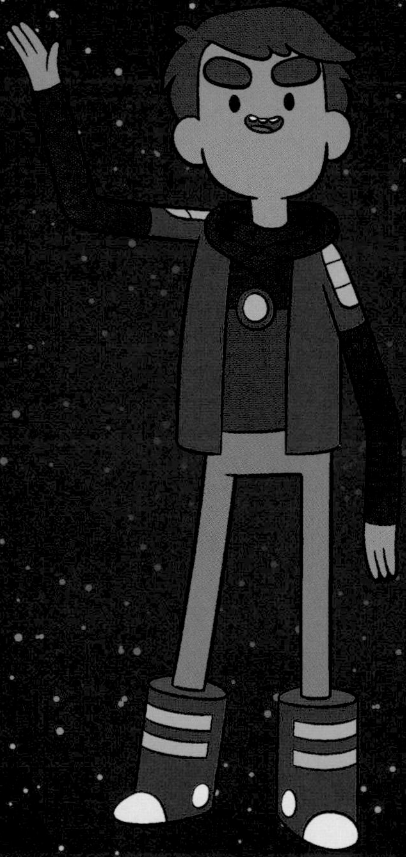

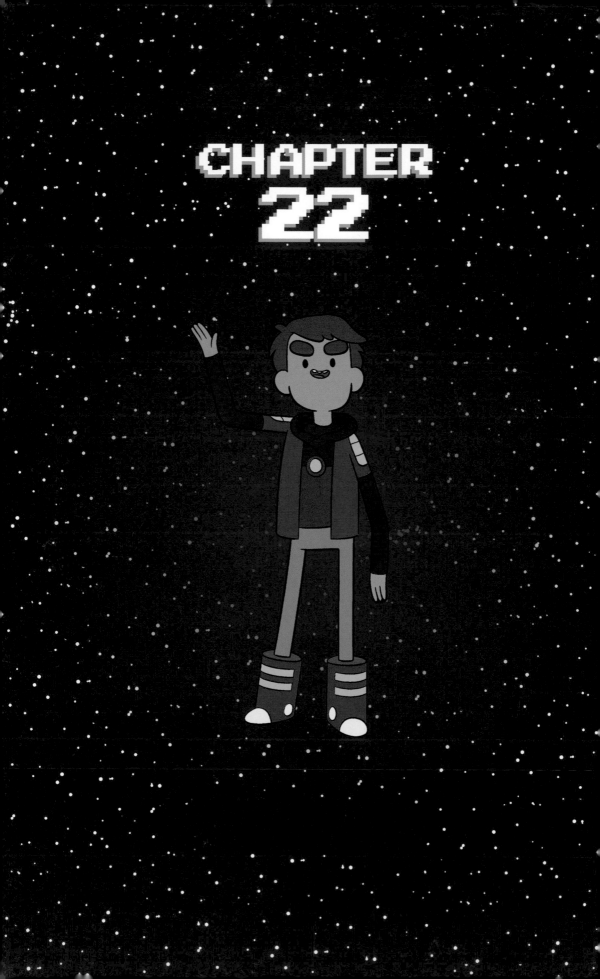

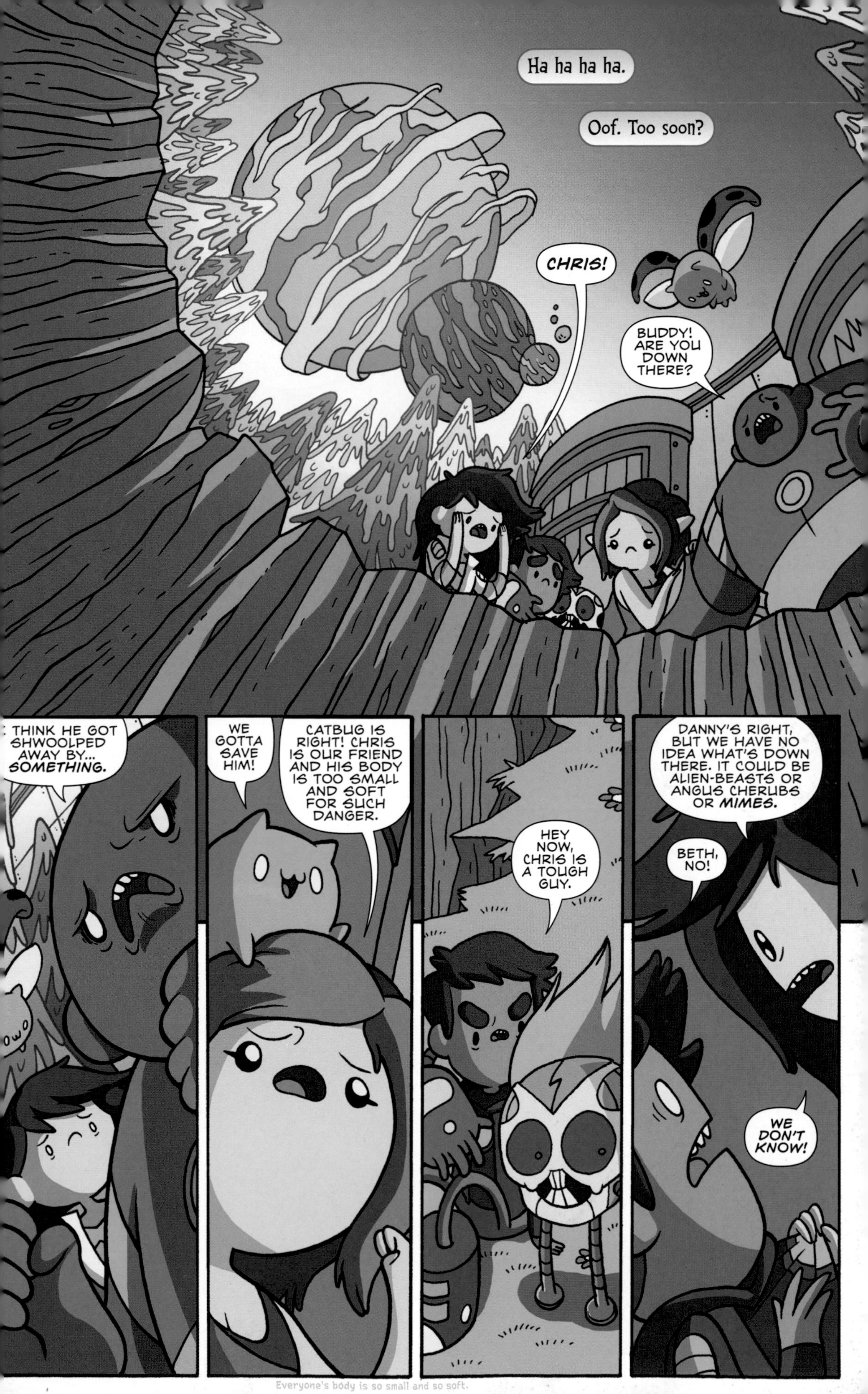
Ha ha ha ha.
Oof. Too soon?
CHRIS!
BUDDY! ARE YOU DOWN THERE?
THINK HE GOT SHWOOLPED AWAY BY... **SOMETHING.**
WE GOTTA SAVE HIM!
CATBUG IS RIGHT! CHRIS IS OUR FRIEND AND HIS BODY IS TOO SMALL AND SOFT FOR SUCH DANGER.
HEY NOW, CHRIS IS A TOUGH GUY.
DANNY'S RIGHT, BUT WE HAVE NO IDEA WHAT'S DOWN THERE. IT COULD BE ALIEN-BEASTS OR ANGUS CHERUBS OR **MIMES.**
BETH, NO!
WE DON'T KNOW!

Everyone's body is so small and so soft.

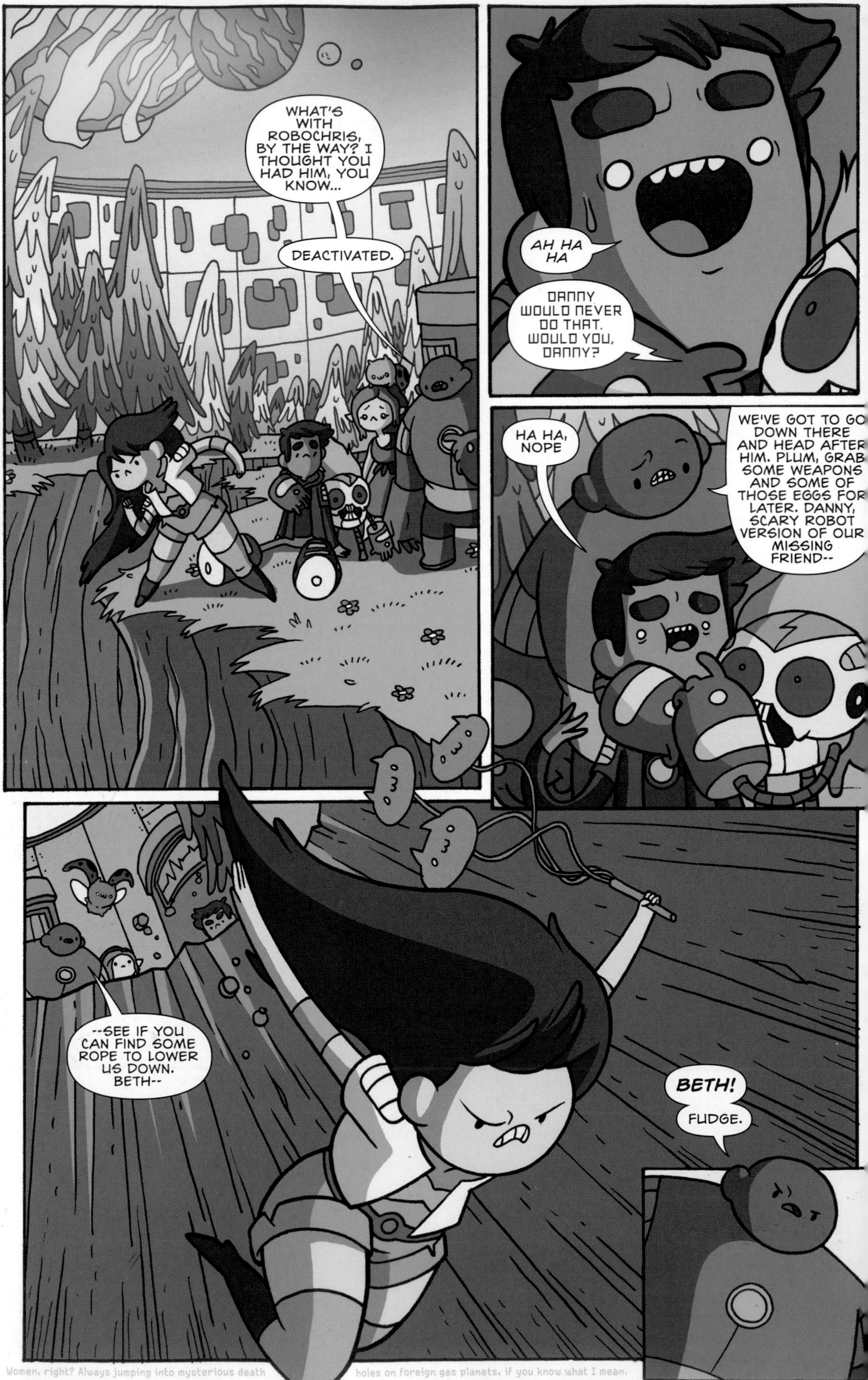
WHAT'S WITH ROBOCHRIS, BY THE WAY? I THOUGHT YOU HAD HIM, YOU KNOW...
DEACTIVATED.
AH HA HA
DANNY WOULD NEVER DO THAT. WOULD YOU, DANNY?
HA HA, NOPE
WE'VE GOT TO GO DOWN THERE AND HEAD AFTER HIM. PLUM, GRAB SOME WEAPONS AND SOME OF THOSE EGGS FOR LATER. DANNY, SCARY ROBOT VERSION OF OUR MISSING FRIEND--
--SEE IF YOU CAN FIND SOME ROPE TO LOWER US DOWN. BETH--
BETH!
FUDGE.

Women, right? Always jumping into mysterious death holes on foreign gas planets, if you know what I mean.

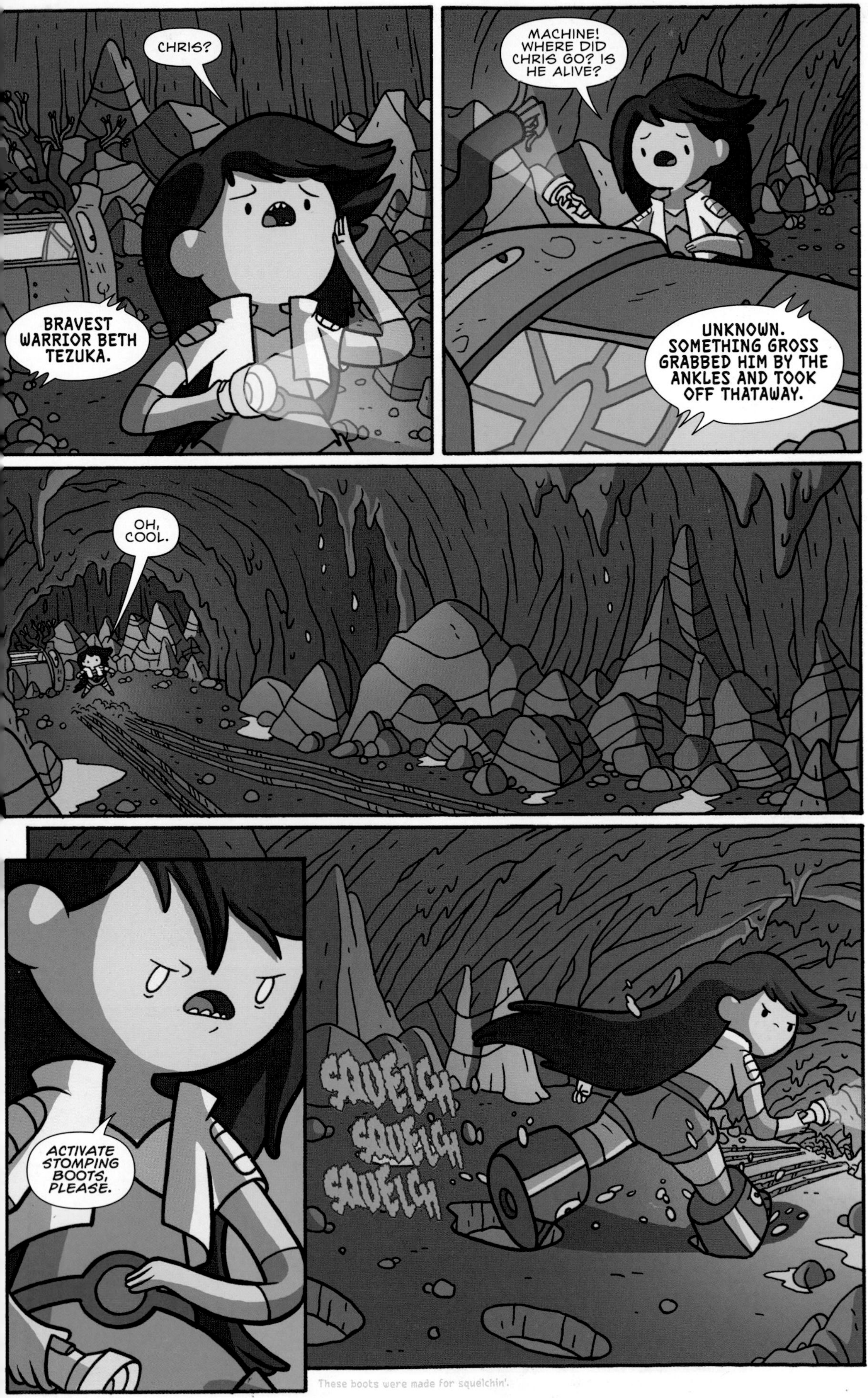
CHRIS?
BRAVEST WARRIOR BETH TEZUKA.
MACHINE! WHERE DID CHRIS GO? IS HE ALIVE?
UNKNOWN. SOMETHING GROSS GRABBED HIM BY THE ANKLES AND TOOK OFF THATAWAY.
OH, COOL.
ACTIVATE STOMPING BOOTS, PLEASE.
SQUELCH
SQUELCH
SQUELCH

These boots were made for squelchin'.

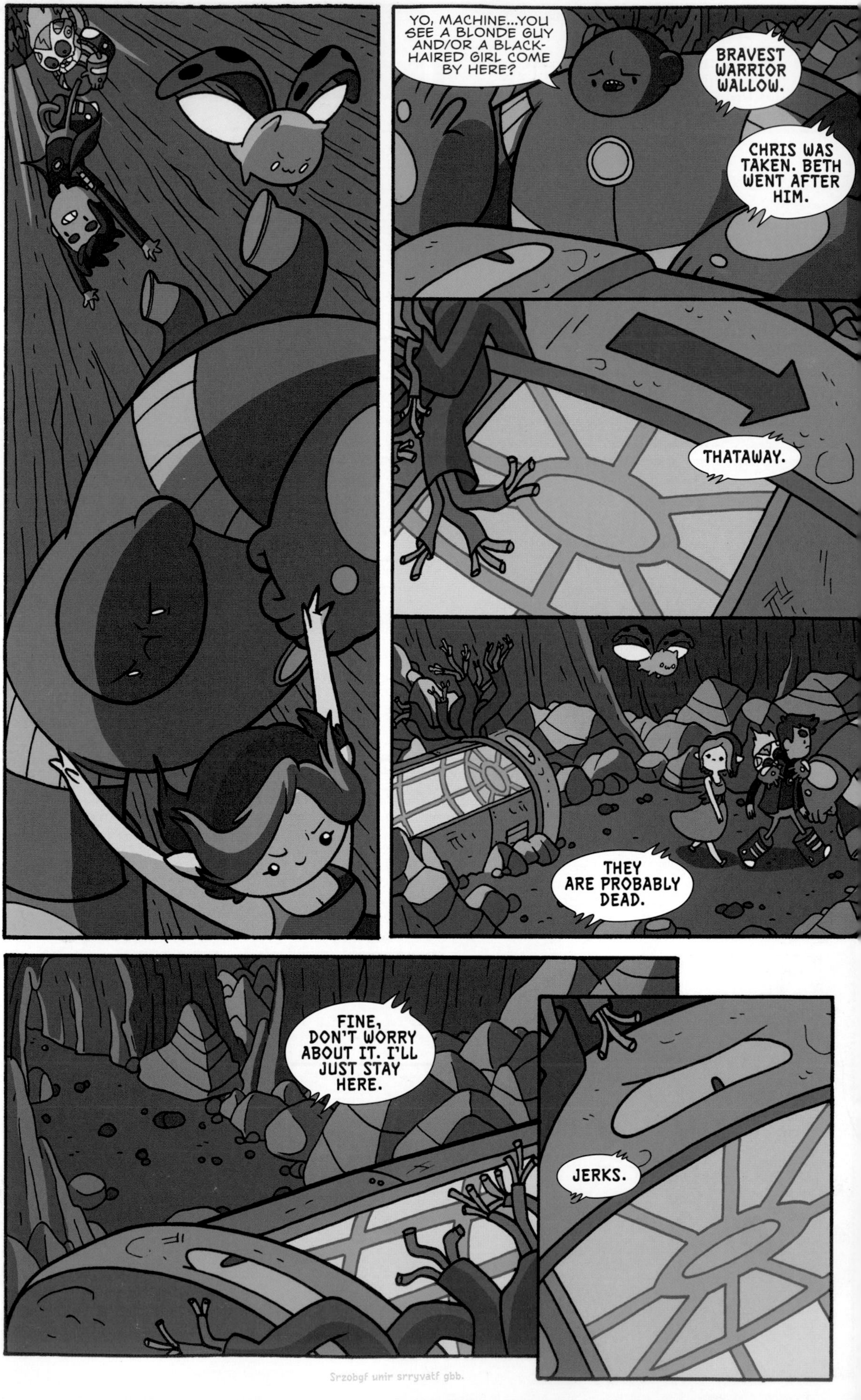
YO, MACHINE...YOU SEE A BLONDE GUY AND/OR A BLACK-HAIRED GIRL COME BY HERE?
BRAVEST WARRIOR WALLOW.
CHRIS WAS TAKEN. BETH WENT AFTER HIM.
THATAWAY.
THEY ARE PROBABLY DEAD.
FINE, DON'T WORRY ABOUT IT. I'LL JUST STAY HERE.
JERKS.

Srzobgf unir srryvatf gbb.

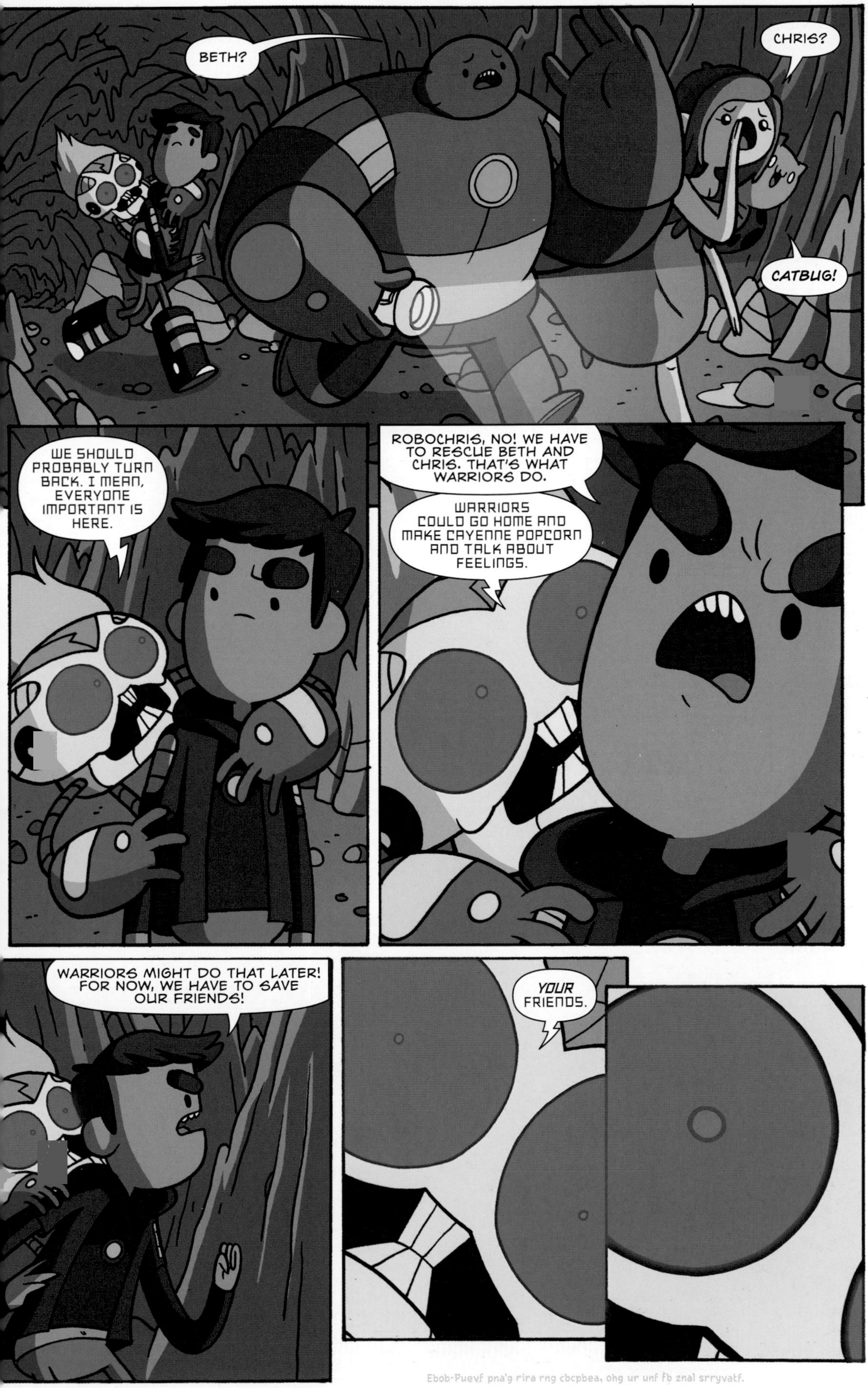
BETH?
CHRIS?
CATBUG!
WE SHOULD PROBABLY TURN BACK. I MEAN, EVERYONE IMPORTANT IS HERE.
ROBOCHRIS, NO! WE HAVE TO RESCUE BETH AND CHRIS. THAT'S WHAT WARRIORS DO.
WARRIORS COULD GO HOME AND MAKE CAYENNE POPCORN AND TALK ABOUT FEELINGS.
WARRIORS MIGHT DO THAT LATER! FOR NOW, WE HAVE TO SAVE OUR FRIENDS!
YOUR FRIENDS.

Ebob-Puevf pna'g rira rng cbcpbea, ohg ur unf fb znal srryvatf.

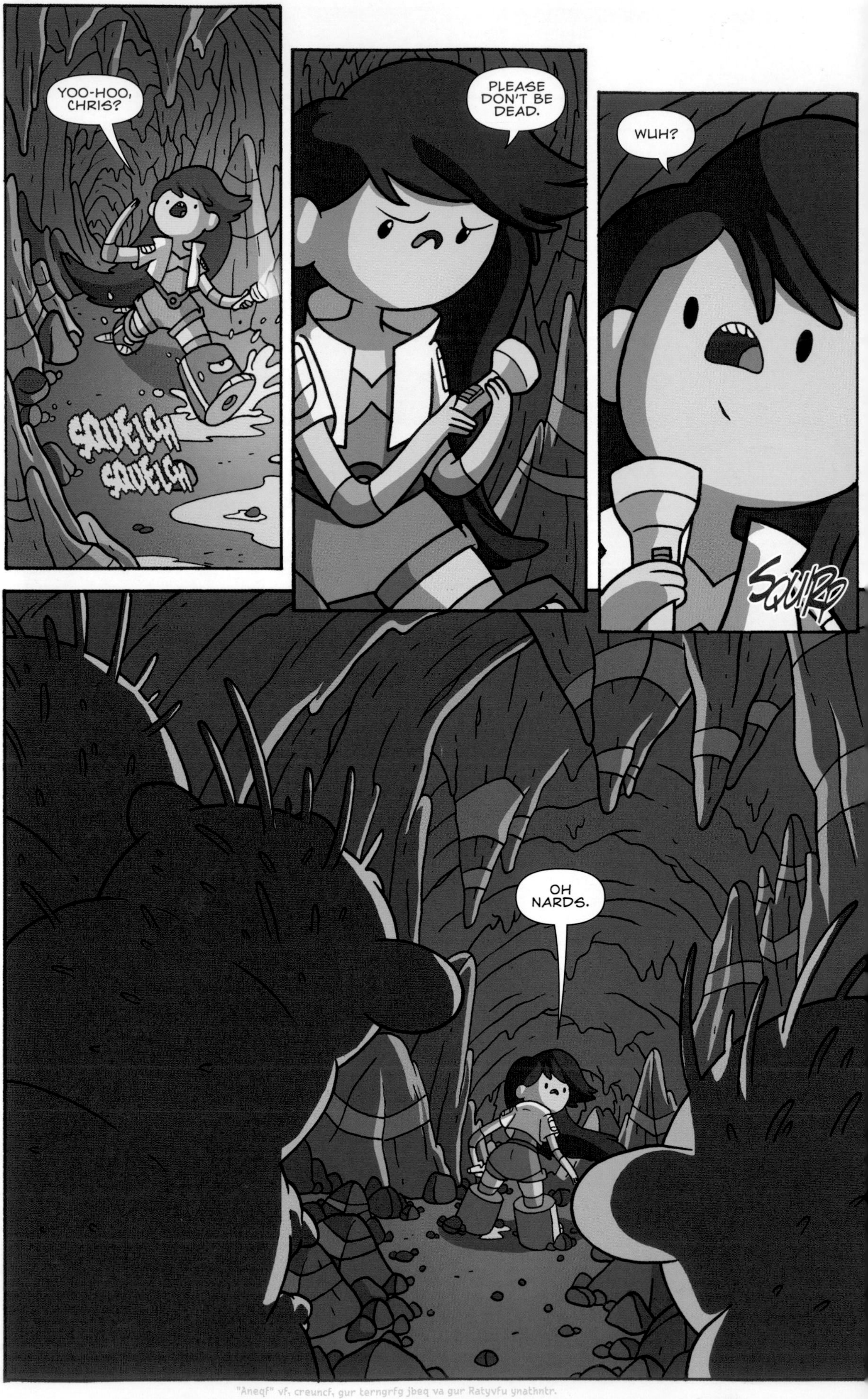
YOO-HOO, CHRIS?
SQUELCH
SQUELCH
PLEASE DON'T BE DEAD.
WUH?
SQUIRP
OH NARDS.

"Aneqf" vf, creuncf, gur terngrfg jbeq va gur Ratyvfu ynathntr.

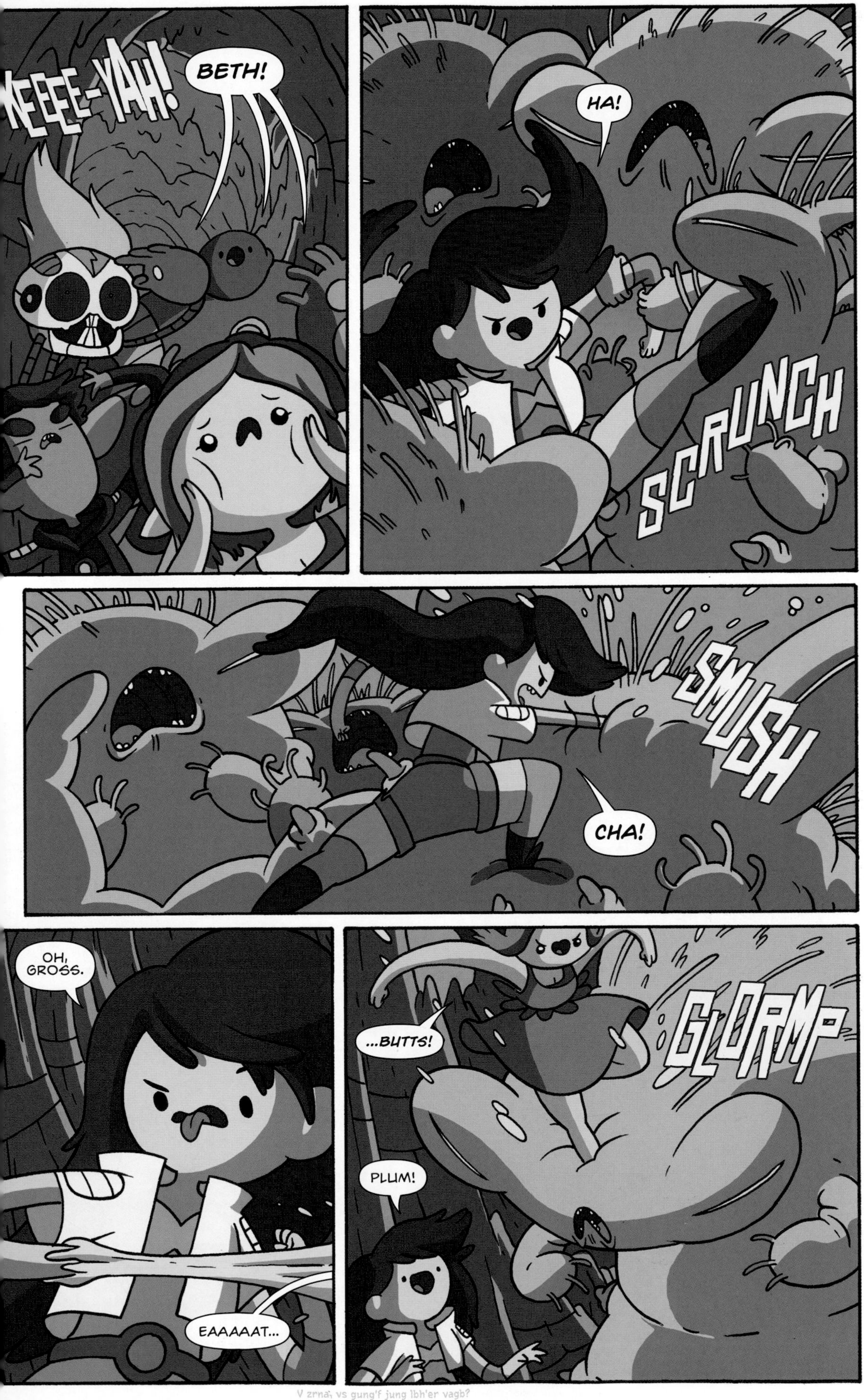
KEEEE-YAH!
BETH!
HA!
SCRUNCH
SMUSH
CHA!
OH, GROSS.
EAAAAAT...
...BUTTS!
GLORMP
PLUM!

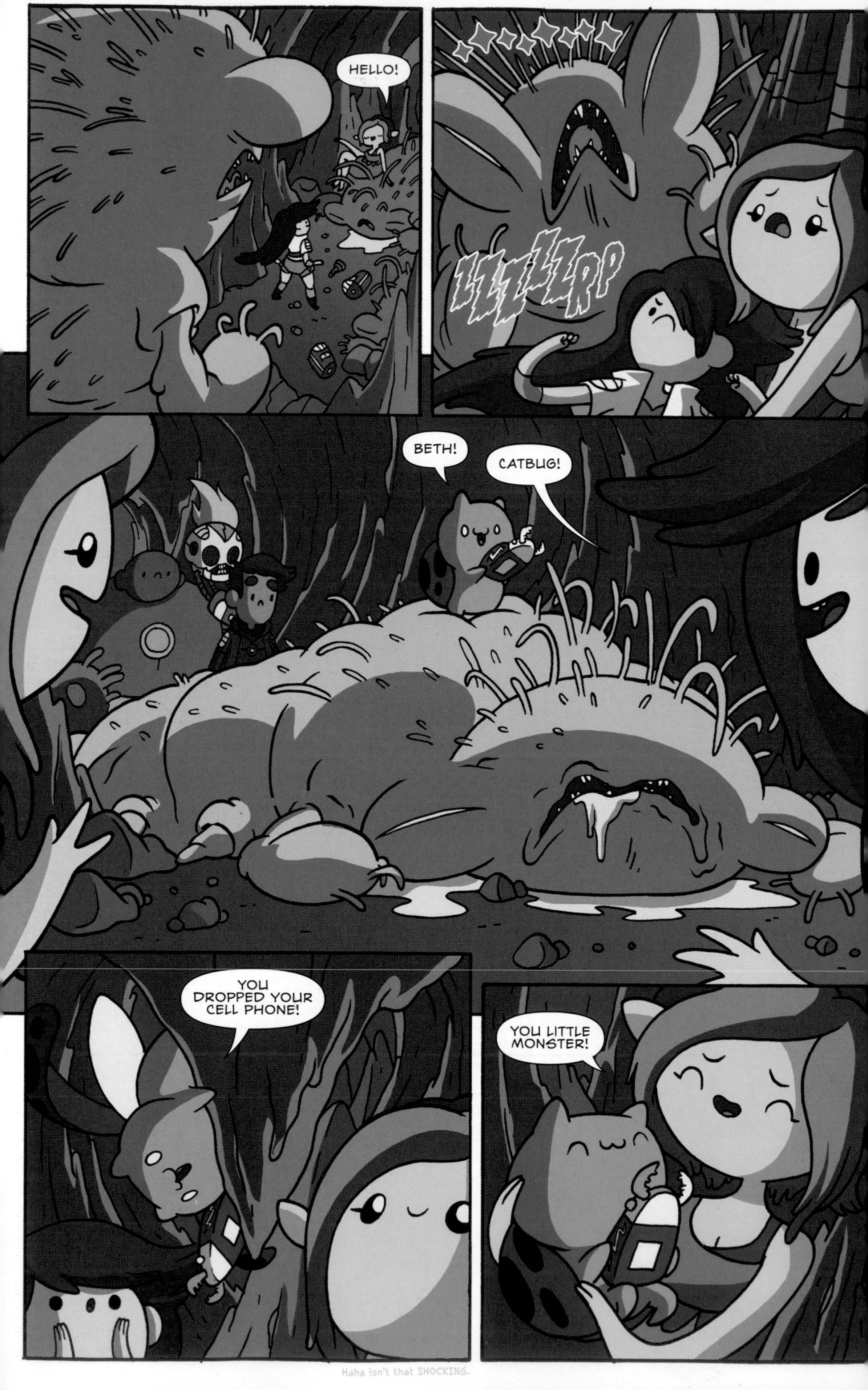
HELLO!
ZZZZZZRP
BETH!
CATBUG!
YOU DROPPED YOUR CELL PHONE!
YOU LITTLE MONSTER!

Haha isn't that SHOCKING.

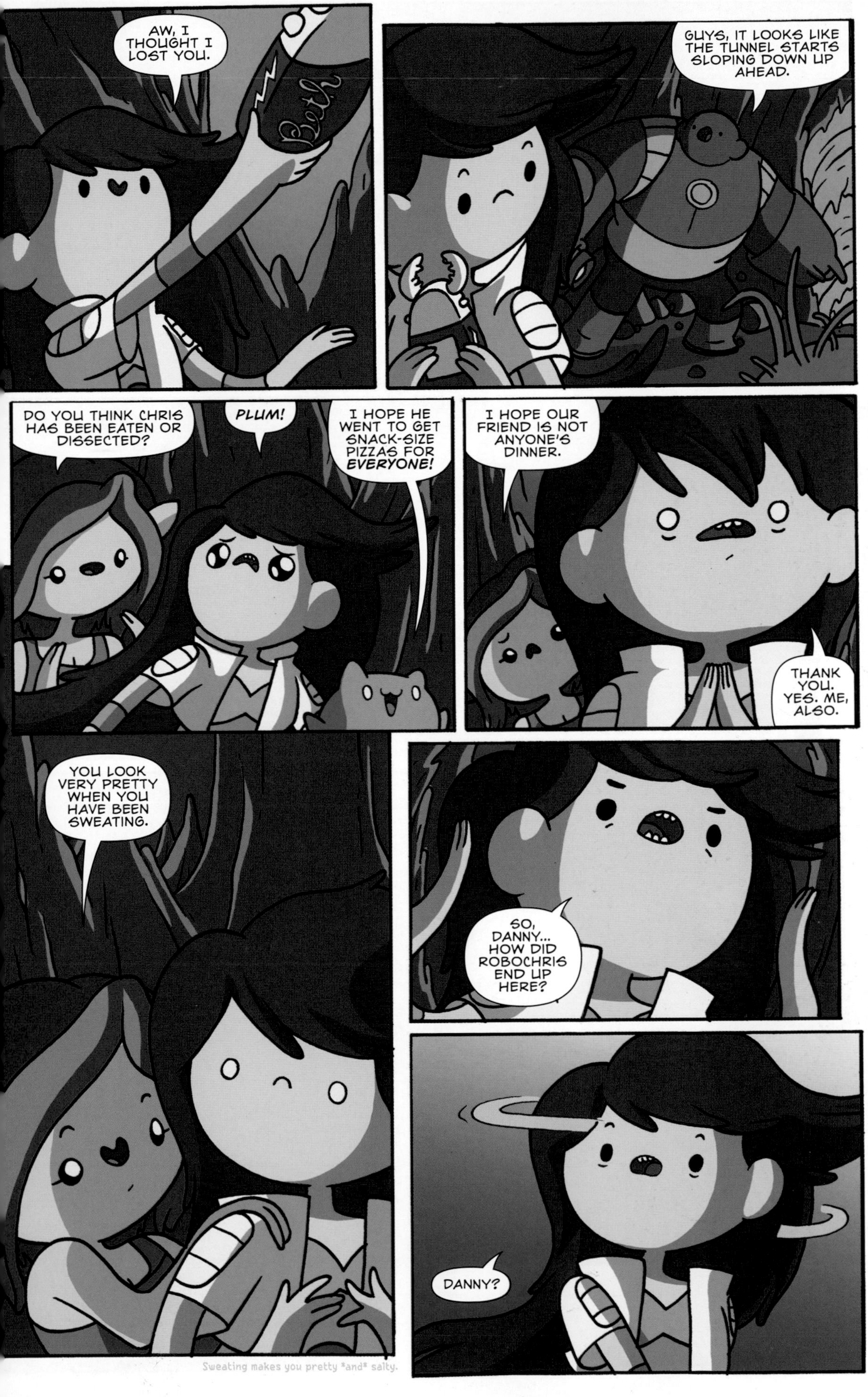
AW, I THOUGHT I LOST YOU.
Beth
GUYS, IT LOOKS LIKE THE TUNNEL STARTS SLOPING DOWN UP AHEAD.
DO YOU THINK CHRIS HAS BEEN EATEN OR DISSECTED?
PLUM!
I HOPE HE WENT TO GET SNACK-SIZE PIZZAS FOR *EVERYONE!*
I HOPE OUR FRIEND IS NOT ANYONE'S DINNER.
THANK YOU. YES. ME, ALSO.
YOU LOOK VERY PRETTY WHEN YOU HAVE BEEN SWEATING.
SO, DANNY... HOW DID ROBOCHRIS END UP HERE?
DANNY?

Sweating makes you pretty *and* salty.

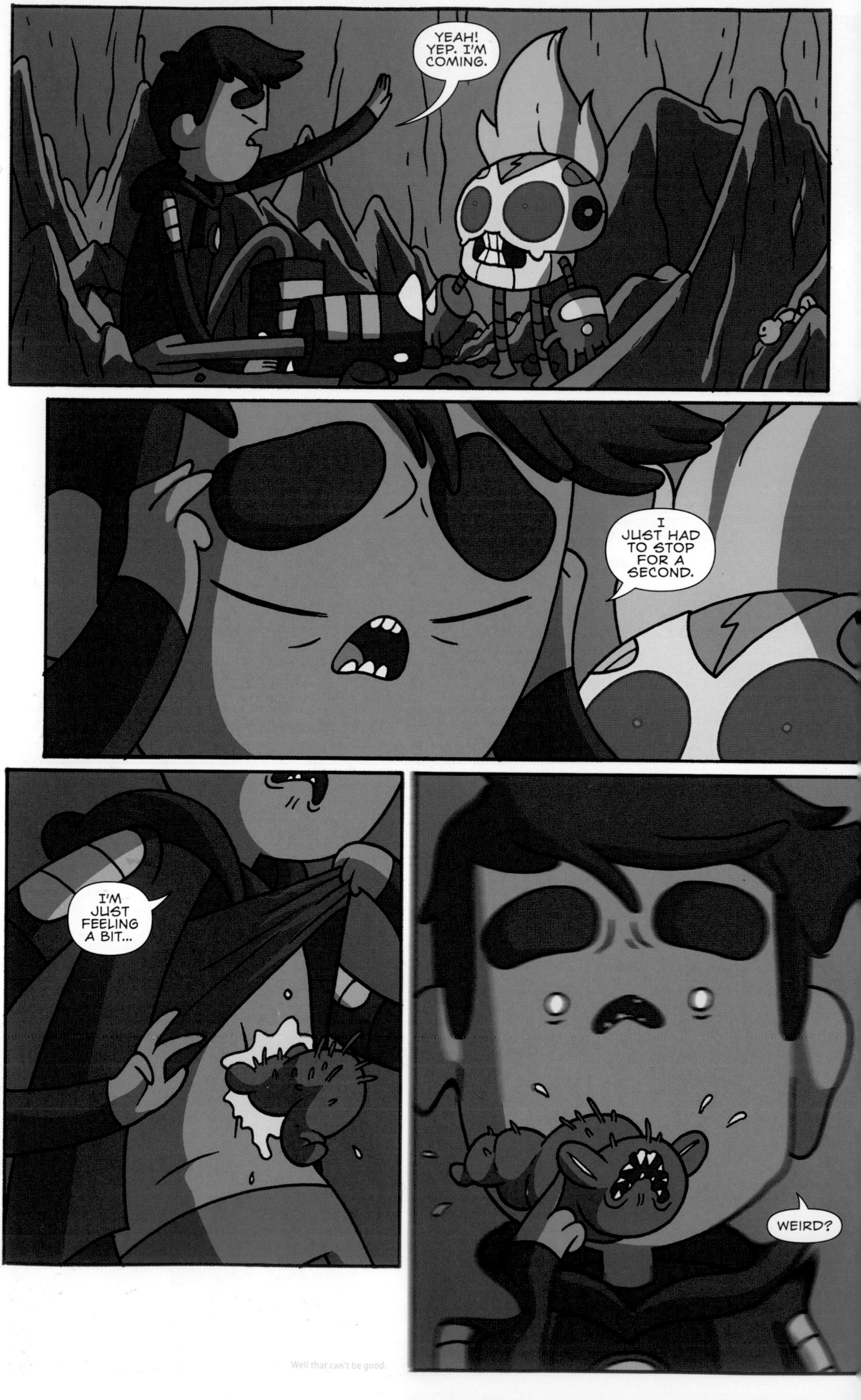
YEAH! YEP. I'M COMING.
I JUST HAD TO STOP FOR A SECOND.
I'M JUST FEELING A BIT...
WEIRD?

Well that can't be good.

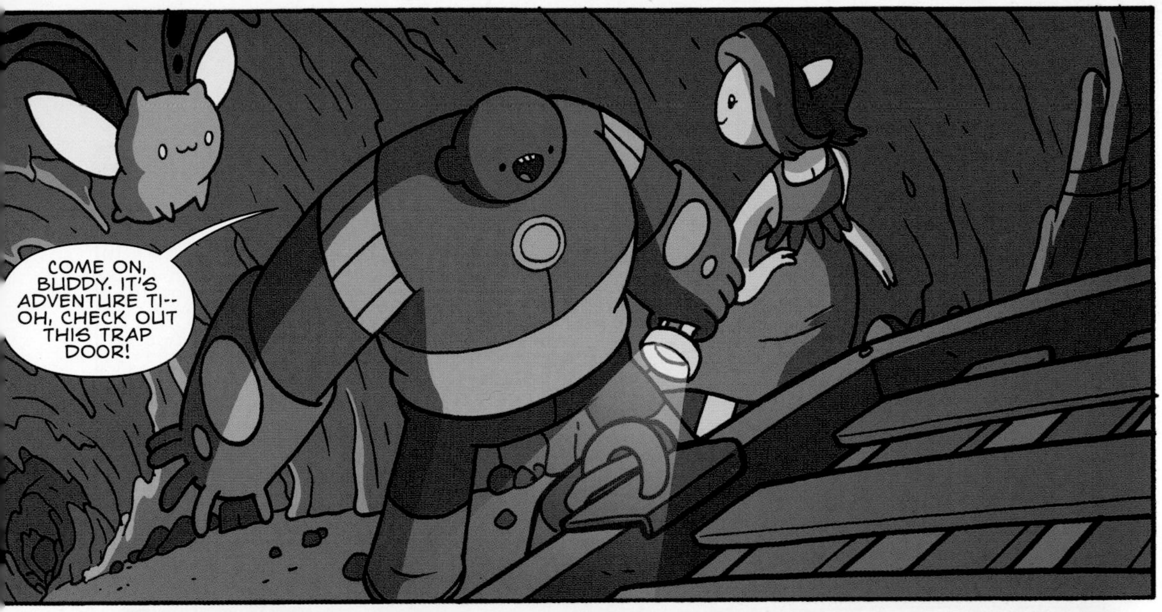
COME ON, BUDDY. IT'S ADVENTURE TI-- OH, CHECK OUT THIS TRAP DOOR!

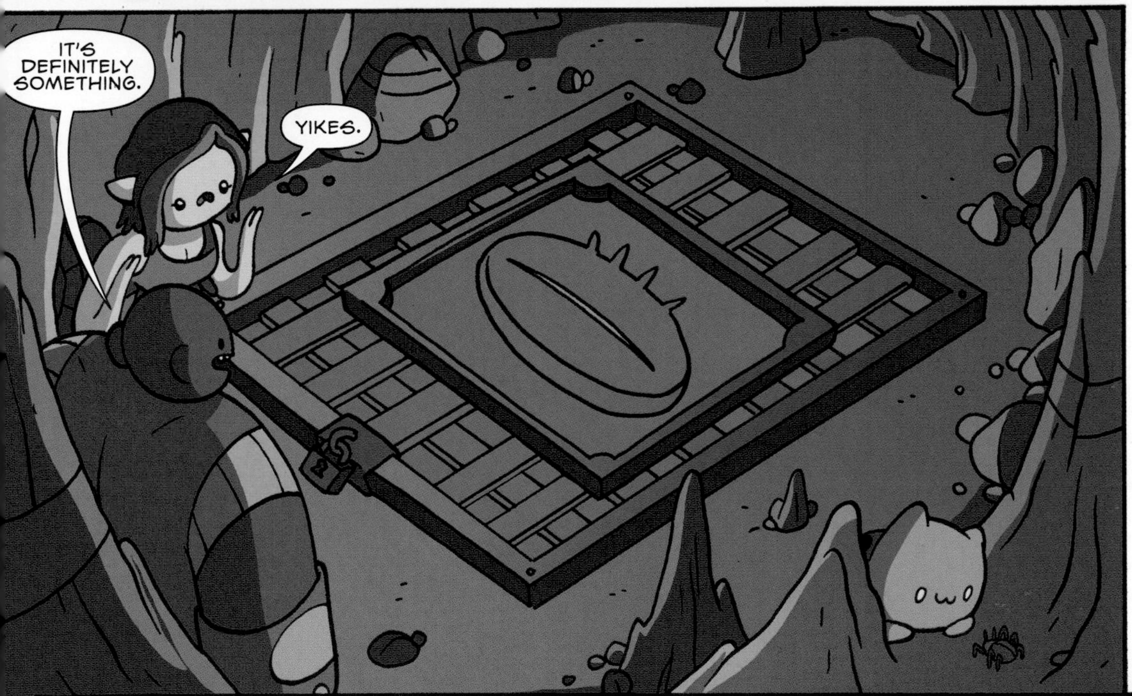
IT'S DEFINITELY SOMETHING.
YIKES.

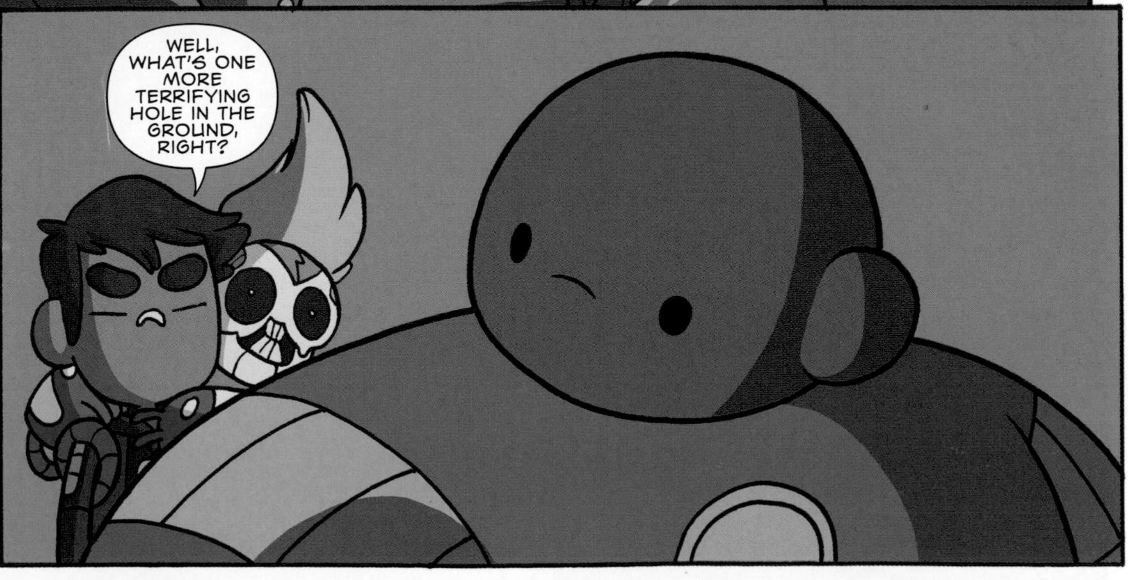
WELL, WHAT'S ONE MORE TERRIFYING HOLE IN THE GROUND, RIGHT?

That's what SHE said! You know, before she was eaten by a sandworm.

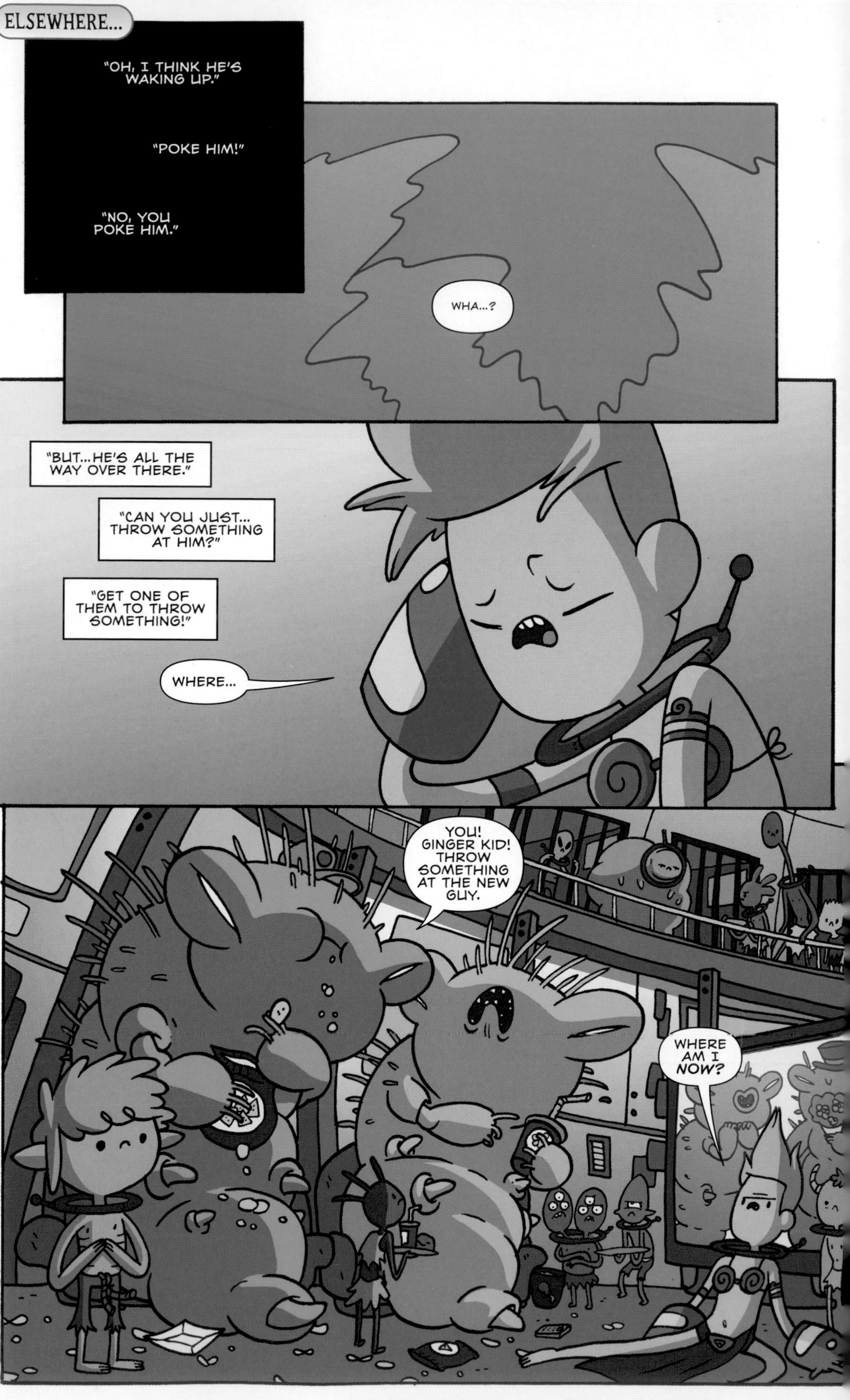
ELSEWHERE...
"OH, I THINK HE'S WAKING UP."
"POKE HIM!"
"NO, YOU POKE HIM."
WHA...?
"BUT...HE'S ALL THE WAY OVER THERE."
"CAN YOU JUST... THROW SOMETHING AT HIM?"
"GET ONE OF THEM TO THROW SOMETHING!"
WHERE...
YOU! GINGER KID! THROW SOMETHING AT THE NEW GUY.
WHERE AM I NOW?

Chris probably shouldn't fall asleep for awhile.

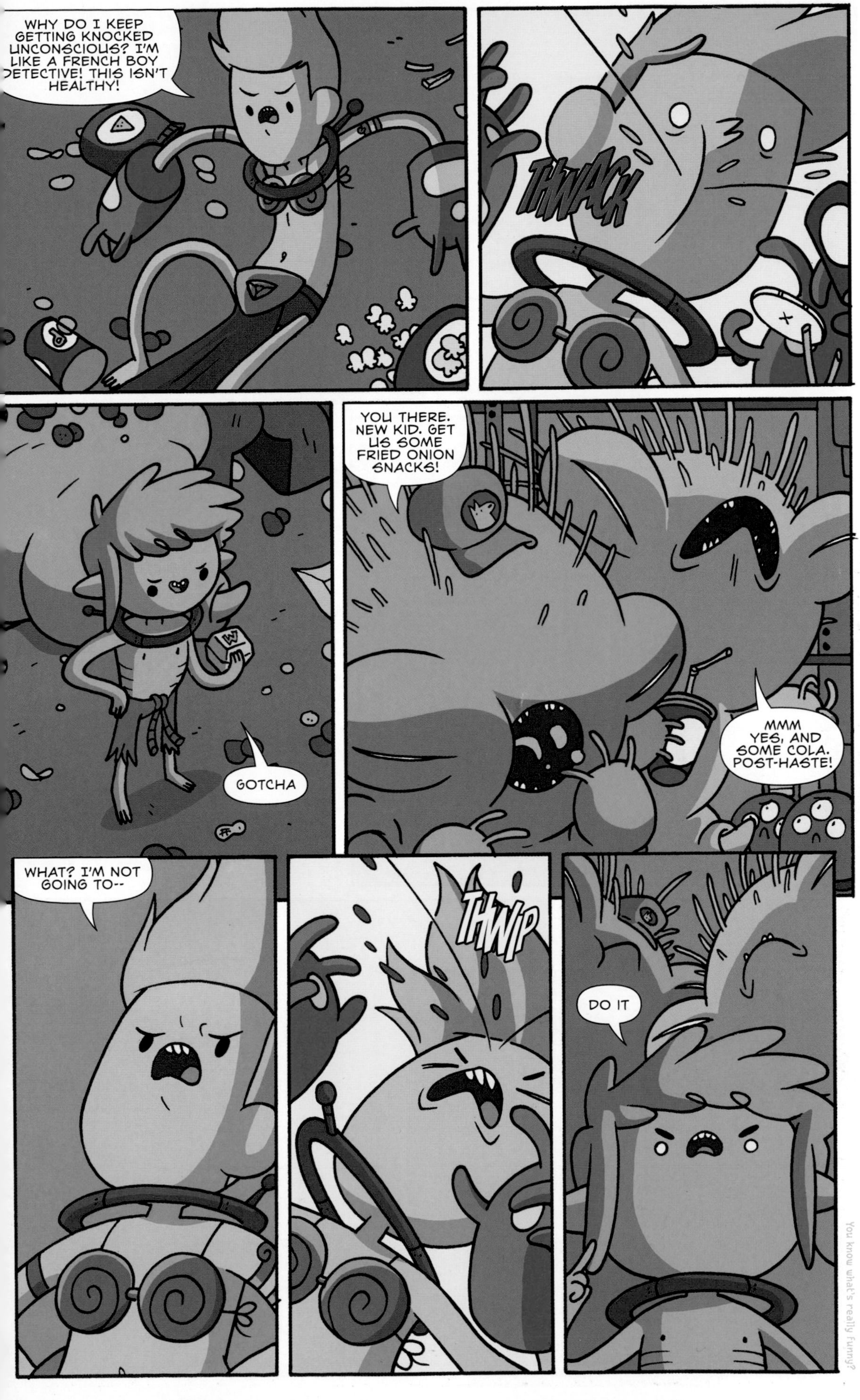
WHY DO I KEEP GETTING KNOCKED UNCONSCIOUS? I'M LIKE A FRENCH BOY DETECTIVE! THIS ISN'T HEALTHY!
THWACK
YOU THERE. NEW KID. GET US SOME FRIED ONION SNACKS!
GOTCHA
MMM YES, AND SOME COLA. POST-HASTE!
WHAT? I'M NOT GOING TO--
THWIP
DO IT

You know what's really funny?

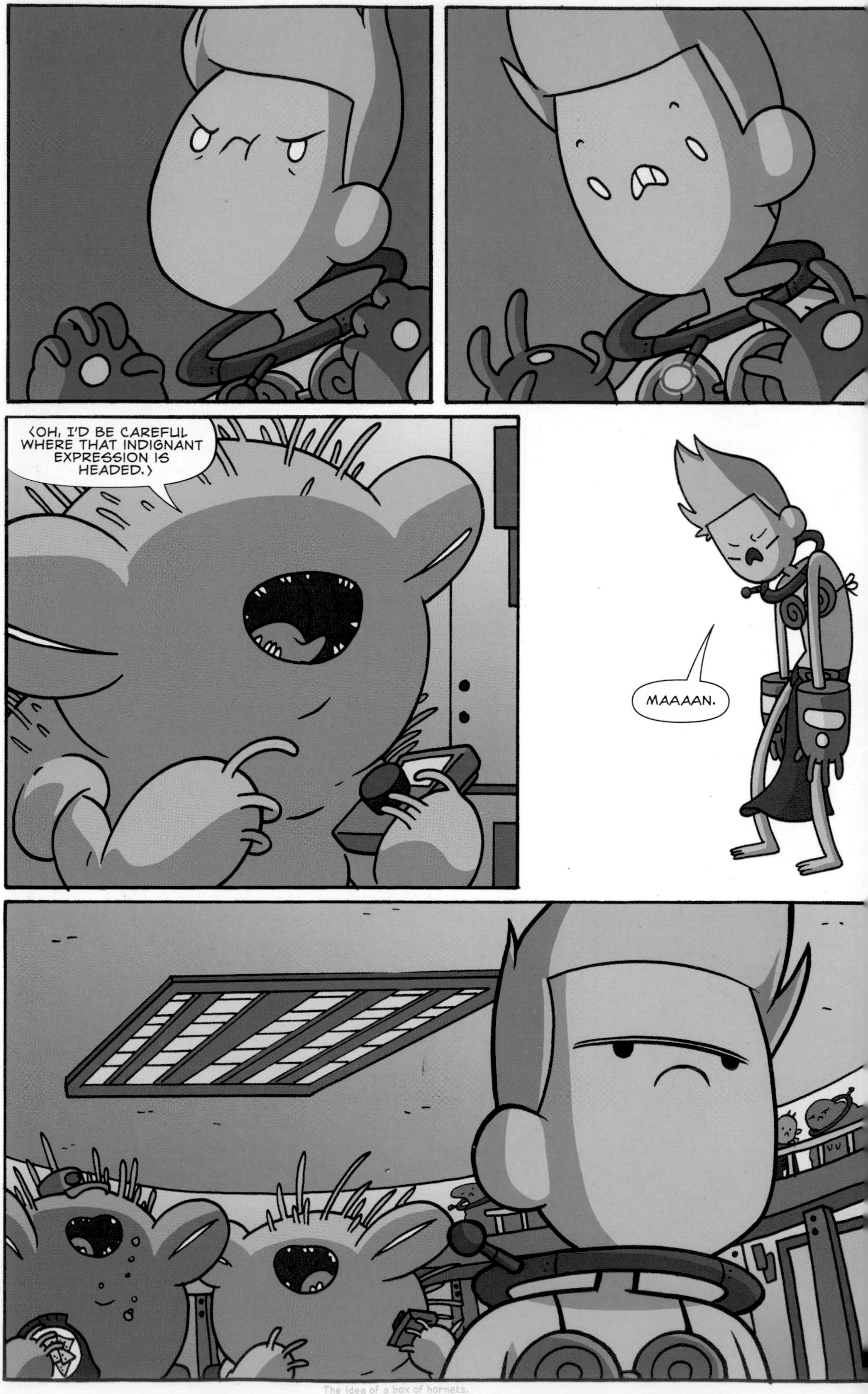

‹OH, I'D BE CAREFUL WHERE THAT INDIGNANT EXPRESSION IS HEADED.›
MAAAAN.

The idea of a box of hornets.

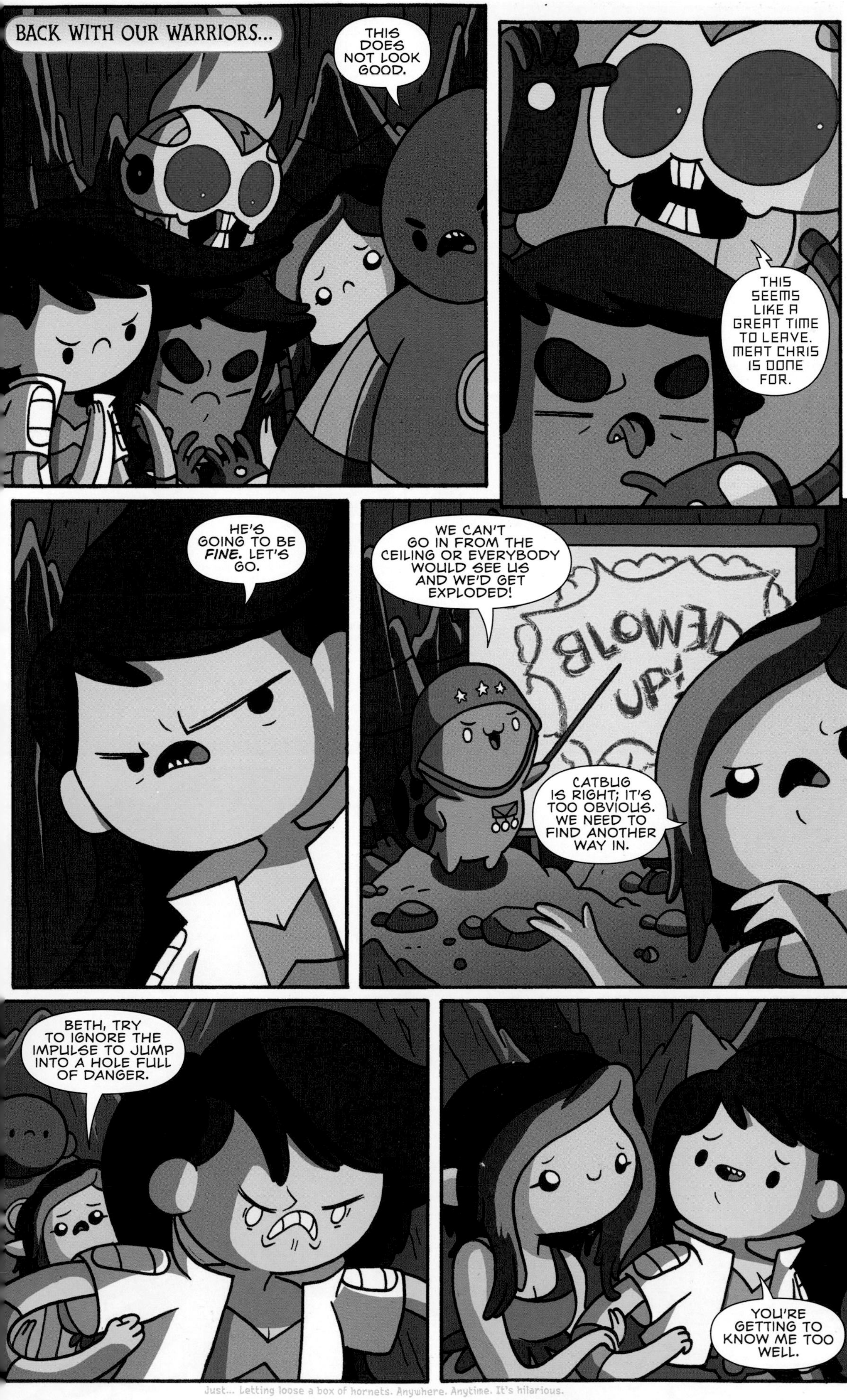

BACK WITH OUR WARRIORS...
THIS DOES NOT LOOK GOOD.
THIS SEEMS LIKE A GREAT TIME TO LEAVE. MEAT CHRIS IS DONE FOR.
HE'S GOING TO BE FINE. LET'S GO.
WE CAN'T GO IN FROM THE CEILING OR EVERYBODY WOULD SEE US AND WE'D GET EXPLODED!
BLOWED UP!
CATBUG IS RIGHT; IT'S TOO OBVIOUS. WE NEED TO FIND ANOTHER WAY IN.
BETH, TRY TO IGNORE THE IMPULSE TO JUMP INTO A HOLE FULL OF DANGER.
YOU'RE GETTING TO KNOW ME TOO WELL.

Just... Letting loose a box of hornets. Anywhere. Anytime. It's hilarious.

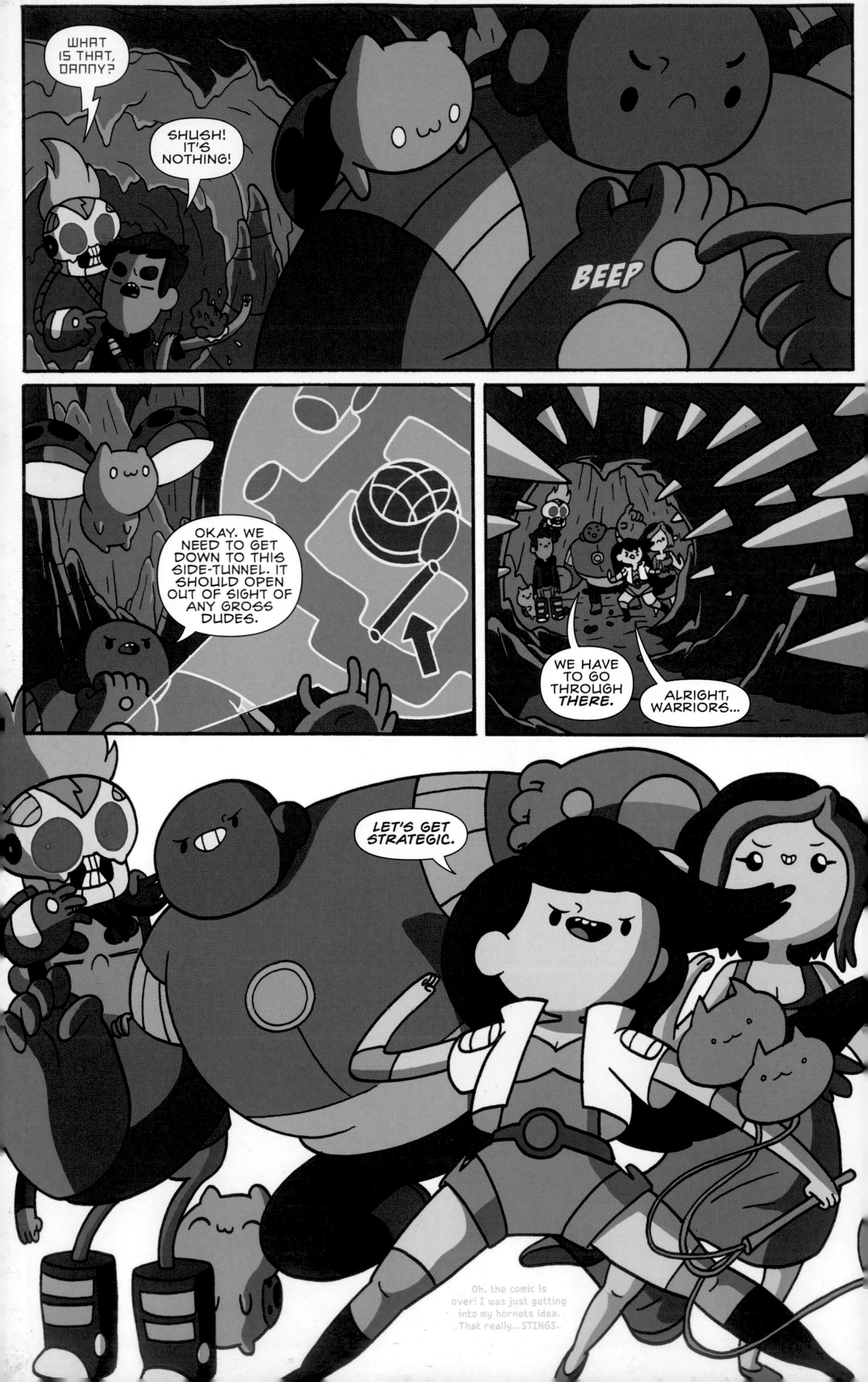
WHAT IS THAT, DANNY?
SHUSH! IT'S NOTHING!
BEEP
OKAY. WE NEED TO GET DOWN TO THIS SIDE-TUNNEL. IT SHOULD OPEN OUT OF SIGHT OF ANY GROSS DUDES.
WE HAVE TO GO THROUGH *THERE.*
ALRIGHT, WARRIORS...
LET'S GET STRATEGIC.
Oh, the comic is over! I was just getting into my hornets idea. That really...STINGS.

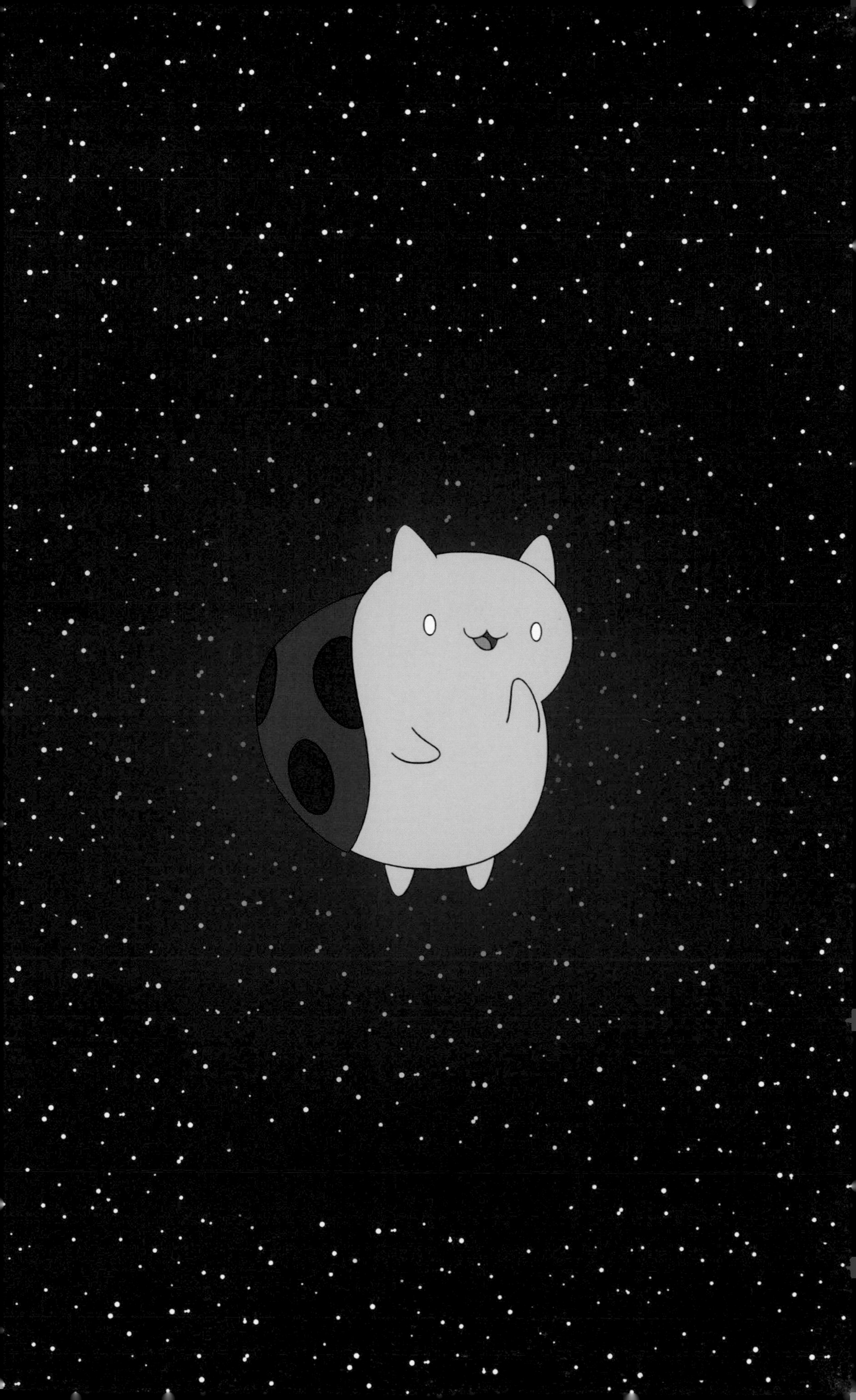

CHAPTER 23

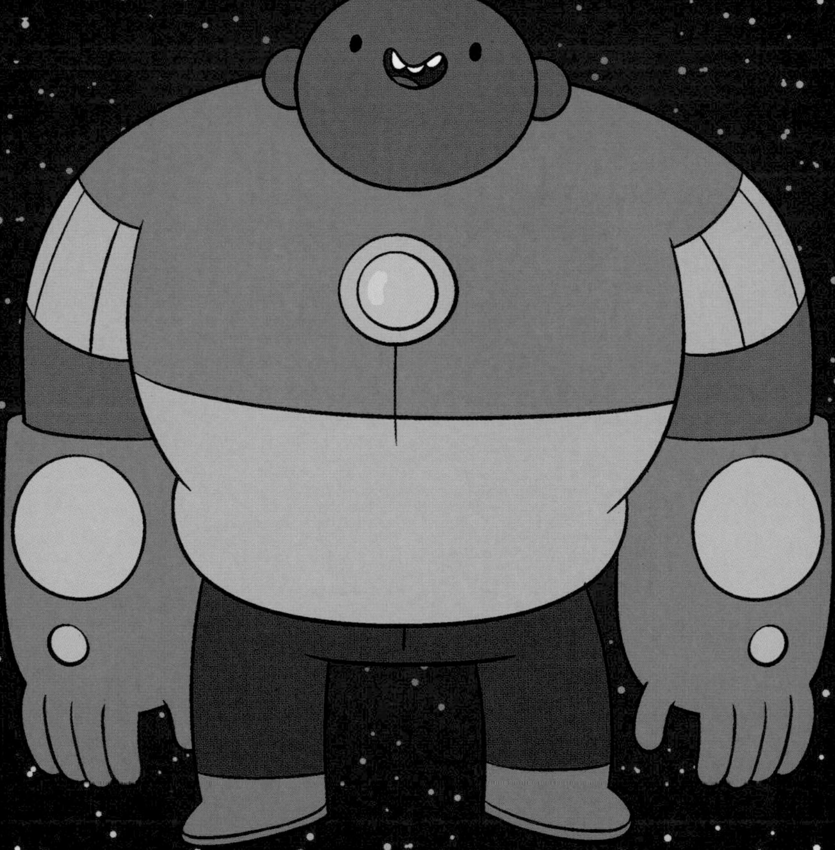

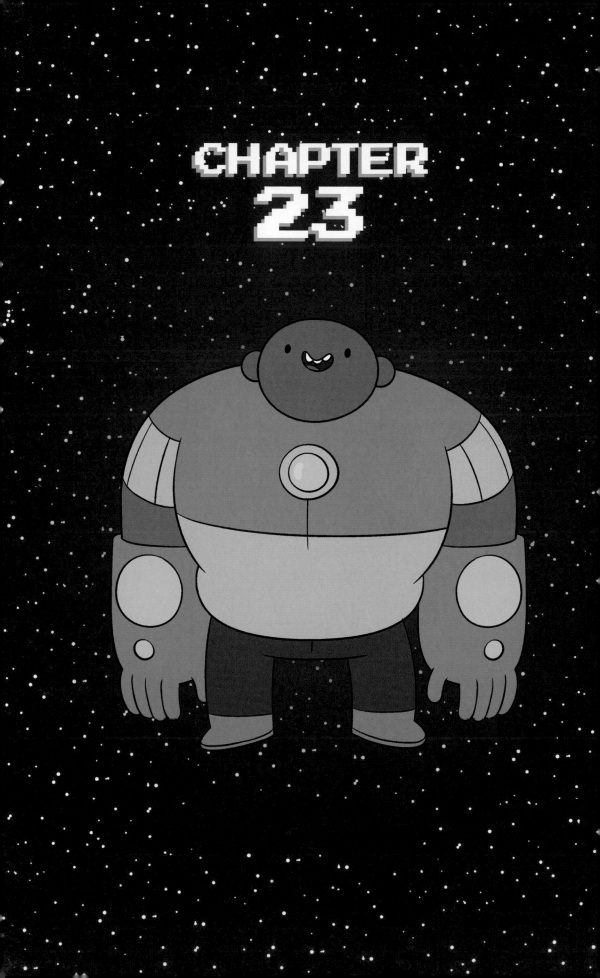

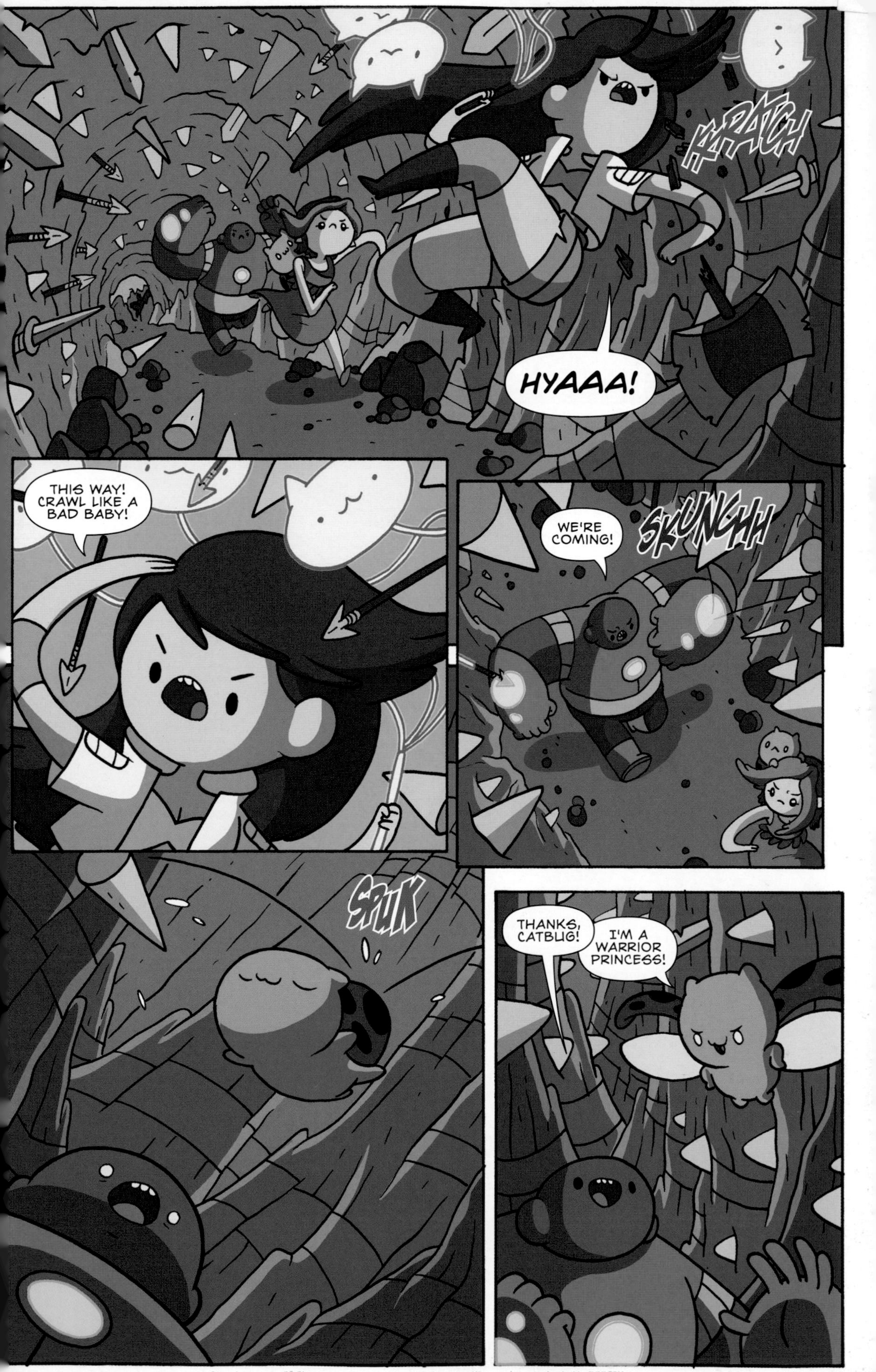
KRATCH
HYAAA!
THIS WAY! CRAWL LIKE A BAD BABY!
WE'RE COMING!
SKUNCHH
SPUK
THANKS, CATBUG!
I'M A WARRIOR PRINCESS!

Ah, where was I? I'm ready. Ian, you ready? You look like you're ready. Let's BEEGIN.

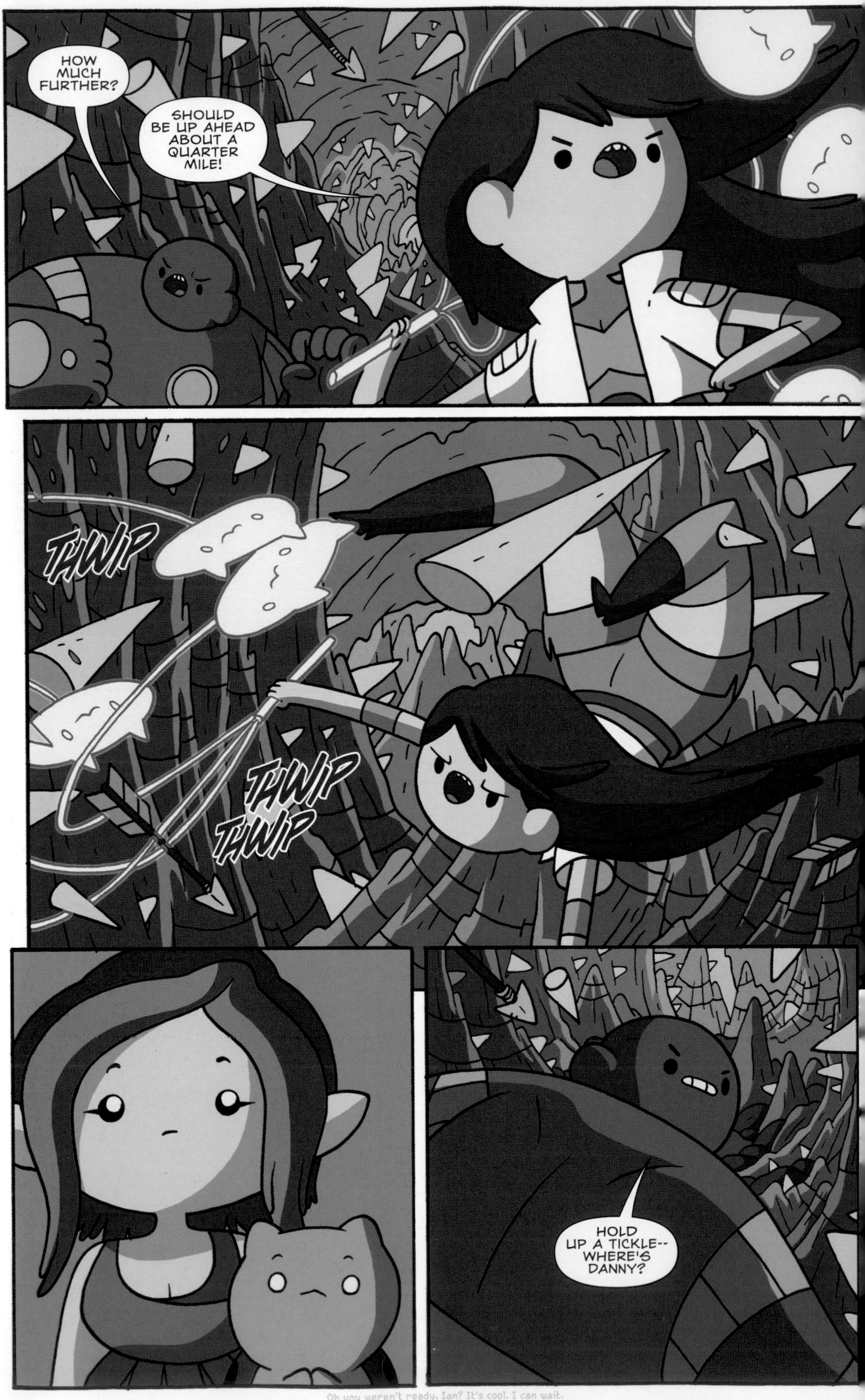
HOW MUCH FURTHER?
SHOULD BE UP AHEAD ABOUT A QUARTER MILE!
THWIP
THWIP THWIP
HOLD UP A TICKLE-- WHERE'S DANNY?

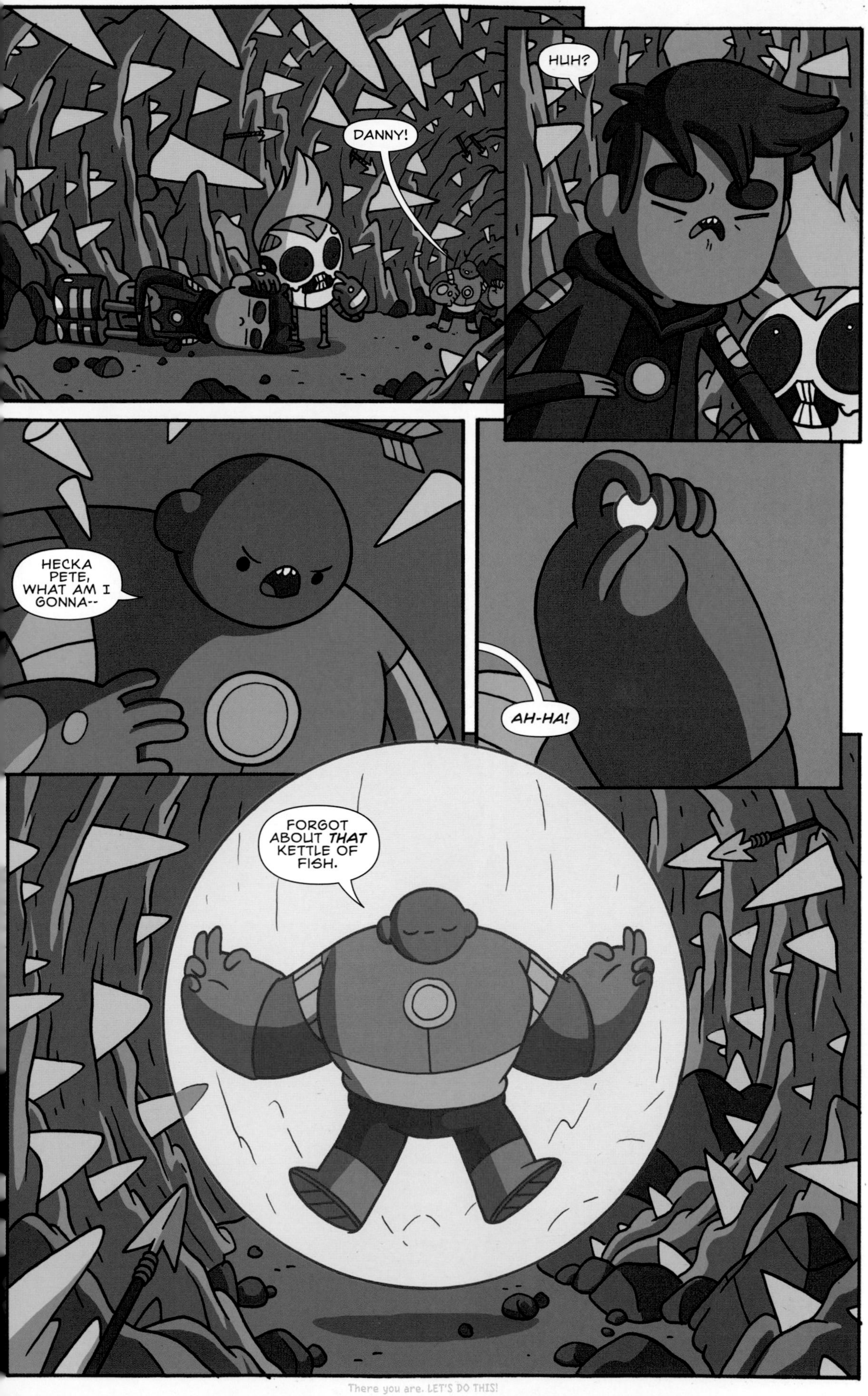
DANNY!
HUH?
HECKA PETE, WHAT AM I GONNA--
AH-HA!
FORGOT ABOUT *THAT* KETTLE OF FISH.

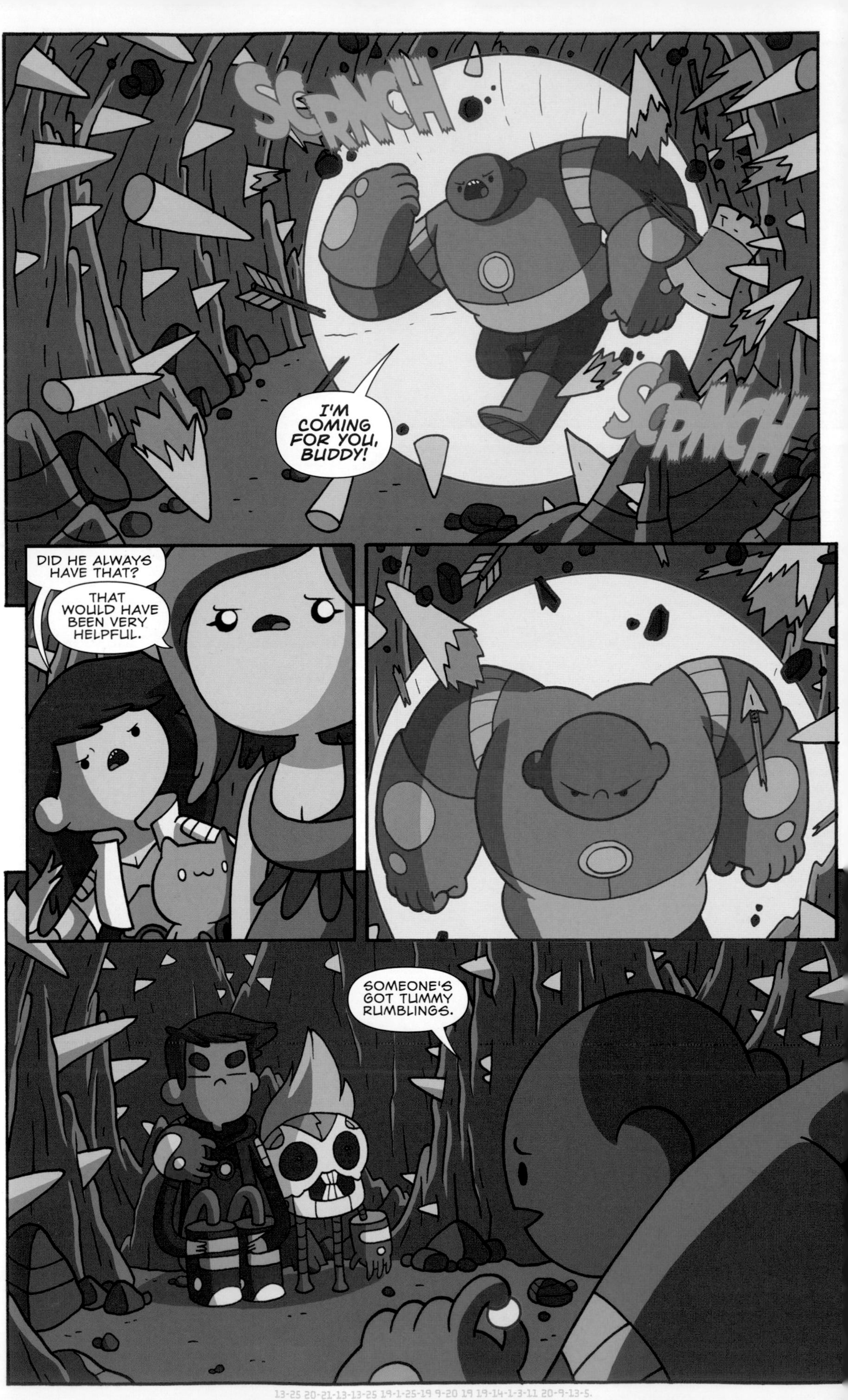
SCRNCH
SCRNCH
I'M COMING FOR YOU, BUDDY!
DID HE ALWAYS HAVE THAT?
THAT WOULD HAVE BEEN VERY HELPFUL.
SOMEONE'S GOT TUMMY RUMBLINGS.

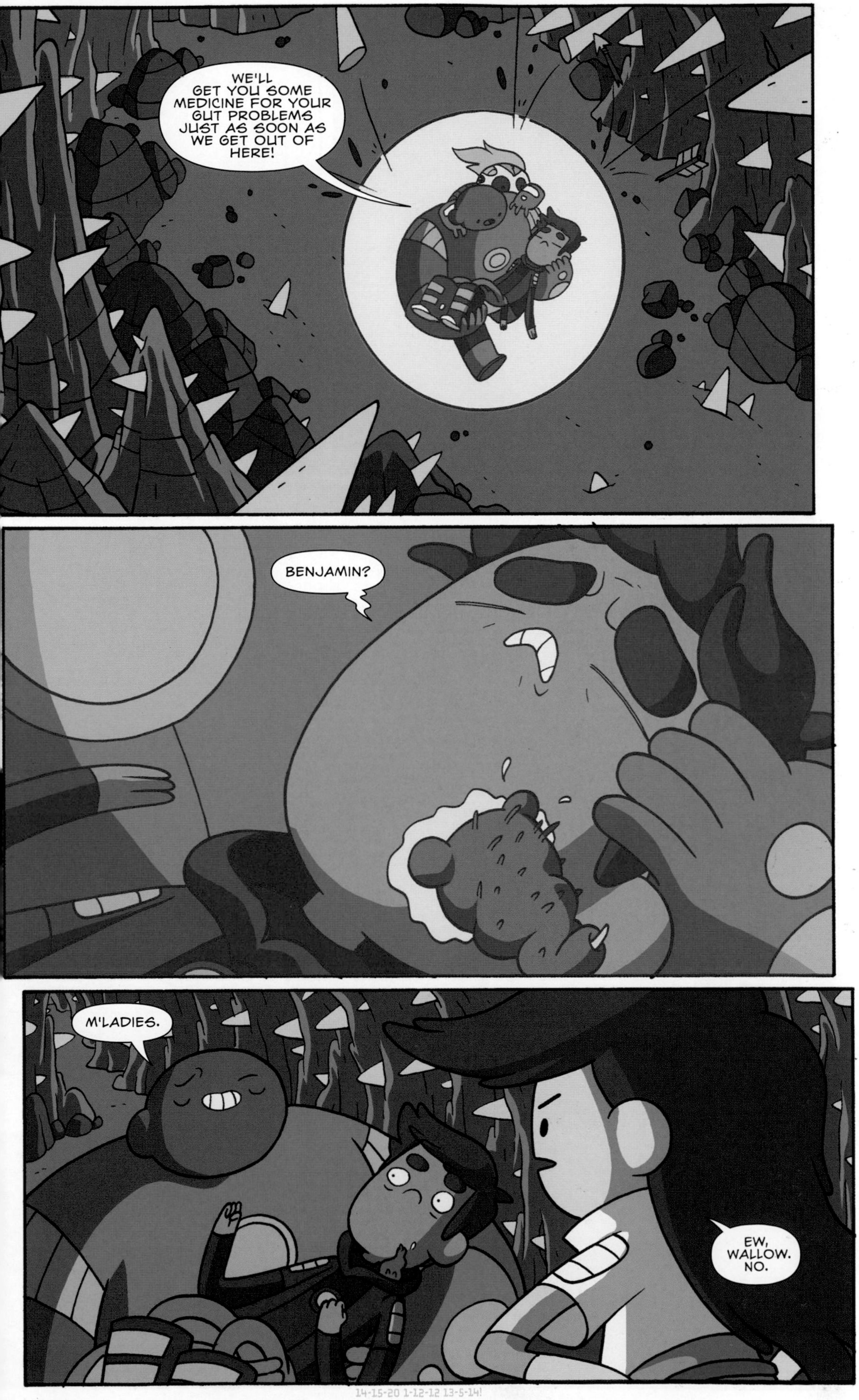
WE'LL GET YOU SOME MEDICINE FOR YOUR GUT PROBLEMS JUST AS SOON AS WE GET OUT OF HERE!
BENJAMIN?
M'LADIES.
EW, WALLOW. NO.

14-15-20 1-12-12 13-5-14!

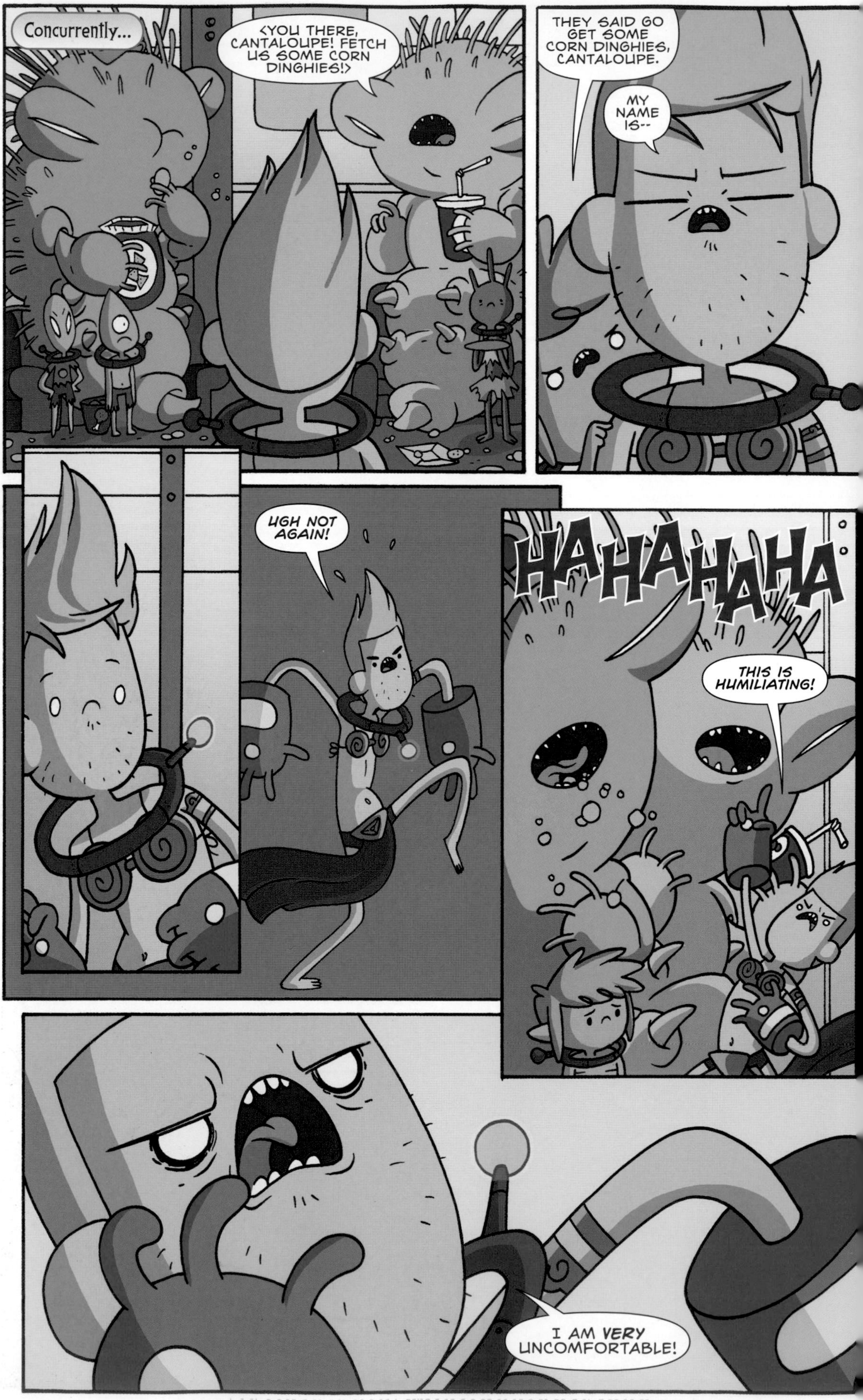
Concurrently...
<YOU THERE, CANTALOUPE! FETCH US SOME CORN DINGHIES!>
THEY SAID GO GET SOME CORN DINGHIES, CANTALOUPE.
MY NAME IS--
UGH NOT AGAIN!
HAHAHAHA
THIS IS HUMILIATING!
I AM VERY UNCOMFORTABLE!

4-1-14-3-5 12-9-11-5 14-15-2-15-4-25'19 5-12-5-3-20-18-15-3-21-20-9-14-7 25-15-21

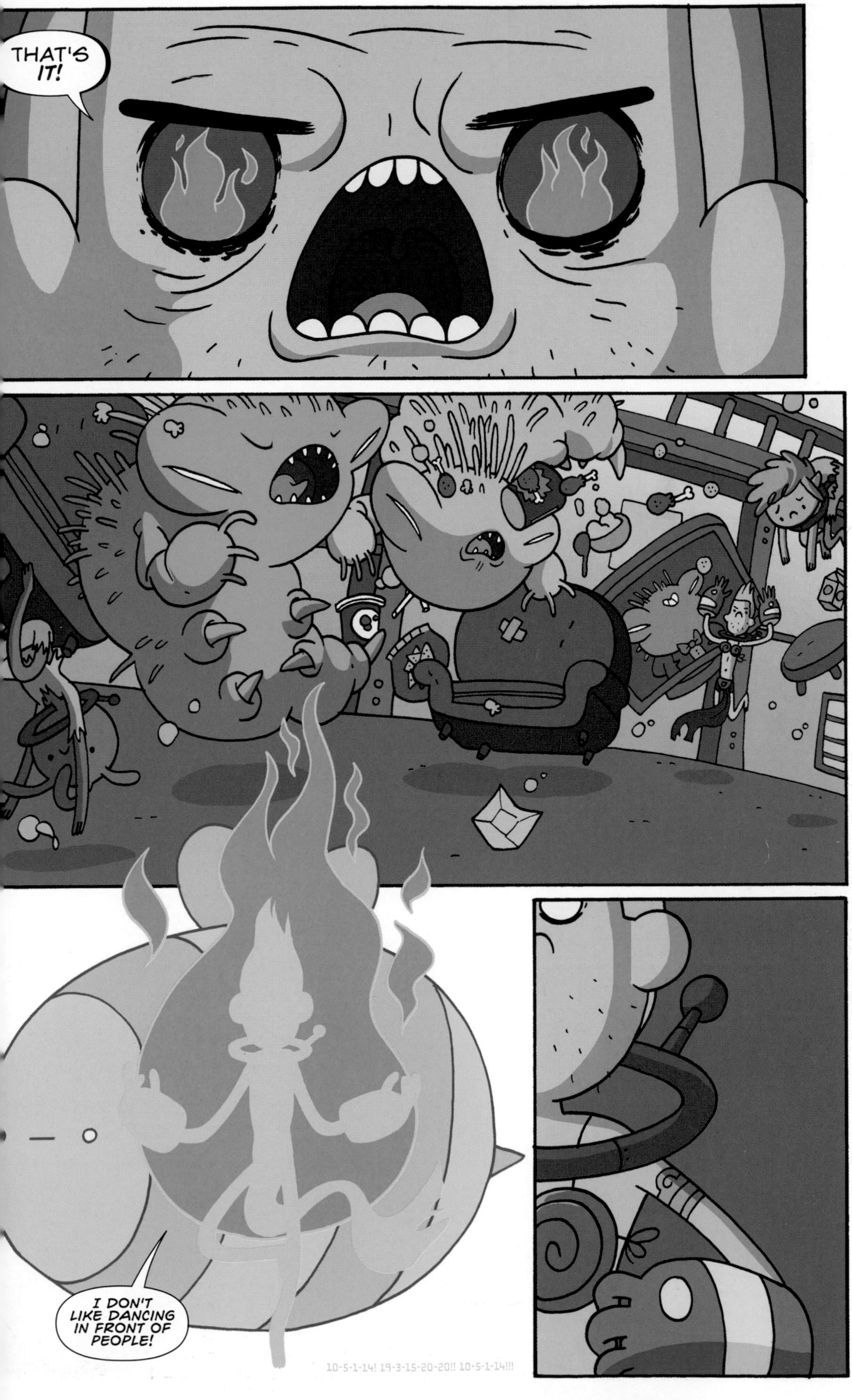
THAT'S IT!
I DON'T LIKE DANCING IN FRONT OF PEOPLE!

10-5-1-14! 19-3-15-20-20!! 10-5-1-14!!!

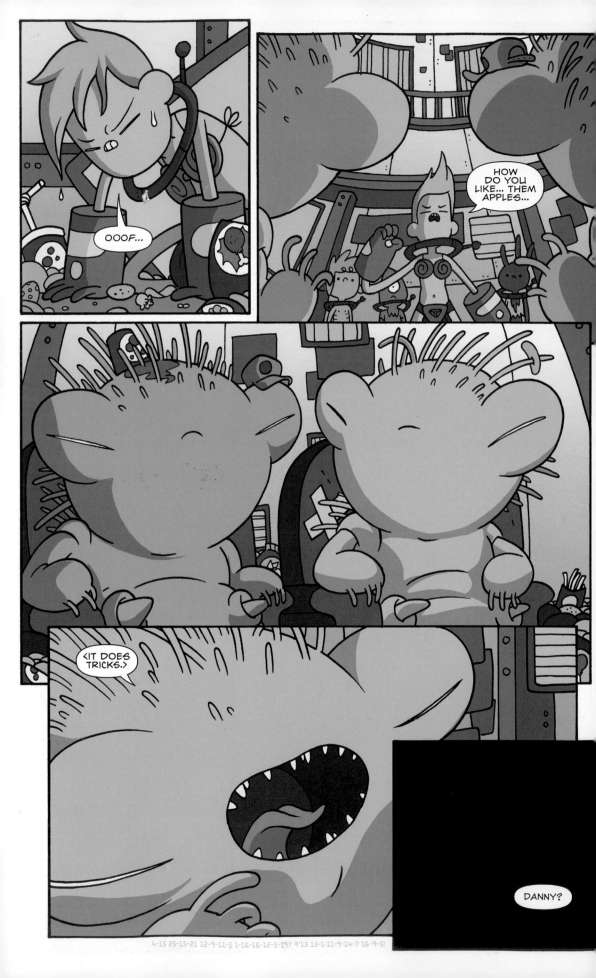

OOOF...

HOW DO YOU LIKE... THEM APPLES...

<IT DOES TRICKS.>

DANNY?

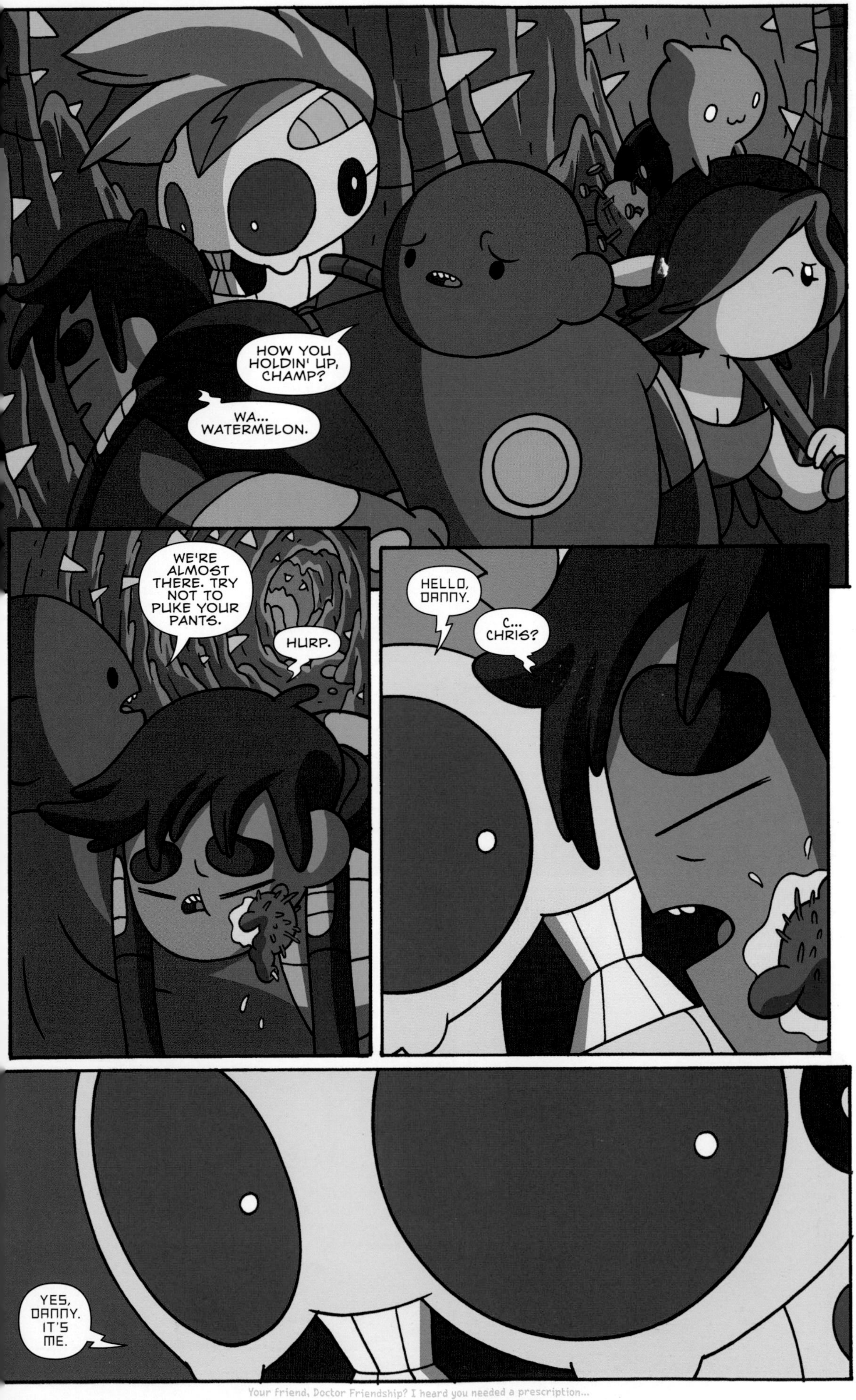
HOW YOU HOLDIN' UP, CHAMP?
WA... WATERMELON.
WE'RE ALMOST THERE. TRY NOT TO PUKE YOUR PANTS.
HURP.
HELLO, DANNY.
C... CHRIS?
YES, DANNY. IT'S ME.

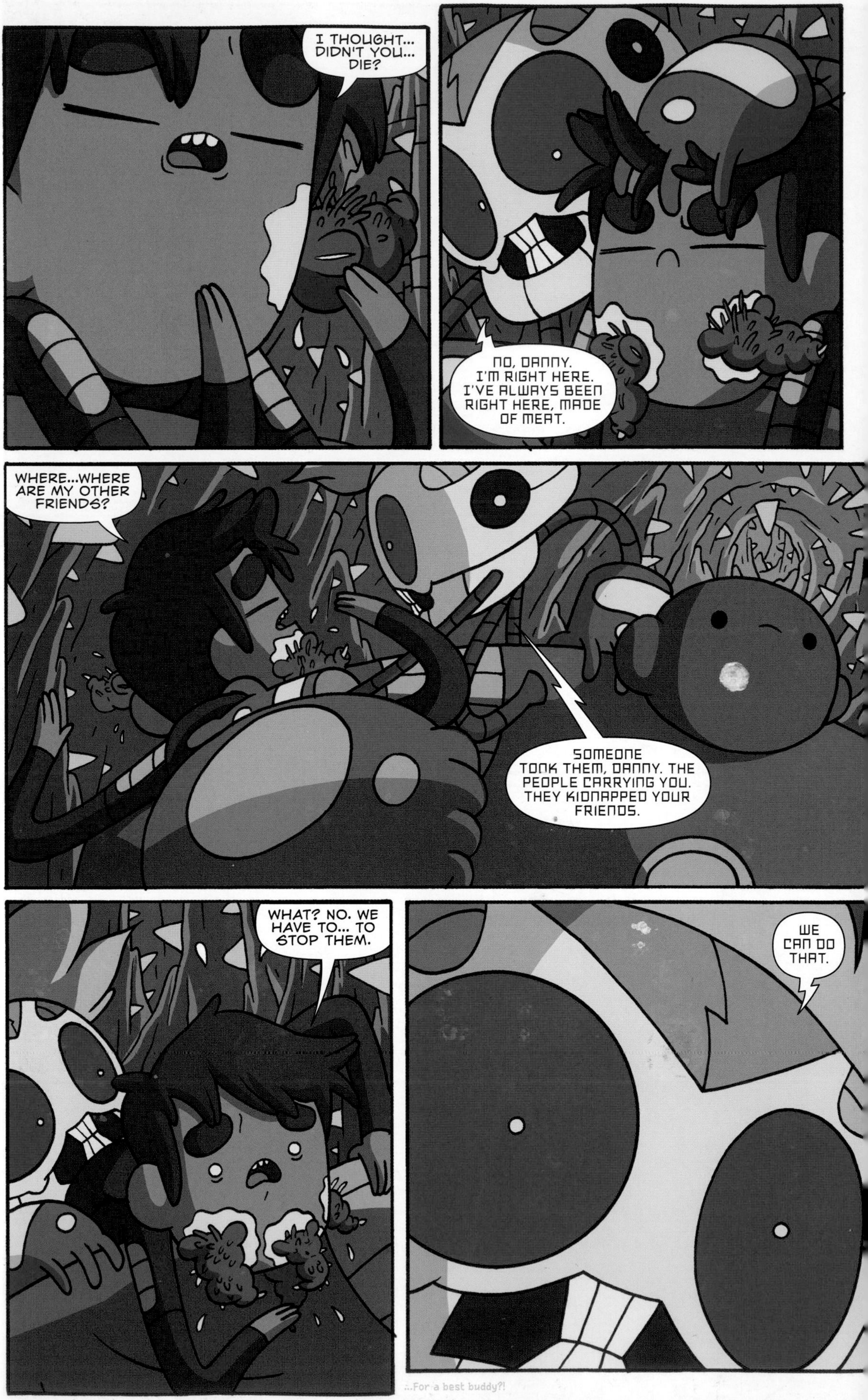
I THOUGHT... DIDN'T YOU... DIE?
NO, DANNY. I'M RIGHT HERE. I'VE ALWAYS BEEN RIGHT HERE, MADE OF MEAT.
WHERE...WHERE ARE MY OTHER FRIENDS?
SOMEONE TOOK THEM, DANNY. THE PEOPLE CARRYING YOU. THEY KIDNAPPED YOUR FRIENDS.
WHAT? NO. WE HAVE TO... TO STOP THEM.
WE CAN DO THAT.

...For a best buddy?!

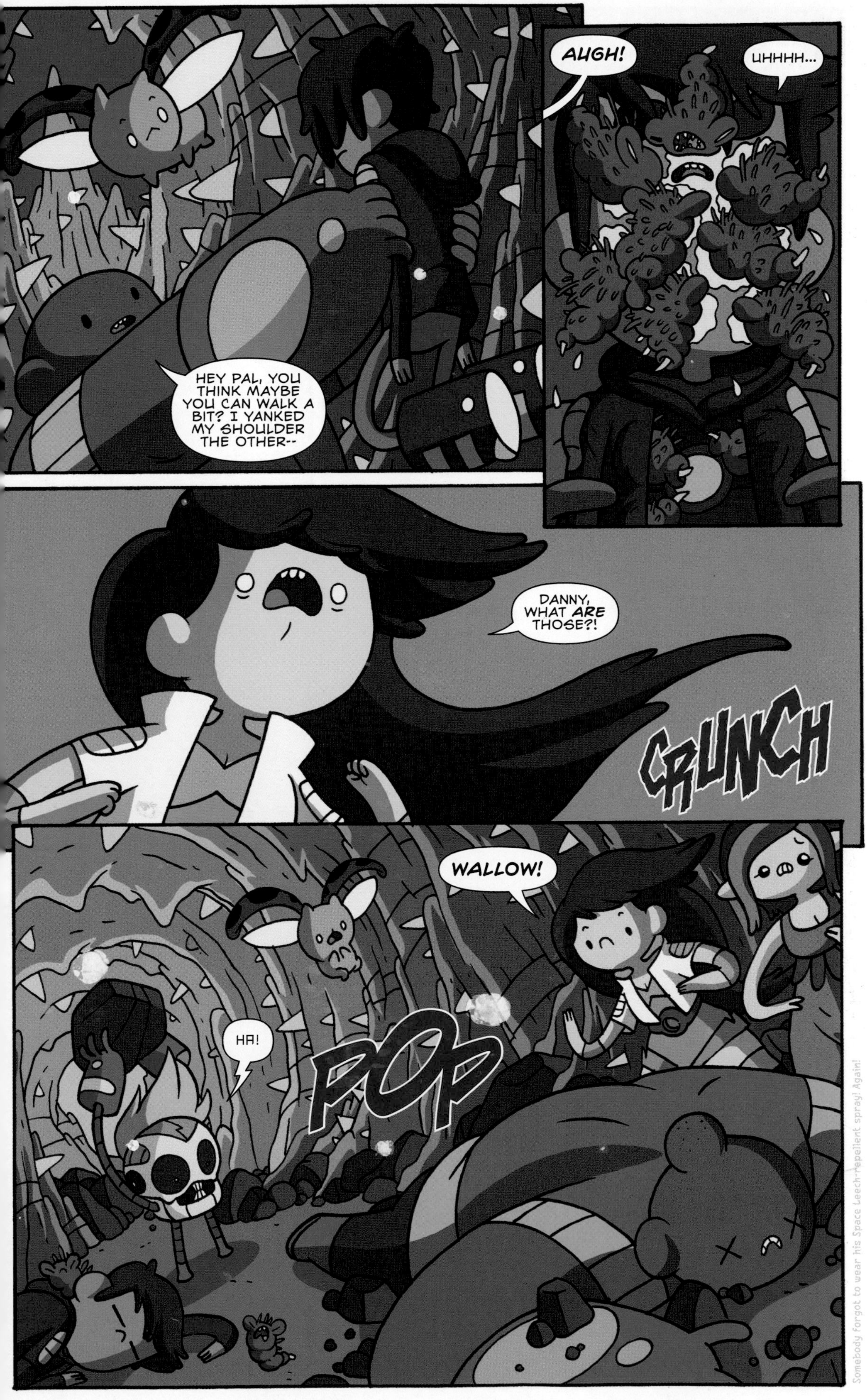
HEY PAL, YOU THINK MAYBE YOU CAN WALK A BIT? I YANKED MY SHOULDER THE OTHER--
AUGH!
UHHHH...
DANNY, WHAT ARE THOSE?!
CRUNCH
WALLOW!
HA!
POP

Somebody forgot to wear his Space Leech-repellent spray! Again!

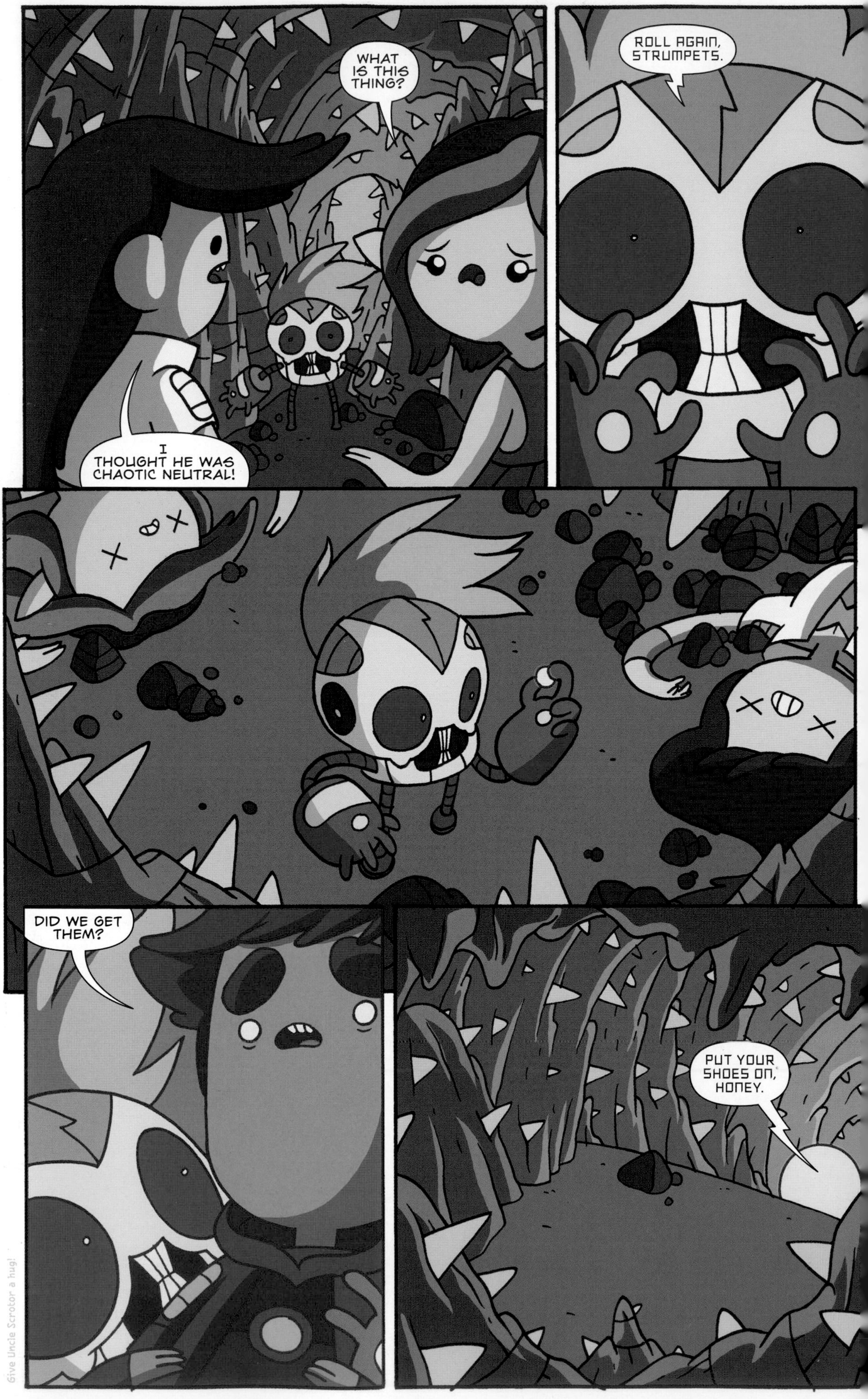
WHAT IS THIS THING?
I THOUGHT HE WAS CHAOTIC NEUTRAL!
ROLL AGAIN, STRUMPETS.
DID WE GET THEM?
PUT YOUR SHOES ON, HONEY.
Give Uncle Scrotor a hug!

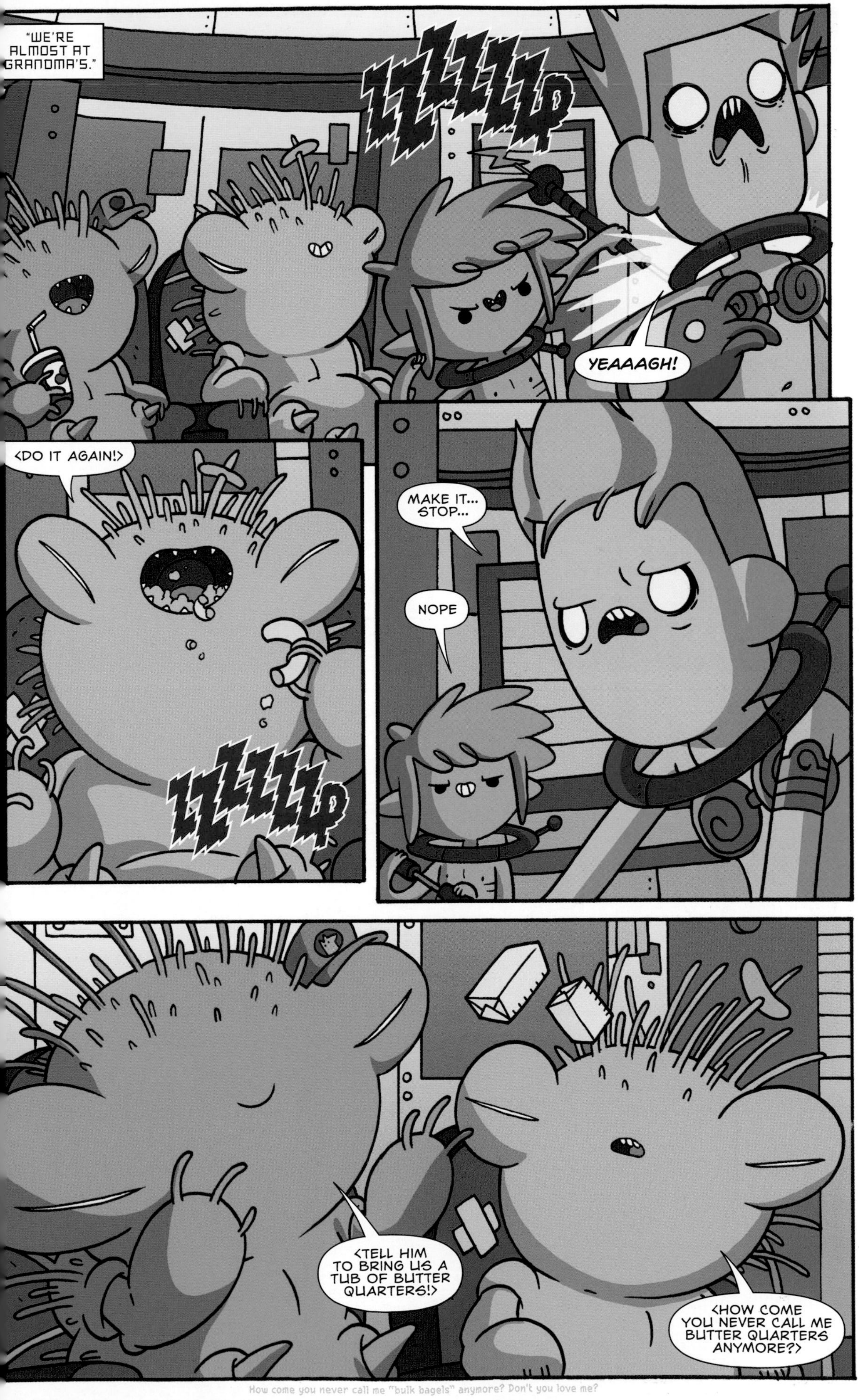
"WE'RE ALMOST AT GRANDMA'S."
ZZZZZZZP
YEAAAGH!
<DO IT AGAIN!>
ZZZZZZP
MAKE IT... STOP...
NOPE
<TELL HIM TO BRING US A TUB OF BUTTER QUARTERS!>
<HOW COME YOU NEVER CALL ME BUTTER QUARTERS ANYMORE?>

How come you never call me "bulk bagels" anymore? Don't you love me?

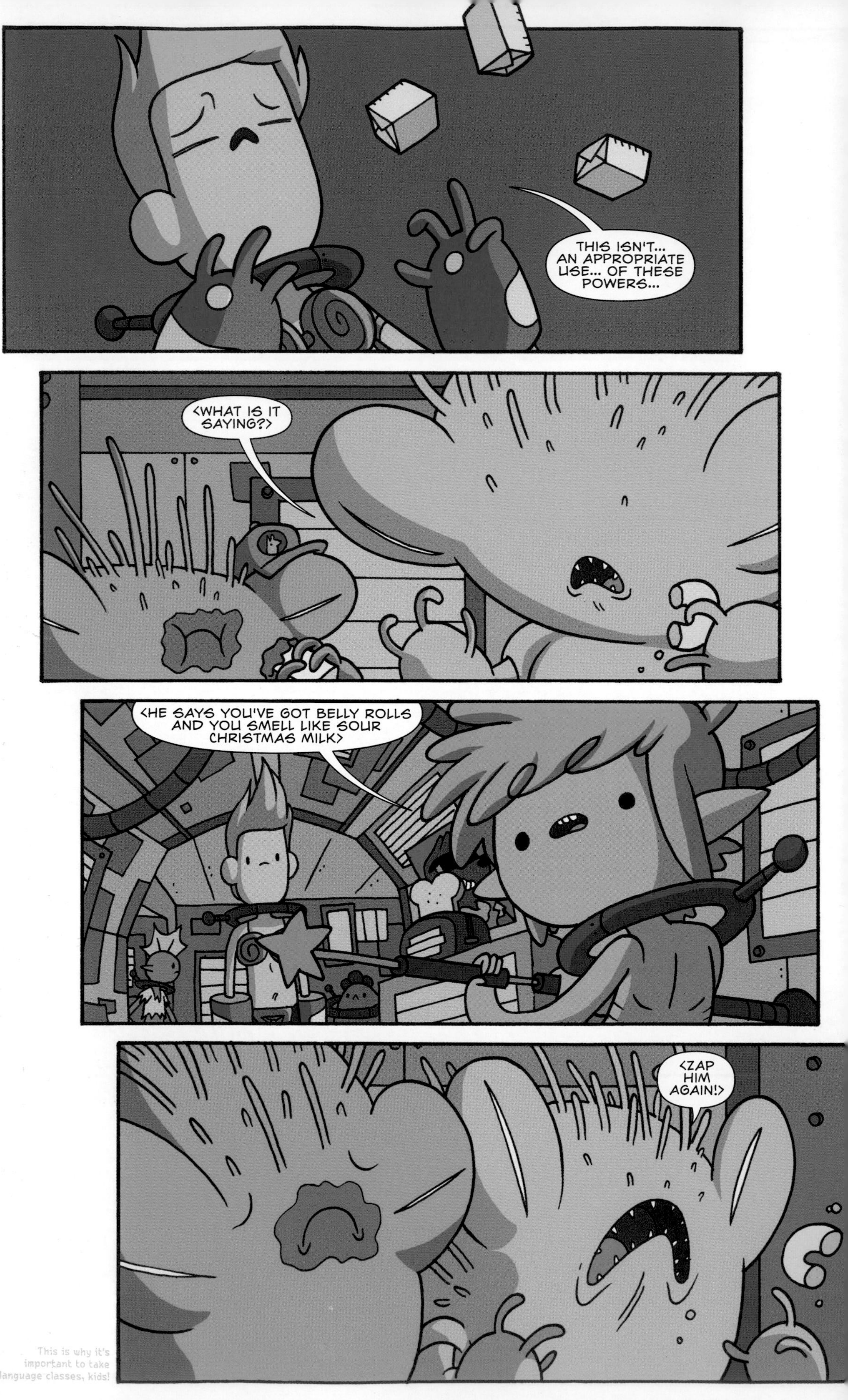
THIS ISN'T... AN APPROPRIATE USE... OF THESE POWERS...
<WHAT IS IT SAYING?>
<HE SAYS YOU'VE GOT BELLY ROLLS AND YOU SMELL LIKE SOUR CHRISTMAS MILK>
<ZAP HIM AGAIN!>

This is why it's important to take language classes, kids!

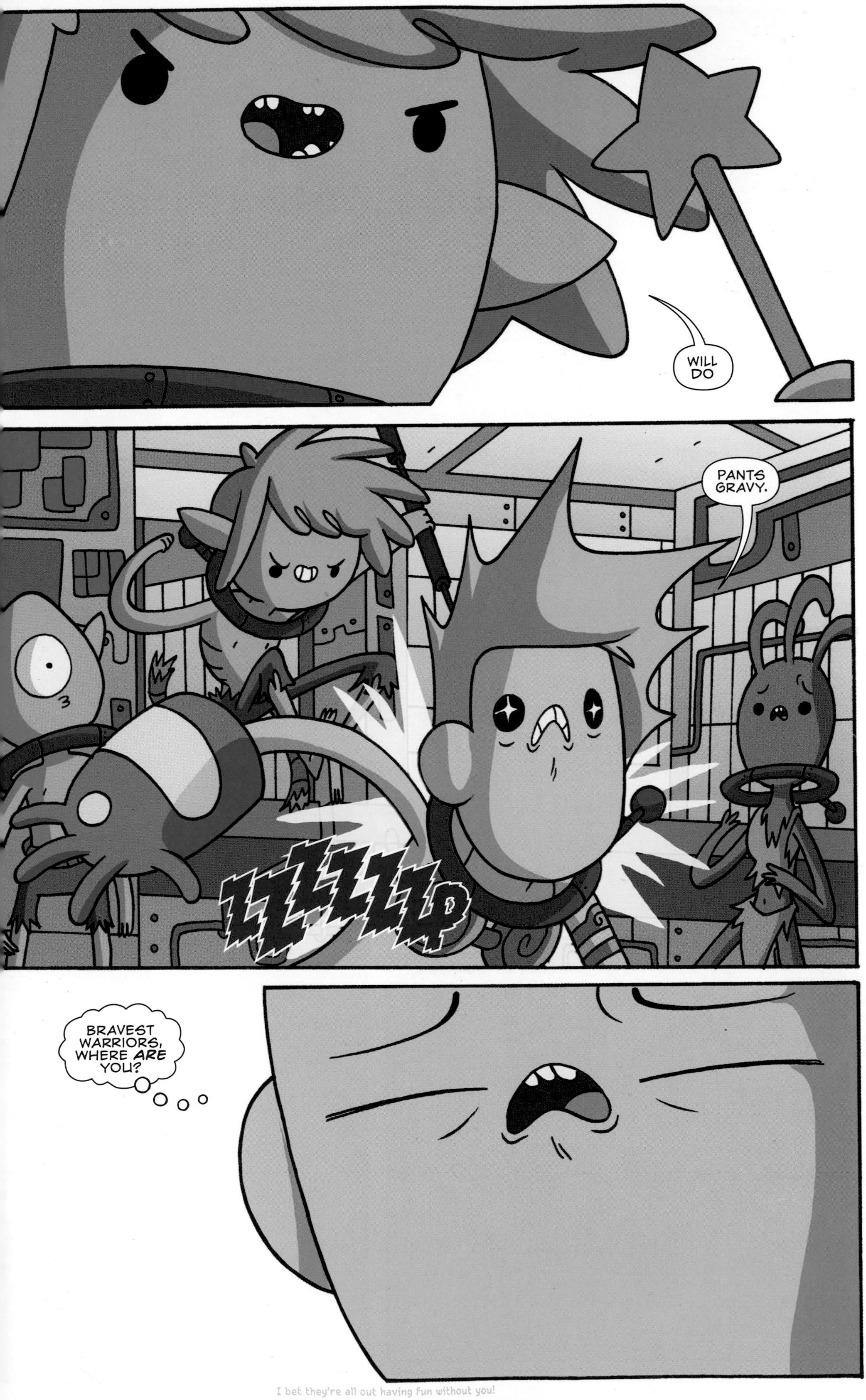
WILL DO
PANTS GRAVY.
ZZZZZP
BRAVEST WARRIORS, WHERE *ARE* YOU?

I bet they're all out having fun without you!

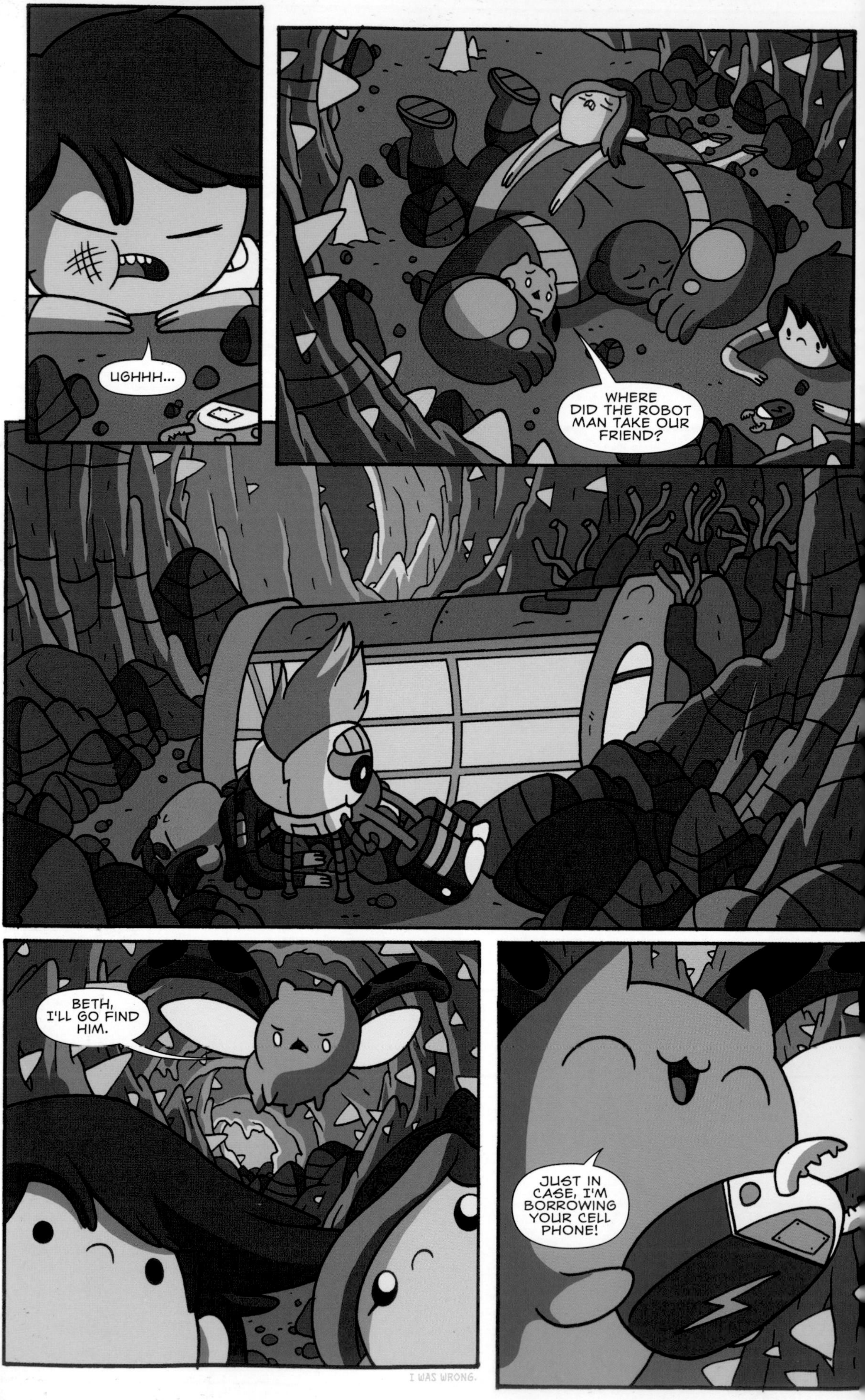
UGHHH...
WHERE DID THE ROBOT MAN TAKE OUR FRIEND?
BETH, I'LL GO FIND HIM.
JUST IN CASE, I'M BORROWING YOUR CELL PHONE!
I WAS WRONG.

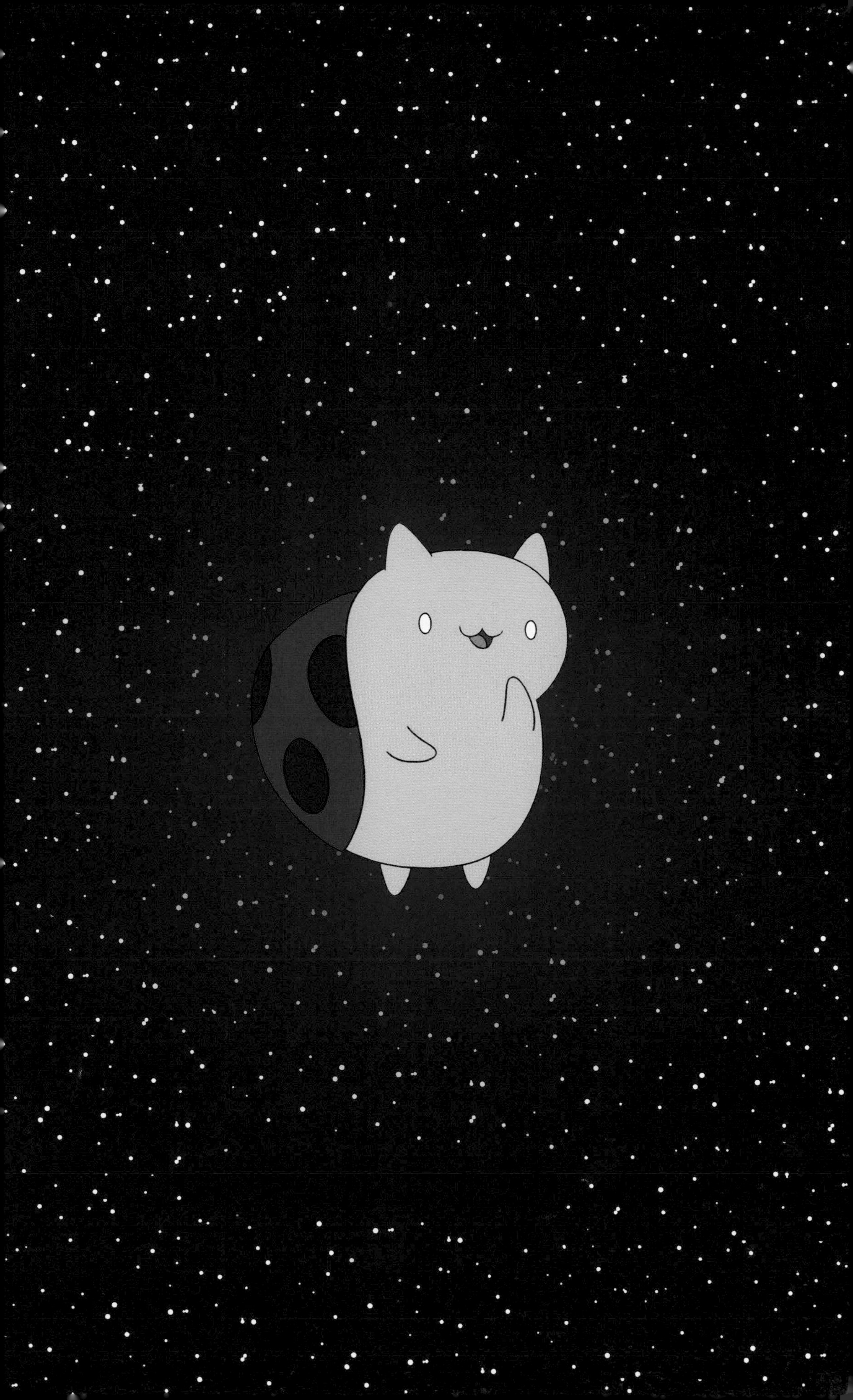

CHAPTER 24

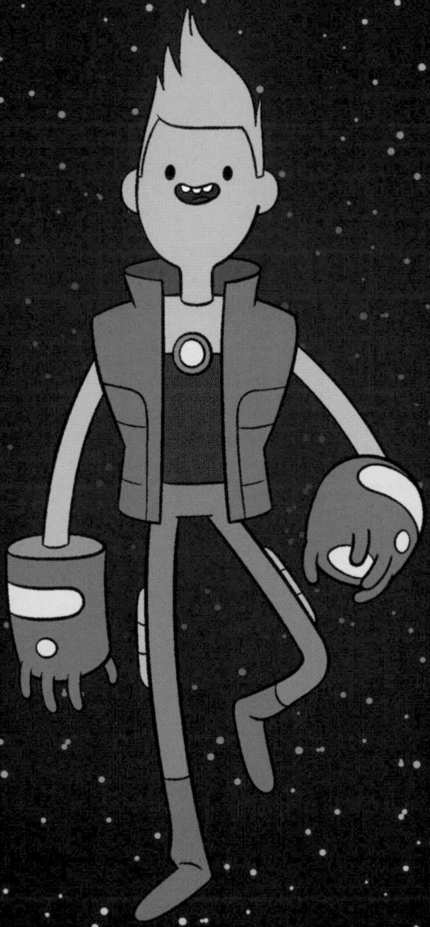

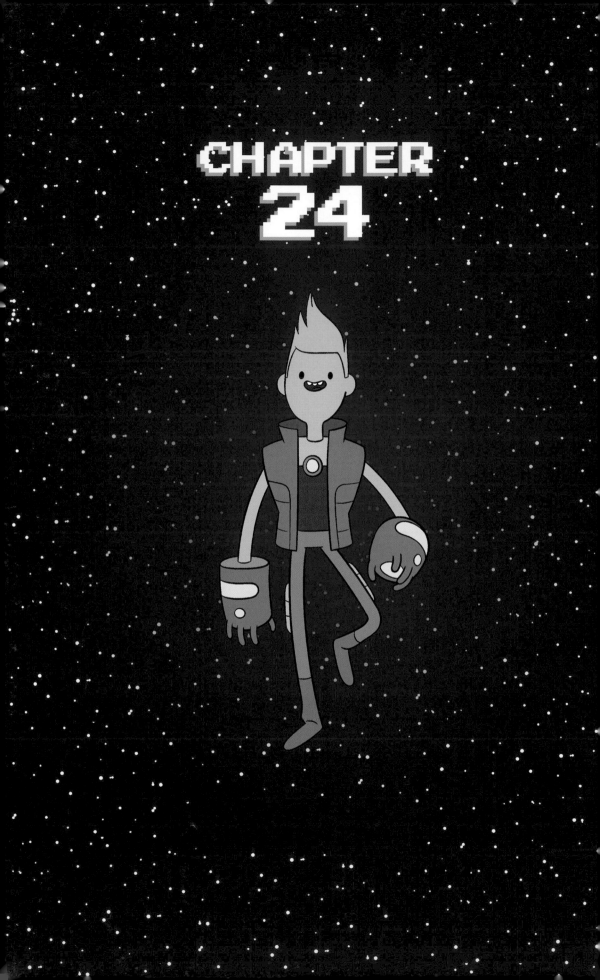

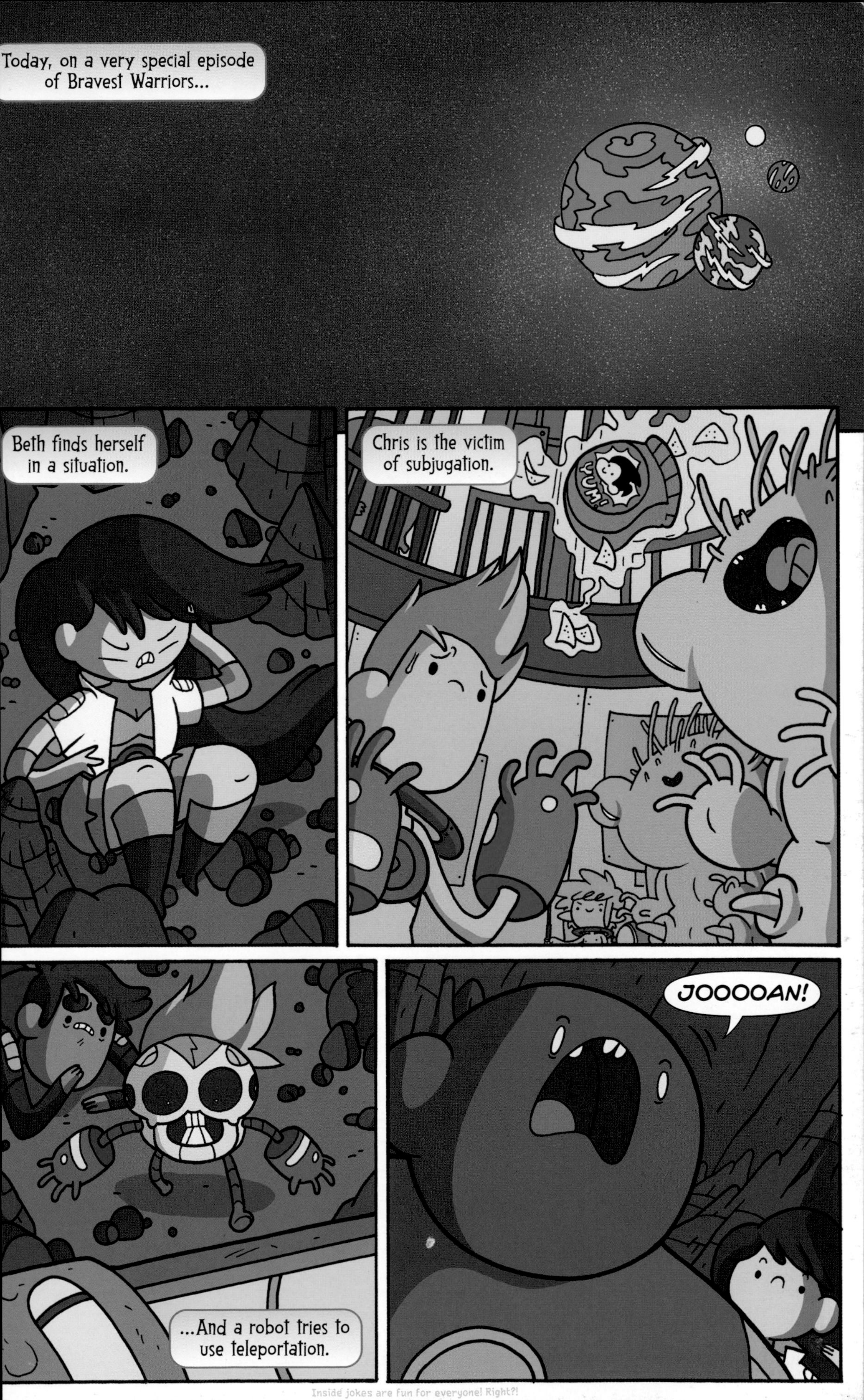
Today, on a very special episode of Bravest Warriors...
Beth finds herself in a situation.
Chris is the victim of subjugation.
YUM!
...And a robot tries to use teleportation.
JOOOOAN!

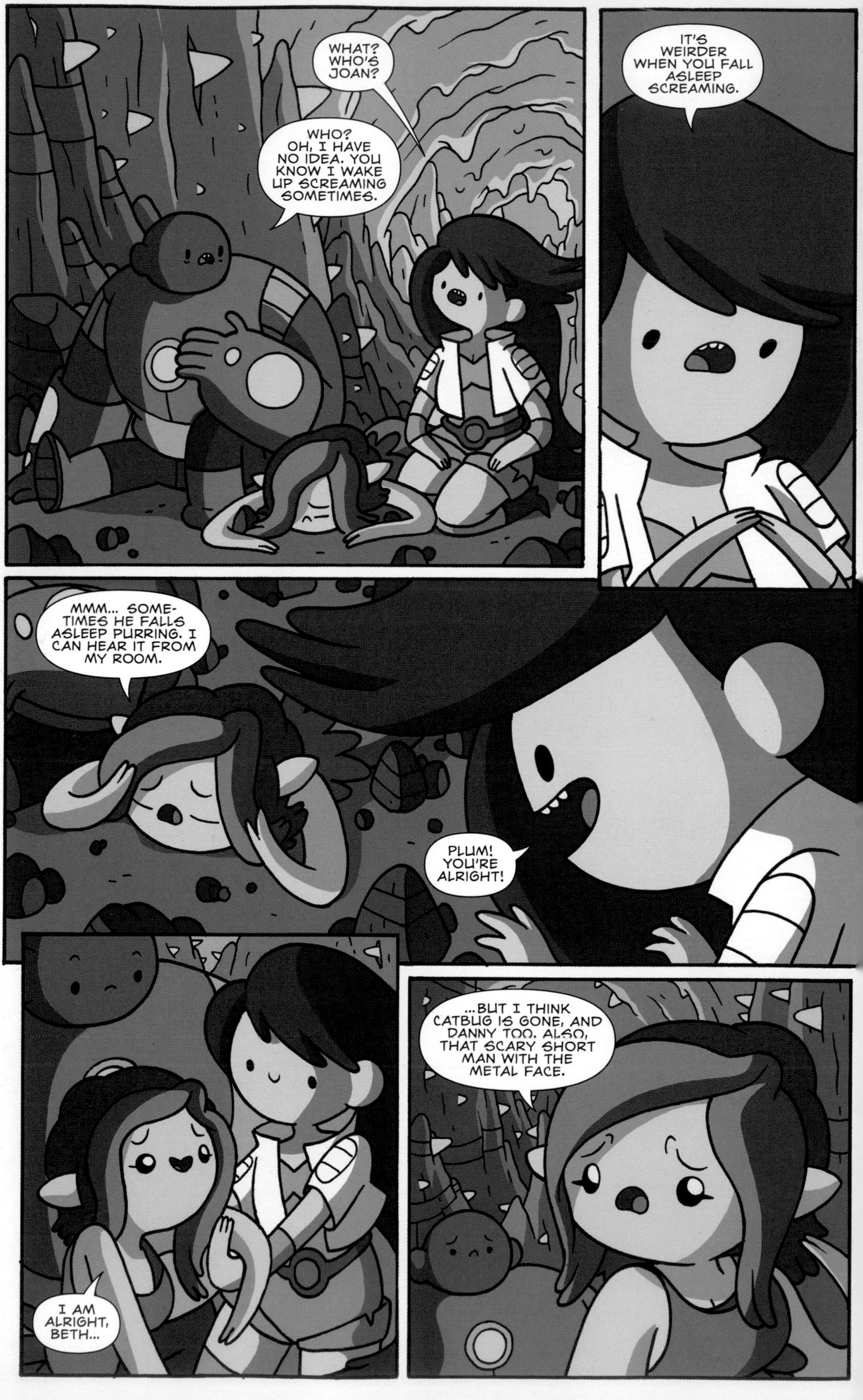

WHAT? WHO'S JOAN?
WHO? OH, I HAVE NO IDEA. YOU KNOW I WAKE UP SCREAMING SOMETIMES.
IT'S WEIRDER WHEN YOU FALL ASLEEP SCREAMING.
MMM... SOME-TIMES HE FALLS ASLEEP PURRING. I CAN HEAR IT FROM MY ROOM.
PLUM! YOU'RE ALRIGHT!
I AM ALRIGHT, BETH...
...BUT I THINK CATBUG IS GONE, AND DANNY TOO. ALSO, THAT SCARY SHORT MAN WITH THE METAL FACE.

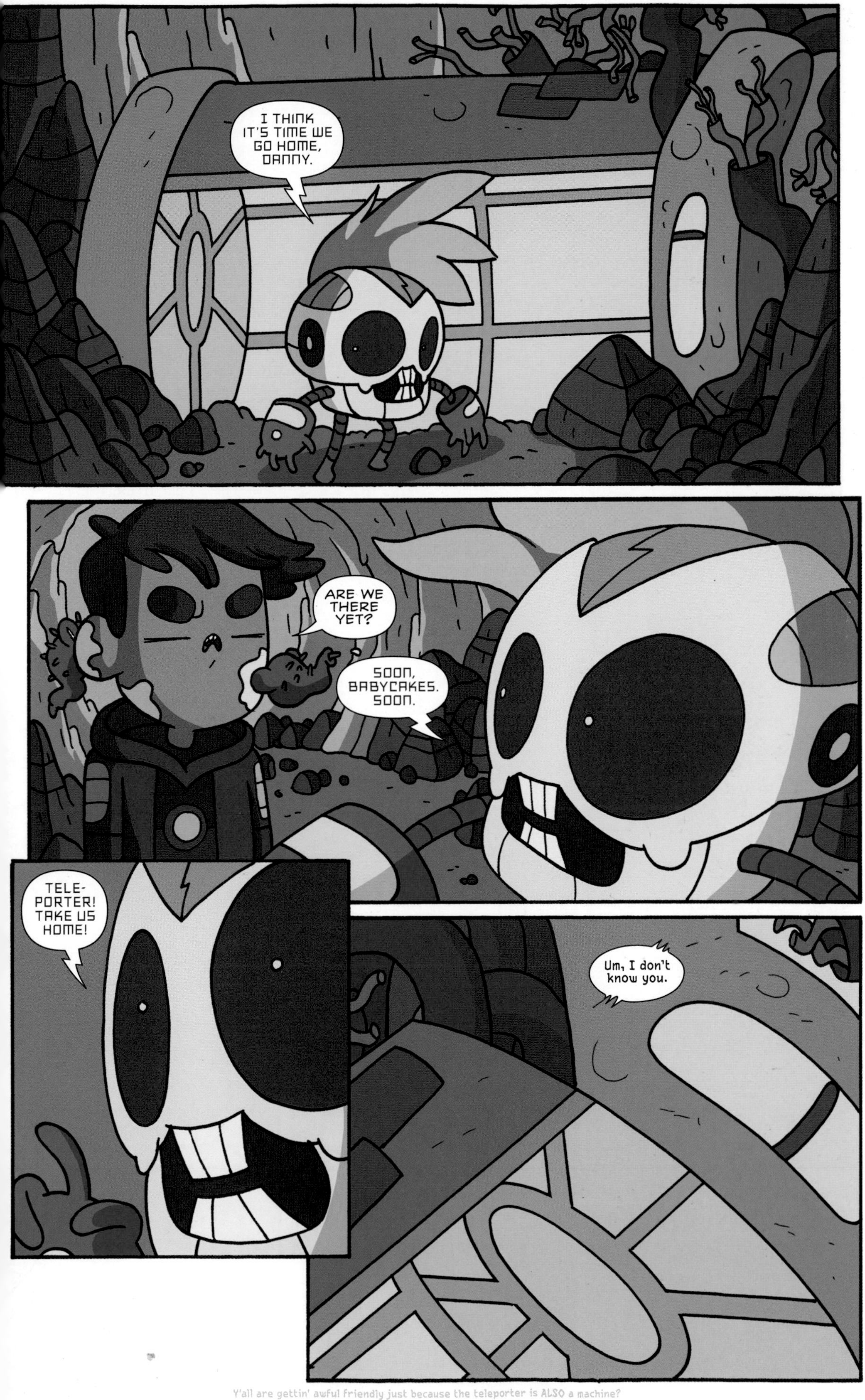
I THINK IT'S TIME WE GO HOME, DANNY.
ARE WE THERE YET?
SOON, BABYCAKES. SOON.
TELE-PORTER! TAKE US HOME!
Um, I don't know you.

Y'all are gettin' awful friendly just because the teleporter is ALSO a machine?

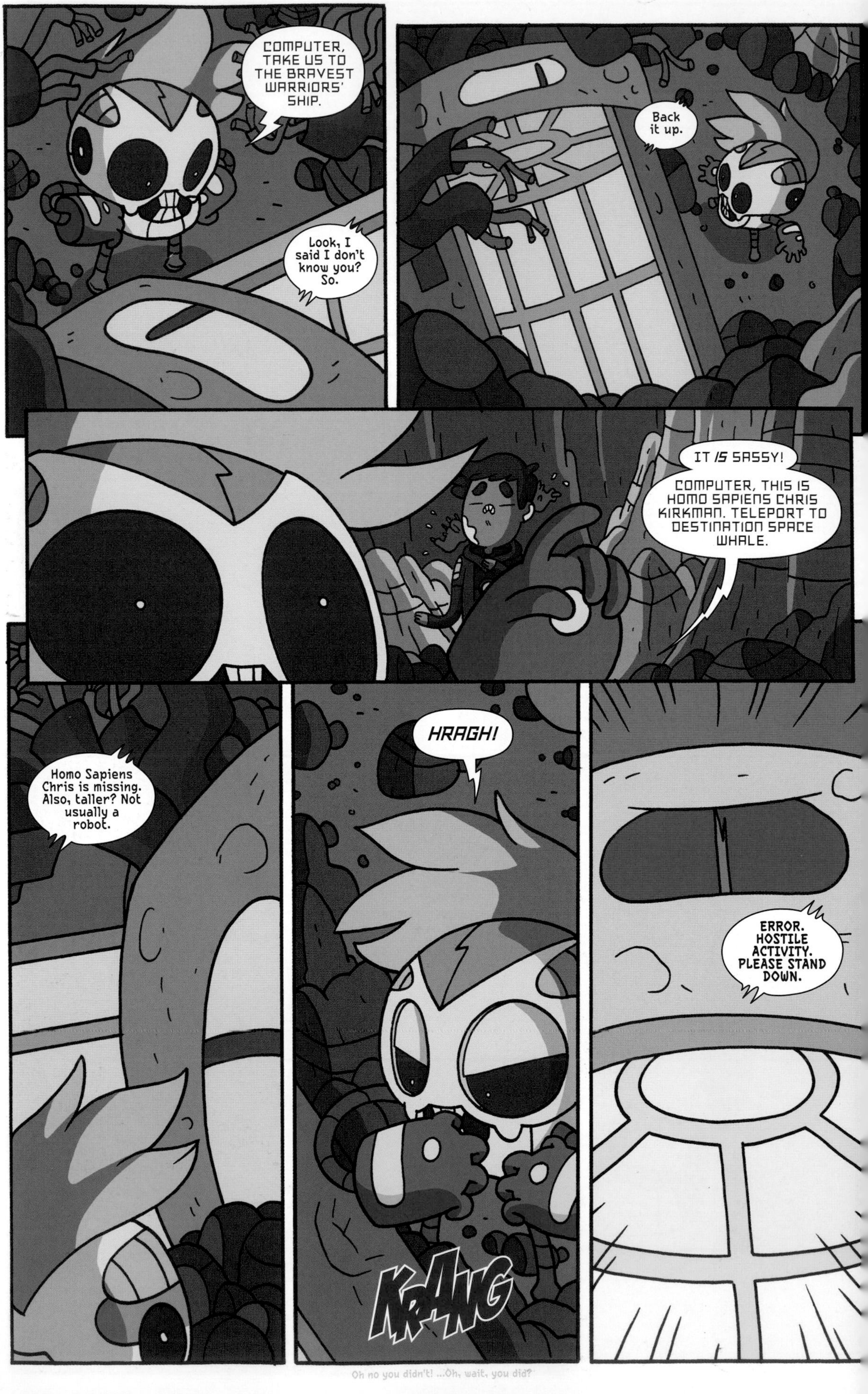
COMPUTER, TAKE US TO THE BRAVEST WARRIORS' SHIP.
Look, I said I don't know you? So.
Back it up.
IT IS SASSY!
COMPUTER, THIS IS HOMO SAPIENS CHRIS KIRKMAN. TELEPORT TO DESTINATION SPACE WHALE.
Homo Sapiens Chris is missing. Also, taller? Not usually a robot.
HRAGH!
KRANG
ERROR. HOSTILE ACTIVITY. PLEASE STAND DOWN.

Oh no you didn't! ...Oh, wait, you did?

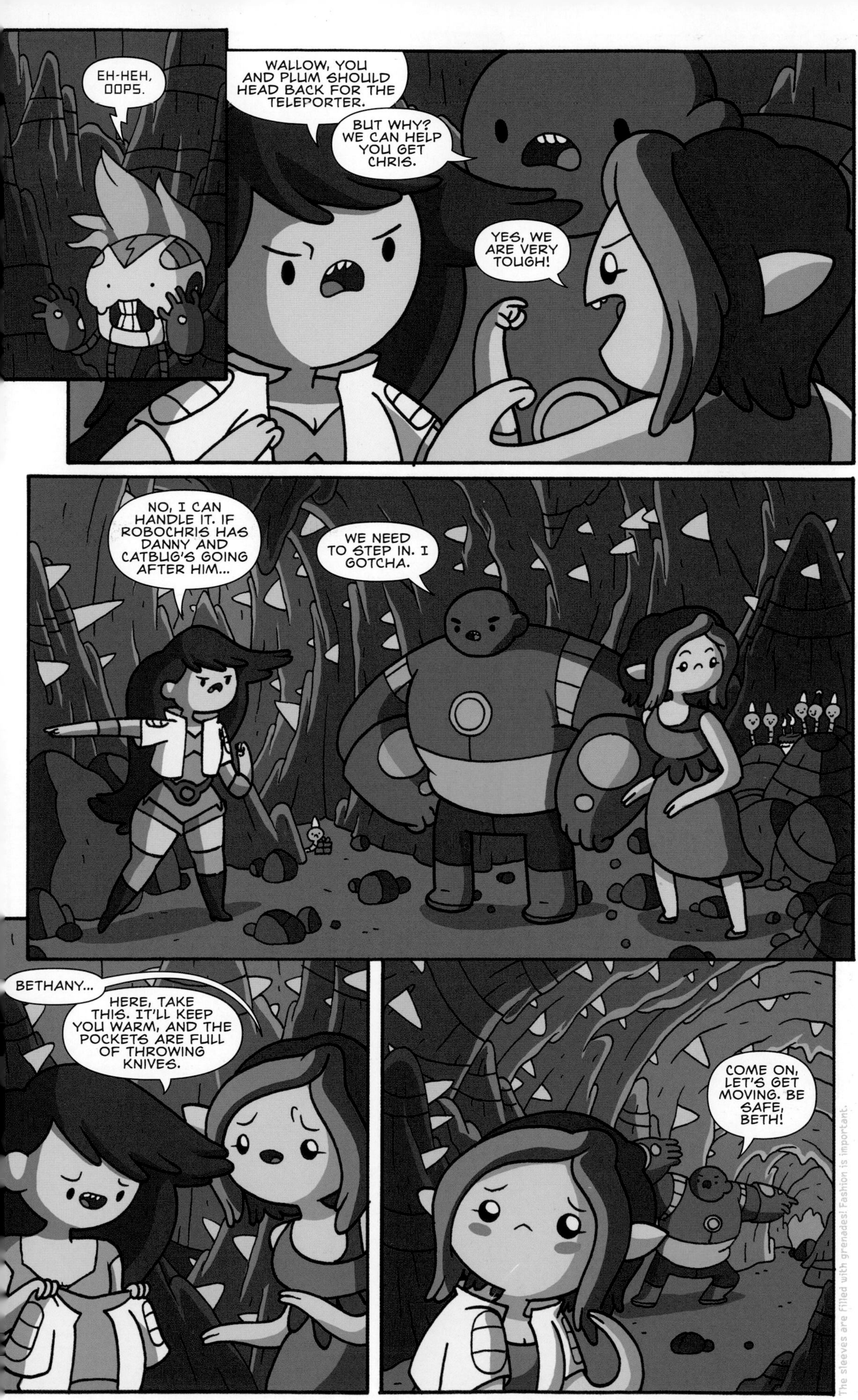
EH-HEH, OOPS.
WALLOW, YOU AND PLUM SHOULD HEAD BACK FOR THE TELEPORTER.
BUT WHY? WE CAN HELP YOU GET CHRIS.
YES, WE ARE VERY TOUGH!
NO, I CAN HANDLE IT. IF ROBOCHRIS HAS DANNY AND CATBUG'S GOING AFTER HIM...
WE NEED TO STEP IN. I GOTCHA.
BETHANY...
HERE, TAKE THIS. IT'LL KEEP YOU WARM, AND THE POCKETS ARE FULL OF THROWING KNIVES.
COME ON, LET'S GET MOVING. BE SAFE, BETH!

The sleeves are filled with grenades! Fashion is important.

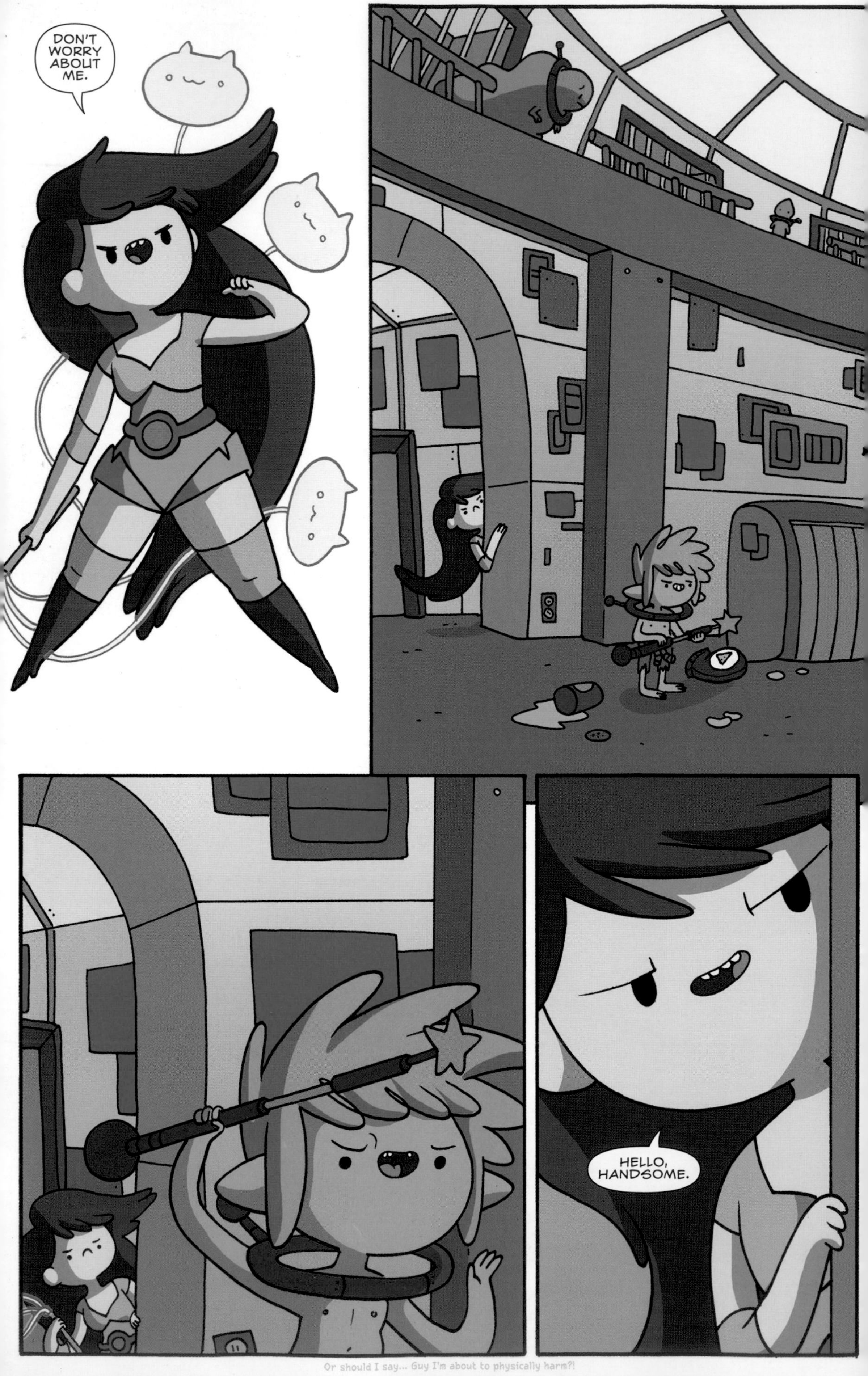
DON'T WORRY ABOUT ME.
HELLO, HANDSOME.

Or should I say... Guy I'm about to physically harm?!

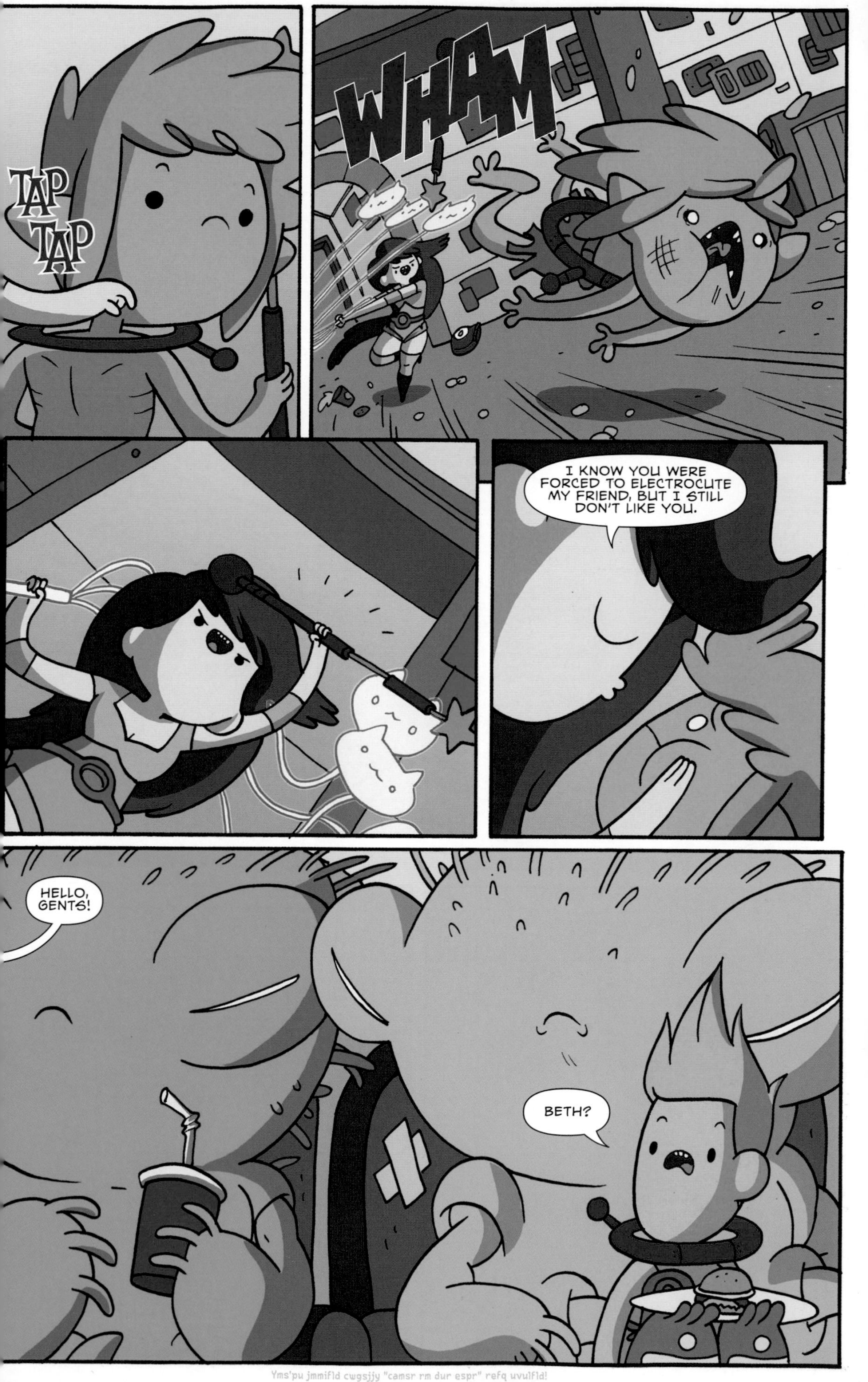
TAP
TAP
WHAM
I KNOW YOU WERE FORCED TO ELECTROCUTE MY FRIEND, BUT I STILL DON'T LIKE YOU.
HELLO, GENTS!
BETH?

Yms'pu jmmifld cwgsjjy "camsr rm dur espr" refq uvulfld!

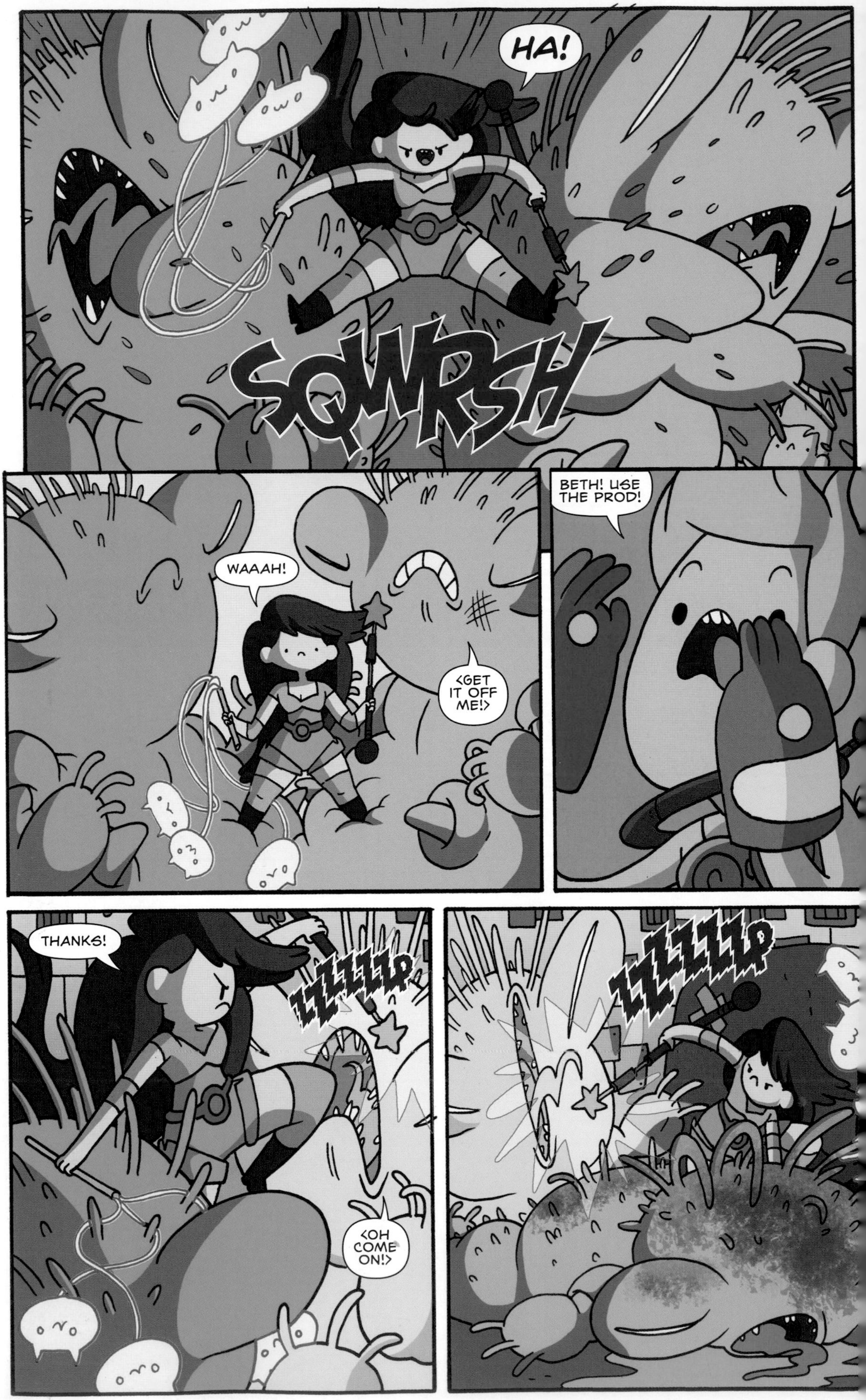
HA!
SQWRSH
WAAAH!
<GET IT OFF ME!>
BETH! USE THE PROD!
THANKS!
ZZZZZZP
<OH COME ON!>
ZZZZZZP

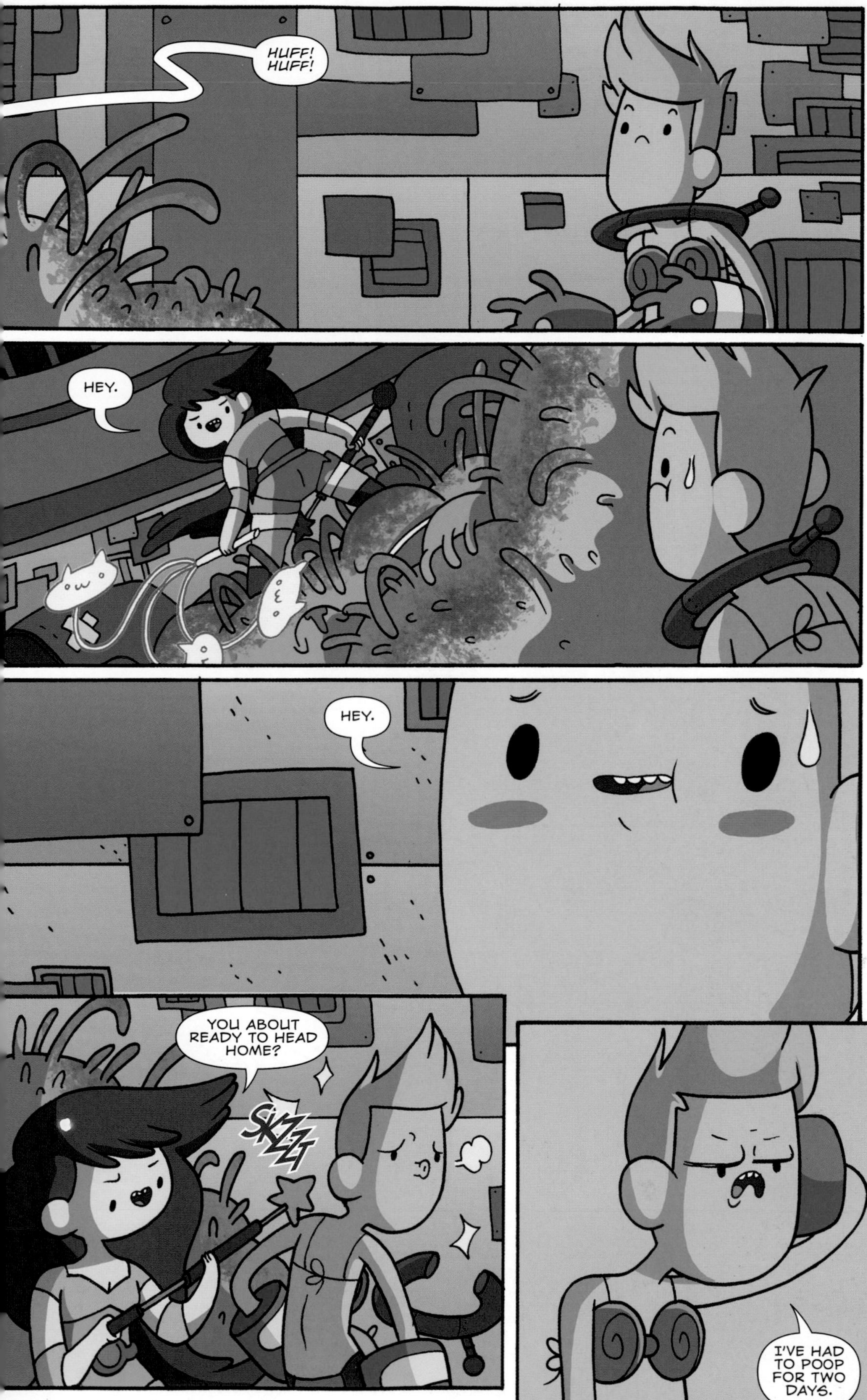
HUFF! HUFF!
HEY.
HEY.
YOU ABOUT READY TO HEAD HOME?
SKZZZT
I'VE HAD TO POOP FOR TWO DAYS.

Refldq cpu camsr rm dur pucj lcqry, Aure.

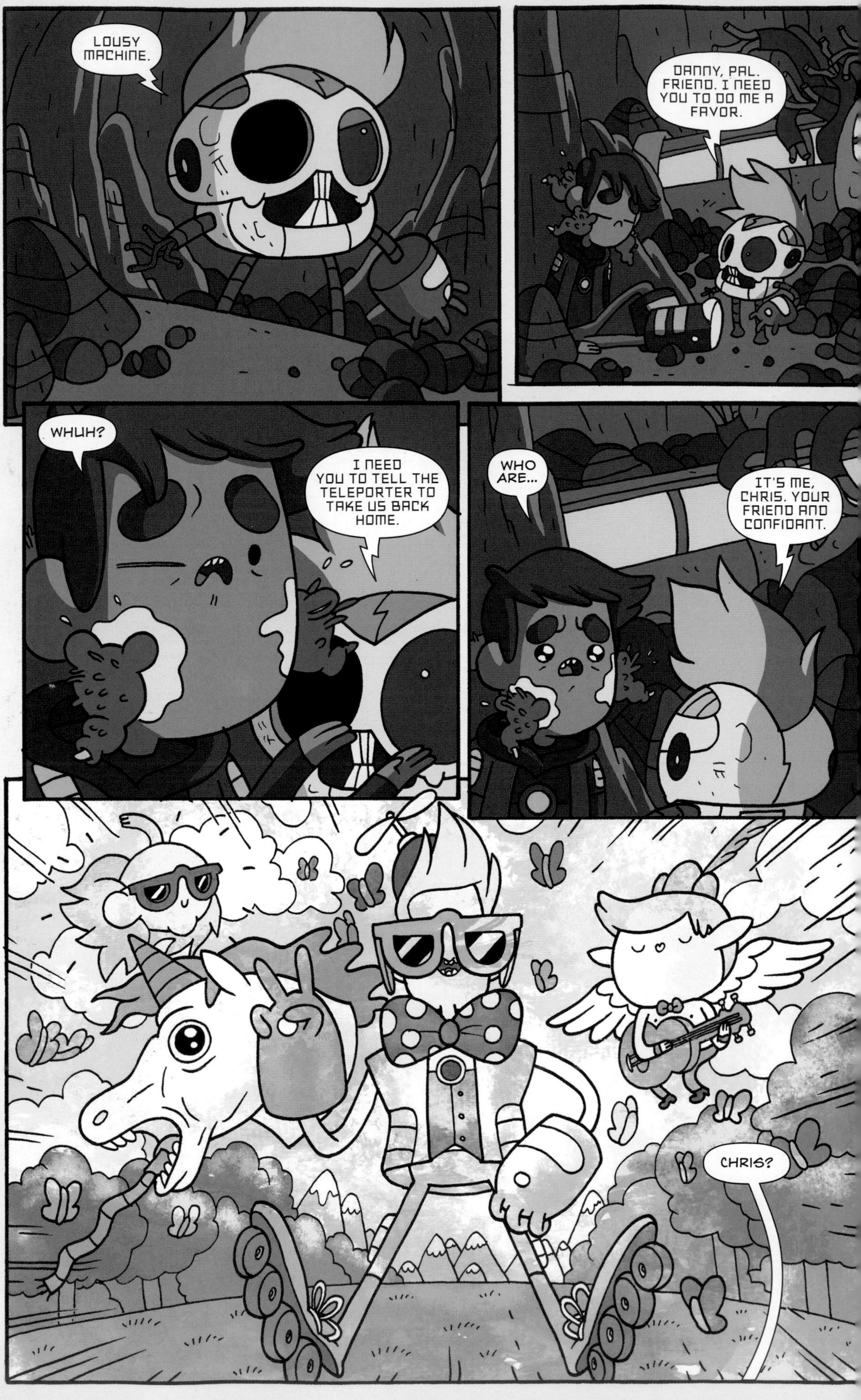
LOUSY MACHINE.
DANNY, PAL. FRIEND. I NEED YOU TO DO ME A FAVOR.
WHUH?
I NEED YOU TO TELL THE TELEPORTER TO TAKE US BACK HOME.
WHO ARE...
IT'S ME, CHRIS. YOUR FRIEND AND CONFIDANT.
CHRIS?

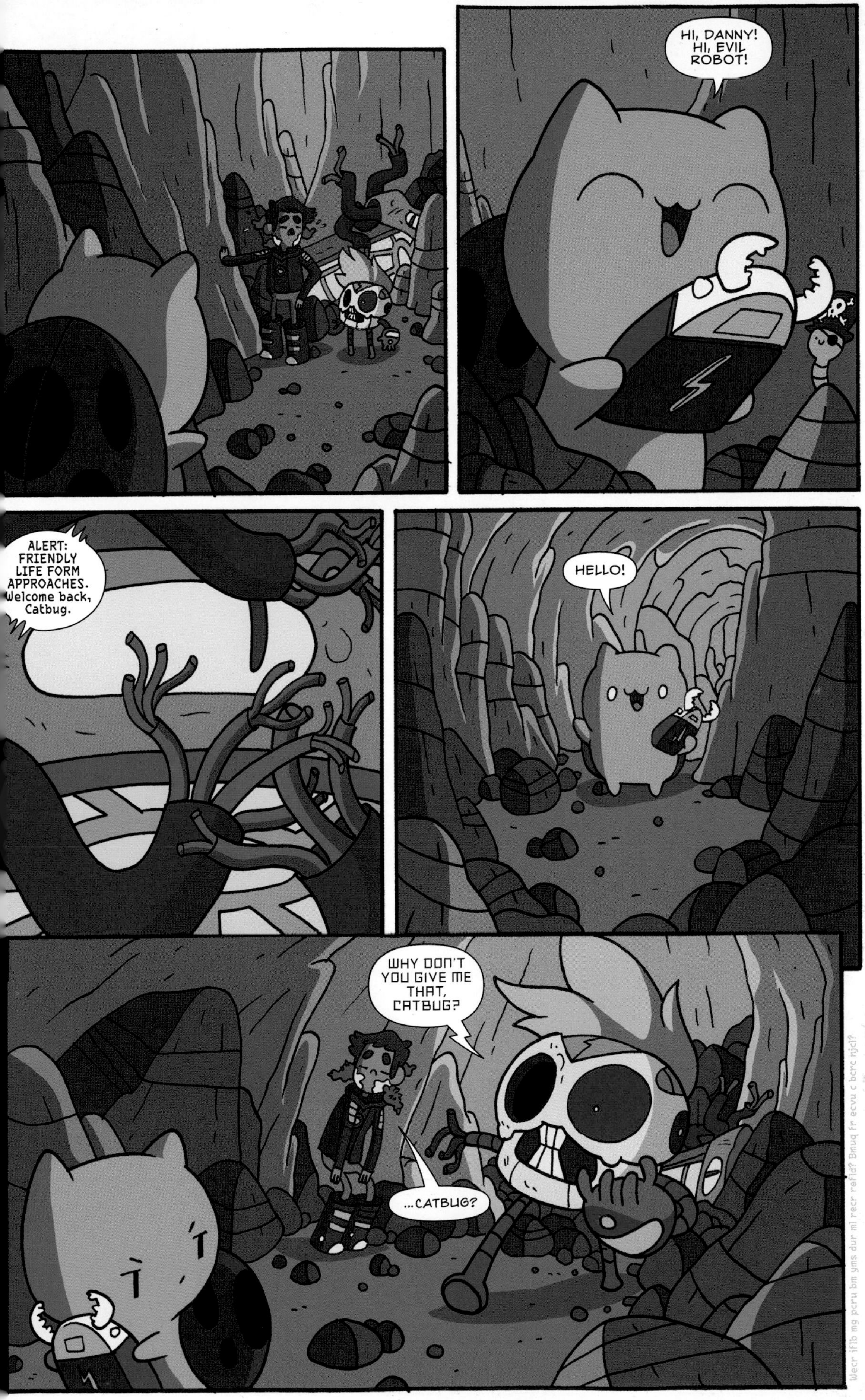
HI, DANNY! HI, EVIL ROBOT!
ALERT: FRIENDLY LIFE FORM APPROACHES. Welcome back, Catbug.
HELLO!
WHY DON'T YOU GIVE ME THAT, CATBUG?
...CATBUG?

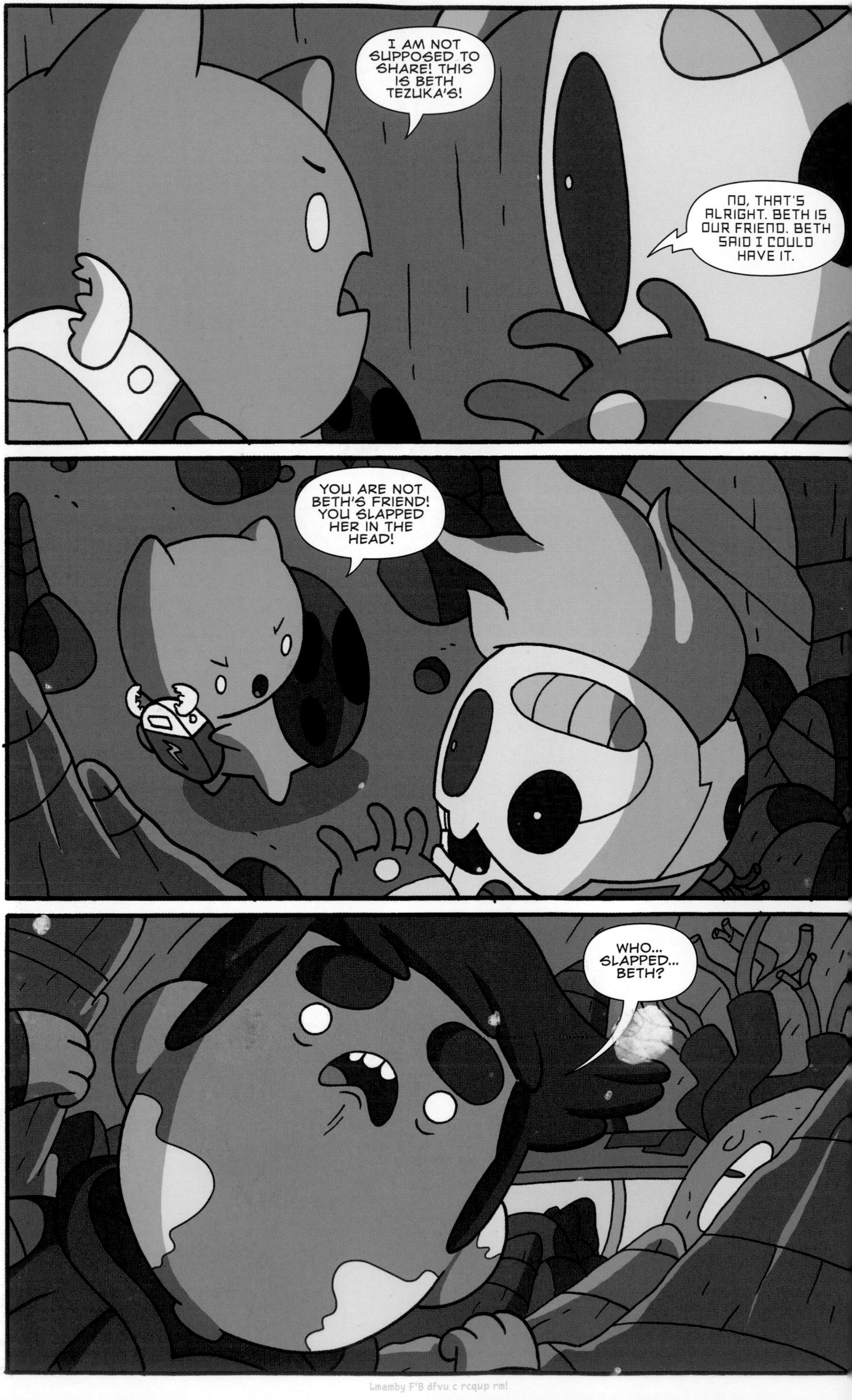
I AM NOT SUPPOSED TO SHARE! THIS IS BETH TEZUKA'S!
NO, THAT'S ALRIGHT. BETH IS OUR FRIEND. BETH SAID I COULD HAVE IT.
YOU ARE NOT BETH'S FRIEND! YOU SLAPPED HER IN THE HEAD!
WHO... SLAPPED... BETH?

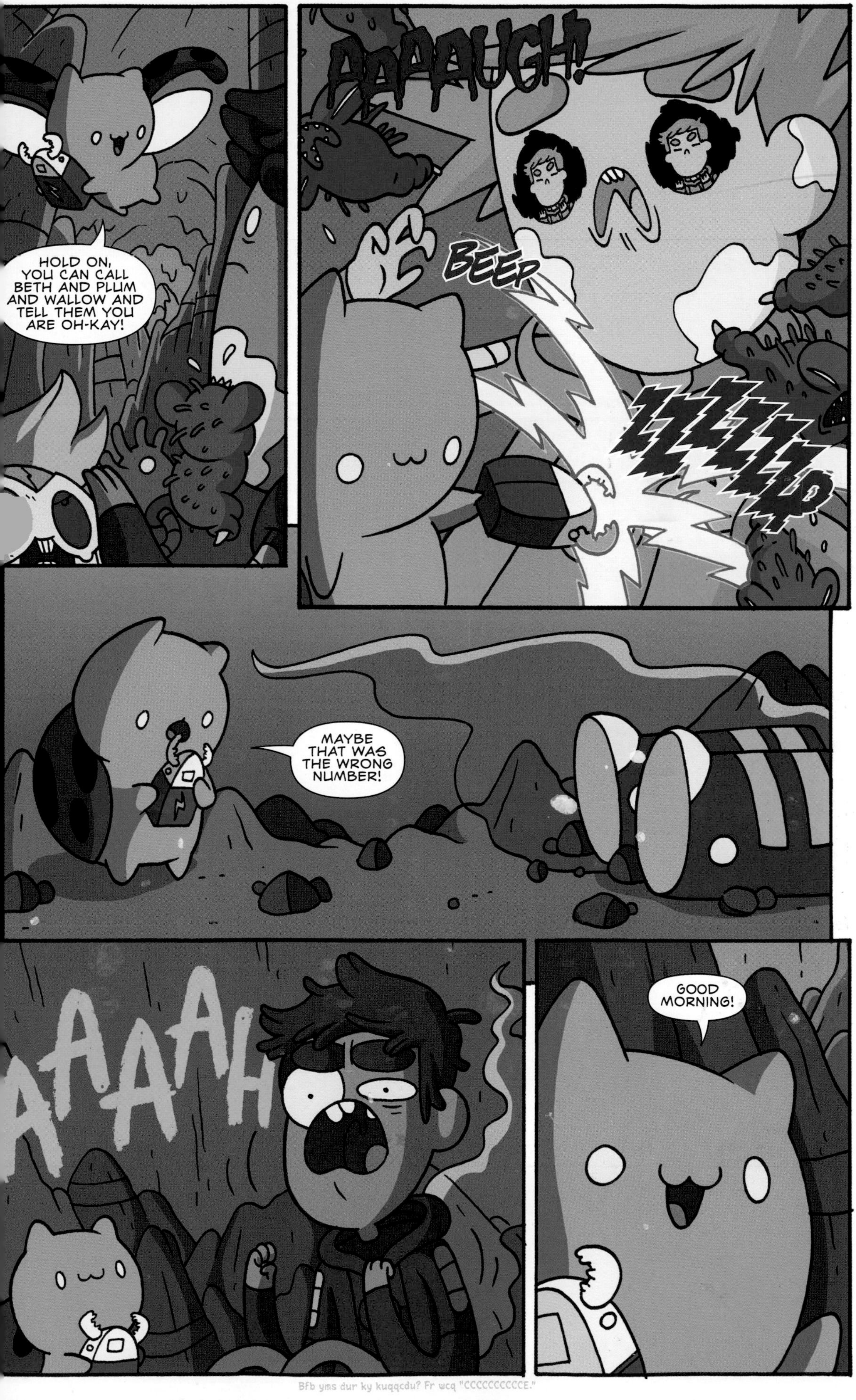
HOLD ON, YOU CAN CALL BETH AND PLUM AND WALLOW AND TELL THEM YOU ARE OH-KAY!
AAAAAUGH!
BEEP
ZZZZZAP
MAYBE THAT WAS THE WRONG NUMBER!
AAAAH
GOOD MORNING!

Bfb yms dur ky kuqqcdu? Fr wcq "CCCCCCCCCCE."

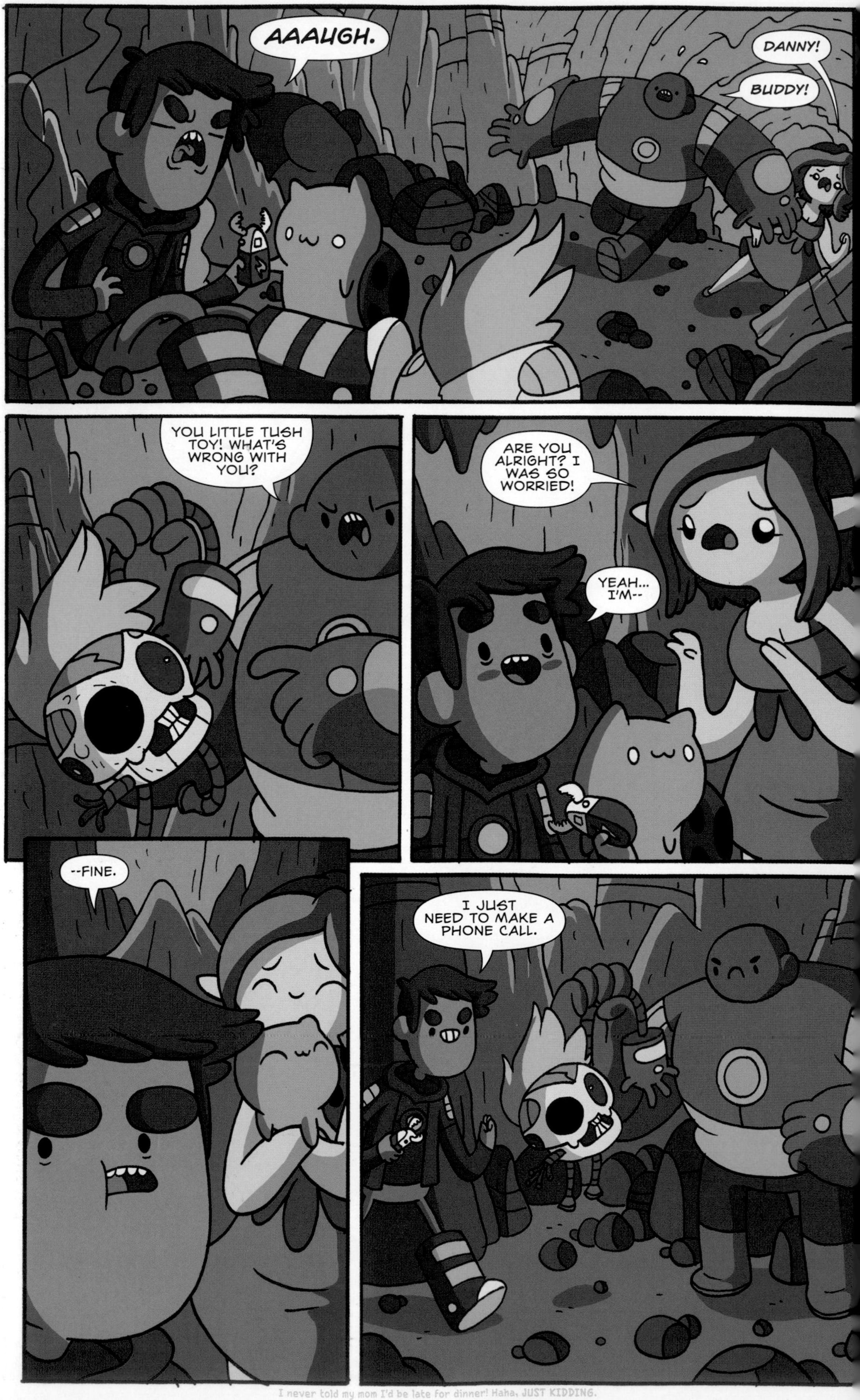
AAAUGH.
DANNY!
BUDDY!
YOU LITTLE TUSH TOY! WHAT'S WRONG WITH YOU?
ARE YOU ALRIGHT? I WAS SO WORRIED!
YEAH... I'M--
--FINE.
I JUST NEED TO MAKE A PHONE CALL.

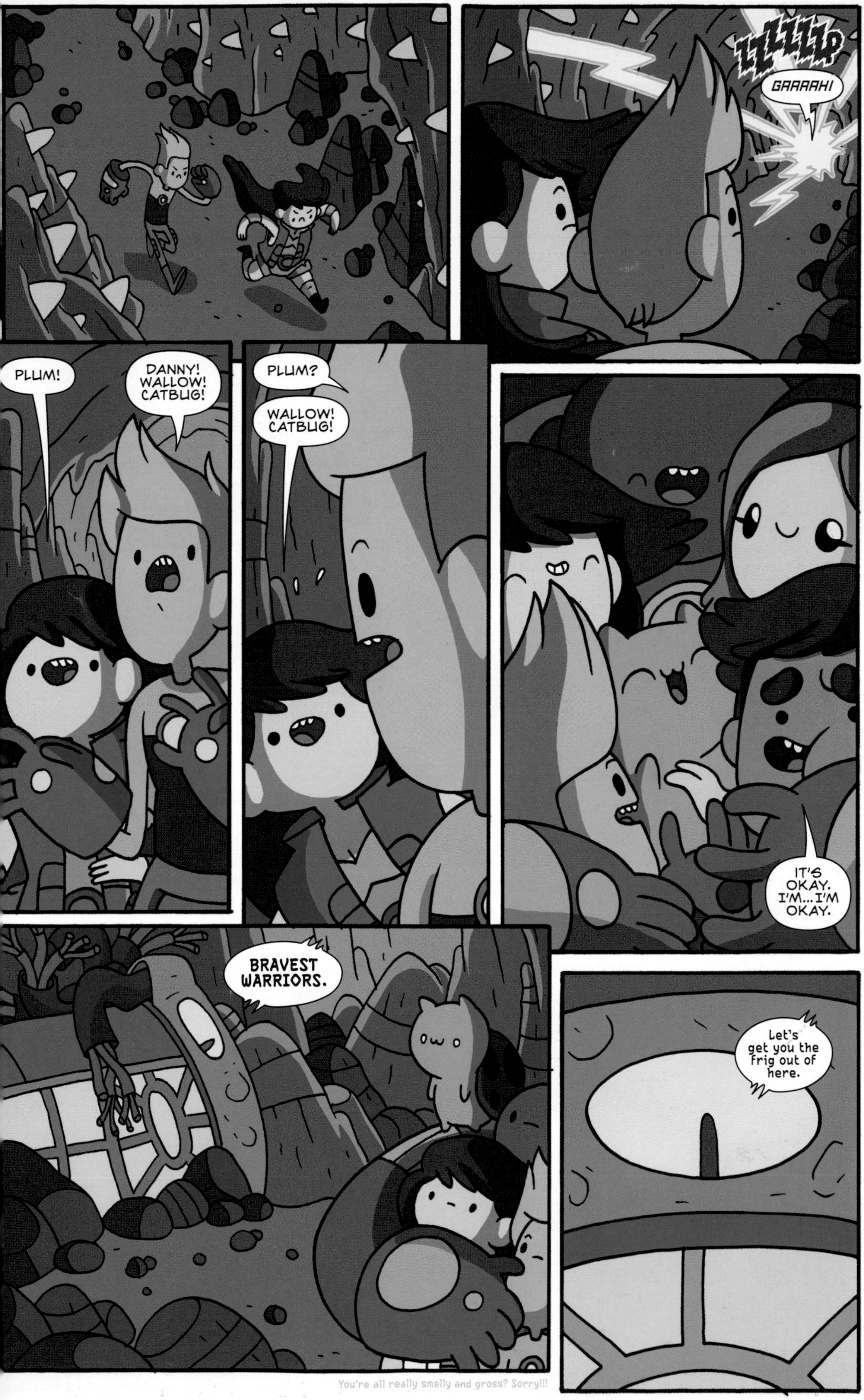
ZZZZZP
GRAAAH!
PLUM!
DANNY! WALLOW! CATBUG!
PLUM?
WALLOW! CATBUG!
IT'S OKAY. I'M...I'M OKAY.
BRAVEST WARRIORS.
Let's get you the frig out of here.

You're all really smelly and gross? Sorry!!!

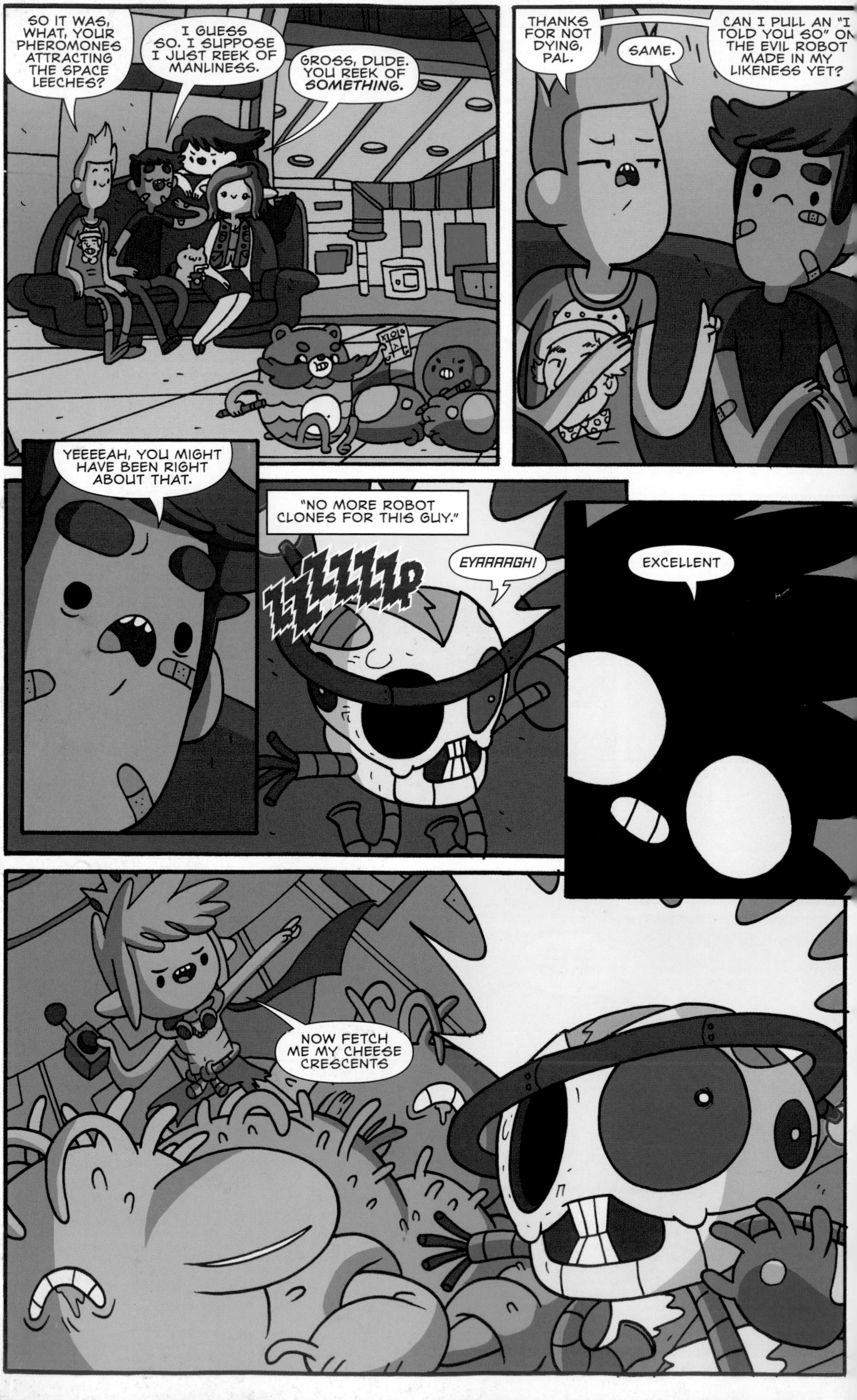
SO IT WAS, WHAT, YOUR PHEROMONES ATTRACTING THE SPACE LEECHES?
I GUESS SO. I SUPPOSE I JUST REEK OF MANLINESS.
GROSS, DUDE. YOU REEK OF *SOMETHING*.
THANKS FOR NOT DYING, PAL.
SAME.
CAN I PULL AN "I TOLD YOU SO" ON THE EVIL ROBOT MADE IN MY LIKENESS YET?
YEEEEAH, YOU MIGHT HAVE BEEN RIGHT ABOUT THAT.
"NO MORE ROBOT CLONES FOR THIS GUY."
ZZZZZZP
EYAAAAGH!
EXCELLENT
NOW FETCH ME MY CHEESE CRESCENTS

SHORT MISSIONS

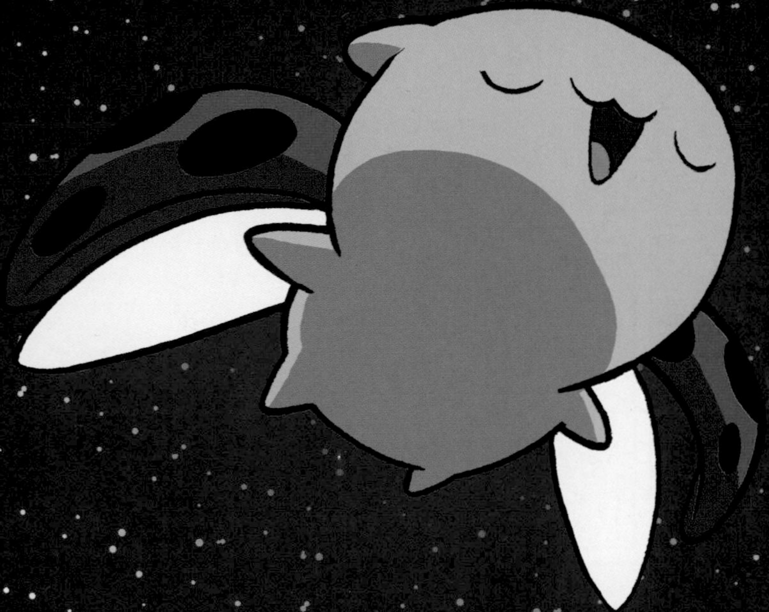

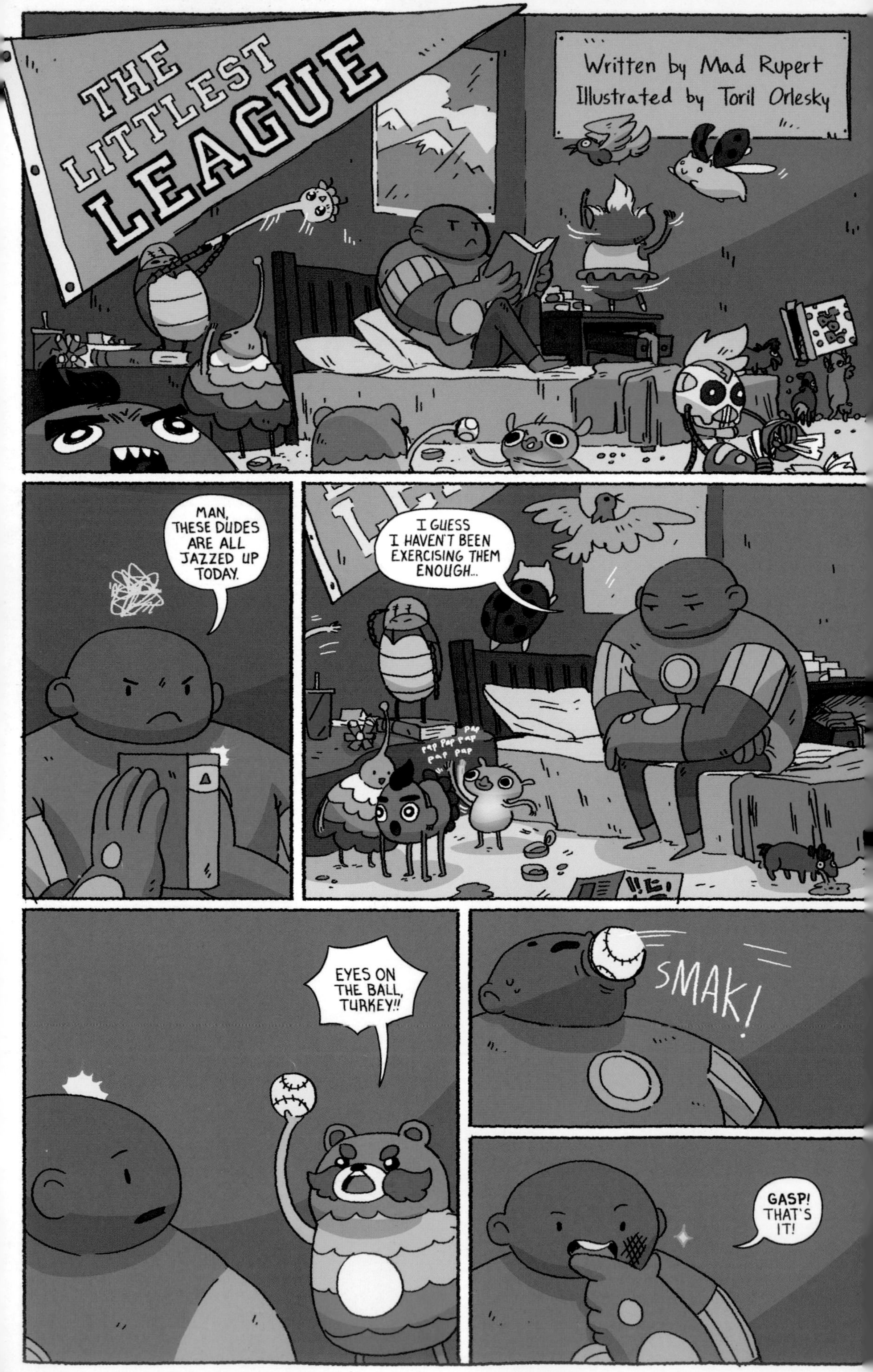
THE LITTLEST LEAGUE
Written by Mad Rupert
Illustrated by Toril Orlesky
MAN, THESE DUDES ARE ALL JAZZED UP TODAY.
I GUESS I HAVEN'T BEEN EXERCISING THEM ENOUGH...
PAP PAP PAP PAP PAP PAP PAP
EYES ON THE BALL, TURKEY!!
SMAK!
GASP! THAT'S IT!

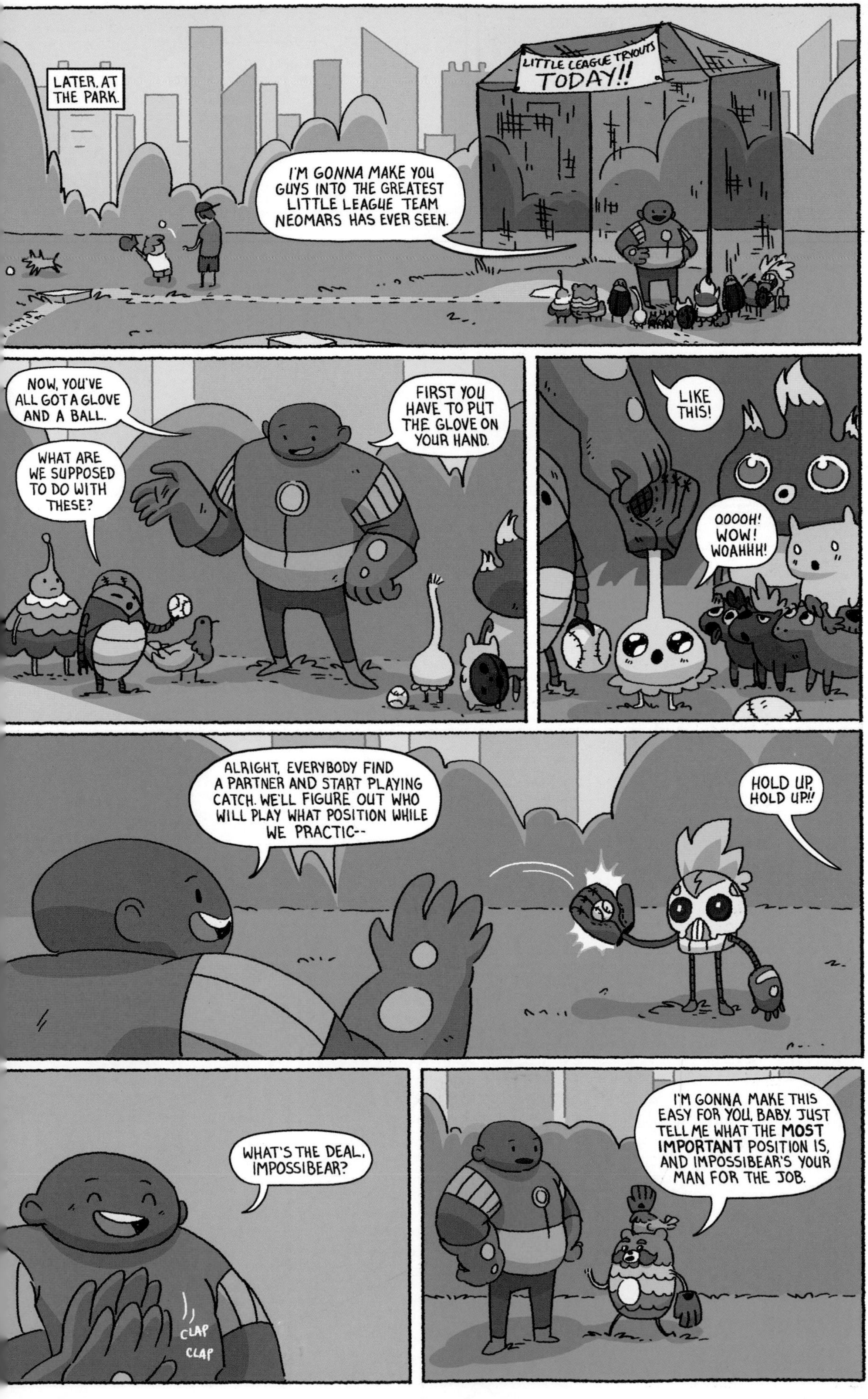
LATER, AT THE PARK.
LITTLE LEAGUE TRYOUTS TODAY!!
I'M GONNA MAKE YOU GUYS INTO THE GREATEST LITTLE LEAGUE TEAM NEOMARS HAS EVER SEEN.
NOW, YOU'VE ALL GOT A GLOVE AND A BALL.
WHAT ARE WE SUPPOSED TO DO WITH THESE?
FIRST YOU HAVE TO PUT THE GLOVE ON YOUR HAND.
LIKE THIS!
OOOOH! WOW! WOAHHH!
ALRIGHT, EVERYBODY FIND A PARTNER AND START PLAYING CATCH. WE'LL FIGURE OUT WHO WILL PLAY WHAT POSITION WHILE WE PRACTIC--
HOLD UP, HOLD UP!!
WHAT'S THE DEAL, IMPOSSIBEAR?
CLAP
CLAP
I'M GONNA MAKE THIS EASY FOR YOU, BABY. JUST TELL ME WHAT THE **MOST IMPORTANT** POSITION IS, AND IMPOSSIBEAR'S YOUR MAN FOR THE JOB.

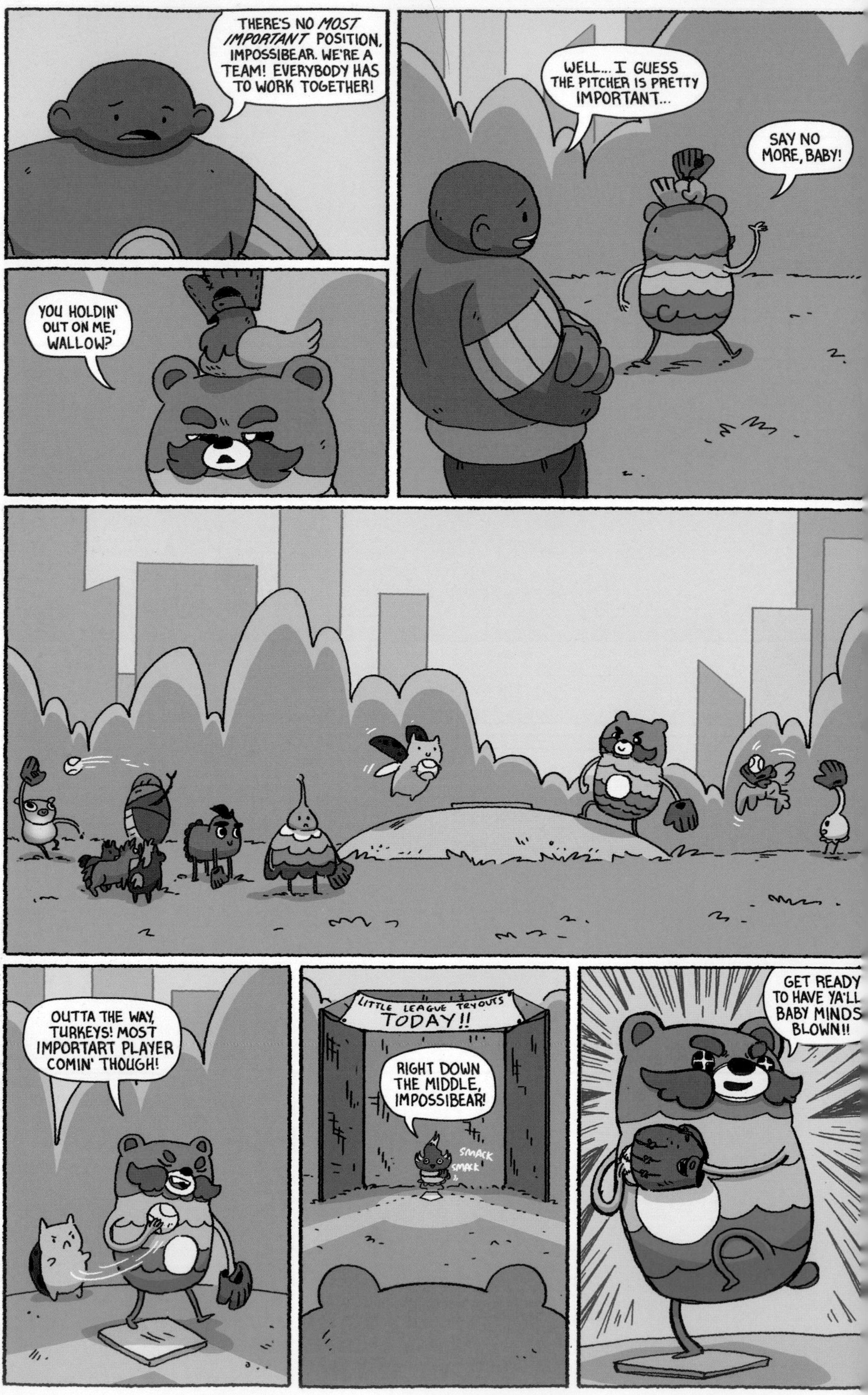
THERE'S NO *MOST IMPORTANT* POSITION, IMPOSSIBEAR. WE'RE A TEAM! EVERYBODY HAS TO WORK TOGETHER!
WELL... I GUESS THE PITCHER IS PRETTY IMPORTANT...
SAY NO MORE, BABY!
YOU HOLDIN' OUT ON ME, WALLOW?
OUTTA THE WAY, TURKEYS! MOST IMPORTART PLAYER COMIN' THOUGH!
LITTLE LEAGUE TRYOUTS TODAY!!
RIGHT DOWN THE MIDDLE, IMPOSSIBEAR!
SMACK
SMACK
GET READY TO HAVE YA'LL BABY MINDS BLOWN!!

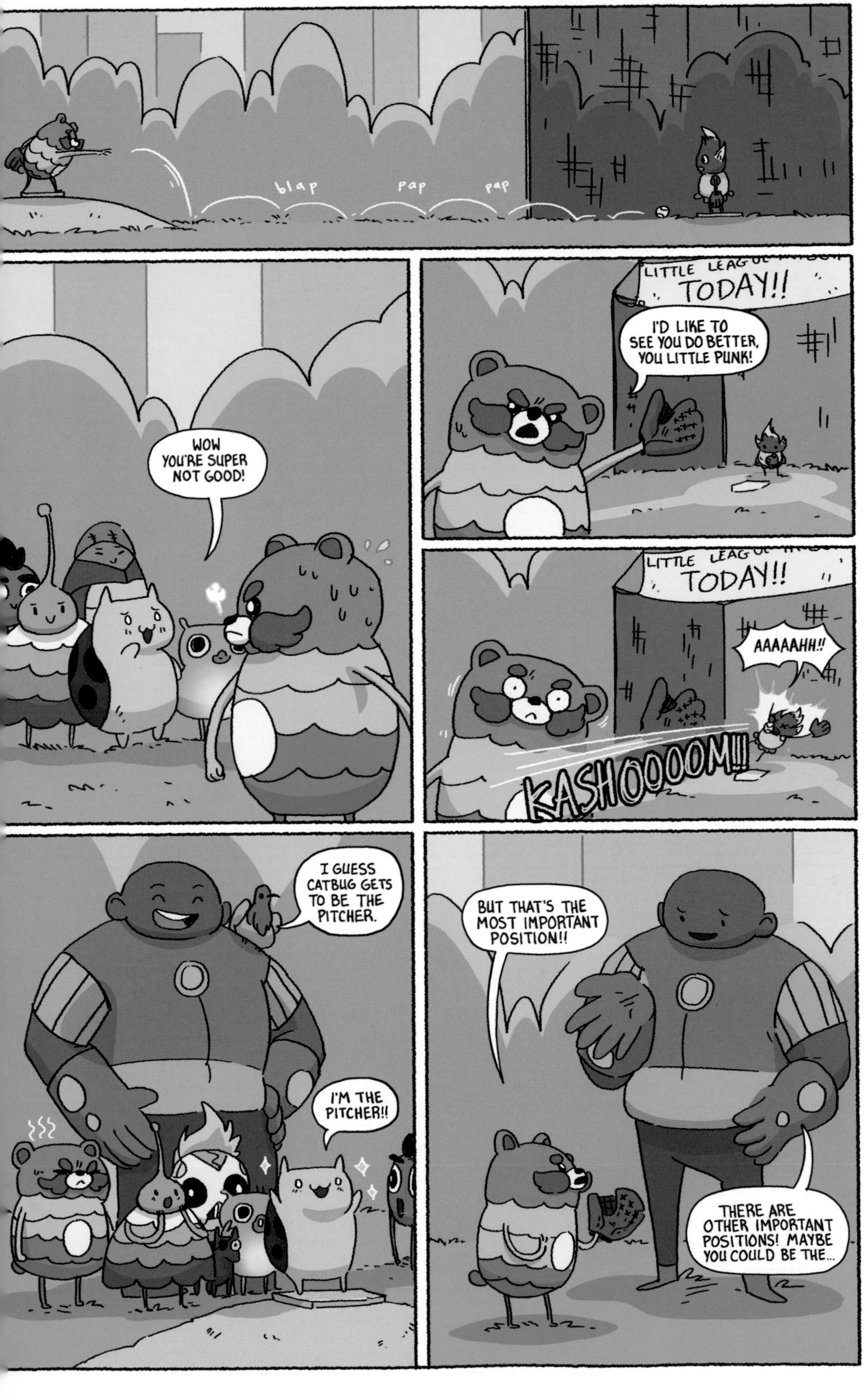
blap
pap
pap
WOW YOU'RE SUPER NOT GOOD!
LITTLE LEAGU
TODAY!!
I'D LIKE TO SEE YOU DO BETTER, YOU LITTLE PUNK!
LITTLE LEAG
TODAY!!
AAAAAHH!!
KASHOOOOM!!
I GUESS CATBUG GETS TO BE THE PITCHER.
I'M THE PITCHER!!
BUT THAT'S THE MOST IMPORTANT POSITION!!
THERE ARE OTHER IMPORTANT POSITIONS! MAYBE YOU COULD BE THE...

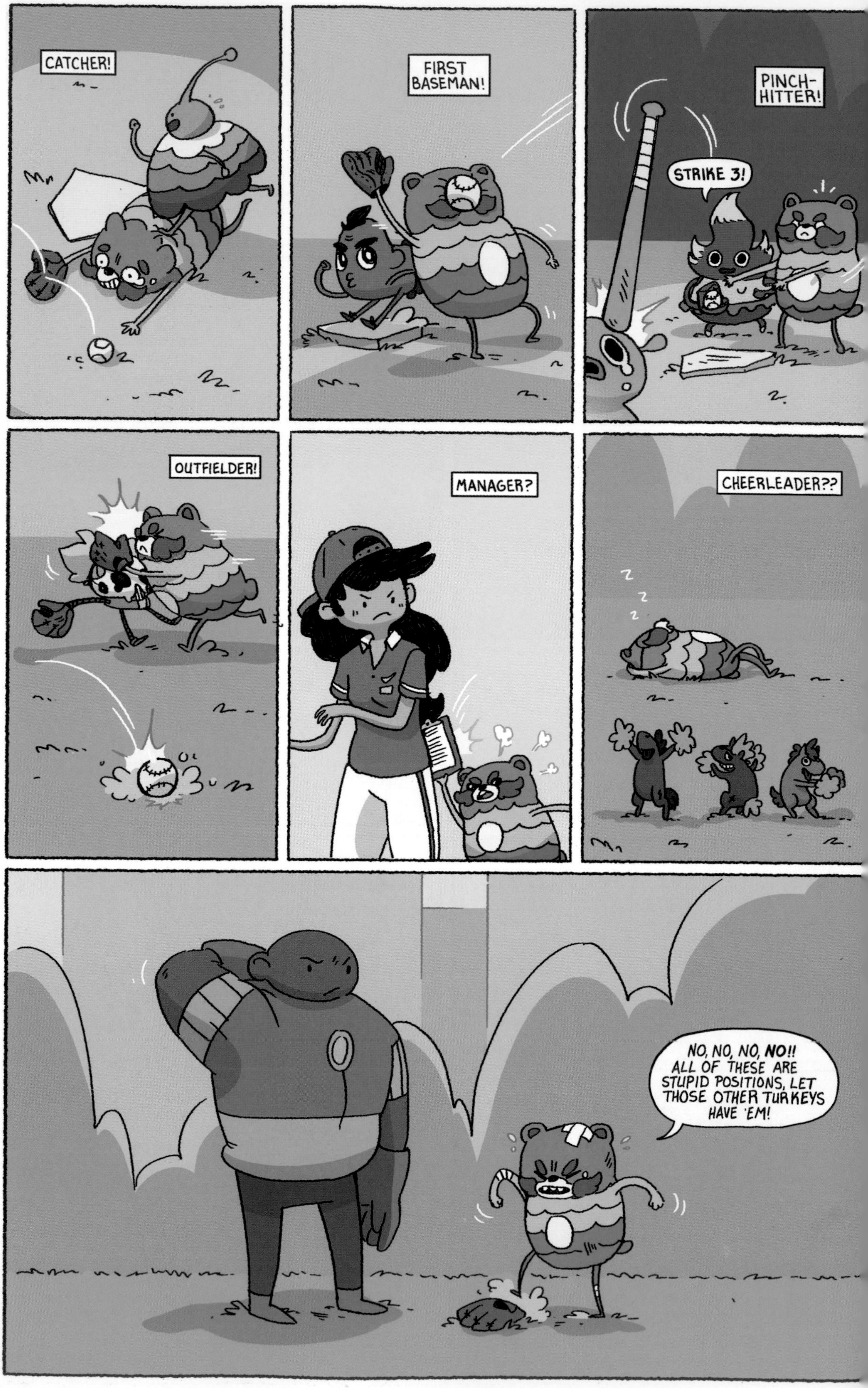

CATCHER!
FIRST BASEMAN!
PINCH-HITTER!
STRIKE 3!
OUTFIELDER!
MANAGER?
CHEERLEADER??
Z
Z
Z
NO, NO, NO, NO!! ALL OF THESE ARE STUPID POSITIONS, LET THOSE OTHER TURKEYS HAVE 'EM!

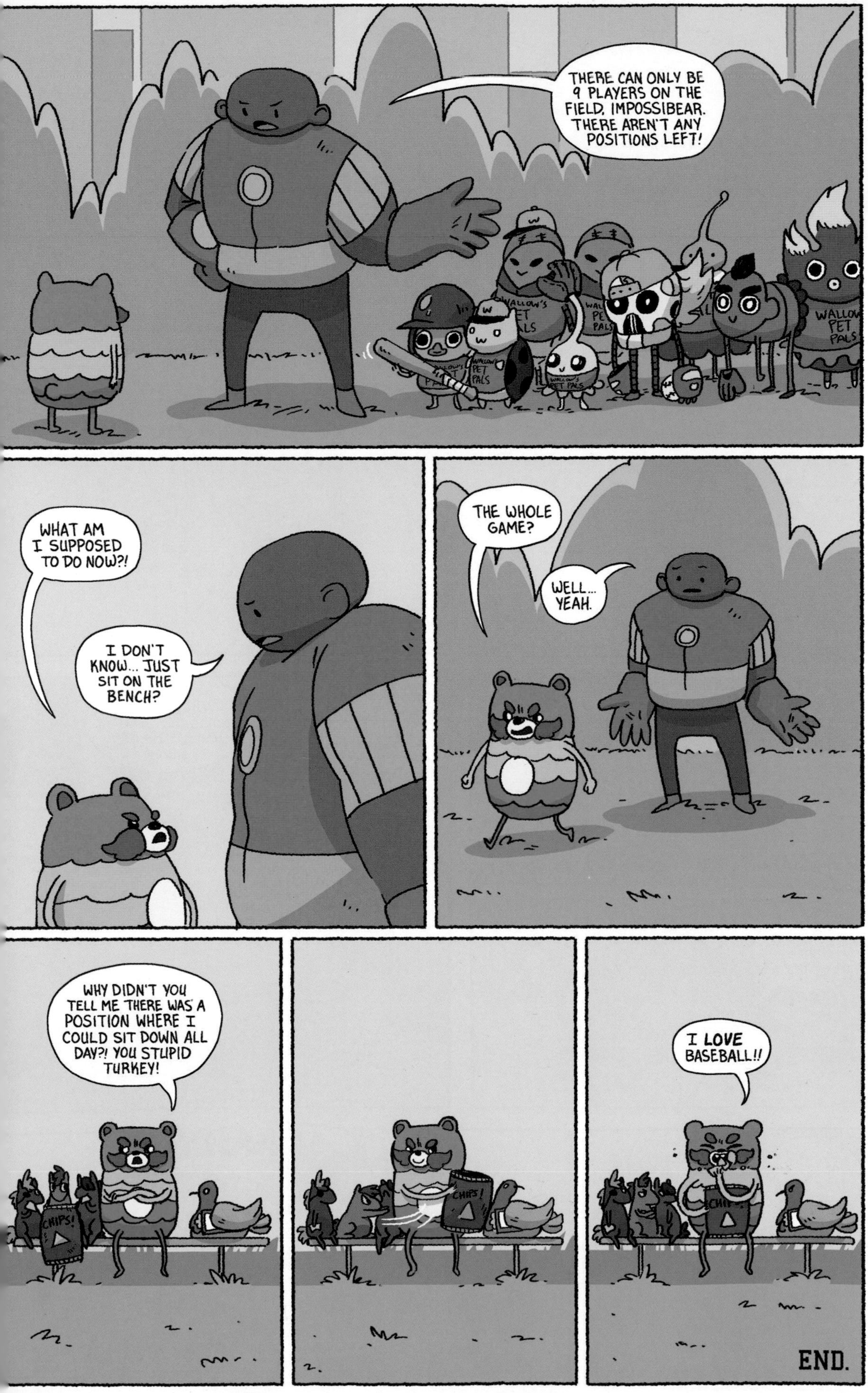
THERE CAN ONLY BE 9 PLAYERS ON THE FIELD, IMPOSSIBEAR. THERE AREN'T ANY POSITIONS LEFT!
WALLOW'S PET PALS
WHAT AM I SUPPOSED TO DO NOW?!
I DON'T KNOW... JUST SIT ON THE BENCH?
THE WHOLE GAME?
WELL... YEAH.
WHY DIDN'T YOU TELL ME THERE WAS A POSITION WHERE I COULD SIT DOWN ALL DAY?! YOU STUPID TURKEY!
CHIPS!
CHIPS!
I **LOVE** BASEBALL!!
CHIPS
END.

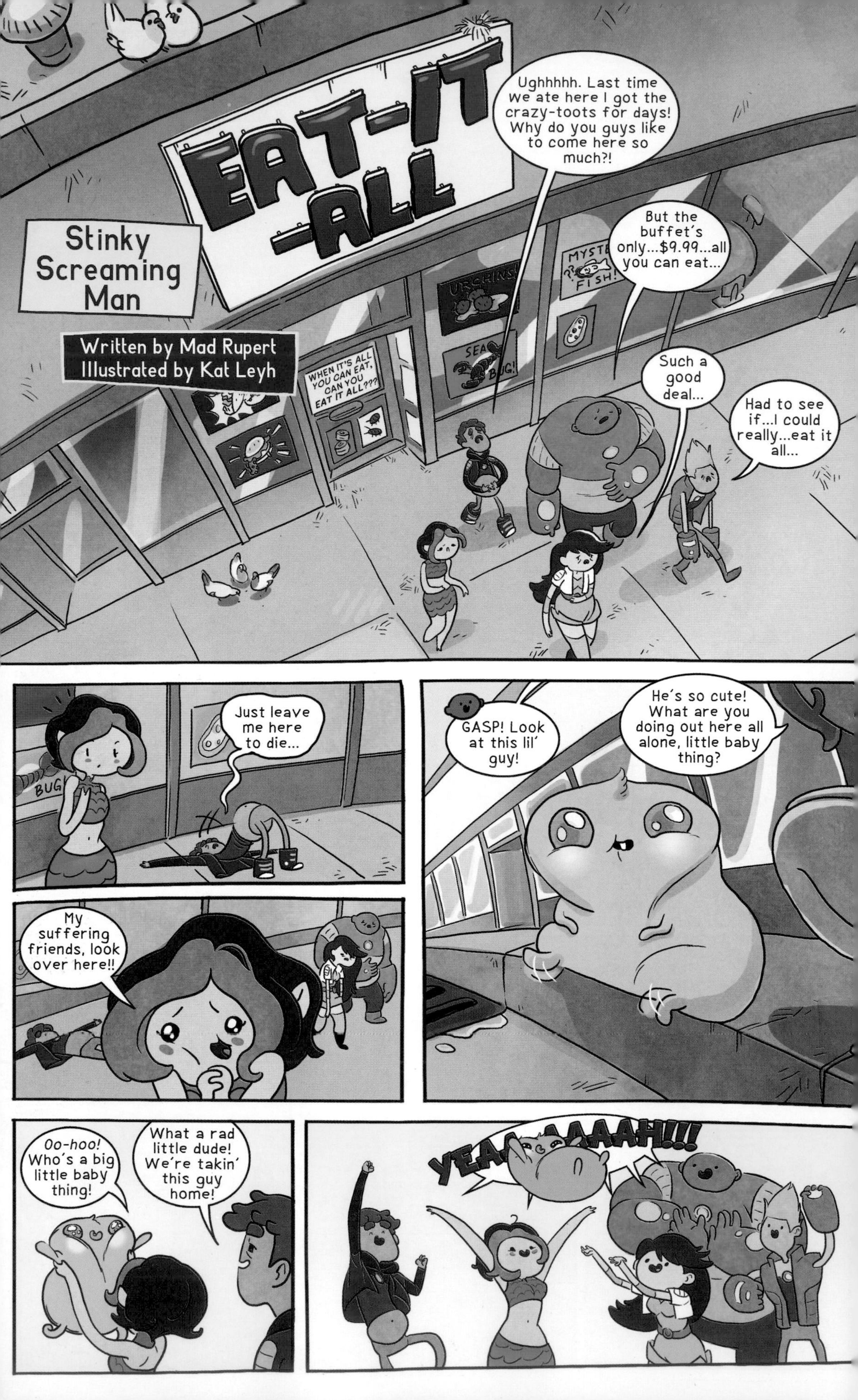
Stinky Screaming Man
Written by Mad Rupert
Illustrated by Kat Leyh
EAT-IT-ALL
WHEN IT'S ALL YOU CAN EAT, CAN YOU EAT IT ALL???
URCHINS!
SEA BUG!
Ughhhhh. Last time we ate here I got the crazy-toots for days! Why do you guys like to come here so much?!
But the buffet's only...$9.99...all you can eat...
Such a good deal...
Had to see if...I could really...eat it all...
Just leave me here to die...
My suffering friends, look over here!!
GASP! Look at this lil' guy!
He's so cute! What are you doing out here all alone, little baby thing?
Oo-hoo! Who's a big little baby thing!
What a rad little dude! We're takin' this guy home!
YEAAAAAAH!!!

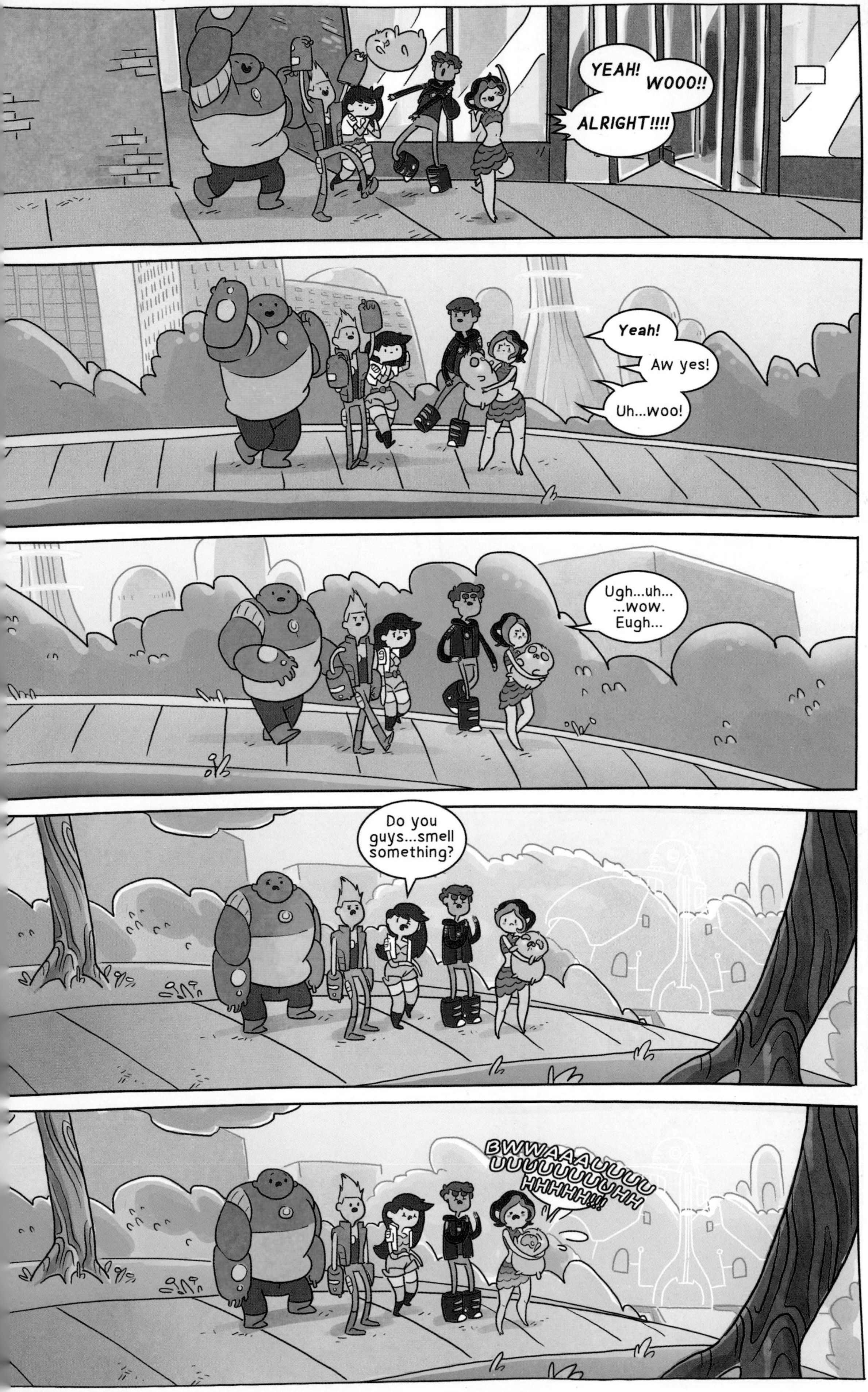
YEAH!
WOOO!!
ALRIGHT!!!!
Yeah!
Aw yes!
Uh...woo!
Ugh...uh... ...wow. Eugh...
Do you guys...smell something?
BWWAAAUUUU UUUUUUUUHH HHHHHH!!!

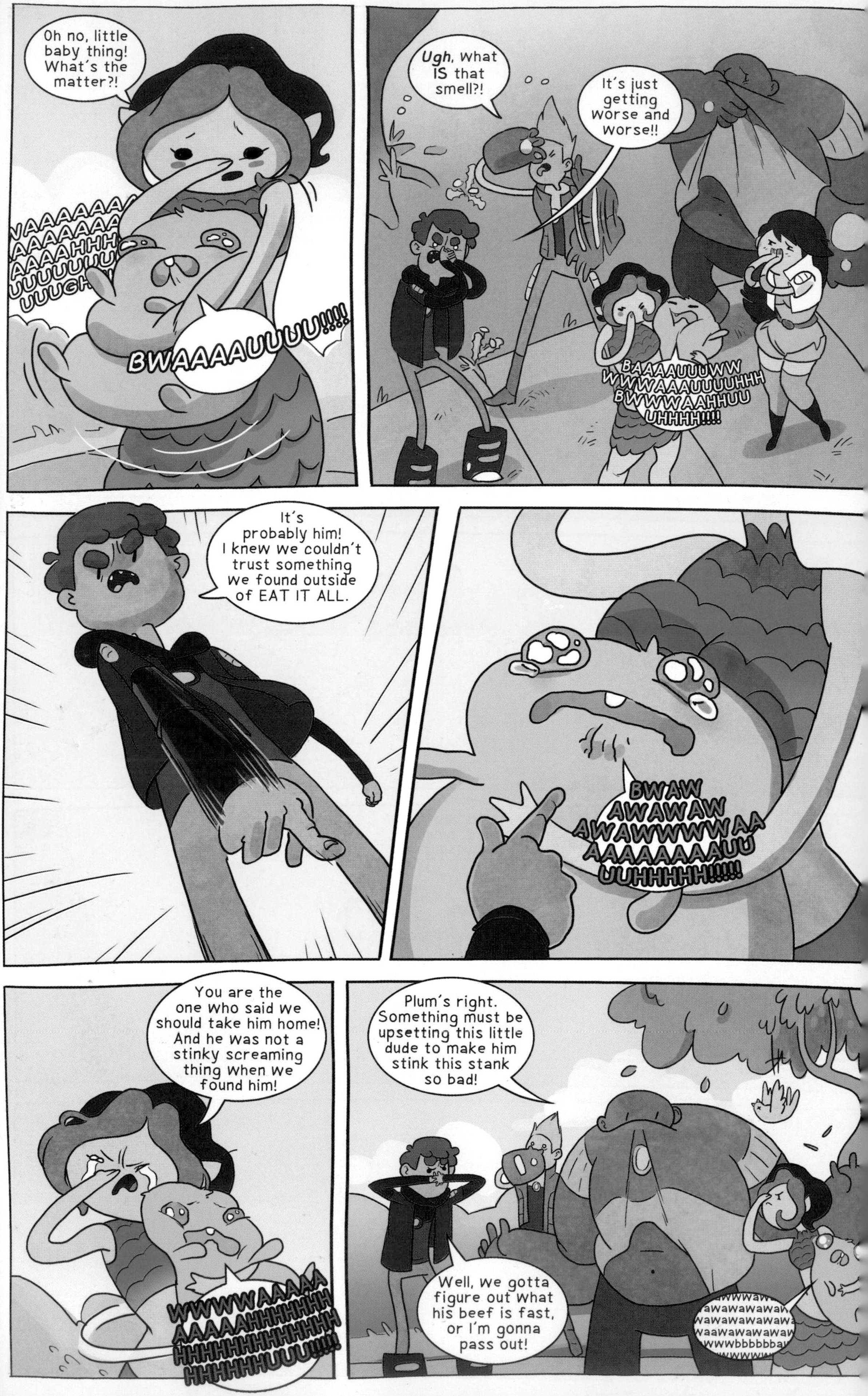
Oh no, little baby thing! What's the matter?!
WAAAAAAA
AAAAAAAAA
AAAAHHH
AAAAUUUUU
UUUUGH
UUUGH
BWAAAAUUUU!!!!
Ugh, what IS that smell?!
It's just getting worse and worse!!
BAAAAUUUWW WWWAAAUUUUHHH BWWWAAHHUU UHHHH!!!!
It's probably him! I knew we couldn't trust something we found outside of EAT IT ALL.
BWAW AWAWAW AWAWWWWAA AAAAAAAAUU UUHHHHH!!!!!
You are the one who said we should take him home! And he was not a stinky screaming thing when we found him!
WWWWAAAAA HHHHH AAAAAHHHHHHHH HHHHHHHHHHHH HHHHHHUUU!!!!
Plum's right. Something must be upsetting this little dude to make him stink this stank so bad!
Well, we gotta figure out what his beef is fast, or I'm gonna pass out!
awawawawawaw
wawawawawawa
waawawawawaw
wwwbbbbbba

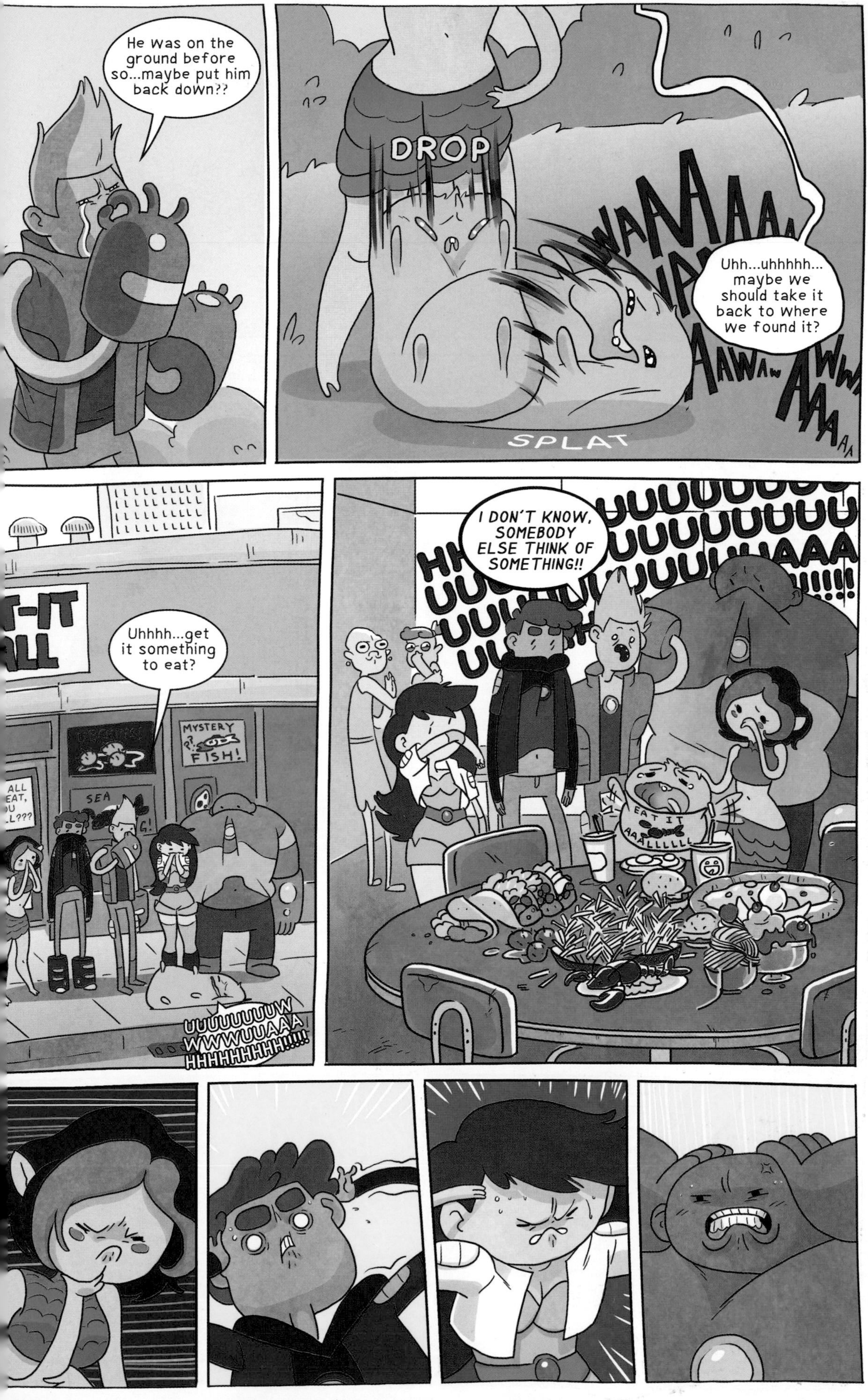
He was on the ground before so...maybe put him back down??
DROP
Uhh...uhhhhh... maybe we should take it back to where we found it?
SPLAT
Uhhhh...get it something to eat?
MYSTERY FISH!
UUUUUUUW WWWUUAAA HHHHHHHH!!!!!
I DON'T KNOW, SOMEBODY ELSE THINK OF SOMETHING!!
EAT IT AALLLLLL

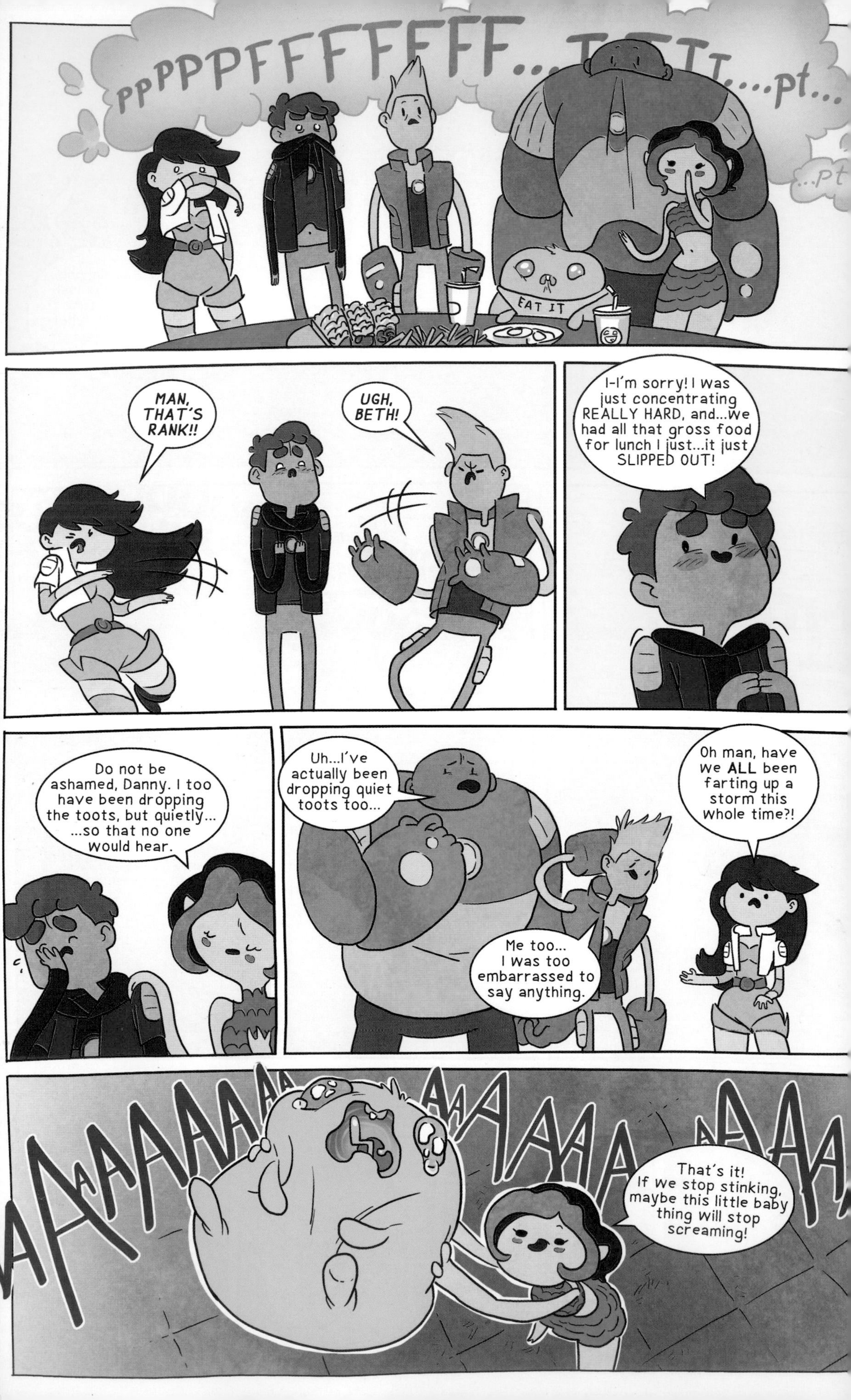
ppPPPFFFFFFF...T...T...T...pt...
...pt
EAT IT
MAN, THAT'S RANK!!
UGH, BETH!
I-I'm sorry! I was just concentrating REALLY HARD, and...we had all that gross food for lunch I just...it just SLIPPED OUT!
Do not be ashamed, Danny. I too have been dropping the toots, but quietly... ...so that no one would hear.
Uh...I've actually been dropping quiet toots too...
Me too... I was too embarrassed to say anything.
Oh man, have we ALL been farting up a storm this whole time?!
AAAAAAAAAAAAAAAAAAAAAAAA
That's it! If we stop stinking, maybe this little baby thing will stop screaming!

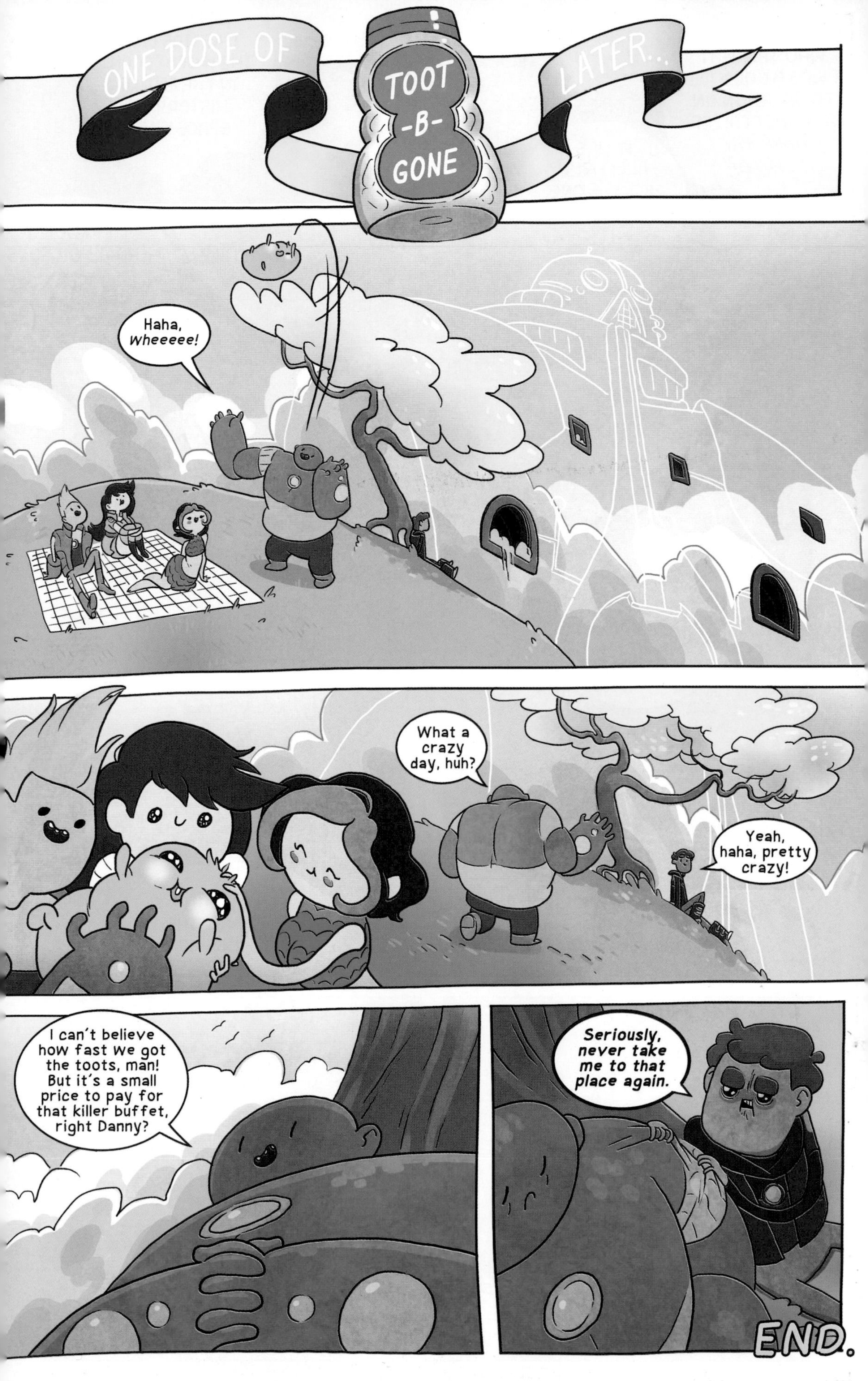

ONE DOSE OF
TOOT -B- GONE
LATER...
Haha, Wheeeee!
What a crazy day, huh?
Yeah, haha, pretty crazy!
I can't believe how fast we got the toots, man! But it's a small price to pay for that killer buffet, right Danny?
Seriously, never take me to that place again.
END.

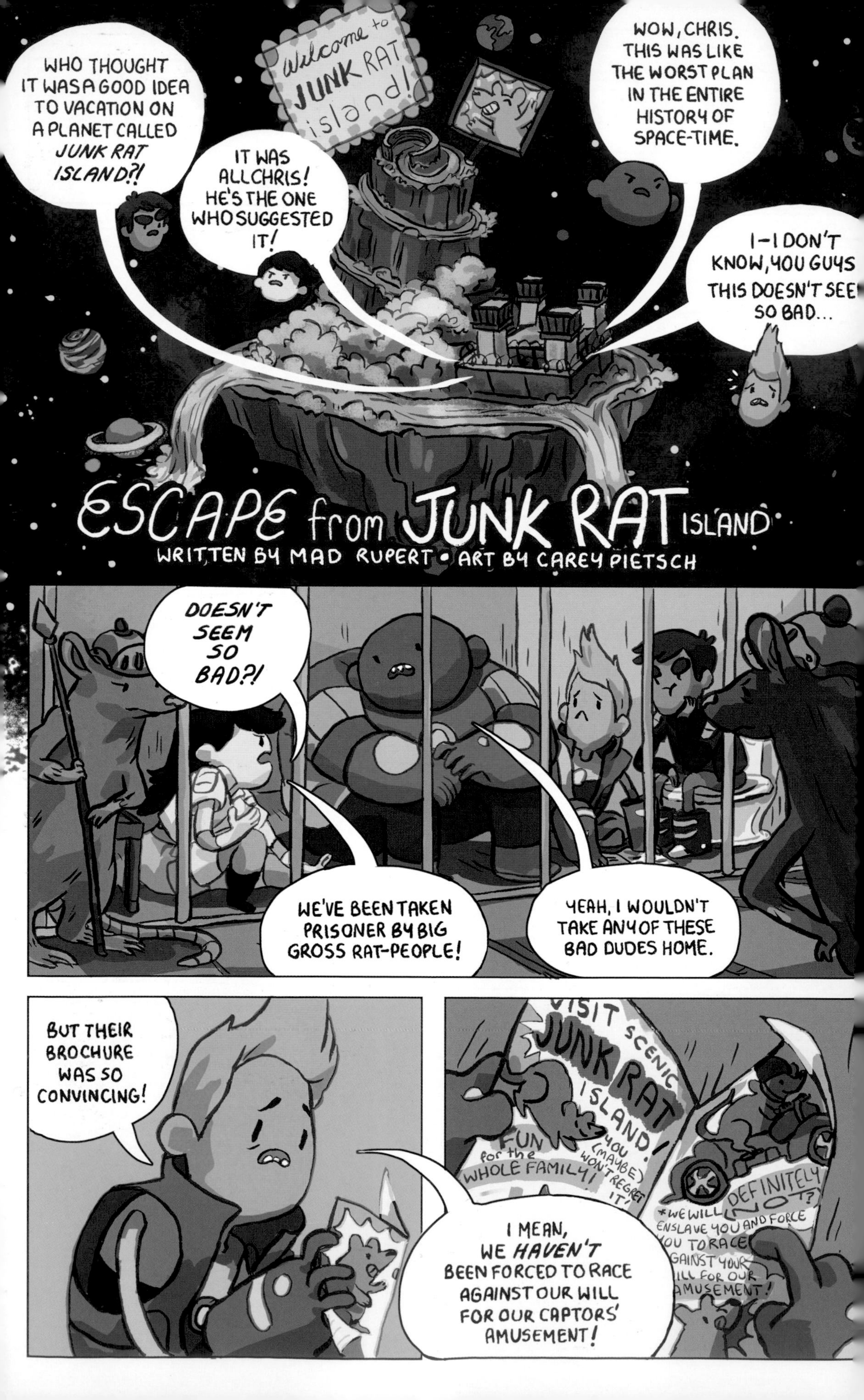
Welcome to JUNK RAT island!
WHO THOUGHT IT WAS A GOOD IDEA TO VACATION ON A PLANET CALLED JUNK RAT ISLAND?!
IT WAS ALL CHRIS! HE'S THE ONE WHO SUGGESTED IT!
WOW, CHRIS. THIS WAS LIKE THE WORST PLAN IN THE ENTIRE HISTORY OF SPACE-TIME.
I-I DON'T KNOW, YOU GUYS THIS DOESN'T SEE SO BAD...
ESCAPE from JUNK RAT ISLAND
WRITTEN BY MAD RUPERT • ART BY CAREY PIETSCH
DOESN'T SEEM SO BAD?!
WE'VE BEEN TAKEN PRISONER BY BIG GROSS RAT-PEOPLE!
YEAH, I WOULDN'T TAKE ANY OF THESE BAD DUDES HOME.
BUT THEIR BROCHURE WAS SO CONVINCING!
VISIT SCENIC JUNK RAT ISLAND.
FUN for the WHOLE FAMILY!
YOU (MAYBE) WON'T REGRET IT!
DEFINITELY NOT?
*WE WILL ENSLAVE YOU AND FORCE YOU TO RACE AGAINST YOUR WILL FOR OUR AMUSEMENT!
I MEAN, WE HAVEN'T BEEN FORCED TO RACE AGAINST OUR WILL FOR OUR CAPTORS' AMUSEMENT!

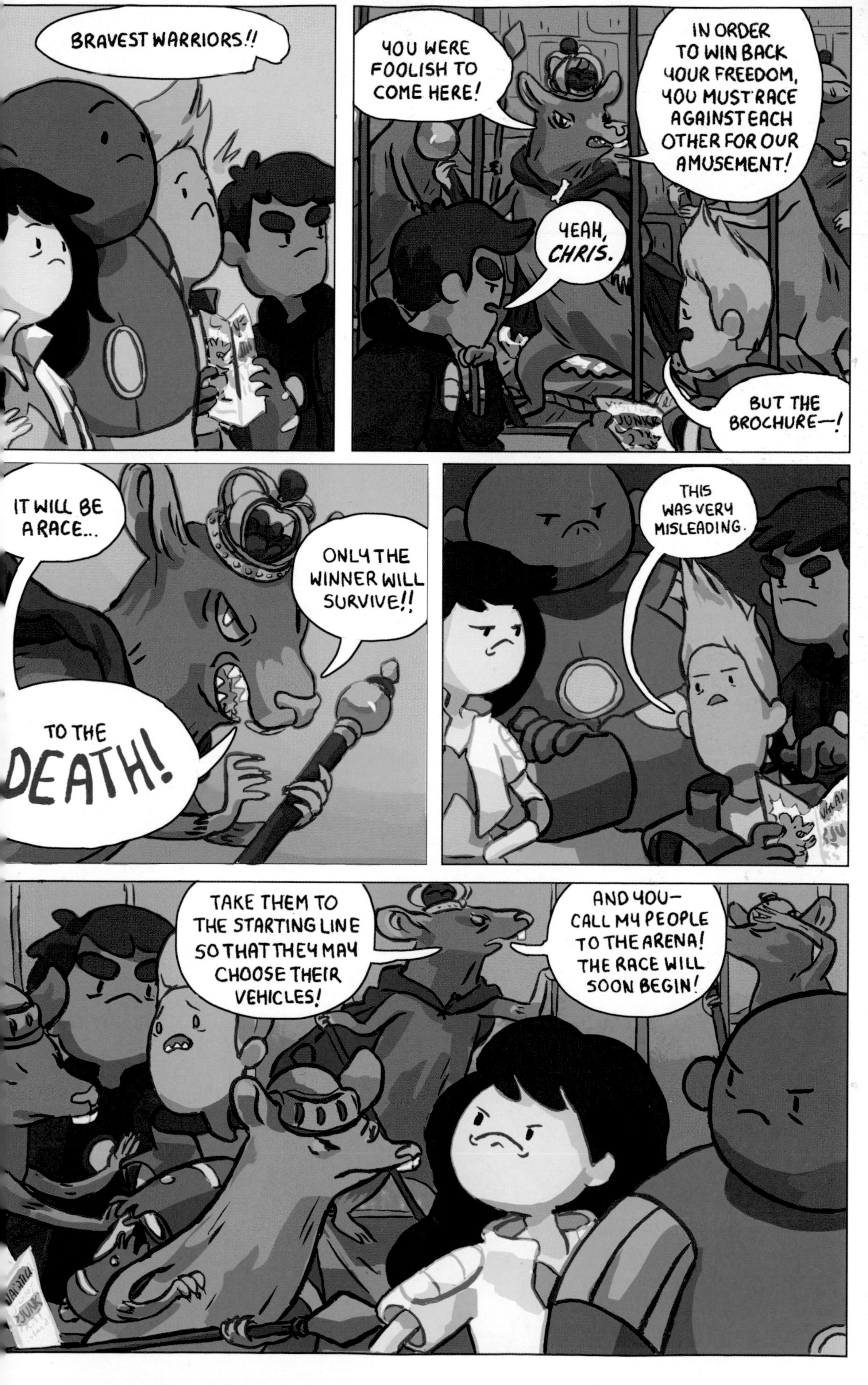
BRAVEST WARRIORS!!
YOU WERE FOOLISH TO COME HERE!
IN ORDER TO WIN BACK YOUR FREEDOM, YOU MUST RACE AGAINST EACH OTHER FOR OUR AMUSEMENT!
YEAH, CHRIS.
BUT THE BROCHURE—!
IT WILL BE A RACE...
ONLY THE WINNER WILL SURVIVE!!
TO THE DEATH!
THIS WAS VERY MISLEADING.
TAKE THEM TO THE STARTING LINE SO THAT THEY MAY CHOOSE THEIR VEHICLES!
AND YOU— CALL MY PEOPLE TO THE ARENA! THE RACE WILL SOON BEGIN!

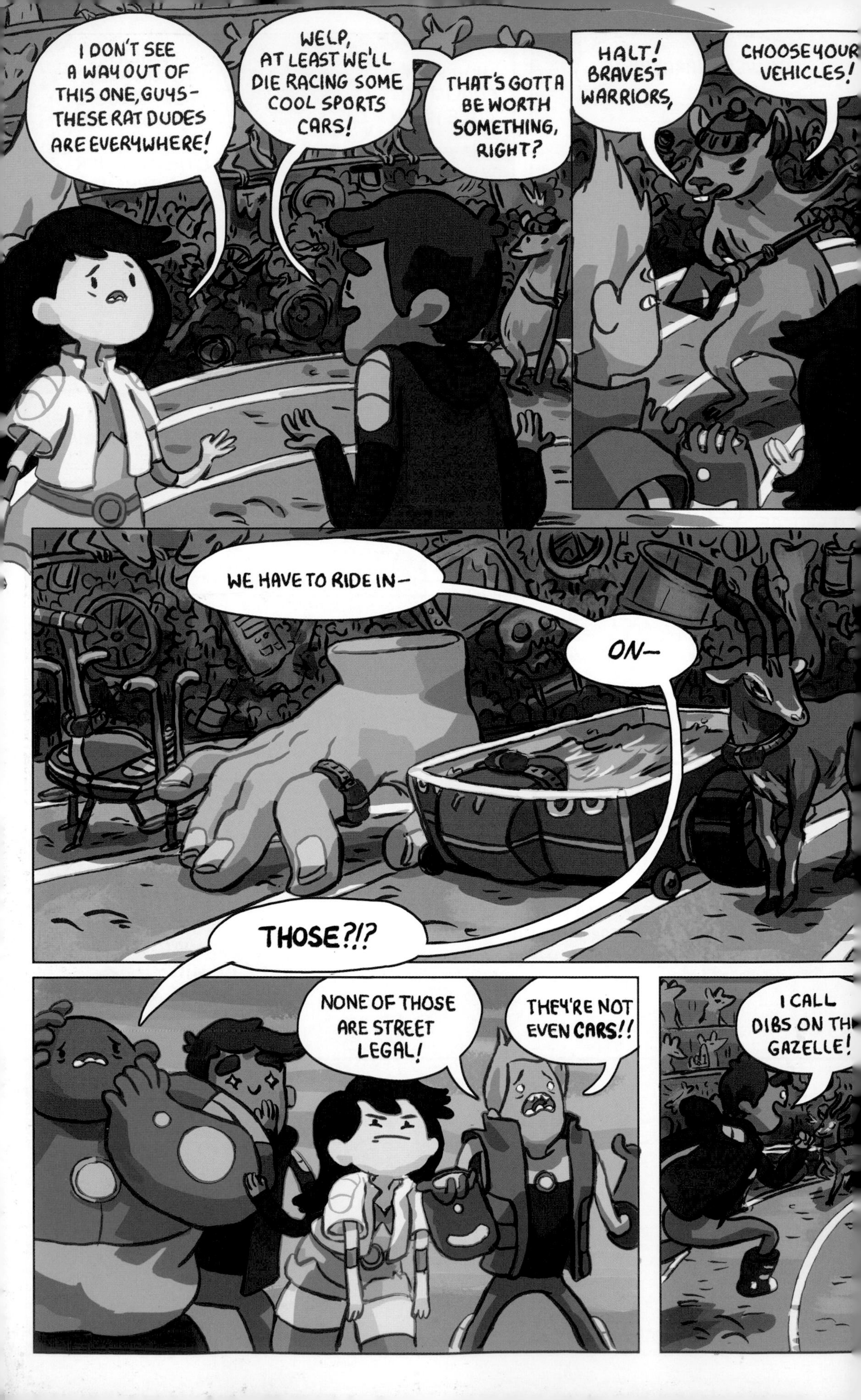
I DON'T SEE A WAY OUT OF THIS ONE, GUYS- THESE RAT DUDES ARE EVERYWHERE!
WELP, AT LEAST WE'LL DIE RACING SOME COOL SPORTS CARS!
THAT'S GOTTA BE WORTH SOMETHING, RIGHT?
HALT! BRAVEST WARRIORS,
CHOOSE YOUR VEHICLES!
WE HAVE TO RIDE IN-
ON-
THOSE?!?
NONE OF THOSE ARE STREET LEGAL!
THEY'RE NOT EVEN CARS!!
I CALL DIBS ON TH GAZELLE!

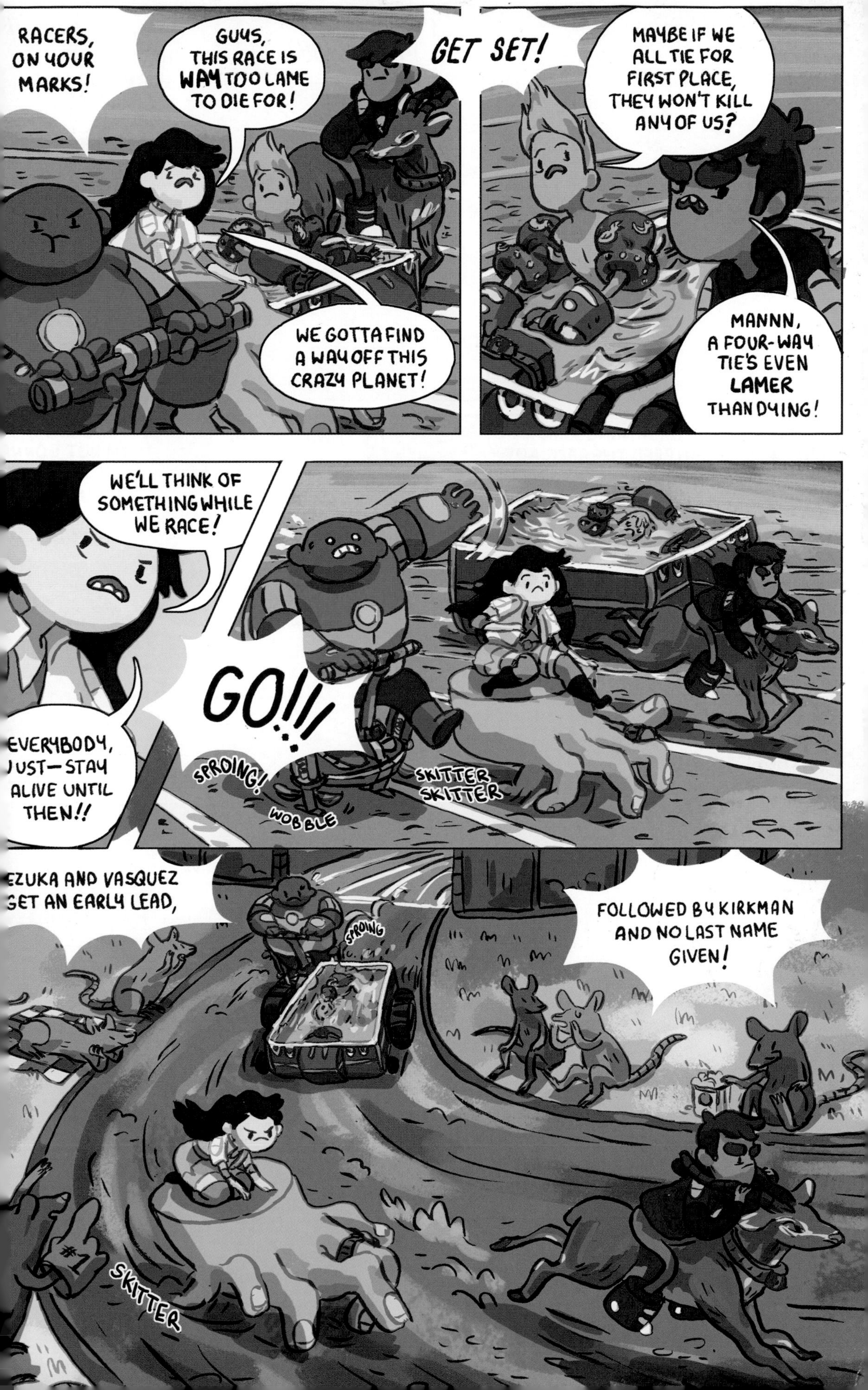
RACERS, ON YOUR MARKS!
GUYS, THIS RACE IS WAY TOO LAME TO DIE FOR!
WE GOTTA FIND A WAY OFF THIS CRAZY PLANET!
GET SET!
MAYBE IF WE ALL TIE FOR FIRST PLACE, THEY WON'T KILL ANY OF US?
MANNN, A FOUR-WAY TIE'S EVEN LAMER THAN DYING!
WE'LL THINK OF SOMETHING WHILE WE RACE!
EVERYBODY, JUST—STAY ALIVE UNTIL THEN!!
GO!!!
SPROING!
WOBBLE
SKITTER SKITTER
EZUKA AND VASQUEZ GET AN EARLY LEAD,
SPROING
FOLLOWED BY KIRKMAN AND NO LAST NAME GIVEN!
#1
SKITTER

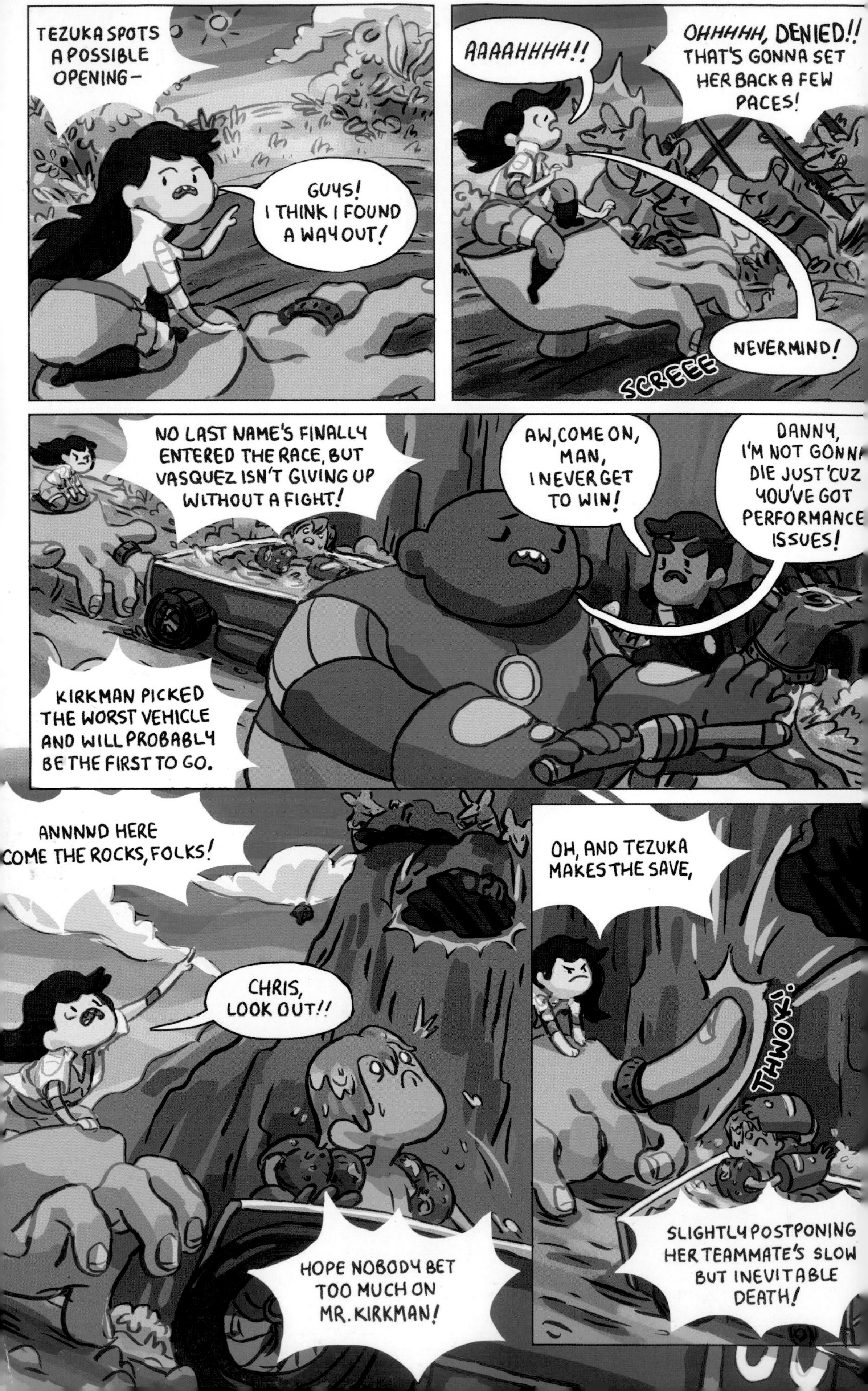

TEZUKA SPOTS A POSSIBLE OPENING–
GUYS! I THINK I FOUND A WAY OUT!
AAAAHHHH!!
OHHHHH, DENIED!! THAT'S GONNA SET HER BACK A FEW PACES!
NEVERMIND!
SCREEE
NO LAST NAME'S FINALLY ENTERED THE RACE, BUT VASQUEZ ISN'T GIVING UP WITHOUT A FIGHT!
AW, COME ON, MAN, I NEVER GET TO WIN!
DANNY, I'M NOT GONNA DIE JUST 'CUZ YOU'VE GOT PERFORMANCE ISSUES!
KIRKMAN PICKED THE WORST VEHICLE AND WILL PROBABLY BE THE FIRST TO GO.
ANNNND HERE COME THE ROCKS, FOLKS!
CHRIS, LOOK OUT!!
HOPE NOBODY BET TOO MUCH ON MR. KIRKMAN!
OH, AND TEZUKA MAKES THE SAVE,
THWOK!
SLIGHTLY POSTPONING HER TEAMMATE'S SLOW BUT INEVITABLE DEATH!

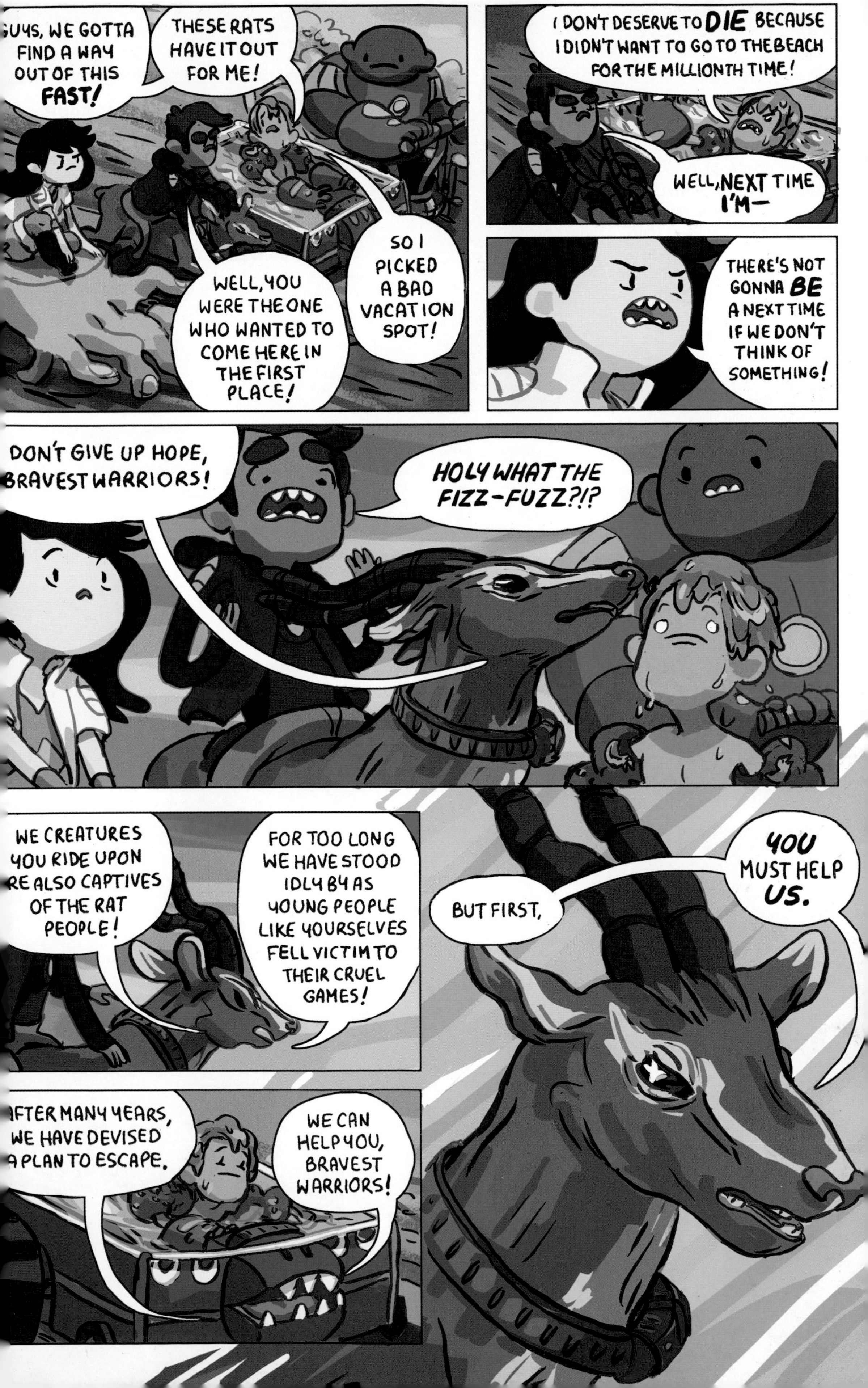
GUYS, WE GOTTA FIND A WAY OUT OF THIS FAST!
THESE RATS HAVE IT OUT FOR ME!
WELL, YOU WERE THE ONE WHO WANTED TO COME HERE IN THE FIRST PLACE!
SO I PICKED A BAD VACATION SPOT!
I DON'T DESERVE TO DIE BECAUSE I DIDN'T WANT TO GO TO THE BEACH FOR THE MILLIONTH TIME!
WELL, NEXT TIME I'M—
THERE'S NOT GONNA BE A NEXT TIME IF WE DON'T THINK OF SOMETHING!
DON'T GIVE UP HOPE, BRAVEST WARRIORS!
HOLY WHAT THE FIZZ-FUZZ?!?
WE CREATURES YOU RIDE UPON ARE ALSO CAPTIVES OF THE RAT PEOPLE!
FOR TOO LONG WE HAVE STOOD IDLY BY AS YOUNG PEOPLE LIKE YOURSELVES FELL VICTIM TO THEIR CRUEL GAMES!
AFTER MANY YEARS, WE HAVE DEVISED A PLAN TO ESCAPE.
WE CAN HELP YOU, BRAVEST WARRIORS!
BUT FIRST,
YOU MUST HELP US.

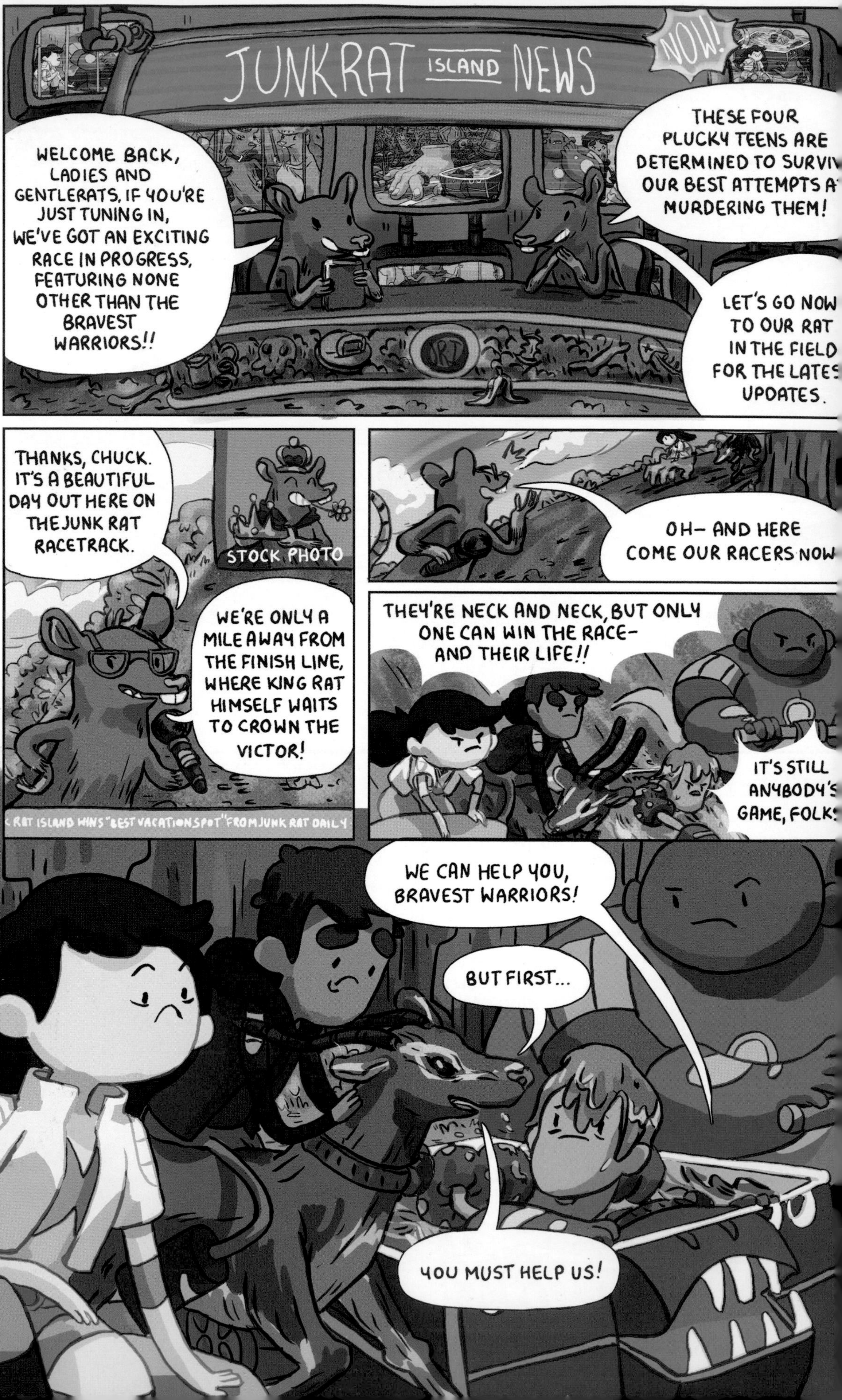
JUNKRAT ISLAND NEWS
NOW!
WELCOME BACK, LADIES AND GENTLERATS, IF YOU'RE JUST TUNING IN, WE'VE GOT AN EXCITING RACE IN PROGRESS, FEATURING NONE OTHER THAN THE BRAVEST WARRIORS!!
THESE FOUR PLUCKY TEENS ARE DETERMINED TO SURVIV OUR BEST ATTEMPTS A MURDERING THEM!
LET'S GO NOW TO OUR RAT IN THE FIELD FOR THE LATES UPDATES.
JRI
THANKS, CHUCK. IT'S A BEAUTIFUL DAY OUT HERE ON THE JUNK RAT RACETRACK.
STOCK PHOTO
WE'RE ONLY A MILE AWAY FROM THE FINISH LINE, WHERE KING RAT HIMSELF WAITS TO CROWN THE VICTOR!
RAT ISLAND WINS "BEST VACATION SPOT" FROM JUNK RAT DAILY
OH— AND HERE COME OUR RACERS NOW
THEY'RE NECK AND NECK, BUT ONLY ONE CAN WIN THE RACE— AND THEIR LIFE!!
IT'S STILL ANYBODY'S GAME, FOLKS
WE CAN HELP YOU, BRAVEST WARRIORS!
BUT FIRST...
YOU MUST HELP US!

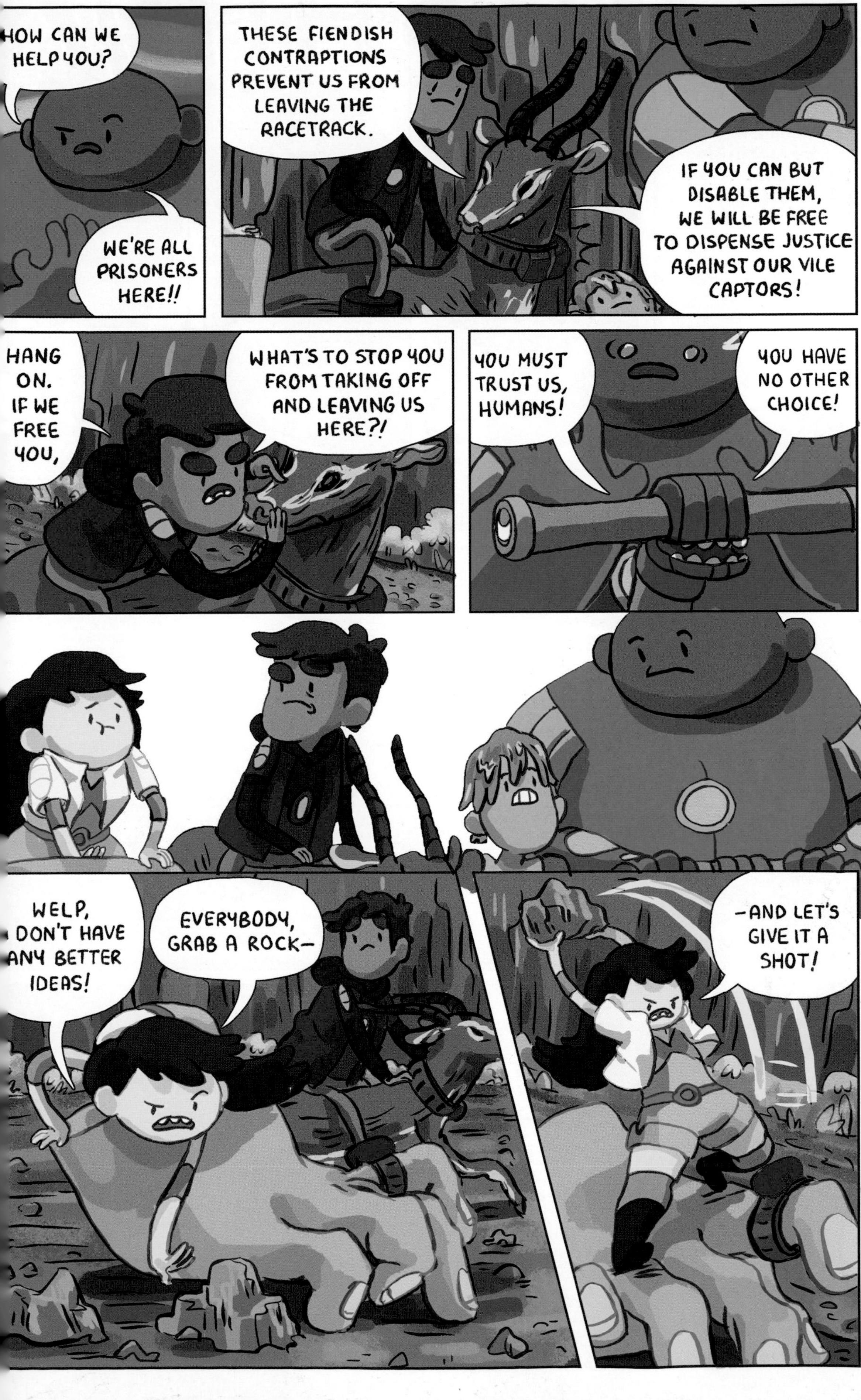
HOW CAN WE HELP YOU?
WE'RE ALL PRISONERS HERE!!
THESE FIENDISH CONTRAPTIONS PREVENT US FROM LEAVING THE RACETRACK.
IF YOU CAN BUT DISABLE THEM, WE WILL BE FREE TO DISPENSE JUSTICE AGAINST OUR VILE CAPTORS!
HANG ON. IF WE FREE YOU,
WHAT'S TO STOP YOU FROM TAKING OFF AND LEAVING US HERE?!
YOU MUST TRUST US, HUMANS!
YOU HAVE NO OTHER CHOICE!
WELP, DON'T HAVE ANY BETTER IDEAS!
EVERYBODY, GRAB A ROCK—
—AND LET'S GIVE IT A SHOT!

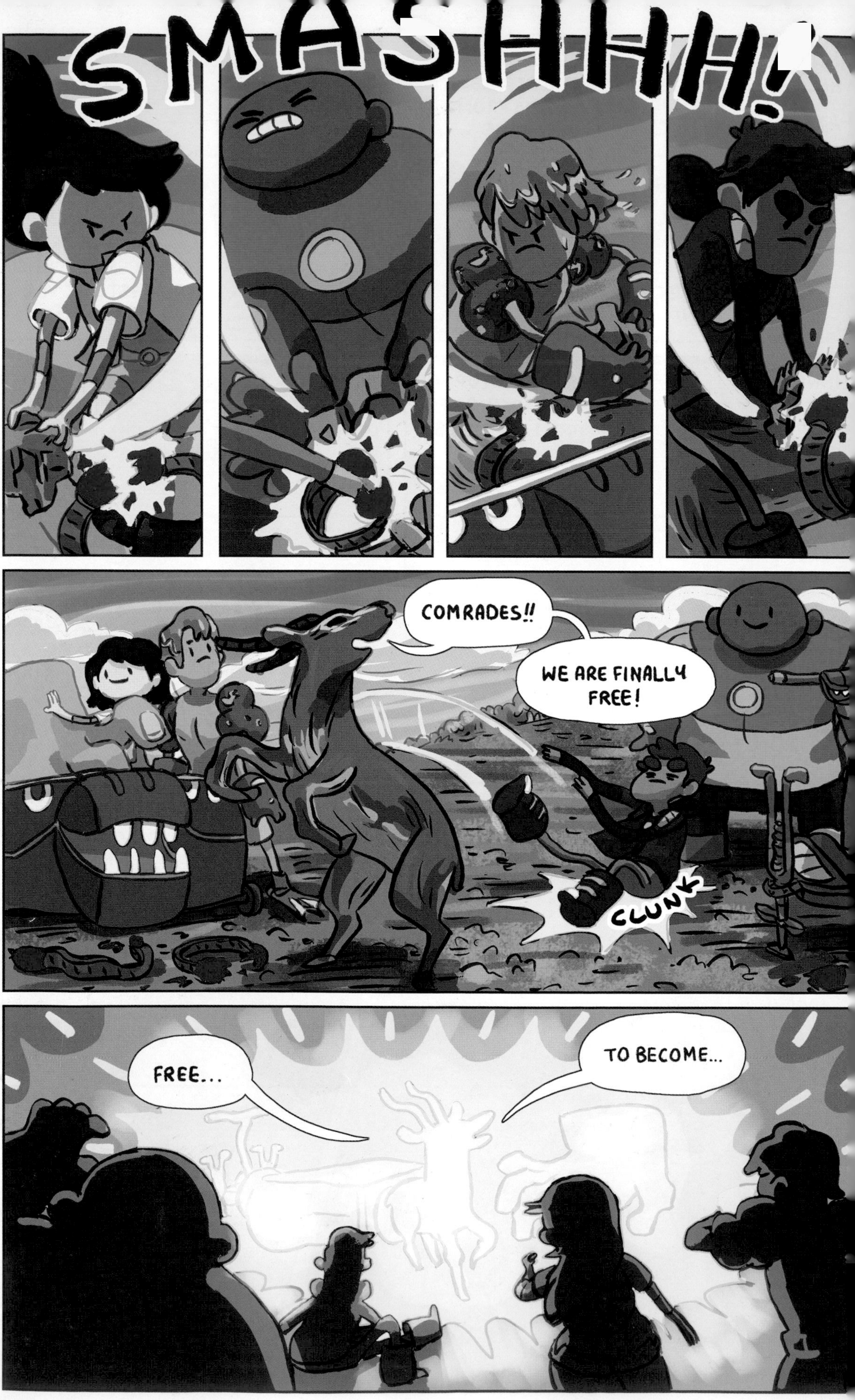
SMASHHH!
COMRADES!!
WE ARE FINALLY FREE!
CLUNK
FREE...
TO BECOME...

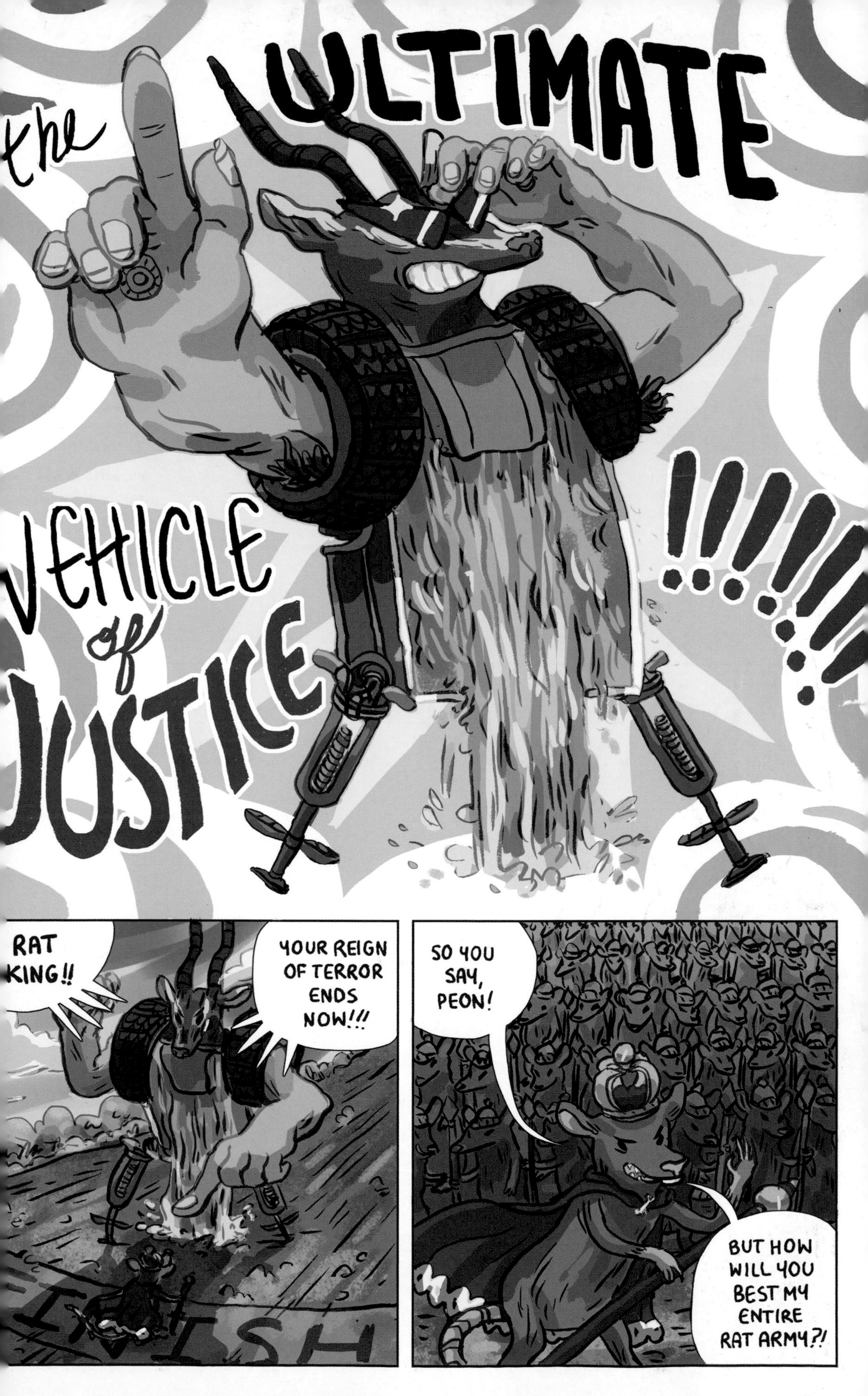
the ULTIMATE
VEHICLE of JUSTICE!!!!!!!
RAT KING!!
YOUR REIGN OF TERROR ENDS NOW!!!
SO YOU SAY, PEON!
BUT HOW WILL YOU BEST MY ENTIRE RAT ARMY?!

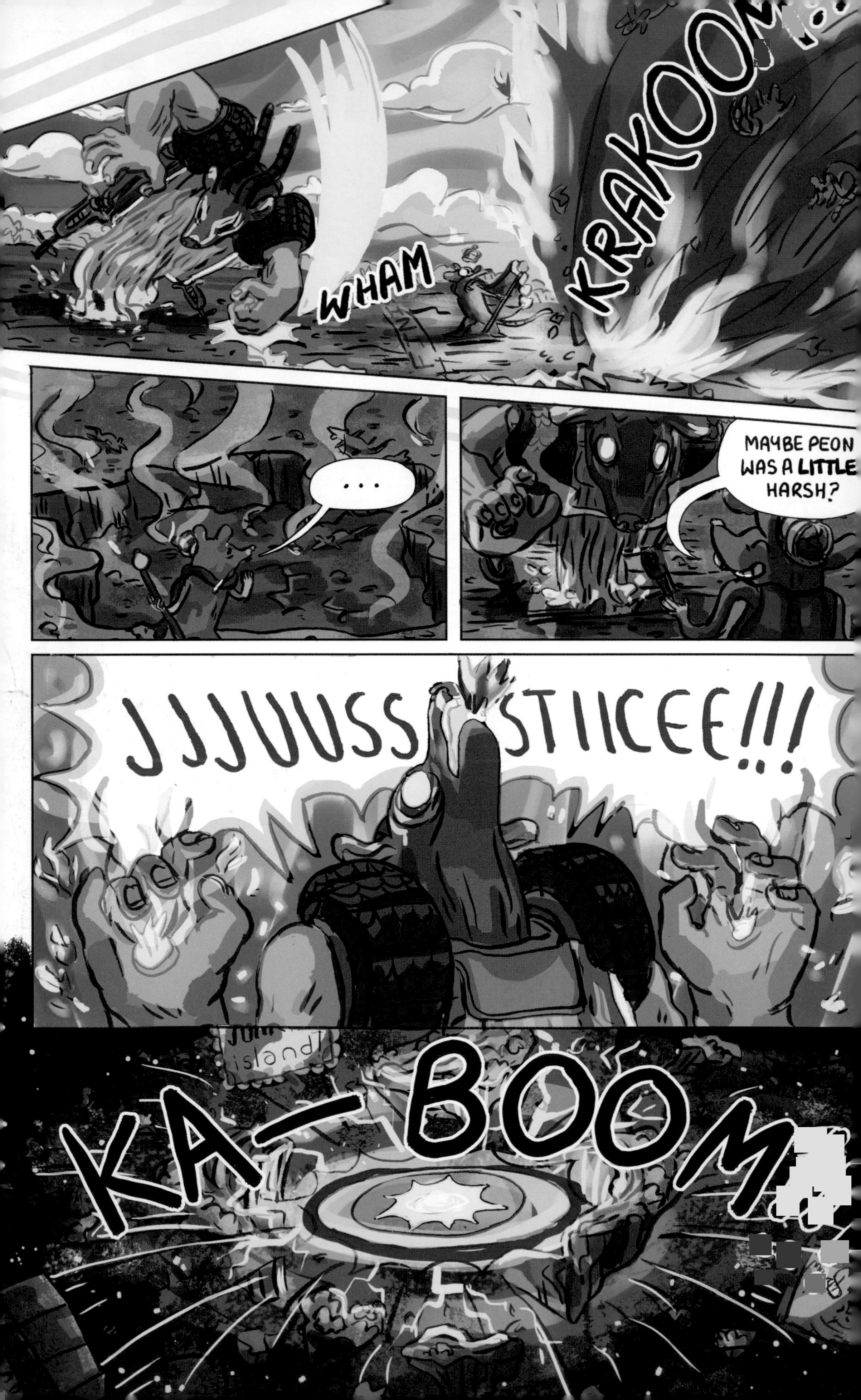
WHAM
KRAKOOM
...
MAYBE PEON WAS A LITTLE HARSH?
JJJUUSS STIICEE!!!
island
KA-BOOM

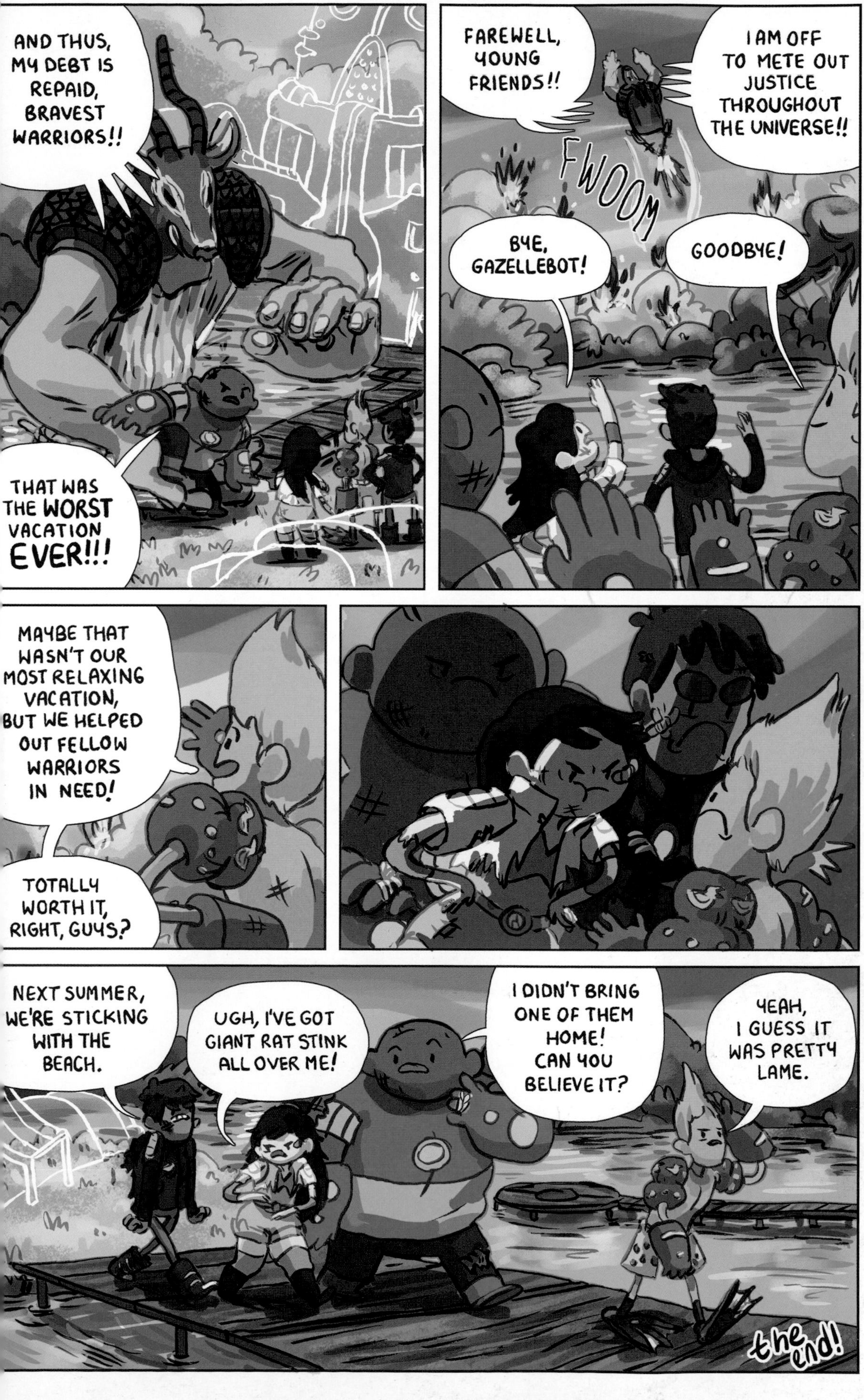
AND THUS, MY DEBT IS REPAID, BRAVEST WARRIORS!!
THAT WAS THE WORST VACATION EVER!!!
FAREWELL, YOUNG FRIENDS!!
I AM OFF TO METE OUT JUSTICE THROUGHOUT THE UNIVERSE!!
FWOOM
BYE, GAZELLEBOT!
GOODBYE!
MAYBE THAT WASN'T OUR MOST RELAXING VACATION, BUT WE HELPED OUT FELLOW WARRIORS IN NEED!
TOTALLY WORTH IT, RIGHT, GUYS?
NEXT SUMMER, WE'RE STICKING WITH THE BEACH.
UGH, I'VE GOT GIANT RAT STINK ALL OVER ME!
I DIDN'T BRING ONE OF THEM HOME! CAN YOU BELIEVE IT?
YEAH, I GUESS IT WAS PRETTY LAME.
the end!

COVER GALLERY

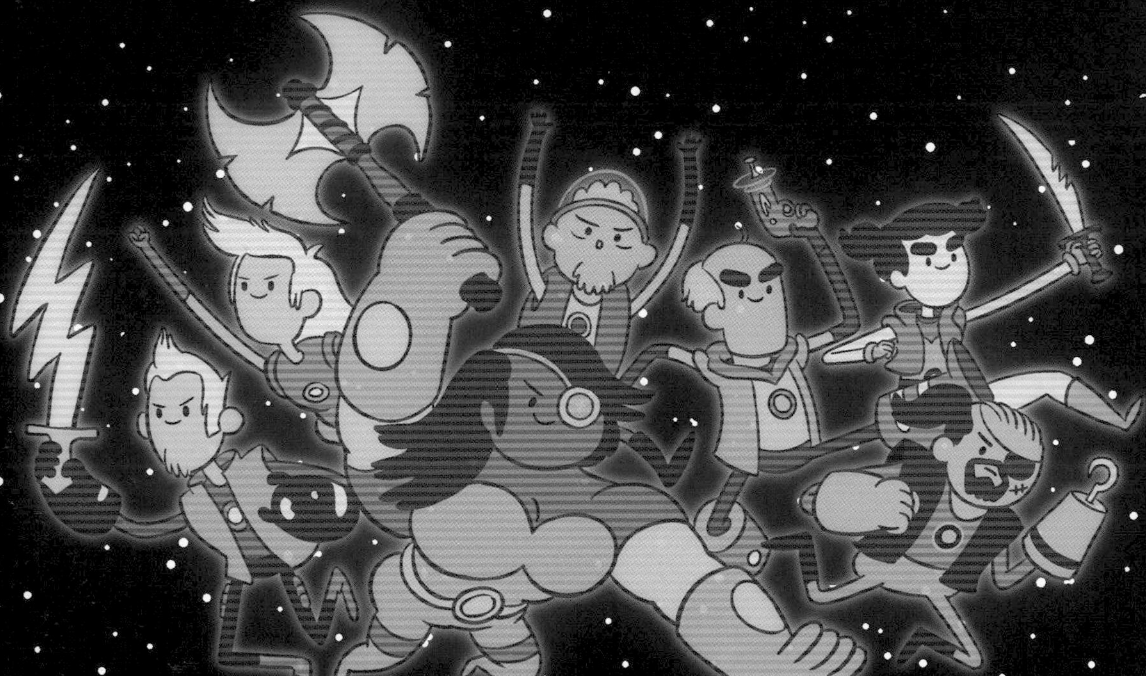

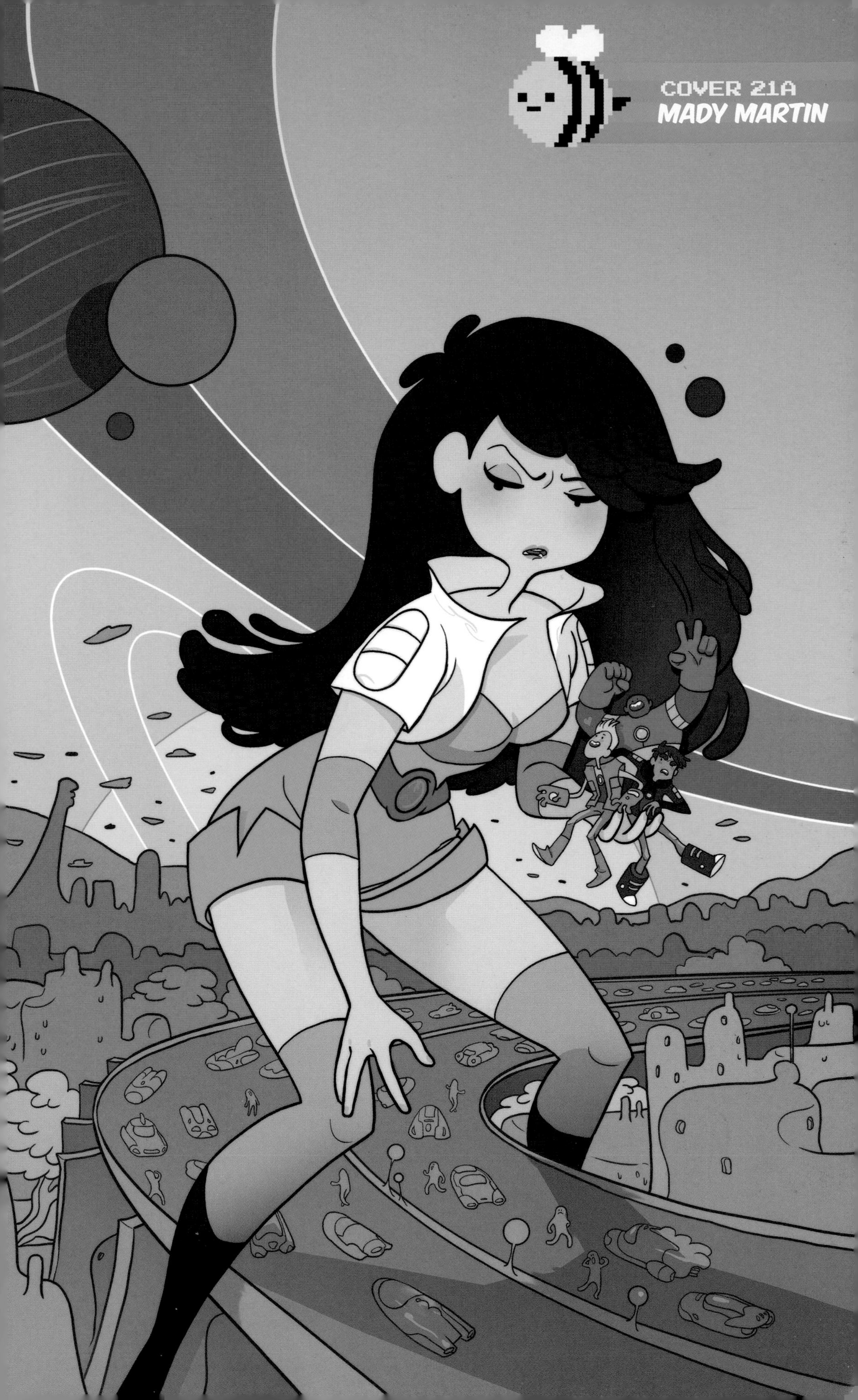
COVER 21A
MADY MARTIN

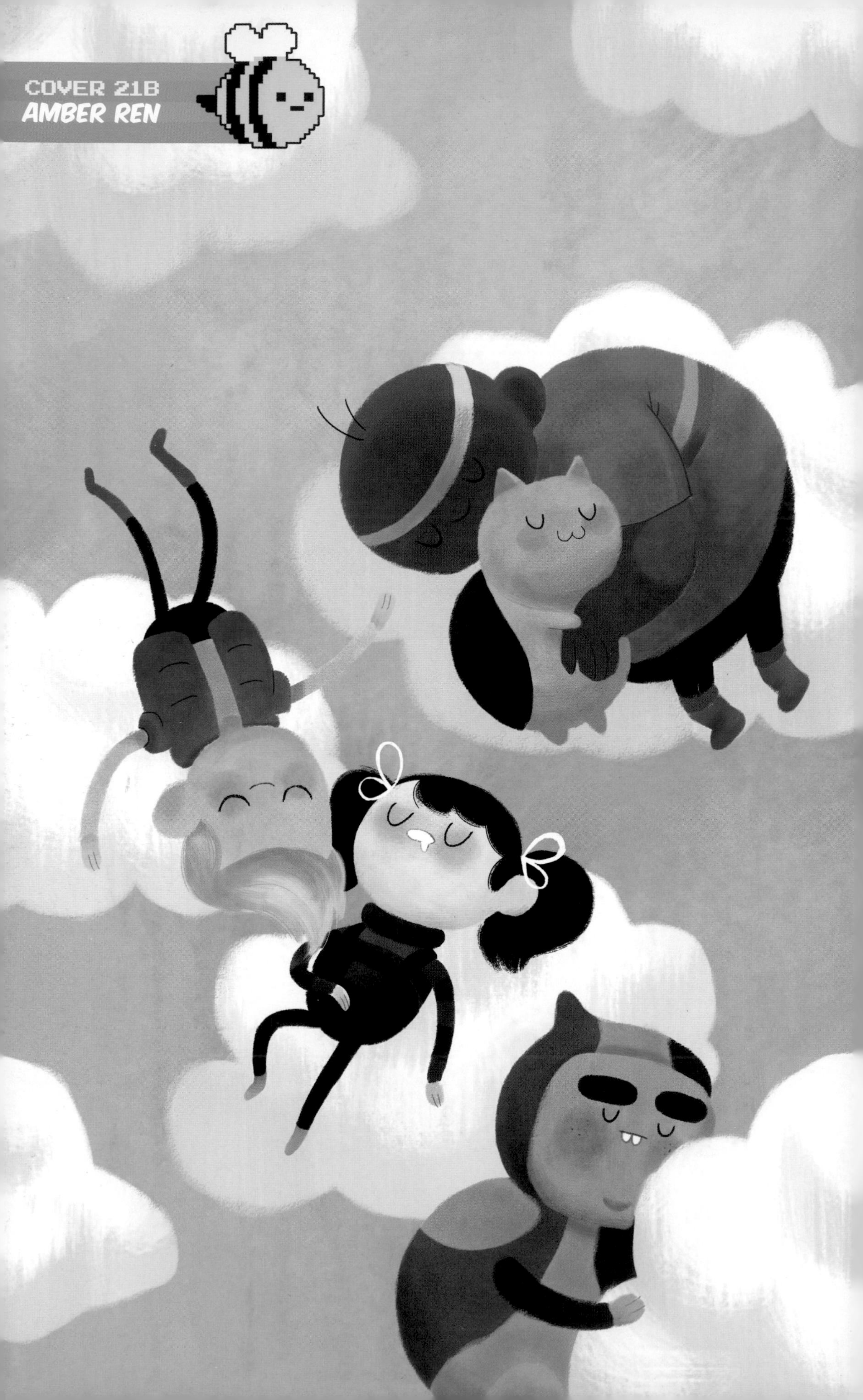
COVER 21B
AMBER REN

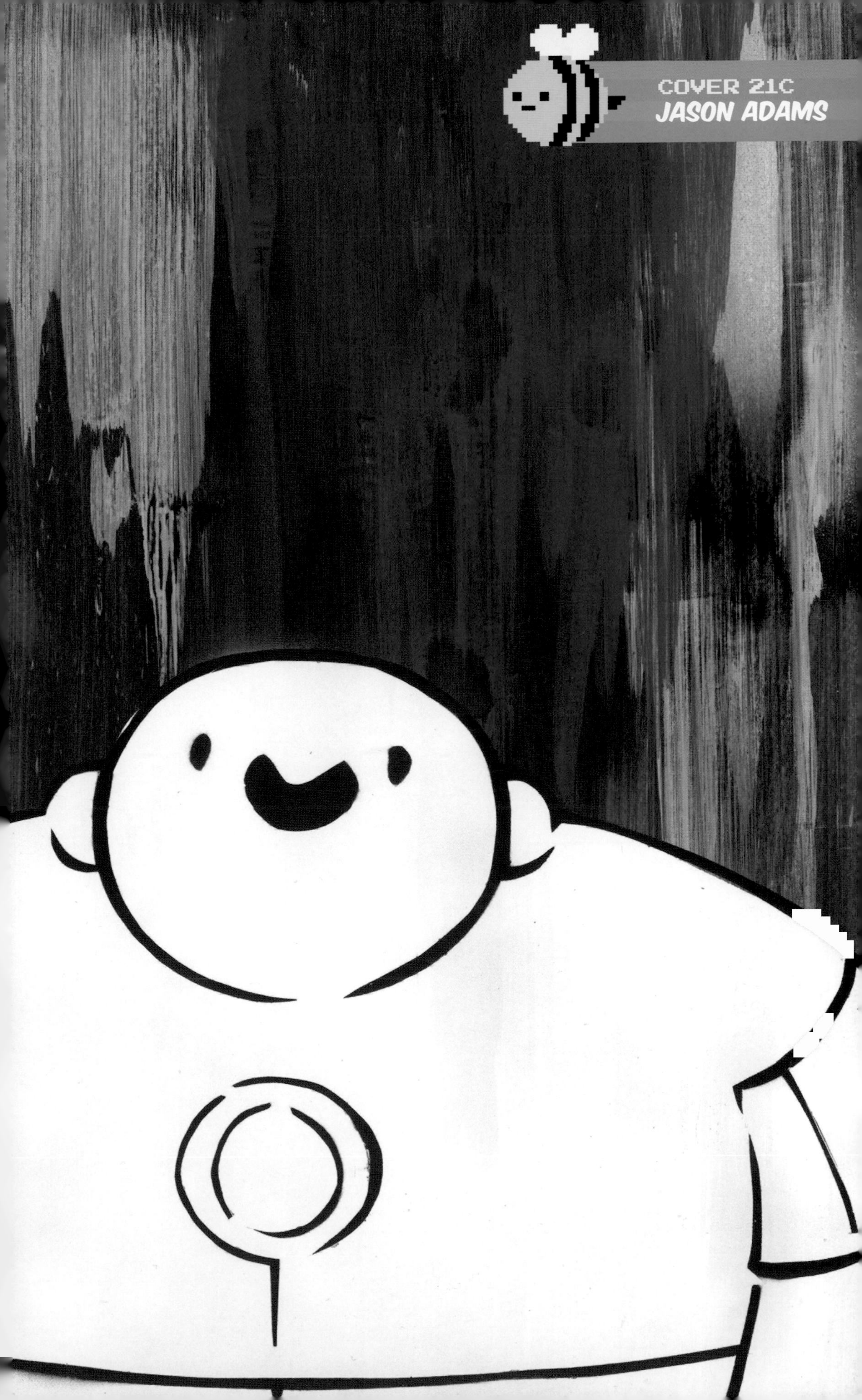
COVER 21C
JASON ADAMS

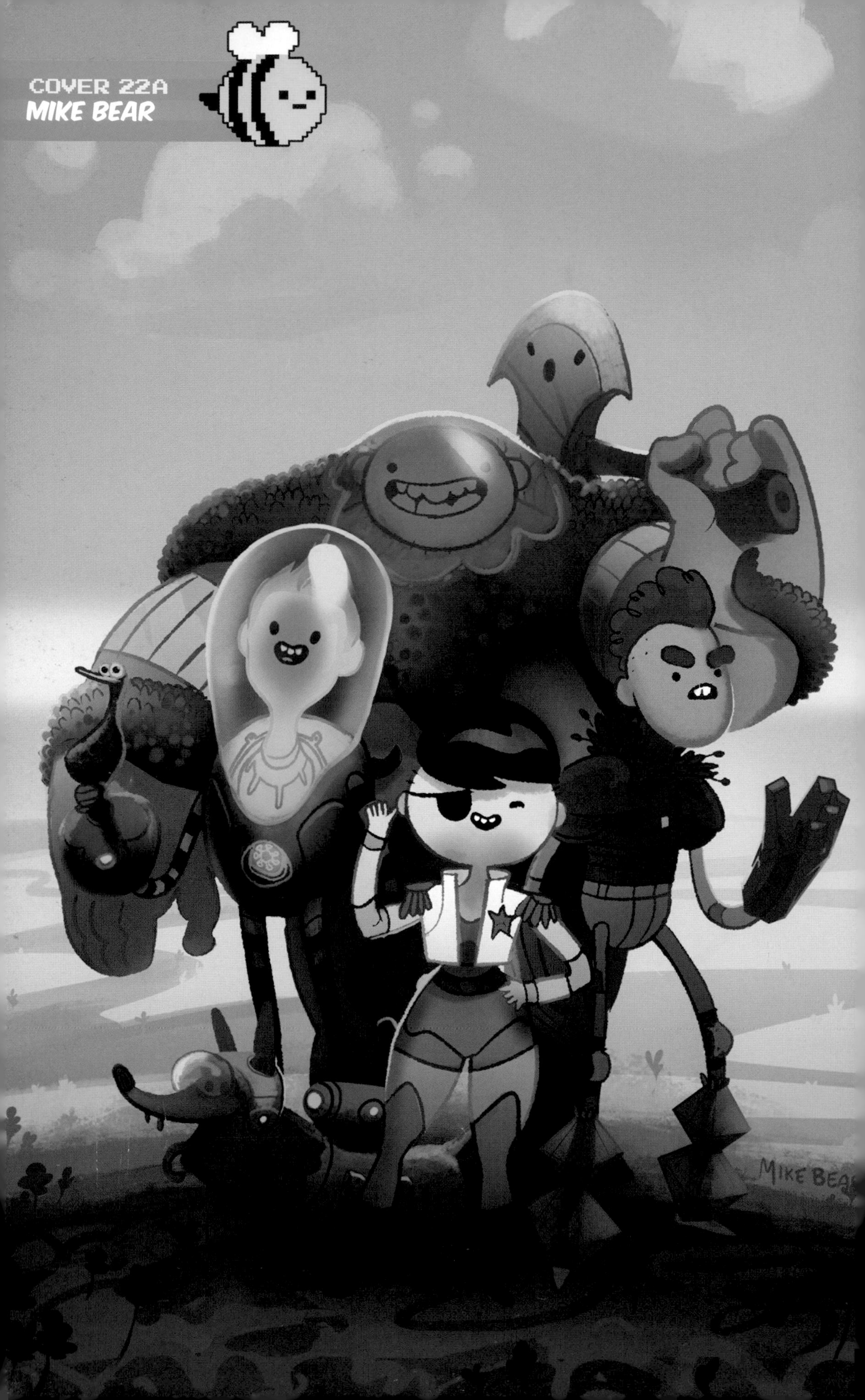
COVER 22A
MIKE BEAR

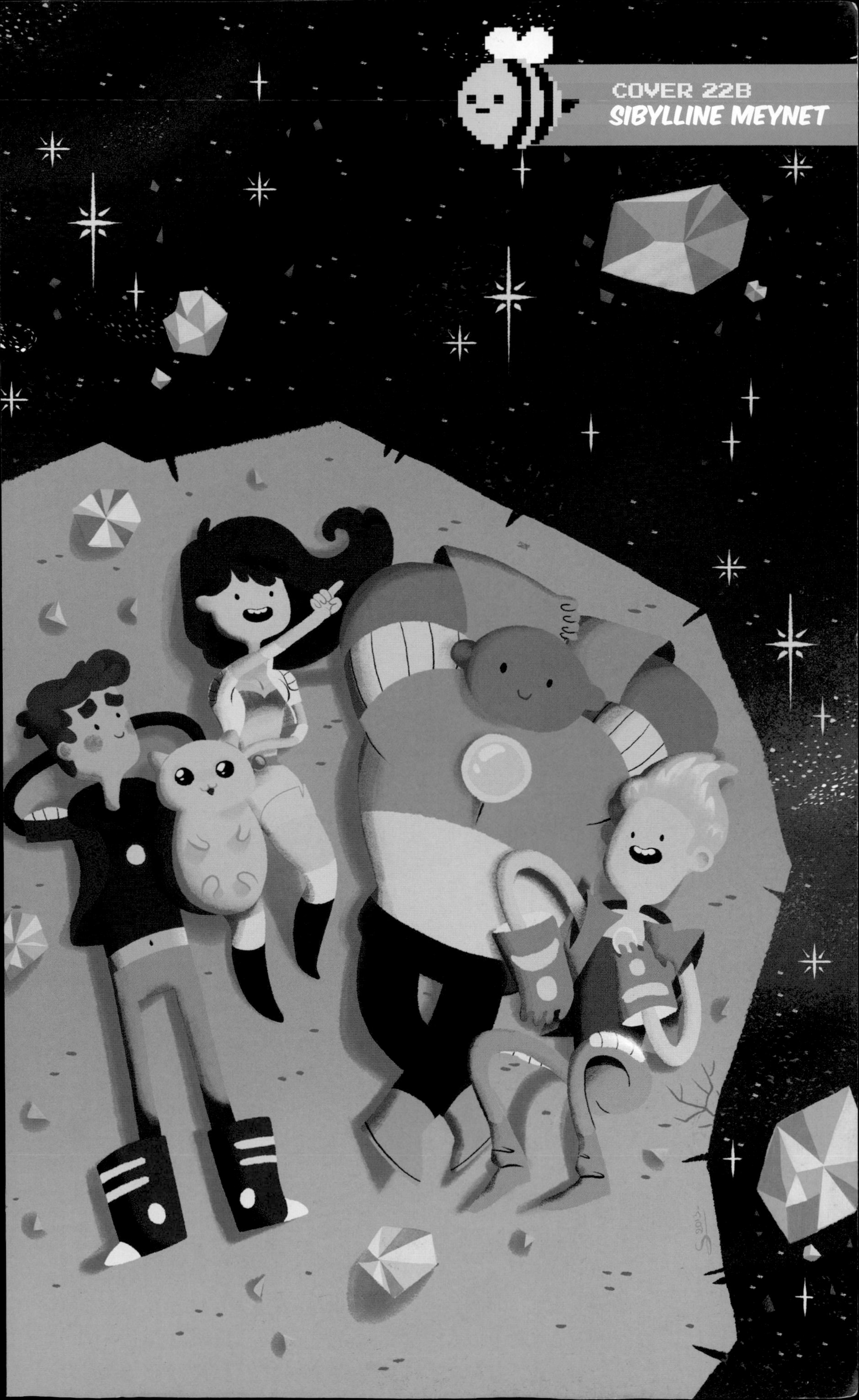
COVER 22B
SIBYLLINE MEYNET

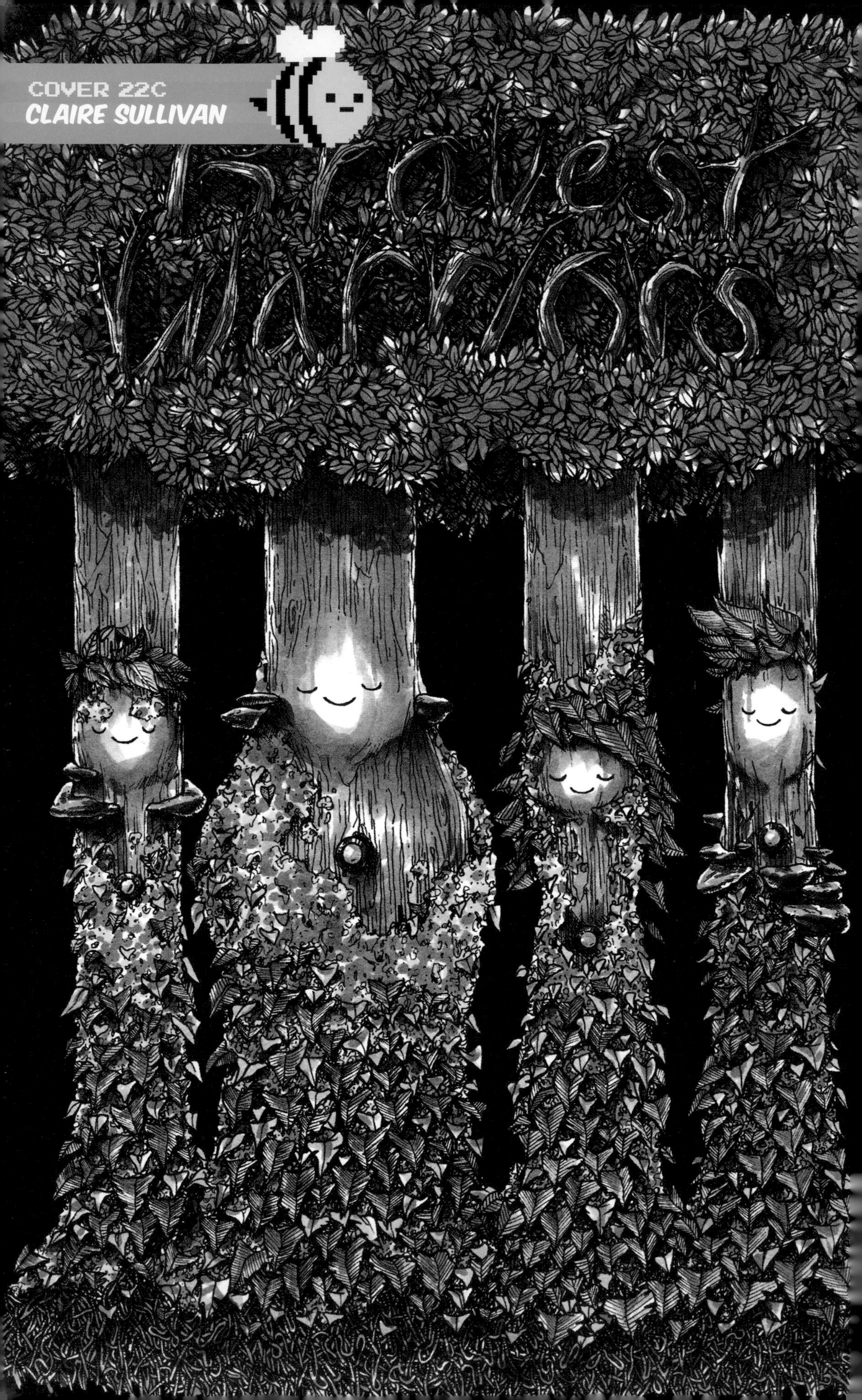
COVER 22C
CLAIRE SULLIVAN
Bravest Warriors

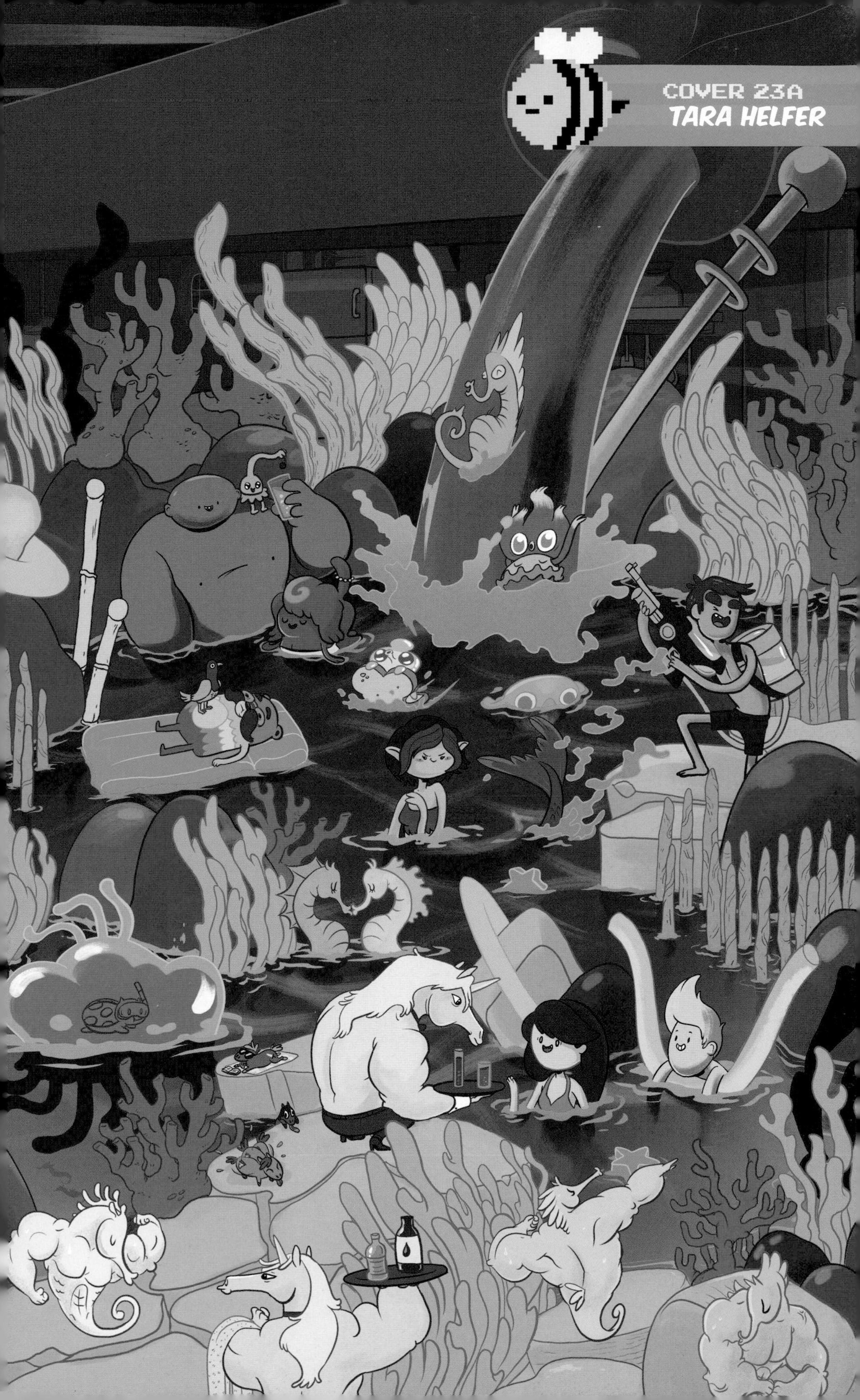
COVER 23A
TARA HELFER

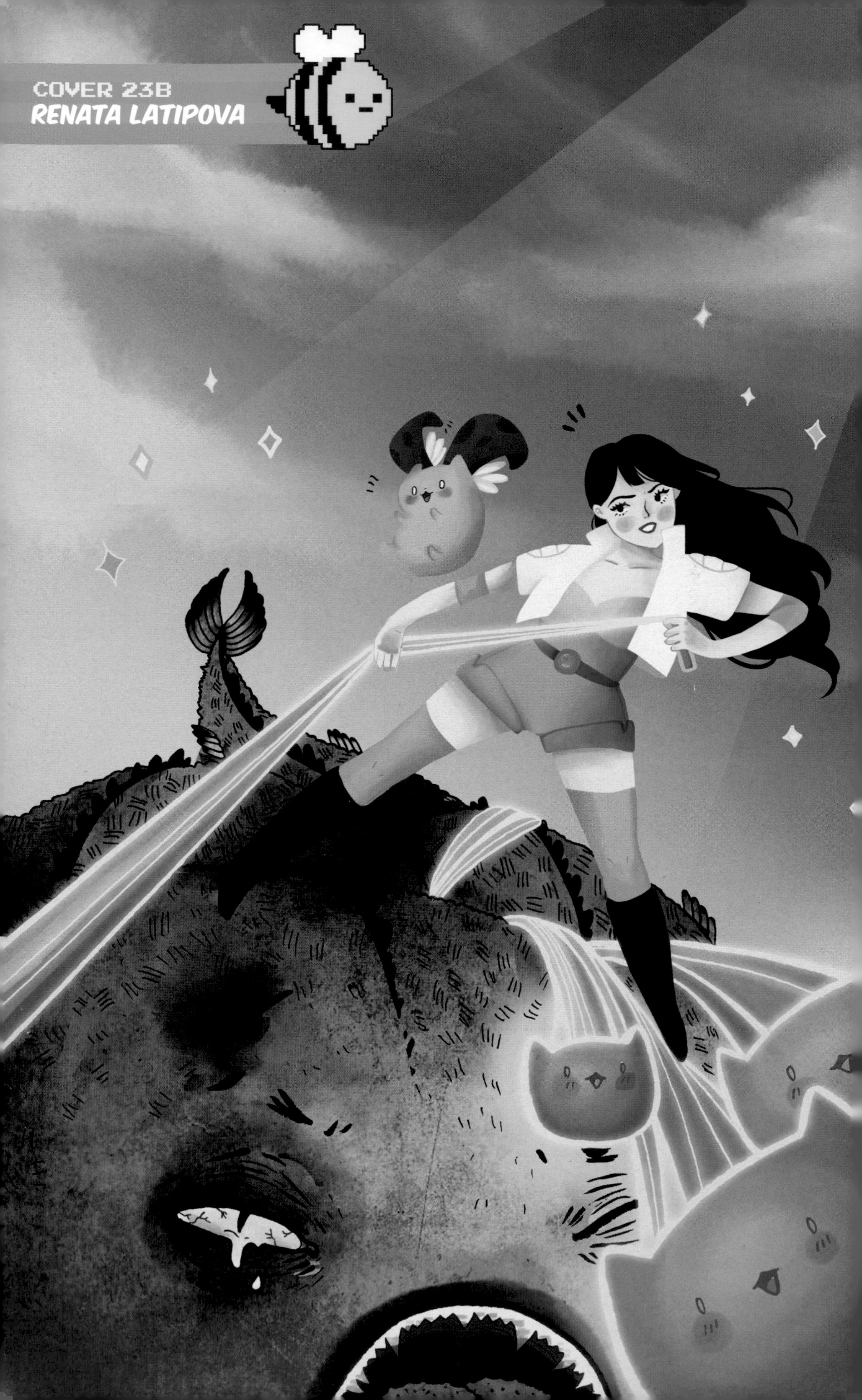
COVER 23B
RENATA LATIPOVA

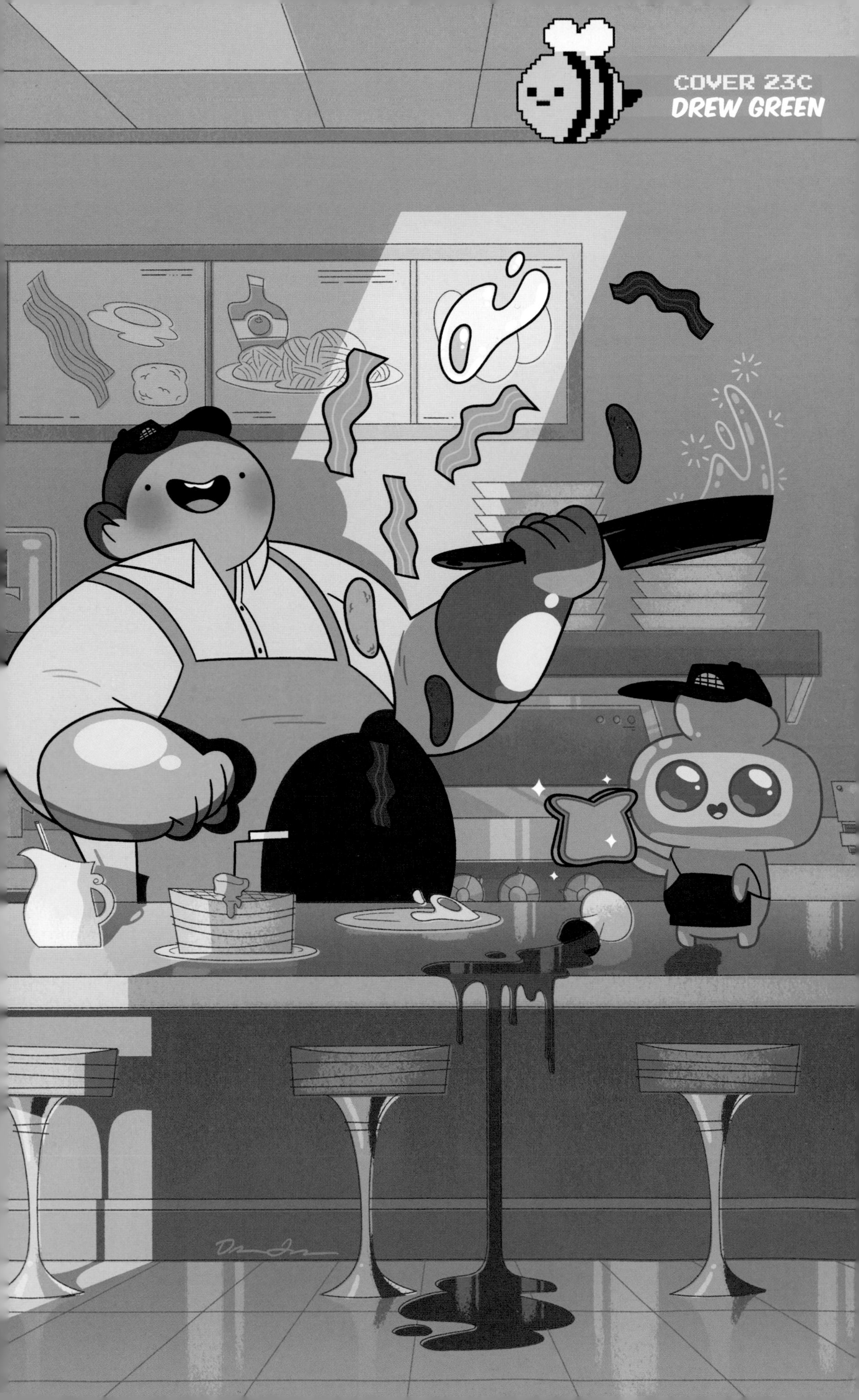
COVER 23C
DREW GREEN

COVER 24A
ANGELICA RUSSELL

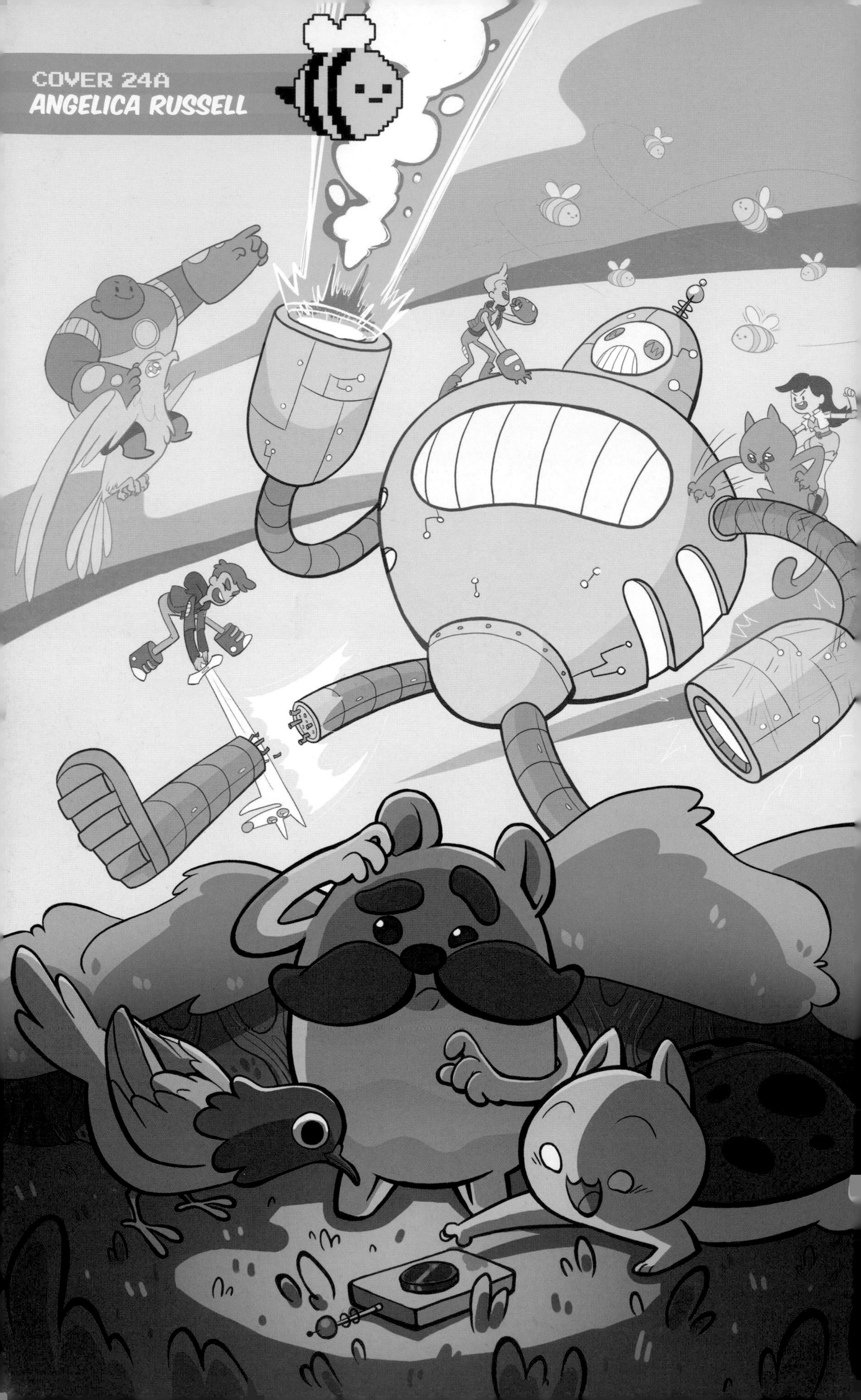

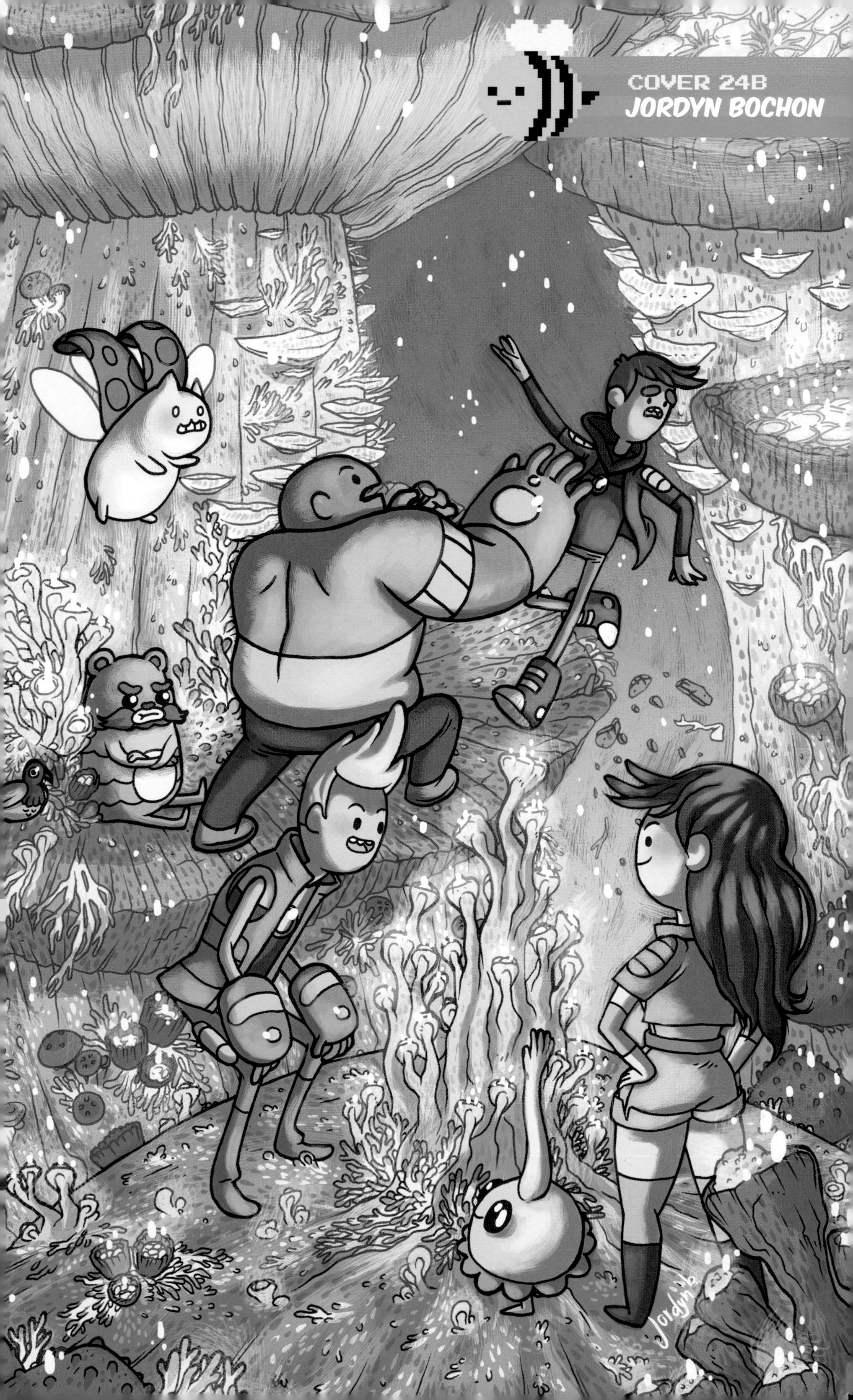
COVER 24B
JORDYN BOCHON

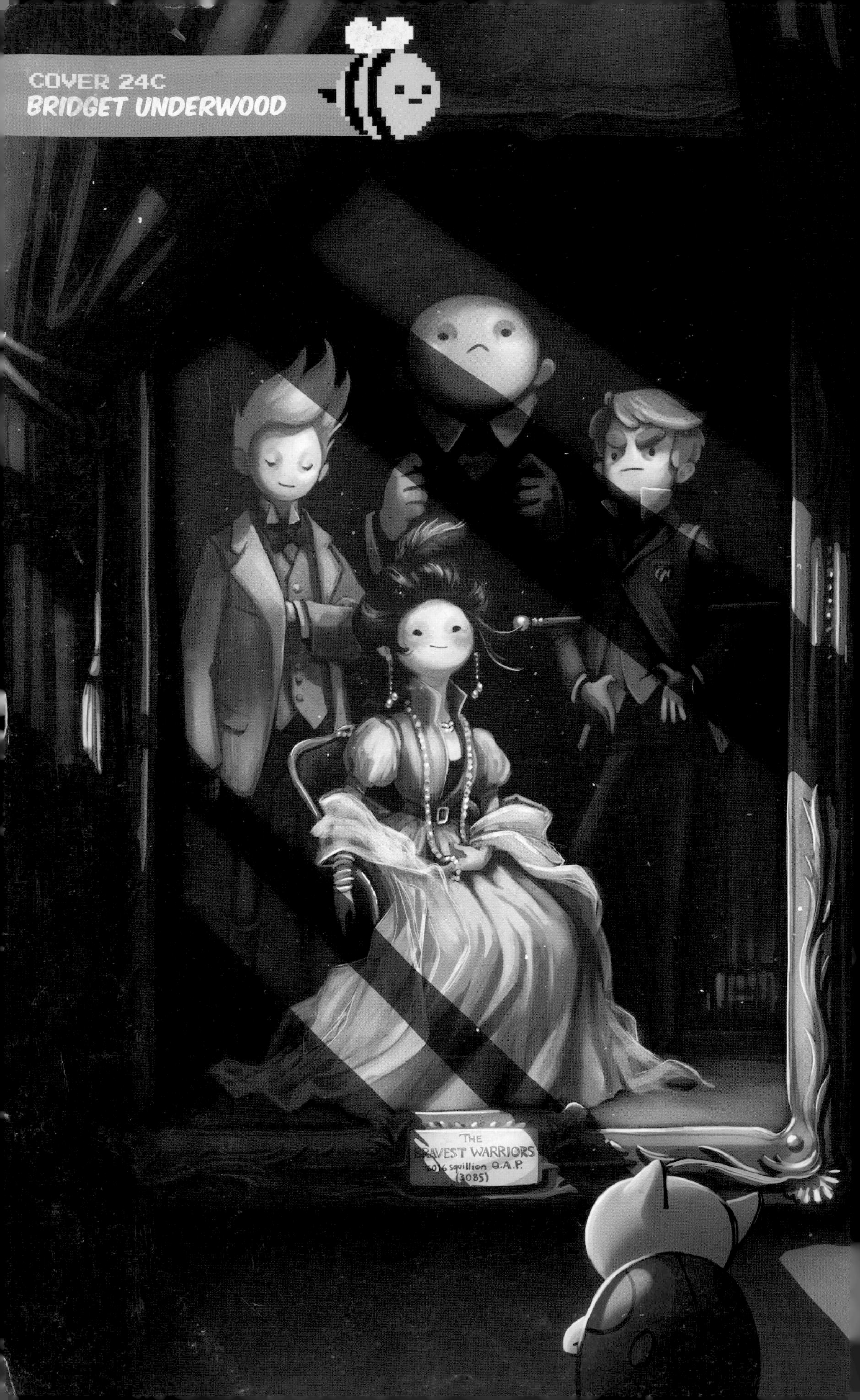
THE
BRAVEST WARRIORS
squillion Q.A.P.
(3085)

COVER 24C
BRIDGET UNDERWOOD